Una-Mary Parker
Drawing extensively
editor of *Tatler* and prominent member of the ...
Una-Mary Parker has written a dramatic and compulsive
novel of sensual suspense. Her previous international
bestsellers, *Riches, Scandals, Temptations, Enticements,
The Palace Affair, Forbidden Feelings* and *Only The Best,*
are all available from Headline and have been extensively
praised:

'A compulsive romantic thriller' *Sunday Express*

'Deliciously entertaining' *Sunday Telegraph*

'Scandal . . . saucy sex and suspense' *Daily Express*

'This novel has everything – intrigue, romance, ambition,
lust' *Daily Mail*

'Blue-blood glitz at its best' *Prima*

'Will keep you glued to the page' *Daily Express*

'The characters ring true and the tension mounts nicely'
Sunday Express

A Guilty Pleasure

Una-Mary Parker

HEADLINE

First published in 1994 by
HEADLINE BOOK PUBLISHING

First published in paperback in 1995 by
HEADLINE BOOK PUBLISHING

10 9 8 7 6 5 4 3 2 1

ISBN 0 7472 4370 0

Typeset by
Avon Dataset Ltd., Bidford-on-Avon, B50 4JH

Printed and bound in Great Britain by
Cox & Wyman Ltd, Reading, Berks

HEADLINE BOOK PUBLISHING
A division of Hodder Headline PLC
338 Euston Road
London NW1 3BH

This is for Sue Fletcher, to whom I owe so much and to whom little Holly owes her life, and to Clare Going, with thanks for helping me to see Holly on her way.

Chapter One

When David announced, after they'd made love, that they were expected to spend Christmas with his parents in Wiltshire, Charlotte looked at him blankly.

'This Christmas?'

'Well, not next,' he replied, laughing. 'What's wrong?' He picked up the glass of champagne he'd been drinking when they'd first got into bed, and sipped it.

'But that's only four days away!' she exclaimed.

'So?' He planted a kiss on her bare shoulder. 'I thought we could drive down on Christmas Eve and then come back on the twenty-seventh; the day after Boxing Day.'

Charlotte pulled up the duvet and reached for her glass which she'd left on the bedside table. 'I know which is Boxing Day,' she said spiritedly. 'Why didn't you mention it before, for heaven's sake?'

'What's the big deal, sweetheart?'

Charlotte sank back on to the pillows with a sigh. 'I've never met your parents. I don't have any clothes to wear and I feel . . . I feel unprepared.'

'It's only Christmas! I'm not asking you to spend the rest of your life with them!' He laughed indulgently.

'I know . . . I just wish you hadn't taken it for granted that I'd go.' They'd only known each other for three

1

months; Christmas seemed such an intimate family occasion to stay with people she'd never met.

'You'll love it,' David assured her confidently. 'I always go home for Christmas.'

'So do I,' she replied in a small voice. Her own parents lived nearby: she had planned to go there on Christmas Day, and had hoped David would come with her.

'Oh, come on, sweetheart. Don't be like that.' David turned his devastatingly blue eyes on her. 'We can drive down in your car, can't we? I'll look after you, I promise.'

She paused before asking, 'Are they expecting me? Have you actually told them you're bringing me down?' She couldn't resist those eyes.

'Yup! They're looking forward to meeting you.'

Charlotte's heart sank. That was it, then. It was a *fait accompli*.

'I must buy them some presents.' Her mind was racing. Would they like her? Would they approve of her relationship with their son? The thought of meeting them made her feel quite nauseous with nerves.

'Oh, get them a box of chocolates or something!' David replied casually. 'They won't expect you to get them anything at all.' There was a moment's silence. 'I've booked a table for dinner. At nine o'clock,' he added, glancing at his wristwatch. 'We've just got time to finish this bottle before we leave.'

He gave her a dazzling smile, and Charlotte snuggled down contentedly in the bed while he refilled her glass. Perhaps Christmas with his parents wouldn't be so bad. It would certainly be better than spending the holiday without seeing him at all.

Earlier in the evening, waiting for him to arrive, Charlotte had realised just how much he meant to her. Her only past experience of the opposite sex had been a brief affair she'd had when she was twenty-two, which had left her totally crushed and bereft of self-esteem. David had appeared out of the blue, had given her back her confidence, making her aware of her body in a way she never had been before.

An hour before he was due, she had had a leisurely bath, slipped into her best satin undies and then dressed in black trousers and a black top, cut low at the back. It was her favourite evening outfit because it made her look slim, disguising those extra pounds she never seemed able to get rid of. Standing before the long mirror in her bedroom, she had brushed her hair, then added some blusher, a little grey eyeshadow and a touch of lip-gloss. She studied herself critically.

No one would call her pretty. Her jaw was too wide, her nose too short and her mouth, described kindly, was over-generous. But she'd been referred to as attractive, and she had to admit she had a certain vivacious quality that made her face glow. Never in a million years, though, could she ever be described as beautiful. Not even by her mother. Ironically it was beauty, in all things, that she most appreciated in life. Whether in a work of art, the face of a friend or a glorious landscape, beauty was something she valued almost more highly than anything else. It was wrong, she knew, to like people because of how they looked, but she couldn't help it. And the reason she'd studied interior design and taken a job with Myra Grant was because if she wasn't beautiful herself, at least she could create beauty through her work. And Myra's decorative skills were the best in London. She couldn't have had a more perfect employer.

By the time David had rung the doorbell at seven-thirty, she'd set the scene in readiness for their evening together. Her flat, on the first floor of a large Victorian house in Kensington, was a conversion that had retained the atmosphere of a large, rather grand home, although in fact she only had a bedroom, a living room, a kitchen-cum-breakfast room and bathroom. Having dimmed the lights and turned up the heating, she lit a few strategically placed candles and arranged a bowl of early-flowering hyacinths on the glass coffee-table before a flickering fire. There was also chilled champagne, white wine, mineral water, and even a bottle of vodka in the deep freeze. She wanted everything to be perfect.

'Hi-ya!' He'd greeted her with a tender kiss. Then he'd felt the warmth of the flat envelop him.

'That's better!' he remarked approvingly, peeling off his overcoat and jacket. 'It's bloody cold out there.'

'Would you like a drink?' Suddenly feeling formal and nervous now that he was here, her voice was low and tentative.

'Ummm. It's been a hell of a day in the office.' Those startlingly blue eyes gazed into hers, making her heart twist with excitement. David was the best-looking man she'd ever seen. Even after three months, one look from him could still make her legs turn to jelly.

'Champagne?'

'Great.' Loosening his tie and undoing his shirt, he kissed her again and smiled wickedly. 'Let's have it in bed.'

Charlotte's hands trembled as she placed two glasses on

a tray with the Moët & Chandon she'd bought at the local off-licence that morning. By the time she entered the bedroom, he was already undressed and lying on top of the white coverlet.

'I'll open it,' he said huskily. 'You get undressed.'

His voice was like a caress. Swiftly, she took off her clothes and climbed on to the large bed beside him. He released the cork with the gentlest of pops and then he filled one of the glasses. Charlotte reached to take it from him, but instead he pressed the chilled glass against first one of her nipples and then the other. Then he tipped it carefully sideways, and a froth of sparkling bubbles trickled between her legs, making her gasp.

'David . . . !'

'That was just for starters,' he murmured, filling his own glass. They drank in silence, their eyes locked. Deliberately, he avoided touching her, but his close proximity was enough to make her long for him. He lay there beside her, aroused himself, and she knew it would be a while before he made a move. He'd taught her the art of foreplay, sometimes making it last for several hours, so that at times her mind seemed to break loose from its moorings as he pushed her to heights of passion she hadn't known existed. Tonight, though, she wanted him quickly.

'David . . .'

He was kissing her now, lingeringly and slowly, and with his forefinger tracing the line of her shoulder, her breast, her hip and the length of her thigh. Then he moved closer, putting his arms around her so their bodies seemed to merge and become one, like a sculpture of two figures carved from the same block of marble.

Dizzily she clung to him. 'I love you . . .'

His blue eyes, looking into hers, were like blue glass marbles in the dim light. 'I love you too,' he whispered back, his lips on hers.

She tried to pull him closer, moving herself into a better position.

'Not yet, sweetheart.' His voice was thick as honey. 'Not for a long time yet.'

'Oh, please . . . David . . .' The torture was exquisite. He was parting her legs now, stroking her with gentle hands. Then he kissed her throat and sucked the lobes of her ears. Her hands sought him with urgency, but he moved beyond her reach, kneeling on the pillow above her head, cradling her face in his hands as he kissed her eyelids.

'Please . . .' Her voice was a thin wail of longing. He buried his face in her neck and his hands slid down to cup her breasts.

'I want you,' she begged. But with unhurried deliberation, savouring each sensation, he tasted her body, letting his tongue seek out every part of her so she felt as if she were being bound up in skeins of silk. Again and again he excited her until she was at breaking point, only to deny her fulfilment for a moment longer.

'David . . . !' She felt she was going crazy, losing her reason, craving for him to fill her with his love . . .

Just when she thought she couldn't bear it a moment longer, he took her with a suddenness that caught her by surprise, entering her swiftly as he cried out her name.

David had booked a table at *Roma di Notti*, the local trattoria, where the food was good and the atmosphere lively. Antonio, a rumbustious emigré from Naples, greeted all the customers in his loud, portentous voice, clapping his large hands together to welcome each new arrival, and bellowing to his staff to jump to it. Charlotte and David dined there regularly, because in spite of the excellence of the menu, Antonio managed to keep the price to an affordable level.

'Good evening, Signorina!' he shouted, when he saw Charlotte. 'And Signor Farrell! How are you tonight? I have nice table for you. Please, come this way.' His stout body, sporting scarlet braces to hold up his baggy grey trousers, weaved a path between the candlelit tables to an intimate alcove on the far side of the restaurant.

Charlotte slipped into her seat while David engaged in light-hearted badinage with the proprietor.

'How's life, Antonio?'

'It not so bad! How's the beeg city treating you, Signore?'

'I'm over-worked and underpaid, as usual,' David smiled.

'I pay myself and yet I'm underpaid too! Life, it's not fair, is that right?'

'Definitely, Antonio.'

'So what you going to have to eat tonight?' Antonio waved two large menus in front of them. 'I suggest you start with the *Zuppa di pesce alla Genovese*. It is the most fragrant of fish soups; pure poetry!'

Charlotte giggled. Antonio winked a beady brown eye at her.

'Then you go on,' he continued, 'to the *Scaloppine al Marsala*. We fry the veal until it is crisp, and it is served on a bed of wild rice with a rich marsala sauce.'

David nodded. 'Sounds great.'

'You will enjoy! Very much!' he said, gesticulating. 'You have a bottle of our chilled Frascati to go with it?'

David nodded again and Charlotte thought how nice it was to have a man take charge of everything. Her father had always been the one in control when she'd been small, and it gave her a safe feeling.

'Very good, Signor Farrell,' said Antonio, pleased with his performance. Then he strolled away, singing at the top of his voice.

Charlotte leaned toward David. 'He's nice, but God, why does he have to be so noisy?' she whispered.

'One day I'll take you somewhere better, darling, but at the moment I'm afraid I can only afford to go halves on the bill, even in a place like this.' He smiled wryly and Charlotte laid her hand on his arm.

'It's all right, David. Really it is. I was joking; I think the atmosphere's great here.'

'One day I'll be rich and successful and we'll go to the Connaught or the Savoy, or one of those grand places,' he grinned.

'No doubt you'll be running Flight Records soon, anyway,' she observed lightly.

'Yes, I'm in line for promotion actually,' he continued. He'd worked for Flight Records for the past year, in the accounts department. Flight was almost as glamorous as Virgin, with a string of hit records and some very big names in the pop world under contract.

Charlotte's face lit up. 'That's wonderful.'

'Yes. They want me to run the sales side. The pay's much better, and of course I'll have a large staff under me.'

Her eyes widened. 'When will you know?'

He leaned back and spread his hands expansively. 'Early January, I should think.'

'That's very exciting.'

'Well, you know, the directors are beginning to realise my potential.' His tone was careless. 'I could make Flight as big as Virgin or HMV, and I'm well in with Don Gabriel.'

'Don Gabriel?' Was he a pop singer?

'The managing director,' David replied with a patient smile.

Charlotte nodded, smiling proudly. She suspected David bragged a bit in order to impress her; she thought it rather sweet. Not that he needed to, she reflected. She was always telling him he was wonderful, but some people needed more reassurance than others.

'At least we're going to be together at Christmas,' she said in a low voice, reaching across to squeeze his hand.

He grinned fondly at her. 'I hope you like my parents,' he said.

'I'm sure I will.' She tried to ignore the apprehensive knot in her stomach. 'Tell me about your home.'

He hardly ever mentioned his family. She only knew that they lived in Wiltshire and that he hadn't seen much of them since he'd come to London.

'There's not much to tell. They live on the outskirts of a village called Barrow, near Devizes. It's a very old house which will be mine one day. With the surrounding land, it's probably worth well over a million.'

Charlotte looked at him, surprised. Somehow she'd imagined his parents to be poor; David himself was always short of money.

'Chelwood Manor was built in 1665 as a nunnery.' He

drained the last of his wine. 'I'll sell it, eventually. I hate living in the country.'

'Has it always been in your family?'

'God, no. They bought it after I was born. Dad made a fortune in timber. He's retired now. My mother never worked, of course.'

Charlotte was amazed. 'You never told me you came from a wealthy background,' she said jokingly.

'You might have been after my money,' he teased her. 'And I wanted you to like me for myself.' His face took on a more serious expression. 'No, my mother and father felt we should fend for ourselves, though of course in the end they had to help Chris.'

'Who's Chris?'

'My younger brother.'

Charlotte felt another start of surprise. David had never mentioned him before either. 'I didn't know you had a brother!'

He shrugged. 'To be honest, we're not very close. They've helped him out a couple of times, though. Paid for him to go to the best clinics.'

'What's wrong with him?' She had visions of a younger version of David, racked by illness or maimed by accident.

David's tone was flat; Charlotte saw anguish in his eyes. 'He's a junkie: drugs, drink, all that sort of thing. He's overdosed accidentally, on several occasions.'

'My God, how sad.'

'After watching someone you love destroy themselves year after year, it's difficult to feel sadness. It's more a frustration at their persisting in shooting up, or whatever, when it's so obvious what it's doing to them.'

10

'I suppose that's the point: addicts just can't help themselves,' she said mildly.

'Who knows?' David sighed. 'All I know is that he's cost my mother and father a fortune, not to mention all the worry.'

David shrugged, but Charlotte could see he'd been disturbed by the conversation. She couldn't imagine what it must be like to see your own brother deliberately destroying himself, your parents trying in vain to help him. She ate in silence, sharing David's pain.

Charlotte was up early the next morning to get herself organised for the day ahead. With Christmas only a few days away, Myra had a dozen clients who wanted the finishing touches put to their houses and flats before the festive season. The day before she'd given Charlotte a list and, looking at it now, Charlotte felt dismayed. How on earth was she going to get through all the jobs in time? There was a house in Chelsea where she had to supervise the laying of carpets, a flat in Eaton Place waiting to have its windows festooned with extravagant drapes, shelves to go up in a kitchen in Fulham, table-lamps to be bought and installed in a study in a house in Campden Hill, and mirrors fixed to the walls of a bathroom in Paddington. Myra had a team of workers who could do anything from installing a central-heating system to making a set of chair covers, so Charlotte's task was to ensure that every job was being carried out to the client's specifications. It was an exacting job, calling for sharp observational powers; everything from the wallpaper to the light-switches had to be carefully checked.

Charlotte loved the work, though. She had dreams of starting her own interior design company in a few years' time, with maybe a shop where she could sell her own brand of merchandise; so no matter how hard Myra made her work, she knew it was all invaluable experience.

This morning, however, as she finished her coffee before stepping into the bath, her thoughts kept straying to David. As each day passed, she was falling more deeply in love with him, and wondering too, how anyone like him could really be in love with her. She felt the luckiest person alive.

Looking back, their first meeting had been so clichéd, yet at the same time extraordinary. Charlotte had been waiting to catch a flight to Rome, where she was going to buy silk for curtains in a Chester Square mansion, when a spectral voice had drowned out all other sounds in the departure lounge at Heathrow, announcing that the flight had been delayed for two hours.

'Damn and *blast*!' she heard a voice exclaim and, glancing across to the seating opposite, saw an incredibly handsome man scowling at the monitor which hung above her head. With his regular features, blond hair and extraordinary pale blue eyes, she supposed him to be a male model or a film star. Something else struck her also. In spite of his obvious aggravation, his mouth had a humorous tilt at the corners and there were laughter lines around his eyes. He looked to be in his late twenties, and she liked the casual yet stylish way in which he was dressed.

Suddenly he became aware of her looking at him and he grinned. 'Bloody typical, isn't it! I hate delays.'

She nodded, almost struck dumb by his friendly manner, and the fact that he was talking to her in such an easy way.

12

'I know.' She smiled fatuously. 'It is a bore.'

'You're going to Rome, too?'

'Yes.'

'God, I hope it's not more than a two-hour wait.'

'I'm glad I've brought something to read.'

He grimaced ruefully. 'I haven't. Are you being met at the other end?'

'No. I'm on a business trip.' She paused. 'It doesn't actually matter when I arrive.'

'Same here,' he admitted. 'I've never been to Italy, so I thought I'd take a few days off and have a look at the sights.' As he spoke he moved across the space between them and seated himself next to her.

'You'll love it.'

He looked at her with interest. 'You know it well, do you?'

Charlotte longed to lie, tell him she could give him a splendid conducted tour and that she knew all the best places, but he was looking at her so penetratingly with those amazing eyes that she knew she'd never be able to get away with it.

'I know bits of Rome,' she said honestly. 'I usually stay near the Spanish Steps and I've seen the Colosseum, of course, and the Vatican . . . but usually I've been so busy I haven't had much time to go exploring.' She didn't add that she was too nervous to roam by herself anyway. She'd seen *The Roman Spring of Mrs Stone*, and often wished she had the courage of the woman Tennessee Williams had written about. She also wished she had the looks of Vivien Leigh, who had played Mrs Stone in the film. With that face one would never be alone anywhere, she reflected wryly.

The young man was looking around the crowded departure lounge now, no doubt thinking up an excuse to get away. She was wondering how she could make it easier for him when, to her joy and amazement, he suddenly asked her to join him for a drink.

'There are several bars to choose from. Which one shall we try?' he asked.

That was how it had all begun. By the time they'd arrived in Rome, having managed to exchange seats so they could sit together, it seemed to Charlotte she had known David Farrell for years. He told her he was twenty-eight, worked for a recording company called Flight Records, was unattached and living in London.

Charlotte could hardly believe her luck and yet, in the days that followed, she'd remained cautious, frightened of getting her fingers burnt again. After three years, she still suffered the awful doubt that comes with rejection. Even now, after three months of loving David, there were moments when she feared she lacked the ability to hold on to him for ever; moments when the consequences of losing him seemed too terrible to contemplate.

The phone ringing brought her back to the present with a start. Clients sometimes phoned her and Myra at home.

'Good morning. Can I help you?' she asked in her professional manner.

'La, darling, it's Mummy. Have you got a moment to spare or is this a bad time?'

'Hi, Ma!' She greeted her mother affectionately. 'How are you?'

'I'm fine, but frantically busy. Listen, darling, I thought of getting Susan one of those skirts from Jigsaw for

Christmas, and I wondered what colour I should get. They've
got them in—'

'Ma.' Charlotte interrupted her.

'Yes?'

'I'm afraid I've got bad news for you about Christmas.'

'What?' Margaret Taylor sounded alarmed.

'Oh, it's not quite the end of the world, but David wants
me to spend Christmas in Wiltshire with his parents and—'

'But that will be lovely for you, sweetheart.' Charlotte
could hear her mother struggling to keep the disappointment
out of her voice. 'You'll have a wonderful time! How nice
of them to invite you. Have you got enough clothes to wear?'

Charlotte giggled. 'It's only a country house, Ma. Not
the Ritz in Paris! Can David and I spend New Year's Eve
with you and Daddy, instead?'

'Of course you can, darling. We'd love to see you. I'm
experimenting with a new way of doing pheasant – *en croute*
– so we can try it out then.'

'Thanks, Ma. I'm sorry about Christmas. I'd much rather
be with you and Daddy and Susie.'

'Don't worry about it, La! You must be with David. It's
only right. We'll all miss you dreadfully, but there'll be the
New Year to look forward to, so that's all right.'

As usual, Charlotte thought, her mother was making the
best of everything. She was a naturally cheerful and resilient
woman, still young looking and energetic at fifty, and always
pleased for her daughters when something nice happened
to them.

'I'll come round with my presents for you all,' Charlotte
promised. 'Would tomorrow be OK?'

'Any time you like, darling. And I'll give you ours. I've

also got a little something for David, too.'

'You're a star, Ma.'

'Now, what about this skirt for Susie?'

They talked for several more minutes; they had always enjoyed a harmonious relationship and, now Charlotte was twenty-six, were the best of friends.

When Charlotte hung up several minutes later, she felt a pang of regret that she was going away, even if it was with David. This would be the first Christmas in her life, she realised, when she'd be away from her family, and it felt strange and unsettling. Then she spoke sternly to herself.

'Come on,' she said briskly. 'Time to grow up, for God's sake!'

Chapter Two

Christopher Farrell rang the door bell of his ex-wife's Islington house and hoped she'd got Holly ready for their trip to stay with his parents in Wiltshire. This was the first Christmas he'd spend with his four-year-old daughter since the divorce, and he was anxious to be off. Tall, comfortably shaped, and with a light brown beard, he pulled his sheepskin coat tighter and leaned into the wind as it rushed down Mulberry Avenue. Christ! It was cold! He rubbed his hands and looked at his wristwatch again, wondering why the hell Linda didn't open the door.

He'd have liked to have seen Holly more often, but their relationship, fragile and infrequent, was ruled by Linda's 'conditions'. She was hot on conditions, he thought. Linda had stipulated he could only see Holly if he gave her several days' notice, and Holly could only stay with him if he was at his parents' house, not his own flat in Battersea. He must take her to Wiltshire in the train and not in his car, and he wouldn't ever be allowed to have her again if he was drinking or doing drugs in her presence. Not that he did drugs any more. Drinking was different. He'd nodded silently in agreement, but knew that he wouldn't be able to resist the odd drink when Holly was in bed at night.

The dark blue painted door of the small but elegant

nineteenth-century house opened, and Linda stood there smiling at him in such a friendly way he couldn't help feeling guilty that he'd been cursing her a few minutes before.

'Hi, Chris! Come in. Holly's just about ready.' She was a motherly-looking woman in her early thirties, with curling brown hair and a cheerful expression. Wearing cream corded trousers and a long loose red sweater which suited her curvaceous figure, she led the way into the living room.

'Like some coffee?'

He glanced at his watch again, worried about the waiting taxi, worried about missing the train.

'Better not, thanks.'

At that moment a short, thick-set man with dark hair and humorous eyes emerged from the direction of the kitchen carrying a ten-month-old boy in his arms.

'How are you doing, Chris?' The men shook hands. Christopher quite liked Linda's new husband, probably because he hadn't come on the scene until after they'd split.

'I'm fine, Denzil.' Chris looked at the baby and felt a momentary pang. He adored Holly, but it would have been nice to have had a son.

'How are you today, Ben?' he asked the child, speaking breezily to hide his longing. Ben blew bubbles and snuggled deeper into his father's arms.

'Daddy!' A small girl, her curly, shoulder-length blonde hair tied back with a ribbon, came tearing down the stairs, jumping the last two steps before flinging herself at Christopher.

'Hi, sweetheart!' He swept her up in his arms, holding her aloft because she was so light, grinning up into her face as she dangled above him. 'How's my girl?'

18

'Are we going to Granny's for Christmas?'

'Yes, we are, Holly.' He lowered her until she was level with his chest, and then he hugged her close.

Holly hugged him back, but she was eager to be off. 'Can we go now?' She wriggled down to the ground and then rushed over to a suitcase which stood ready by the front door.

'This is my luggage,' she announced importantly.

Linda and Christopher looked at their only child with fond eyes. They found her irresistible with her heart-shaped face and forget-me-not-blue eyes which twinkled with merriment. There was an almost permanent giggle in her throat, which broke into rich, milky laughter when she was happy, and she had an endearing habit of saying, 'Oh, *Mummy*!' or, 'Oh, *Daddy*!' and winding her arms round their necks. Linda dropped to her haunches and held out her arms, her eyes suddenly glistening with unshed tears. 'Come and say goodbye to Mummy.'

Holly ran and flung herself at Linda. 'Aren't you coming to Granny's too, Mummy?'

'Not this time, love,' Linda replied, keeping her voice light. 'Be a good girl and give my love to Granny and Grandpa.'

'I want you to come too, Mummy.' Holly looked crushed. She gazed into Linda's eyes and nodded her own head in encouragement. 'Say yes. Say you'll come,' she persisted, nodding.

'Then who would look after Denzil? And Ben?' Linda stood up quickly, her face pinched with pain.

'And you'll be with Mummy for the New Year,' Christopher pointed out with forced cheerfulness. He caught

Linda's eye and they exchanged wry smiles, united in their effort to make Holly understand that her time would always have to be divided between them in the future.

'We'd better hurry or we'll miss the train,' Christopher coaxed, 'Granny is expecting us for tea.' He picked up her case while Linda buttoned up her red anorak. Suddenly Holly stood still in the middle of the hall. Her expression was appalled.

'Does Father Christmas know I'm going away? Will he know where Granny's house is?' she asked in a quavering voice.

Denzil came to the rescue as both Linda and Christopher struggled with their emotions. Bending down he spoke earnestly and gravely. 'Don't worry, Holly. I sent Father Christmas a fax, marked "urgent" and "important", and I gave him your granny's address in Wiltshire.'

Holly only looked partially convinced. 'Are you sure he'll get it? Will he know where to go?'

Denzil nodded vigorously. 'He faxed me back! Don't worry about a thing. Now, you'd better hurry before that taxi gets fed up with waiting! You don't want to miss your train, do you?'

Reassured, Holly brightened visibly and grabbed Christopher's hand.

'Thanks, old chap,' Christopher murmured. 'Bye, Linda. Have a good Christmas.'

'You, too.'

'Bye-bye, Mummy.'

'Goodbye, sweetheart. See you very soon. Take care and be a good girl.'

The quiet tree-lined street echoed to their voices as, with

a shuddering start, the taxi pulled away from the kerb. Linda watched it go, unable to speak. Denzil, standing beside her, still holding Ben, looked at her sympathetically.

'Cheer up, love. You've got us.'

'I know.' She was hoarse with choking tears. 'It never gets easier, though, does it? In fact, it gets more painful all the time.' Then she leaned forward to kiss him, to reassure him that, in spite of her sadness, she really loved him and Ben. 'What would I do without you?'

He kissed her back, putting Ben in her arms at the same time. 'I think your son and heir needs changing.'

Linda patted Ben's padded bottom fondly. 'Come on then, sweetheart. Up to the nursery.'

Ben gurgled and clapped his hands, something he'd only recently learned to do. Linda carried him up the stairs and, as they passed Holly's bedroom – a confection in various shades of pink, with a stencilled border of dancing elephants created by Denzil – Linda averted her eyes. She would never get used to having to share Holly with Christopher. It had to be done and she tried to make the best of it, but she'd never get used to it.

Carol and Neil Whittaker loaded the last of their luggage into the boot of their old Bentley, and did a final check to make sure the house was locked up and the burglar alarm set.

Since Neil's retirement the previous year, as headmaster of a leading public school, they'd moved to a modern redbrick house near a golf course in Berkshire. Now their time was devoted to improving the garden, and pursuing their respective hobbies. Life was leisurely and comfortable.

In many ways they'd rather have stayed at home for Christmas, but both had a deep, in-built sense of duty. Every alternate year they stayed with her sister and brother-in-law in Wiltshire. It was expected of them, and this was the year they were due to go again.

'At least Virginia has a wonderful cook,' Neil had remarked as they'd finished packing the previous night.

'And Edmund has an excellent cellar,' Carol reminded him, wishing they'd been able to have children of their own. Apart from everything else it would have been a perfect excuse for staying at home. The fact was, they were only going away in order to please her sister and brother-in-law who, being richer, liked to dispense biennial hospitality to the poorer members of their family.

'I like sleeping in my own bed,' Neil grumbled. He was a man of habit, who liked his wife's cooking better than anyone else's, his regular whisky and soda at six o'clock (Edmund Farrell refused to offer anyone a drink before six-thirty), and to have his bath after breakfast, not before.

'It can't be helped, dear,' Carol commiserated, thinking how she was going to miss being able to watch her favourite television programmes. At least they'd be in their own home next year, able to do exactly as they liked.

'I hear Christopher is coming down for Christmas and bringing Holly with him,' Carol remarked as they set off along the M3 for Devizes. 'She must be quite a big girl now.'

'How old is she?' Neil drove carefully, checking in the mirror every thirty seconds.

'Four, I think. Yes, she must be. Poor little thing. I don't approve of breaking up marriages where children are involved.'

'I don't think you can blame Linda for wanting a divorce, dear,' he said mildly.

'She should have put up with it.'

'What, his drinking? And drugs?'

'Other women sometimes have to.'

'I dare say, but with Holly . . . ! I'm sure she felt it was bad for the child being in that environment. They never had any money, either, because he spent it all getting the stuff. I don't think you can blame her.' Neil shook his bald head and changed gear with vigour.

'I'm sure she could have managed if she'd tried,' Carol said stiffly. 'I think she wanted to get away from Christopher so she could marry Denzil Blake. I believe he's quite well off.'

'But Linda met Denzil after she'd left Christopher.'

Carol looked at him and said darkly, 'That's what she says.'

Neil sighed inwardly. There was no changing his wife's viewpoint when she was set on something. She'd never liked Linda, and nothing was going to alter that fact, even though they'd not seen her since she and Christopher had divorced.

'Edmund told me on the phone yesterday that David's bringing a girlfriend down this year,' Neil observed, changing the subject.

Carol shot him a surprised look. 'Really? What sort of girl?'

'How should I know, dear? Presumably one with two legs, two arms and a woman's body.'

'Don't be silly, Neil. What did Edmund say about her? Who is she?'

'All he said was that her name is Charlotte and that David

has been going out with her for several months. Oh, yes, and that she's an interior decorator.'

'Is she from a good family?' *Debrett's Peerage* was to Carol Whittaker what the Bible was to a Jehovah's Witness.

'Edmund didn't actually go into her antecedents,' Neil said drily.

'David's too young to get seriously involved.'

'He's twenty-eight.'

'Yes, but he never sticks at anything. How many jobs has he had since he failed to get into university? Six? Seven? Eight?'

'I think he's got a good job now, with a recording company.'

Carol snorted. 'And how long is that going to last? It'll be all pop stars and concerts and that sort of trash.'

Neil put his foot down hard on the accelerator and gritted his teeth. In their own home Carol was a very amenable woman: active, cheerful, involved in playing tennis and golf several times a week, and a gracious hostess. Yet as soon as they went to see her sister, she changed completely, becoming unbearably snobbish and intolerant of her peers. Was it a deep dissatisfaction within herself that suddenly made her critical of everyone else? Or was it jealousy that Virginia had so much more than her materially. He sighed inwardly, and hoped he wasn't going to have to listen to her carping all over Christmas.

'I wonder what David's girlfriend is like?' she continued.

'No doubt we shall soon find out,' Neil replied. 'They're arriving at about the same time as us. Driving down from London, Edmund said.'

Carol looked cross again. 'David doesn't have a car.'

'No, but she does.'

'How much further is it?' Charlotte asked, wriggling her toes. She'd slipped off her shoes as soon as they'd left London, and now her feet were wonderfully warm from the powerful car heater.

'We'll be there in ten minutes,' David replied. 'It's on the outskirts of a village called Barrow, but because we have a high walled garden, one gets the feeling it's more isolated. It's an interesting old place.' He'd taken it for granted he'd do the driving, and Charlotte hadn't minded because it meant she could relax. Slipping another tape into the cassette, she snuggled back in her seat, feeling safe and cocooned from the bleak-looking countryside that surrounded them. A grey shroud enveloped the damp landscape and, to Charlotte, who had always lived in London, it was the most depressing sight in the world. Then she had a sudden thought, and she turned anxiously to David.

'We will be sleeping in the same room, won't we?'

David raised his fair eyebrows and answered decisively, 'Not a chance.'

'Really?' She tried to keep the disappointment out of her voice. 'Oh well, I suppose you can always visit me in the night, after everyone's gone to sleep?'

'Yeah, course I can.' He turned to her briefly and smiled. 'Don't worry about it, love.'

Charlotte felt rather put out. But, she reminded herself, people in the country were far more fussy about that sort of thing when you were unmarried; probably something to do with the neighbours knowing and it not looking good.

'Is anyone else staying?' she asked.

David changed gear as they came to a steep hill. 'This might be the year for Aunt Carol and Uncle Neil to stay,' he said. 'She's Mum's sister and they come every other year.'

Charlotte said nothing. The whole thing was becoming more nerve-racking by the moment, and when David announced, 'Here we are,' as he turned left and swung the car up a wide gravel drive, edged with lime trees, she felt positively sick. Then the drive curved to the right and she saw it: a low, L-shaped building of old grey stone with a dusky pink slate roof and tall, lead-paned windows. Three pillars supported a jutting-out section above the main entrance, giving a portico effect. Beneath it the heavy oak front door was firmly shut.

The dark panelled hall was dominated at the far end by a Christmas tree of immense height and lushness, its blue spruce branches stretching elegantly outwards like long velvet gloves. Charlotte moved closer to get a better look at the decorations that hung from it and then gasped with pleasure.

'Oh, David! It's exquisite! I've got clients who would kill for a tree like this!'

Hundreds of tiny Victorian wooden figures dangled on tarnished gilt threads; Charlotte marvelled at how detailed was the carving and how exquisitely they'd been painted. Angels with scalloped wings and round, rosy cheeks hung in close proximity to jaunty sailors, prancing dapple-grey horses, clambering monkeys and cheeky, brightly coloured parrots. Black cats, clowns, fairies and gnomes swung gently alongside striped tigers and snowmen. To complete the nineteenth-century look, old-fashioned cream candles were held in place by little painted tin holders.

'Have you always had these carved figures in your family?' she asked, examining a minutely carved jack-in-the-box. 'They must be very valuable. I've never seen anything so enchanting.' Then she sighed. 'It does make all the glittery stuff we put on our trees nowadays seem trashy, doesn't it?'

David had brought their cases in from the car and had put them down in the middle of the hall, where dark blue velvet sofas and polished oak furniture gave it an air of grand formality. 'Where is everyone, I wonder?' The house was quiet, as if it had been deserted.

Then they heard quick, light footsteps trotting along the corridor that led off the hall, and a moment later a little girl with the face of an angel stood framed in the archway. She wore a denim mini-skirt that revealed sturdy legs in red woollen tights. The child glanced at them both with a serious expression, but her eyes seemed to dance with merriment.

'Hello, Uncle David.' She turned to Charlotte. 'Hello! What's your name?' she asked in a clear little voice.

'I'm Charlotte. Who are you?' Charlotte dropped on to her haunches in front of Holly and looked into her face. Holly immediately dropped on to her haunches in imitation and gazed back earnestly.

'I'm Holly.'

'Hello, Holly,' said Charlotte, falling in love.

'Have you come to stay?'

'Yes, David and I have come for Christmas.'

'So have I! Denzil said he'd faxed Father Christmas so he'd know I was staying here.'

Charlotte looked desperately in David's direction for

27

guidance. Holly was obviously his niece, but who was Denzil?

'Where's your granny?' David asked Holly. 'Where is everyone?'

'Granny's in the kitchen and my daddy is helping her 'cos there's a lot to do,' Holly replied without drawing breath. She gulped. 'And Grandpa's in the cellar. He's getting wine to drink.'

Holly grabbed Charlotte's hand. 'I'll show you the cellar.'

'I think we'd better say hello to your granny first,' Charlotte replied. She would ask David for a full 'who's who' when they were alone.

'Let's go then,' said David suddenly and decisively, pushing past them, and striding off down the corridor. The kitchen stood at the end of it and Virginia Farrell looked up in surprise as they entered.

'David! I never heard you arrive . . . ! And you must be Charlotte!' Her face, deeply etched with wrinkles, lit up. She smiled warmly as she came towards them, hands outstretched.

'Did you have a good journey? The weather hasn't been too good, I was worried about you. The roads get very icy at this time of day. Carol and Neil haven't arrived yet, although they said they'd be here in time for tea. I wonder what can have happened to them? Chris, darling, put on the kettle, will you? I'm sure everyone is dying for a cup of tea.' Talking non-stop, Virginia Farrell flitted around the kitchen, a slim woman in her late fifties. She seemed rather highly strung, with an anxious expression and a flustered manner.

Christopher came forward, grinning and wiping his hands on a cloth. In contrast to his mother, he appeared laid back and relaxed.

'Sorry I can't greet you in the proper manner, but I've had my hands up a turkey's backside for the last hour, and I can think of more attractive places to be.'

Charlotte laughed, liking him instantly, but there was something debauched about his bearded, smiling face. His slightly rotund body showed signs of indulgence, too, as he ambled over to her in baggy trousers and a chunky sweater. She watched as he and David greeted each other, their lack of affection reflecting what David had told her about the brothers' relationship. Her family were extremely effusive, had always been very close, but then they hadn't been through the difficulties that the Farrells had.

'Is the turkey ready, Daddy?' Holly piped up, kneeling on a kitchen chair so she could get a better look at the bird which was now sitting in a large roasting pan by the sink.

'Yes. I've stuffed it with chestnuts and it's going to be tucked up for the night in the Aga so it will be ready for lunch tomorrow,' Christopher informed her.

Holly digested this piece of information with satisfaction. 'After Father Christmas has been?'

'Yes, sweetheart.' He caught Charlotte's eye and smiled.

Virginia swooped around the kitchen, putting out things for tea. 'Bread and jam? Biscuits? Scones? Fruit cake? What do you like, Charlotte? I think there are some muffins we could toast . . . and, oh, there's some homemade damson jam in the larder. Do you like Indian or China tea?'

Charlotte's head reeled. 'Whatever everyone else is having, Mrs Farrell,' she replied lamely.

'Do stop fussing, Mother,' David said in a flat, weary voice.

Virginia Farrell looked rebuffed. 'I'm only trying to get

29

a nice tea for you all,' she replied, hurt.'

At that moment the kitchen door opened. A tall man with thick white hair and strong, tanned features stood there, carrying a large gardening trug. It was filled with bottles of wine. He looked round the kitchen at the assembled company, his penetrating dark eyes taking in everything at a glance. Virginia's nervousness seemed to increase, and she dropped a jam spoon with a clatter.

'Grandpa!' Holly shrieked in delight. 'Have you got the drink?'

'Hello, everyone.' His eyes lingered on Charlotte for a moment, and she couldn't tell whether his expression was friendly or not.

'Hi, Dad.' David went over to him and they shook hands while Holly jumped up and down and tried to take the trug from her grandfather. 'This is Charlotte,' David added.

'No, Holly, it's too heavy for you,' Edmund Farrell remonstrated, though not unkindly. Then he looked up again. 'Hello, Charlotte.' He shook her hand. 'Glad you could come and stay with us. Had a good journey?' It was a rhetorical question, to which he expected no answer. Lifting the trug on to the kitchen table, he turned to Virginia.

'Why did you tell me to bring up more port? I checked in the dining room and there's plenty in the decanters.'

'I thought with so many people . . .' Her voice drifted off into silence as she fussed with a large white teapot.

Edmund smiled thinly at Charlotte. 'Christmas, eh? Weeks of shopping and preparation, hours of work and worry, and it's all over in a few hours! Who needs it?'

'Oh, come on, Dad!' Christopher laughed jovially. 'Don't be such an old Scrooge! You've got your whole family around you, including your granddaughter! What more do you want? We're going to have a fabulous time, aren't we?' He turned to Charlotte. 'Here's a girl who I'm sure knows how to have a good time!'

Charlotte laughed. Christopher's good humour really was infectious and she felt her doubts about the next few days dwindle. 'I make it my business to enjoy myself!' she replied stoutly. 'Life's too short for anything else.'

'Exactly my sentiments,' Christopher agreed. 'Come on, Mum. Pay no attention to the old man, and let's have a cup of tea.' As he spoke he scooped Holly up in his arms, tickled her playfully, then seated her on one of the wooden kitchen chairs.

'Milkshake!' she demanded.

This threw Virginia into a deeper spin. 'Oh, darling, I don't know if we have . . . Would a chocolate drink do? Or would you like orangeade? Or a nice hot cup of Horlicks . . . ?'

'Ma,' said Christopher with cheerful patience. 'Holly will have plain milk and that's an end of it.'

'No, no . . . milkshake!' Holly repeated with determination. 'Banana milkshake.'

'There isn't . . .' Virginia paused and then her tired face lit up. 'All right, darling! I can do that! I've got bananas, and milk, and if we put them in the liquidiser . . . What do you think, Chris? That would be a milkshake, wouldn't it? We could add a little sugar . . . ?'

Charlotte could see that Christopher was torn between exasperation and amusement. 'Sit down, Ma. I'll do it.' He rose, moving neatly for someone of such comfortable build.

David and his father were engrossed in conversation, so

Charlotte turned to talk to Virginia, who was making a jam sandwich for Holly.

'What a beautiful house this is,' she observed conversationally, although she realised she'd hardly seen anything of it yet.

'Thank you, my dear. It's very old. Not very convenient, but Edmund loves it. In the summer the garden is very pretty.'

Charlotte looked round the expensively equipped kitchen, confirming her suspicions that the Farrells were rich.

'You don't look after if all by yourself, though, do you?' she asked. From the outside it looked enormous.

Virginia handed Holly her sandwich and then absently stroked her curling blonde hair. Charlotte noticed her fingers were still sticky with jam, but Virginia seemed oblivious of this as she twisted Holly's curl round and round.

'We have Fred, the gardener, and of course I have Gladys and Ruby for the house. They'll be here in a few minutes to do dinner tonight, and they'll be here most of tomorrow.'

'On Christmas Day?' Charlotte asked in surprise. Even in London her mother found it difficult to hire help on Christmas Day.

Virginia dropped her voice to a conspiratorial whisper. 'Gladys is a widow, and Ruby is her daughter. They live in the village. Ruby has a baby, although I'm afraid there's no husband. One of Gladys's many sisters looks after the baby when Ruby's here, and so it works very well. They need the money and I need the help. They even do all the washing and ironing. Such a joy, my dear.' For a brief moment the older woman seemed to relax, and her blue eyes looked almost tranquil. Then she sighed. 'This is *such* a large house, Charlotte.'

Charlotte nodded. And gloomy too, she thought. Not to mention rather oppressive.

' . . . The private sector will never make a go of the railways,' Edmund was booming from the other side of the round pine table.

'It'll make them a damn site more efficient, though,' Christopher replied with fervour.

'But there needs to be a massive injection of capital put into rolling stock,' David interjected.

Impressed by his knowledge, Charlotte nevertheless hoped the whole of Christmas wasn't going to be spent listening to David discussing railways.

When they'd had tea, Charlotte turned to Virginia. She was longing to unpack, and maybe have a bath before dinner.

'Is it all right if I go to my room?' she asked shyly.

Virginia sprang to her feet as if she'd received an electric shock. 'Oh! My dear girl! How perfectly dreadful of me! I'll show you up, right away! Edmund, dear! *Edmund*!'

His expression was resigned. 'What is it now?'

'Can you take Charlotte's cases up to her room? The poor girl doesn't even know where she's sleeping!' She made it sound as if it was his fault.

Edmund spread his large hands, indicating his sons. 'Why can't one of them take up the cases?'

'Honestly, I can easily . . .' Charlotte protested.

David jumped to his feet, nearly knocking over his chair. 'For God's sake! Charlotte and I will do it ourselves! What room have you put her in?' he demanded angrily, obviously appalled at his father's rudeness.

There was a stunned silence, but before anyone had time to reply, there was the sound of voices coming from the hall.

'Oh, it's Carol and Neil! They've arrived! At *last*!' Virginia shot off on her long thin legs to greet them.

'Come on, darling. Let's get settled into our rooms,' David muttered and, grabbing Charlotte's hand, led her towards the hall, where they came face to face with Virginia's sister and brother-in-law.

After brief introductions, David picked up their cases and made for the stairs. Charlotte, still rather stung by Edmund's rudeness, followed him. She would be glad of a few minutes alone with David.

'Charlotte's in the third room on the left,' Virginia called up after them.

It turned out to be a large, old-fashioned room, furnished with a hotch-potch of mixed patterned chintz and odd pieces of furniture which at first glance caused Charlotte to wince; but it was comfortable in a homely way and it was warm. After David had left her, she ran a bath in the adjoining bathroom and hung up her clothes in the big walnut wardrobe. She thought about her own family back in London. They'd be opening the champagne soon, and allowing themselves just one present each before dinner from beneath the tree. The conversation would be warm and witty and the banter affectionate. They might even have invited a few friends for supper, to share in the festivities.

Sighing, Charlotte climbed into the large cast-iron bath and closed her eyes. She loved David and that was why she was here. That was something she had to remember and, if necessary, keep reminding herself of for the next three days.

An hour later, changed into a neat navy blue dress with tights and shoes to match, Charlotte went downstairs again and found everyone in the drawing room, sitting before a smouldering log fire.

David came over to her immediately. 'You've been ages, sweetheart. Are you all right?'

'Yes, of course, I'm sorry . . . I didn't know you were waiting for me.'

'Well, you're here now.' He sounded a little tense. 'What do you want to drink?'

She glanced at the tray of drinks arranged on a side table. There was no sign of champagne.

'Gin and tonic, please,' she replied. As he mixed the drink, adding a lump of ice, she whispered, concerned, 'What's wrong?'

'Nothing's wrong. I was missing you. That's all!' His smile was boyish and apologetic. When she smiled back, he reached out and squeezed her hand.

Glowing with happiness now, Charlotte went over to join the rest of his family.

'There you are, Charlotte,' Virginia greeted her warmly. She'd changed into a smart red dress and brushed her hair into a woolly fluff of curls around her head. 'I want you to meet my sister properly . . .'

She grasped Charlotte's wrist with a bejewelled hand and led her over to the stocky woman she'd met briefly in the hall. She had grey hair cut short and straight, and was wearing a thick tweed dress and clumpy shoes.

'Carol, you've met Charlotte briefly . . .' Her voice faded as she looked at them both. 'This is my sister, Carol Whittaker,' she continued, starting up again. 'Carol and Neil live near Newbury and Carol's the sporty one in the family. Always was, even when we were girls, weren't you, dear? Oh, my goodness, your glass is empty! Edmund, give Carol another drink, will you, dear? Dinner won't be ready for a while, I'm afraid, so do have another drink.'

'Is there anything I can do to help, Mrs Farrell?' Charlotte asked politely.

Virginia's blue eyes stared at her, wide open and with a faintly blank look, as if not much was registering. 'It's all right, thank you, dear. Gladys and Ruby are here and they've got everything under control. I don't think dinner will be very long . . . I suppose if we . . .' But the words faded away again as she looked over at Edmund who was deep in conversation with Neil and looked as if he had no intention of topping up people's drinks. It suddenly dawned on Charlotte why Virginia never seemed to finish a sentence, why her voice always trailed off; it was because Edmund never listened to anything she said.

'What do you do with yourself, Charlotte?' she heard Carol Whittaker ask. 'You live in London, I gather?' There was a note of criticism in her voice, and her mouth, slightly whiskered, drooped disapprovingly at the corners.

'I'm an interior decorator.'

'What does that entail?'

'I work for someone who decorates people's houses and flats.'

'Oh!' There was unmistakable contempt in her voice. 'I can't imagine anything worse than having someone do up my house. Haven't these people any ideas of their own? I suppose they're too rich and spoilt to be bothered.' She finished her glass of whisky and soda and then looked hopefully in Edmund's direction.

Charlotte flushed. 'In most cases the clients haven't the

time,' she replied quietly. 'They know what they want and we never impose our ideas on them, but they do need a designer to pull the whole thing together.' But Carol Whittaker's attention was already elsewhere.

Dinner was served at eight o'clock in the formal dining room, where the long oval table was laid with an immense amount of silver, including a pair of ornate candelabra in which flickered dark green candles. Charlotte found herself placed on Edmund Farrell's left as he took his place at the head of the table, and she was relieved to find David was sitting on her other side. If they couldn't sleep together, at least sitting together was allowed.

They were served by Gladys, a rotund, jolly-looking woman in a white overall, and Ruby, even jollier and plumper than her mother, and seemingly almost as old. Edmund poured the white wine into exquisite hock glasses, each a different vivid jewel colour, and Charlotte looked round appreciatively, noting the white damask cloth and table-napkins and the simple arrangement of cotoneaster, heavy with scarlet berries and dark, glossy leaves, in a silver rose bowl in the centre of the table.

They were half-way through the first course, which was salmon mousse, when the dining room door opened and Holly came bursting into the room in her nightdress. She ran over to Christopher; there were large tears rolling down her cheeks.

'What's the matter, my precious?' he asked, concerned, gathering her up in his arms.

'I don't think Father Christmas knows where I am,' she wept. 'Can we phone Mummy and get her to tell him?'

'Sweetheart, I promise you he'll come to see you tonight,' Christopher said gently, dabbing her wet cheeks with his table-napkin.

'But he won't come if you're still awake,' Carol intervened in a brisk, jolly voice.

'That's right,' Neil added, nodding his head and smiling, still wishing after all these years that he and Carol had been able to have a family.

Virginia leaned forward, whispering. 'I'll give you a sweet if you get back into bed.'

Holly regarded her with serious eyes, unsure if she could be bribed.

'Who's a lucky girl?' Christopher coaxed. 'Go with Granny and she'll get you something nice.'

Holly slid off her father's knee, smiling tremulously. Virginia rose and taking her hand, led her to the sideboard. Charlotte watched as Holly gravely examined the contents of a box of chocolates before choosing one. She was unfamiliar with children, but the sight of Holly with her angelic face and soft blonde hair made her suddenly long, for the first time, to have a baby.

'Isn't she adorable?' she said to David, as Christopher carried Holly off to bed.

He smiled, looking into her eyes. 'Don't tell me you're getting broody!'

'Not right this minute,' she blushed, 'but I'd like to have children one day.'

'Meanwhile, you enjoy practising how to conceive?' he grinned, whispering so no one could hear.

'Of course. Don't you?' she responded swiftly looking into his eyes.

Gladys and Ruby brought in the next course, which was roast lamb. Above the sound of general chatter, Charlotte suddenly heard Edmund exclaim irritably: 'What's happened to Christopher? What the hell's he doing now?'

'I expect he's reading Holly a story,' Virginia replied, soothingly. Several drinks seemed to have had a calming effect on her.

Carol seemed anxious to placate her brother-in-law, too. 'He's a very devoted father, isn't he? He's so good with her.'

Edmund scowled. 'Is there any reason why he shouldn't be?'

'Of course not. But you can see she's missing her mother. It's dreadful for a child to have a broken home.'

To Charlotte's horror, she didn't even try to keep her voice low. At any moment Christopher might return and hear what they were saying. She looked at the others. They seemed unperturbed as they helped themselves to mint sauce and gravy.

David leaned forward, staring at his aunt, and said in hushed tones, 'But Linda couldn't stay with him; she had a duty to protect their child.'

'*David*!' Edmund shouted so loudly that they all jumped. 'You've no right to talk about Chris like that. Where's your family loyalty?'

'He never showed any when he was destroying himself and us,' David continued hotly. 'Not to mention his own wife and daughter.' His voice was quavery.

'But he's given it all up! He hasn't touched a drop of drink or been near drugs for the past year. Ever since he went to that clinic for treatment,' Edmund thundered.

'I wish . . . I really wish I could believe that.' The two men were glaring at each other, David's blue eyes glistening suddenly.

Shocked by his distress, Charlotte stole a look at his profile. His jaw was tightly clenched and her heart contracted in sympathy. Much as she liked Christopher his addiction had clearly taken a terrible toll on them all.

'Please, David.' Virginia looked distressed and for a moment Charlotte thought she was going to burst into tears. 'Don't let's have any unpleasantness. Christopher is a changed person. Even Linda agrees the treatment worked. And he is a marvellous father, there's no doubt about it.'

At that moment they heard footsteps clattering down the polished staircase, and Virginia turned to Neil, on her left, and said in a normal voice, 'Are you and Carol going anywhere nice this year? You went to Spain last summer, didn't you . . . ?'

Christopher came back into the room. If he suspected they'd been talking about him, he gave no sign of it.

'Sorry about that,' he said genially. 'We had to leave another note for Father Christmas.' Then he caught Charlotte's eye and smiled, and for a moment she felt ashamed. Perhaps he deserved her sympathy as much as David did.

It was after eleven when Christopher stole into Holly's room and filled the pillowcase at the foot of her bed with presents. She lay asleep on her back, her arms spread wide. To him she was the most beautiful child in the world, and he would gladly, if required, have given his life for her. For a moment his eyes stung in the semi-darkness as he remembered the night she'd been born. He had rushed Linda into Queen Charlotte's Hospital, thinking the baby's arrival was imminent, but then had come the long hours of pain for Linda and anxiety for him. It hadn't been until eight the next morning that Holly had finally appeared, red faced and howling. He'd loved her from that moment.

Four years on, the hurt he felt at no longer being able to see her all the time never left him. It was his own fault, of course. He admitted it. He'd been out of his skull during his marriage, wanting to, yet unable to give up the stuff that had nearly destroyed him. In the end Linda hadn't been able to stand it any longer. She'd walked out, taking Holly with her, and gone back to her mother's, where she'd stayed until she met Denzil Blake. Denzil had been able to give Linda the security she so badly needed, and he adored Holly too, but it grieved Christopher that it was someone else who saw Holly every morning, who kissed her every night, who comforted her childish woes and heard her singing in a sweet but off-key voice her own version of 'Twinkle, Twinkle Little Star'.

Sometimes, in an agony of self-disgust mixed with self-pity, Christopher would curse Linda for leaving him and depriving him of his daughter, but in his heart of hearts he knew she'd had no option; the trouble was he hadn't been able to get through a day without a fix, and he hadn't wanted the responsibility of being married either. By the time he woke up to that fact, it was too late.

He took one last look at Holly and then stole back to his own room. Delving into the bottom of his hold-all he pulled out a bottle of Bell's whisky. Drugs were no longer a part of his life, but drink still was. Not that anyone knew, because he'd learned the art of drinking steadily and secretly so that, whilst he was never completely sober, he was never obviously drunk either. Fetching the tooth-mug from the adjoining bathroom, he poured out a measure and, sitting on the side of the bed, sipped it slowly and appreciatively. After all, it was Christmas, he told himself, and he wouldn't drink during the day while he was with Holly, so what was the harm . . . ? Reaching for one of the paperbacks his mother had left on the bedside table, he opened it and started reading. Ten minutes later, absorbed in the racy thriller, he realised he'd finished his drink. Looking at the empty tooth-mug for a moment, he pondered on whether he should allow himself another shot of whisky? Just a small one? Temptation won over caution. The second drink was rather larger than the first. Downstairs the grandfather clock continued to chime the quarter hours. He'd go to bed as soon as he'd finished his drink because Holly was sure to be up early in the morning.

Along the corridor, Virginia washed her face with a flannel wrung out in very hot water, pressing it to her forehead and temples in an endeavour to help her feel less stressed. Then she patted her skin dry and, looking in the mirror, tried to recall the face of the young girl she'd once been. It was impossible. A strained, anxious woman with a deeply lined face stared back at her. Wrinkles, like straight furrows, fanned out from what had once been a softly tender mouth. Thirty years of being married to a bully like Edmund had left their mark. The trouble was she'd always been too scared to answer back. Too scared to leave him, too, without any money of her own. And then there had been the problem of children. When she hadn't become pregnant during the first few years of their marriage, he'd blamed her. Nothing could be wrong with him. He was all right. The trouble had to lie with her. It stood to reason. There'd never been anything wrong with the men in *his* family. On and on it went, driving her crazy. Now, looking back on those early years, she realised it might have been better if they'd never had David and Christopher. As unalike as chalk and cheese, the boys had caused problems, in their different ways, ever since puberty. Only small children are nice, she thought sadly. If only they stayed small, like Holly, how much more pleasant the world would be.

When she re-entered her bedroom, a bleak, unlovely room with beige walls and carpet, she went over to the chest-of-drawers by the window and opened the top left-hand drawer. From this she extracted, after nervous groping among a selection of tired-looking Marks and Spencer underclothing, a small bottle. Inside, turquoise and white capsules glistened reassuringly, reminding her that, with their help, life could be made bearable; well, almost. These weren't 'happy' pills, of course. Her doctor had told her there was no such thing. These were – she took out two with care – these were *blunting* pills. They blunted the jagged edges of life, insulating her somewhat from Edmund's sarcastic manner.

Gazing up at the ceiling as she lay in bed waiting for him, she knew that if he didn't come up soon, she'd fall asleep. She always seemed to fall asleep these days as soon as her head touched the pillow. It was a way of escaping reality, of course, of taking refuge in blessed oblivion, and she embraced the blackness that overcame her with a sigh of welcome.

* * *

Edmund walked quietly into the kitchen to make the call. Virginia, Carol, Neil and Christopher were all upstairs in their rooms now, and only David and Charlotte remained downstairs, engrossed in some rubbish on television. There was no risk of him being disturbed, and so he dialled the local number he knew so well, he could have dialled it blindfold.

A woman's voice answered swiftly, as if she'd been waiting by the phone. 'Yes?'

'It's me,' Edmund whispered, although he knew he couldn't be overheard.

'How's me?'

He could tell by the way she spoke that she was smiling. In his mind's eye he could picture her lying in bed, her lustrous black hair tumbling about her creamy shoulders, her dark eyes gleaming. Everything about Olivia was seductive. Even her bedroom was an oyster satin haven of luxury, and she herself the pearl lying in its midst. He closed his eyes and sighed deeply.

'I'm missing you dreadfully, darling. God, Olivia, how am I going to get through Christmas without you?'

'You *could* be with me, sweetie.' Olivia's voice was husky.

'You know it's impossible.'

'Nothing's impossible if you want it enough.'

'Christ, you know how much I want you.'

'But not enough, apparently. Otherwise you'd be here with me now . . . in bed.'

Edmund groaned, and Mackie, in his dog basket in the corner, looked up with pricked ears. 'Jesus, Olivia, I'm

44

getting an erection just thinking about you.'

'Then what are you going to do about it?'

'What *can* I do?'

Her laugh was richly deep. 'Poor Edmund. Christmas Eve and you're reduced to a quick hand-job in the bathroom.'

'Don't joke about it,' he said, distressed. 'I don't just need you in that way. I love you, damnit.'

'I know.' She sounded almost sad. 'And I love you too, but if you won't leave Virginia, what are we to do? Meet secretly two or three times a week for the rest of our lives? I want to be with you, sweetheart. All the time. Meeting you only now and again is driving me crazy.'

'You know how difficult it is, Olivia. I'd ask for a divorce tomorrow if I could. You know that. I love you more than anything else in the world, believe me.'

She sounded slightly sullen. 'Couldn't she go and live with that sister of hers?'

'I'd still have to make a settlement. After all these years it would be a fortune!' Edmund began to sound flustered. 'I might have to sell this house.'

'I'm sorry, darling . . . I'm sorry,' Olivia said contritely. 'I didn't mean to upset you. I know how difficult it is for you. It's just that I'm so miserable without you, tonight of all nights.'

They'd been through this a hundred times, Edmund reflected, and it never got them anywhere. Occasionally he liked to entertain the fantasy that one day he and Olivia, who was a divorcée of thirty-two, would get married and set up home together at Chelwood Manor. But it was only a fantasy. If he asked Virginia for a divorce it would cost him half of everything he'd worked for, including the house, and not even the sexiest woman in the world was going to force him to make those sorts of sacrifices. Meanwhile, he spoke coaxingly.

'Shall I come and see you now?' It was a cold night, but dry. A brisk walk across the fields to the far side of Barrow, and then up Burchfield Lane to Magnolia Cottage, would take less than ten minutes.

Olivia gasped with pleasure. 'Really? You'd come and see me now?' Her voice was tremulous with joy. 'Oh, yes, please! Please, darling. That would be wonderful.'

Edmund glanced at his wristwatch. It was eleven-thirty. The thought of Olivia lying in bed waiting for him, smooth skinned and scented and so skilled at making love she made his head reel, was a temptation he couldn't resist.

'I'll be right over,' he whispered. But first he must go upstairs and check that Virginia had gone to sleep.

'Who was that you were talking to?' Carol asked Neil as he came into the bedroom. Their bathroom was on the opposite side of the corridor, and she'd heard voices droning on for the past few minutes.

'Edmund. He was going to check the thermostat in the cellar or something. I asked if I could help but he said it was all right.'

'At this time of night?'

Neil shrugged. 'You know what he's like; always fussing over something.' He slid into the large bed beside her, his flannel pyjamas striped like a schoolboy's.

Carol put down her book of *Tips for the Advanced Golfer*. 'I like David's girlfriend, don't you?'

'Yes. I'd say she's quite bright.'

'Do you think she's well off? David needs someone with money; someone who will get him kick-started in life.'

'I've no idea.' *I'm not very interested either,* he thought, turning on to his side and shutting his eyes.

'She told me, when we were chatting after dinner, that her father works for a large finance company. Her mother's very successful, too.'

Trust Carol, Neil thought, to go poking her nose into other people's affairs.

'Don't you want to know what her mother does?' Carol demanded. 'She's very well known.'

Neil sighed. It was no good. He wouldn't be allowed a wink of sleep until Carol had unburdened herself of this riveting piece of information.

'So what does she do?' he asked.

'She's Margaret Taylor!'

'Who the hell's Margaret Taylor?'

'She's a famous cookery writer! She's written *Suppers on a Shoestring*, *Lunch for Loungers*, *Elegant Entertaining*, and a whole lot more. I've got them all at home.'

'Bully for you.'

Carol sighed heavily. 'Why are you never interested in people, Neil?'

'I am, if I like them. But I've never met or even heard of Margaret Taylor, so why should I be interested?'

'Supposing David marries Charlotte?'

Neil opened weary eyes and stared at his wife. 'You're being a bit premature, aren't you?'

'Virginia told me they've been going out for three months. This is also the first time he's brought a girl home. I'd say it looks hopeful.'

'Hopeful for whom?' he asked drily.

'Both of them, if they marry . . . You know what I mean perfectly well, Neil! And it would be rather fun if David married the daughter of someone famous.'

Neil rolled on to his back, abandoning all thoughts of immediate sleep. The trouble with Carol was that she completely lacked any sense of logic. Where was the fun, he asked himself, in having a nephew – by marriage in his case – who married a girl whose mother wrote cookery books?

'Well, if it makes you happy, dear,' he said finally. He was beginning to detect a headache starting and he wished he hadn't drunk so much port after dinner.

'Well, if David *does* marry Charlotte,' she continued unabashed, 'I think it will be the making of him. Already I can see a change since he's known her. I gather his company are going to promote him in the New Year. Maybe he'll be able to afford a flat then, unless of course he moves into Charlotte's place. Neil? Neil?' She leaned towards her husband but he was fast asleep. Or at least pretending to be, she thought crossly. Why was it that both she and Virginia, who so loved to converse, had married silent types?

As soon as David and Charlotte had wished Edmund goodnight, and he'd shut the study door firmly 'so that the noise of the television won't disturb us all', David slumped back on the sofa, as if in relief.

Charlotte moved closer.

'Are you all right?' The row at dinner had upset him badly, but he turned towards her and smiled faintly.

48

'Yes, I'm OK, sweetheart. It's just such a strain being here,' he replied. His blue eyes were intense. 'As you may have gathered, it's not the easiest family in the world to live with. And Christopher's problems have always demanded so much of my parents' attention that it's hard not to feel ignored sometimes.' He laughed self-consciously and hugged her. 'But I've got you to myself now, so let's forget them.'

'Oh darling,' Charlotte sighed. 'I can see how hard it must have been for you all, but I don't believe for one minute that they don't care at least as much about you as they do about Christopher. You're their elder son! Maybe they're just not very good at showing it.'

'You're so good for me, La.' He pulled her towards him. 'You're the best thing that's ever happened to me.'

'Oh, David . . .' Tears sprang to her eyes: he needed her as much as she needed him. The warm feeling of security the thought gave her made her press herself closer to him.

Then he was kissing her demandingly, pulling her down on to the sofa, his hands fumbling with the buttons down the front of her dress.

'David . . . ! Your family,' she protested weakly.

'Shush,' he whispered between kisses. 'It's all right.'

She tried to get off the sofa but he held her fast with unexpected strength, sliding his thigh between her legs so that she couldn't move.

'David!' Charlotte turned her face away. 'Your family might come down again! We can't do it here . . .'

'Of course we can, my angel.' His breath was hot on her neck, his hands powerful as they explored inside her dress, caressing her with skill. Suddenly she felt excited. The risk of being caught added a new dimension to their love-making,

making her want him with urgency.

'I don't know what I'd do without you,' he was whispering seductively.

'You'll never have to do without me . . .' she whispered back, her arms wound round his neck. 'I love you.'

David looked down into her eyes, and his expression was tender.

'I love you, too, little angel.' He kissed her deeply, passionately, and she pressed herself closer, feeling breathless, dizzy, transported to some heavenly paradise, which was inhabited by only the two of them.

Fleetingly, she wondered if he would ask her to marry him, over Christmas. They were the words she most longed to hear, the words that would transport her forever to a state of bliss. Her need to belong to him was acute. If she couldn't be a part of his life, the most important part, then she wouldn't want to go on living.

He was pushing up her dress now and pulling off her white satin panties. Then he buried his face between her legs, driving her crazy with his tongue, arousing her so much that she groaned aloud and then remembering there were other people in the house, sank her teeth into one of the velvet cushions that was on the sofa.

'Oh, baby.' His voice was throaty, ardent. 'Oh, baby angel, you're so wonderful. I want to go on making love to you all night.' David undid his trousers. 'I want you. I must have you. Oh dear God, always be here for me, won't you?'

'Oh, I will, David. I promise.' She parted her legs, guided him inside, pressing down so that he could go deep, gasping and convulsing as he probed even deeper, filling her with his love, transporting her to a world of ecstasy, where pleasure filled her whole horizon and all she wanted was to be part of him forever.

He came before she did, in a great throbbing explosion of released desire, but it did not matter, for he still stayed inside her, strong and hard, thrusting again, working himself up into another orgasm, moaning with the pleasurable pain of coming again so quickly, but determined to satisfy her, too. She could feel the rising tide beginning deep inside her, rising quickly, feverishly, consuming all her other senses so that all she was capable of was feeling; feeling her body linked to his, feeling his strength, feeling the bliss as the tide broke its banks and she was left shuddering on the shore, replete and spent.

'I suppose we'd better go upstairs, before we get caught,' David murmured a few minutes later. He smiled down at her, as he braced himself on his hands. He looked hot and dishevelled, but sublimely happy.

Charlotte nodded. 'I wish we were sleeping together,' she said wistfully, as they clambered off the sofa and straightened their clothes.

He leaned forward to kiss her lightly on the lips.

'I wish we were, too, sweetheart, but it's only for a few nights, and then we'll be back in London.'

'I know,' she nodded, smiling. 'It's just that I miss you so, when you're not beside me.'

'Me too.'

Hand in hand they went up to bed, lingering on the landing for a moment to exchange kisses, before Charlotte went into her room.

' 'Night,' David whispered, as he headed off down the corridor to his own room.

After she'd undressed, Charlotte turned off the lights and, going to the window, pulled back the curtains. Born and brought up in a city, she was intrigued by the countryside at night. The emptiness and stillness filled her with awe. The fact that there were no people, only thousands of animals and birds and insects out there in the silent darkness gave her an eerie feeling. Opening the casement she leaned out and took a deep breath. The cold air smelled of damp earth and the darkness seemed solid. Then, bit by bit, as her eyes got used to it, the outline of trees and bushes became etched against a pewter sky.

Looking up she saw a single star and remembered this was, after all, Christmas Eve. Then something on the ground caught her attention. There was a movement. Suddenly a man, tall and broad shouldered, came striding swiftly across the lawn in the direction of the house. For a moment Charlotte held her breath, thinking it must be an intruder, but then something familiar about the figure made her frown. As he disappeared among the shrubbery that edged the path to the back door, she realised with a shock that it was Edmund Farrell. At that moment the clock in the hall chimed once.

Chapter Three

Christopher awoke with a start, the agonising crick in his neck causing him to give a sharp yelp of pain. He was also frozen. Peering at his watch he saw it was five o'clock in the morning.

'Jesus!' He jumped to his feet, head pounding, trying to assess the situation as quickly as his addled senses would allow. The whisky bottle, three-quarters empty, stood on the floor by the side of the bed. Beside it, neatly placed, was the empty tooth-mug.

'Oh, *shit*!' He clapped the palm of his hand to his forehead. How *could* he have done such a thing? Christ, what had happened to his good resolutions? Worse still, supposing Holly had come into his room in the middle of the night and found him out cold, still fully dressed and lying on top of the bed?

Christopher rubbed his beard in guilty anguish. If he went on like this he'd blow it. All the 'conditions' had to be adhered to if he was going to be allowed to see Holly – and he could just picture Linda's expression of horror if she saw him now. Why the hell had he drunk so much the previous night? he thought, in self-disgust.

Slipping out of his clothes, he struggled into his pyjamas. He wished his parents had a better central heating system:

the room was icy. He could almost see his breath vaporising as he blew on his cold fingers. Then he hid the whisky bottle in his hold-all again and rinsed the tooth-mug under the cold tap in the hand-basin.

Once in bed, sleep evaded him. In an hour or so Holly would appear, her face alight with the innocent pleasure of finding Father Christmas had visited her after all. Meanwhile, he was going to have to pull himself together and at least pretend he was the man he would really like to be.

Virginia was down first the next morning, fortified against the coming stress of the day by two more white and turquoise capsules, and a couple of aspirins as well, since her consumption of white wine the previous night had left her with a slight headache.

'Good morning, Gladys. Good morning, Ruby.' She greeted the two women, who were already hard at work in the kitchen. An aroma of grilling bacon and fragrant coffee permeated the air, and she sniffed appreciatively. 'How does the turkey look?' she asked.

'Grand,' Gladys assured her. 'It'll be just right for one o'clock.'

Virginia looked around with approval, finding the well-organised activity in the kitchen soothing to her turbulent inner feelings. While Gladys prepared breakfast, Ruby was busy doing the vegetables by the sink, chopping and slicing them with practised ease. On the kitchen table, mince pies and brandy butter, crystallised fruit and bowls of nuts stood in readiness to be carried into the dining room. Nevertheless, within moments of surveying the busy scene,

Virginia's natural agitation surfaced again.

'Have you found the boxes of crackers?' she asked Gladys, who was arranging fried eggs on a dish with artistic precision. 'And you've remembered the cranberry sauce? And what about the cream to go with the mince pies? We did get double cream, didn't we?' Flitting nervously from fridge to Aga and back again, Virginia already looked worn out. Gladys regarded her with patient sympathy.

'Everything's been taken care of, Mrs Farrell,' she said, as gently as if talking to a child. 'There's no need to worry.'

Useless to say that, Virginia thought, her heart thumping as she contemplated Edmund's anger if anything went wrong. It was his sarcastic turn of phrase that was so wounding. 'One would at least expect you to be able to remember to order cream,' she could hear him say in that cold, mocking voice of his.

'Good . . . good,' Virginia muttered distractedly. As she loped off in the direction of the dining room, her tweed skirt falling from her narrow hips in heavy folds, Gladys regarded her back view pityingly.

'She's in ever such a state, isn't she?' she whispered to Ruby. 'Gawd, it'll be tears before bedtime. It's too much for her, having all these people to stay.' She shook her head knowingly. In her opinion, Mrs Farrell had a lot to put up with.

Gladys had been born in Barrow fifty-seven years ago, and she knew everything that went on in the village, as did her sister, Mabel. They'd both been in service since the age of sixteen, and they'd both married young farm-workers who also lived locally. Between them there was a network of gossip and information that would do credit to government intelligence. Mabel, in particular, had a lot to talk about, because for the past year she'd worked at Magnolia Cottage, the home of the exotic Mrs Olivia Middleton. It was rumoured Mrs Middleton had been divorced – more than once, in fact – and that she'd had a string of men 'friends'. For the past year, however, she'd got her claws stuck into Edmund Farrell. She wasn't going to let him go, neither, Mabel declared darkly. Ambitious like, was Olivia Middleton and she'd set her sights on Chelwood Manor and all the trimmings that went with it, right from the start. Mabel was of the opinion she wouldn't let go until she got what she wanted.

Everyone in the village knew that several times a week Edmund Farrell visited the 'dark divorcée' as she was called locally because of the colour of her hair, and the only person who didn't seem to know what was going on was Virginia Farrell.

'It's a shame,' Mabel said reprovingly. 'A nice lady like her.'

'It seems to me Mrs Farrell would be better off without him,' Gladys assured her sister. Neither of them would have dreamed of saying anything to Virginia, though. That would be interfering. There were some things that were better left alone, in their opinion.

Breakfast was ready. Carrying a tray with several silver racks of toast into the dining room, Gladys found Virginia hovering uncertainly near the sideboard.

'Thank you, Gladys. That looks very nice, but where is everyone? There's so much still to be done and we've got to lay the table for lunch. Perhaps you'd better sound the gong.'

It was still only half-past eight, Gladys reflected privately.

'Very well, Mrs Farrell. There's eggs and bacon and grilled tomatoes on the hotplate, and grapefruit for whoever wants it.' Gladys turned to leave the room with Virginia close at her heels.

'Don't worry about the gong, after all, Gladys. You get on in the kitchen.'

Virginia overtook Gladys, crossing the hall with hurried strides. Then she took the polished stick with the leather padded head, and struck the large brass gong with several short sharp beats. Booming waves of sound reverberated round the hall.

There was a roar from the staircase behind her. Startled, she spun round and saw Edmund coming down the stairs.

'What the bloody hell do you think you're doing, woman?' he yelled. 'That thing goes right through my head!'

Abashed, she looked at him with small pale eyes. 'I was just letting everyone know breakfast was ready.'

'What? For the entire village? You're supposed to *tap* it, Virginia. Not knock the hell out of it.'

At that moment Charlotte appeared at the top of the stairs.

Virginia moved forward to greet her, immediately the gracious hostess.

'My dear, I hope you slept well? Oh, and a Happy Christmas! Come and have breakfast.' A deep flush suffused her face and she pointedly avoided looking at her husband as she hustled Charlotte past him into the dining room.

'Any sign of David yet?' she continued conversationally.

'I haven't seen him,' Charlotte replied, eyeing the silver dishes of eggs and bacon with longing. Pulling in her stomach she helped herself to a grapefruit, and felt very virtuous.

'Is that all you're having, dear?' Virginia fussed. 'There's toast on the table . . . and jam, or do you prefer marmalade?'

While Virginia chattered on, Edmund lumbered grumpily around the dining room, complaining the coffee was too weak.

At that moment Holly came running into the room, a red ribbon in her hair and an ecstatic expression on her face.

'Father Christmas came!' she announced. She was clutching an armful of toys to her chest and her eyes were shining. Charlotte smiled, enchanted.

'Did he fill your stocking with lovely presents?'

Holly shook her head so her golden curls bounced. 'Not a stocking,' she said importantly. 'A *pillowcase*.'

'You lucky girl. So he *did* know you were staying here, after all?' Charlotte caught Christopher's eye as he followed Holly into the room. He looked terrible. 'Disturbed night?' she asked.

Christopher looked rather shifty. 'Madam here was up before six,' he said carefully, 'and it's been all go ever since.' He helped himself to coffee; she noticed he took it black, without sugar.

'I want Coco-pops!' Holly announced, clambering on to a dining room chair. 'Coco-pops with milk *and* sugar!'

'OK, darling.' Christopher looked at the boxes of cereal. 'How about a bowl of nice Nutty-Crunch?' he asked tactfully, seeing there were no Coco-pops.

Holly shook her head.

'Don't be like that, sweetheart. You could have Alpen . . . that's very nice. Or All Bran?'

'I want Coco-pops,' she said determinedly, pressing her lips together.

'There aren't any . . .'

'I *always* have Coco-pops . . . !'

'Spoilt little girls end up getting nothing,' Edmund boomed down the length of the table. 'When I was a little boy I had to eat what was put in front of me.'

Holly's mouth dropped at the corners and her eyes were stricken. 'But I *always* have Coco-pops . . .' she quavered.

Charlotte came to the rescue. 'I have an idea,' she said to Holly. 'Why don't I fix you a bowl of Nutty-Crunch with a sliced banana on top? And a little cream?'

Miraculously, Holly's face broke into a radiant smile. 'All right,' she said, instantly mollified.

'Hello! Hello!' Carol and Neil appeared in the doorway, all smiles and carrying beautifully wrapped parcels. Charlotte wondered why they'd brought them into the dining room when all the presents were being placed under the tree in the hall, but then their motive became clear as she heard Carol pointedly ask Virginia where she'd like them put.

'I've been up half the night, wrapping everything!' she gushed, extending her arms. 'I thought I'd run out of red ribbon at one point!' It was obvious she wanted everyone to be impressed by her efforts, and Virginia rose splendidly to the occasion, leaping up from her chair and clapping her hands in a girlish way.

'Oh, my *dear*! How *too* exciting! Yes, do put them under the tree . . . Oh, honestly, you *shouldn't*!'

Gratified, Carol beamed and turned back into the hall, murmuring something about 'it-was-the-least-she-could-do'.

'Happy Christmas, everyone,' Neil said amicably as he helped himself to eggs and bacon.

Amid a chorus of reciprocal greetings, everyone sat round the breakfast table. With a stab of longing, Charlotte realised that, at this moment, her sister would be sitting on her parents' bed and they'd all be drinking Bucks Fizz and opening the stockings they all gave each other.

Holly interrupted her thoughts. 'What did you get from Father Christmas?'

Charlotte shook her head, feeling suddenly absurdly and childishly homesick. 'He doesn't visit grown-ups.'

Holly digested this thoughtfully. 'How old are you?'

'Twenty-six. How old are you?'

'Nearly five.'

Christopher leaned over the table, smiling. 'Not quite, sweetheart. You were only four two months ago.'

'That's nearly five,' she protested stoutly.

Charlotte grinned. 'So your birthday's in October?'

'How did you know?' Holly asked suspiciously.

Everyone laughed, with the exception of Edmund, who was solemnly spreading butter on a piece of toast.

'Charlotte knows because she's a clever lady,' Christopher said, gravely.

'That makes a change; having an intelligent woman around the place,' remarked Edmund in an unpleasant tone. There was an awkward silence.

'Mummy's married to Denzil,' Holly piped up, which at least, Charlotte thought gratefully, created a diversion.

'But this is my daddy,' Holly continued, nodding her head knowingly. Then she turned to Christopher. 'Aren't you?'

'Of course I am, sweetheart.'

'Grandpa?' She switched her dazzling blue-eyed gaze across to Edmund.

'Yes?'

'What were you doing in the garden in the night?'

There was silence, and everyone looked at her.

'In the garden?' Virginia echoed.

Out of the corner of her eye, Charlotte saw Edmund stiffen and an ugly flush stained his neck. So she hadn't been the only one to see Edmund in the garden last night.

'I was probably gardening! Isn't that what one usually does in a garden?' he retorted, angrily, unthinkingly.

'In the dark?' queried Holly, stuffing a finger of toast and Marmite into her mouth with both hands.

'What time was this?' Virginia asked, anxiously.

Holly waved another piece of toast. 'When I woke up it was all dark.' Then a fat chuckle broke from her throat as she looked at Edmund. 'Funny Grandpa! Gardening in the dark!' She chanted this several times, and then paused and beamed at the assembled company, pleased with her performance, looking for adult praise.

'Well, wasn't that a funny thing to do,' Christopher remarked in a once-upon-a-time voice, nevertheless glancing askance at his father. Carol and Neil looked first at Virginia and then Edmund, sensing something was wrong.

'What *were* you doing, Dad?' Christopher asked, slyly.

Virginia broke in hurriedly. 'I expect he was taking Mackie for his last walk.'

'Don't I always?' Edmund said drily, pouring himself another cup of coffee. He'd forced his mouth into a smile, but it looked more like he was baring his teeth.

'Mackie wasn't there,' Holly said stubbornly. 'Grandpa was on his own.'

Suddenly Edmund flung down his table-napkin with a petulant gesture.

'You don't know what you're talking about,' he snapped harshly. 'Little girls should be taught to behave, and not answer back! You're a rude, spoilt, naughty child and you're not coming to stay again unless you can behave.'

There was a moment's stunned silence, and then a forlorn wail filled the air.

'I want Mummy,' Holly wept, her eyes stricken. Then she covered her face with her small hands in a gesture of such mature distress that Charlotte reached out and put her arm round Holly's shoulders.

Christopher glared at his father. 'Was that really necessary?'

'She shouldn't be allowed to be rude and answer back grown-ups.'

'She wasn't being rude! And this is Christmas.' The atmosphere between the two men was icy.

At that moment David entered the dining room, but only Charlotte seemed to notice. The others were too intent on Holly, who was still crying bitterly, and the fight going on between father and son. Helping himself to coffee, David sat down, facing Charlotte, gave her a reassuring wink, and listened as Edmund and Christopher continued their furious exchange.

'If you're going to bring her to stay she's *got* to learn to behave,' Edmund shouted, his face scarlet, the veins in his temple standing out.

'But she hasn't *done* anything!' Christopher was both angry and bewildered. 'You're being totally unreasonable, Dad.'

'I won't have mischief-makers in my house!'

Charlotte looked at the four-year-old child and wondered

how anyone could remotely label her a mischief-maker. More likely, she thought, whatever Edmund had been doing in the garden last night was something he didn't want anyone to know about. Guilt was stamped on his face as clearly as the mark of a branding iron.

'Oh, for God's sake stop it you two!' David exclaimed loudly. Then he turned to Charlotte with a boyish grin of apology. 'I'm sorry about this, La. My family do go stark raving mad from time to time, so just ignore it! Now, who's for more coffee?' Trying to diffuse the atmosphere, he rose and fetched the percolator from the sideboard.

Everyone started talking at once, except for Edmund, who sat in silence, his face dark and brooding. Holly, who was still giving hiccuping sobs, had gone back to munching toast, while she gripped Christopher's arm with one hand. Then Charlotte caught sight of Virginia's face as she rose and hurried from the room. Her mouth was twisted in an ugly moue of anguish, and her cheeks were awash with tears.

'I'm fine, Ma. Having a wonderful time,' Charlotte lied, as she watched David throw more logs on the study fire. 'How are you and Daddy?'

Breakfast over, she'd asked if she might phone her family to wish them a happy Christmas.

'We're having terrific fun, but we're missing you, darling,' Margaret Taylor replied, her voice warm and affectionate. 'Daddy's in the shower and Susie and I are finishing off the champagne with our croissants! And guess what?'

'What?'

'Daddy's taking us to lunch at the Savoy! Can you

imagine?' Her mother sounded excited, like a young girl. 'I'm cooking dinner tonight . . . I've invented an *incredible* sauce with juniper berries and kirsch to go with the turkey, and we've invited the Motcombs and the O'Sullivans; but as it's only the three of us for lunch, and we're missing you so much, Daddy said he'd cheer us up by taking us out.'

'Lucky you,' Charlotte replied, making a determined effort to sound bright. Her mother was not deceived.

'Are you all right, La?'

'Of course.'

'You're probably not alone, am I right?'

'Yeah, you're right.'

'Then just answer "yes" or "no". Are you really having a good time?'

'No.' Charlotte gazed out at the window, watching Holly trying to catch a ball as Christopher kept patiently throwing it to her.

'Oh, sweetheart, I'm so sorry. Is it David?' Margaret Taylor was whispering now.

'Oh, no, not at all.'

'Good. Then it's his family?'

Charlotte grinned suddenly at their coded conversation. Somehow, it made her feel close to her mother. 'You could say that!'

'Oh, dear. Any chance of your getting back to London any earlier?'

'No.'

Margaret Taylor sighed. 'Oh, what a pity, darling. Never mind. You'll be able to stay at home next year, maybe?'

Charlotte laughed outright this time, feeling much better. 'I'll make a point of it! And David and I'll see you on

New Year's Eve. About eight o'clock?'

'I can't wait! Now, look after yourself, sweetheart, and lots of luck. Don't let it get you down. *No one's* worth it.'

With her mother's words still filling her thoughts, Charlotte hung up. There was only the rest of today and tomorrow to get through, and then she'd be on her way back to London. The thought was terrifically cheering. She also reminded herself that none of this was David's fault. Beneath his jolly manner at breakfast, she knew the little scene between his father and Holly had made him as miserable as it had everyone else.

Going over to the fireplace where he was sitting reading a newspaper, she dropped on to her haunches and looked smilingly into his face. 'Shall we go for a walk?'

David looked up, eyebrows raised comically. 'To get away from my dreadful family?' His voice was teasing; nevertheless she quickly denied the suggestion.

'I'd like to see your garden.'

He glanced out of the window. 'Go ahead, darling. I want to have a talk with Dad, about money.'

'Is this the best time to ask him?'

'Why not?'

'Well, he was in such a bad mood at breakfast . . .'

David turned to her. 'Oh, he'll be all right. Look, darling, I know you and your family are very close, but you're very lucky. Most families have arguments and fights: it's not the end of the world. I'm sorry if it upsets you, though.'

'Oh, it's OK,' Charlotte smiled bravely. 'Just as long as your parents' problems don't affect us,' she said softly.

'I agree.' Grinning broadly again, he reached out to take her hand. 'I love you, you know.'

'I love you, too,' she replied, and suddenly nothing else mattered. Christmas was, after all, only a couple of days in a whole year, and she could easily get through it if she felt confident in their relationship.

At that moment, the sound of Holly's shrieks of delight coming from the garden made them both look out of the window. She was jumping up in the air, trying to catch a ball Christopher was throwing to her; she looked rosy cheeked and gleeful, all tears forgotten.

'Let's go and join them,' Charlotte exclaimed, 'you can talk to your father later. I'll go and get my coat.'

As she hurried up the stairs to her room, she heard a door slam further along the corridor. Then she heard a man's voice, low and angry. A moment later, there was the sound of a woman crying and then, unmistakably, Virginia's voice, quavering hysterically.

'I didn't mean to upset you, Edmund . . .'

Charlotte hurried into her room and shut the door, not wanting to hear any more. She'd seen and heard enough in the past twelve hours to guess what was going on and why Virginia was so unhappy. She glanced at her wristwatch. It was still only eleven o'clock in the morning. If this was going to be a difficult Christmas, it was also going to be the longest one in living memory.

'Look at my new ball! Look at my new ball! My daddy gave it to me!' Holly's voice was filled with pride as she came hurtling across the lawn towards them.

'It's lovely,' Charlotte said admiringly. 'Shall I throw it to you?'

'I throw it,' Holly replied, raising it above her head and

66

dropping it so that it landed a foot in front of her. 'Oh!' Surprise made her blue eyes widen. She stooped to pick it up and flung it in Charlotte's direction again. 'I threw it!' This time it landed five feet away.

'Well done,' Charlotte exclaimed encouragingly, picking it up and tossing it gently into Holly's outstretched arms.

They continued to play with the ball, David and Christopher encouraging Holly to kick it along the ground so they could kick it back to her, and while this version of football was in progress, Charlotte saw Neil strolling across the lawn to join them.

'How's it going?' he called jovially.

'Exhaustingly,' Charlotte laughed, glad of an excuse to stop for a moment. David kept teasing her by kicking the ball to the far end of the lawn when he sent it in her direction, and her legs were aching from running after it. She went and stood by Neil and they watched the two men racing, while Holly shrieked with delight.

'Soon be time for lunch,' Neil observed in a hopeful voice.

'Yes.' Charlotte felt instinctively that he wasn't enjoying his stay with the Farrells any more than she was.

'So, your family live in London?' he asked conversationally. His sympathetic manner suddenly made her feel thankful that he was staying in the house as well. It was as if he understood she was having difficulty adjusting to David's family.

'Yes. I spoke to my mother on the phone and they're off to lunch at the Savoy. It's all right for some, isn't it?' she laughed.

Neil pretended to look impressed, raising his bushy grey eyebrows and pursing his lips. 'The Savoy, indeed! Very nice.' He dug his hands into the pockets of his Barbour, and started to stroll slowly down the side of the lawn, where a herbaceous border lay dormant and droopy in the watery winter sunshine. Charlotte fell into step beside him.

'Known David long, eh?' he asked conversationally.

'Three months.'

'How did you meet?'

Charlotte regaled him with the story of their Heathrow encounter.

'Quite romantic, then?' he observed, chuckling.

'Oh, very.' She looked dreamy for a moment at the memory of that first weekend they'd spent together in Rome, and wished they were there now.

'I gather you're a successful interior decorator? D'you enjoy that? Is it fun?' He sounded genuinely interested, and Charlotte found herself talking to him as if she'd known him for years.

'How's David getting on with that recording company he's with?' he asked.

Charlotte brightened. 'Fantastically! They're going to promote him next month. Put him in charge of sales. He's going to put Flight Records on the map, you know. He's got a great future with them,' she added, proudly.

'Well, isn't that good? I'm so glad,' he said, smiling brightly.

'Yes, he works so hard, he really deserves all the success that comes his way,' Charlotte enthused.

'David's not a bit like his father, is he?' she said, rather too relievedly.

'No . . .' Neil drew out the word.

'He seems to have more of his mother's sensitivity.'

They had reached the bottom of the lawn where a high yew hedge sheltered the borders and blocked from view much of the field beyond, where cattle grazed under the shadow of oak and ash and lime trees.

'Shall we walk back?' Neil suggested. 'It might even be time for a drink before lunch.'

'That sounds like a very civilised idea,' Charlotte agreed. 'I think I've done enough running around for one day.' She glanced over to where the two brothers were playing with Holly, who was now riding on Christopher's shoulders and whooping with excitement.

'Let's go in then.' Neil led the way. 'No doubt my wife and Virginia have been having a chin-wag, as they always do when they get together. Typical sisters! I don't know what they find to talk about.'

'Susie and I are the same,' laughed Charlotte.

They found Virginia and Carol in the dining room, putting the finishing touches to a festive-looking arrangement of crackers down the centre of the table. There was no sign of Edmund, and Virginia seemed to be more cheerful. She was even laughing as Carol teased her about having candles on the table for lunch.

'Absolutely non-U, my dear!' Carol chided. 'Nancy Mitford would have had a fit! She said you must never have candles on the dining room table during the day. It's as bad as using fish-knives!'

'I don't care about being non-U,' Virginia giggled. 'Candles look pretty, so candles we're having.'

'Where's Edmund?' Neil asked, looking around.

Virginia looked at him understandingly. 'Help yourself to a drink, dear. And give one to Carol and Charlotte too.

Edmund's taken Mackie for a walk before lunch.'

'Can I get you a drink, Virginia?'

'I'm all right for the moment,' she replied brightly. She'd taken another two turquoise and white capsules and she wasn't sure how much she dared drink with them.

While Neil fixed the drinks, Charlotte hovered in the dining room, feeling it was only polite to offer to help.

'Is there anything I can do, Mrs Farrell?'

Virginia looked at her with eyes that held such a hidden depth of agony that Charlotte almost winced at the proximity of such obvious pain.

'Everything's under control, my dear,' Virginia replied. 'Gladys and Ruby have got everything in hand; why don't you sit in the drawing room? Where's David?'

'He and Christopher are in the garden with Holly.'

For a moment Virginia's tight features softened and something warm flickered in her eyes.

'The dear child,' she murmured. 'I love that little girl so much. She's an angel.'

'She's rather bowled me over, too,' Charlotte admitted, chuckling at the memory of Holly trying to throw a ball. 'I'm glad my mother's not here, or she'd start nagging Susie and me to get busy producing grandchildren for her.'

'I wish we could spend the day together,' Olivia whispered, looking up at Edmund, her dark hair blowing about her pale, heart-shaped face, her enormous eyes filled with longing. Standing by the stream in Long Meadow, while Mackie circled around them on the trail of a rabbit, she didn't care if anyone from the village saw them. In fact, she'd have been rather glad if they had, because then it would

70

have forced Edmund to admit to their affair.

'I know, darling. God, so do I.' He buried his face in the wind-tossed silk of her black hair, and tried to forget the fight he'd had with Virginia earlier. Not that he felt bad at being unfaithful to her; just a sense of chagrin that she'd found out, making it necessary for him to defend himself against her hysterical accusations.

Olivia leaned against him, his bulk shielding her from the wind. 'I wish we could . . .'

'Oh, Christ, so do I.'

'Last night was so wonderful. Do you think we're ever going to be together, properly?'

Edmund kissed her tenderly, marvelling at her beauty even in the morning. She was thirty-two and yet she didn't look a day more than twenty. Her skin was as fresh and unlined as any girl's, and her body as firm and slim, with perfect breasts and long, slender legs.

'I must go back,' she said sorrowfully, gazing up into his face. Her full mouth was soft and, like a child's, tender and pink.

'Oh, my darling one . . .' He kissed her again.

'I shall be lonely today,' she said wistfully.

'And you think I won't?'

'Will you miss me? Just a little?'

'More than you'll ever know,' he replied passionately. 'Oh, God, Olivia . . .'

'I don't think I can bear this much longer.' There was finality in her tone.

Alarmed, he drew back. 'What do you mean?' The thought of losing her filled him with panic. 'I'll think of something. There must be a way. Oh, don't give up on me, darling. Please don't give up on me!'

There was a long pause and then, like a child, she snuggled close to him, her face buried in his chest.

'But how long will it be before we can be together – live together?' she persisted, reminding him for a fleeting second of Holly when she wanted something.

'As soon as I can manage it.' He thought of Virginia and wondered what a divorce would cost. Would he have to sell Chelwood Manor? Would he be forced to give her a large settlement? In theory, it should be the easiest thing in the world to walk away from his former life and build a new future for himself, but in practice his fear of losing much of what he'd worked for terrified him.

'I'll think of something,' he said weakly.

'Make it soon, Edmund. It's hurting too much, the way things are at present. I can't bear the loneliness. I need someone . . . I can't be on my own.'

The fear that she might find someone else if he couldn't provide a life for them together swept through him like an icy wave. He kissed the top of her head, her musky perfume making his senses reel. He wanted her now, this minute, out here in the meadow, with the wind shimmering through the rushes, turning them to silver blades, and the stream trickling like liquid crystal over the polished stones.

'Oh, dear God . . .' He shut his eyes, the better to concentrate on the sweet heat that fired his loins.

Olivia pressed closer. Her tone was wheedling. 'Come to me again tonight, sweetheart.'

The breath caught in his throat. 'I'll be there,' he said rashly. To hell with everyone. To hell with Christmas. He loved this woman and he must have her.

With one hand she reached inside his coat, stroking him with tenderness.

'Keep it until tonight.' She squeezed gently.

He gripped her tightly. 'I don't know that I can . . .' All he could feel was the surge of desire that was sweeping through him. No other part of him existed except the part that was for her only. He was no longer an individual, a separate entity; he was no longer connected in any way to Virginia or David or Christopher. Chelwood Manor didn't exist. Nothing was real except this burning need to take Olivia and make her his, for ever.

'Olivia . . .' He could hardly speak.

'I'll see you later.'

Then she was gone, running away like a young girl in her high Russian boots, across the meadow and into the woods beyond. And, as Edmund gazed after her, his face was set in rigid lines of pain.

Chapter Four

Only the upper half of Holly's body was visible as she sat on the floor, surrounded by a sea of discarded wrapping paper and gift tags. Christopher tried in vain to keep track of the presents she'd been given, so that the right people could be thanked. Everyone had put gifts under the tree for Holly, and her face glowed like a pink beacon as she excitedly ripped the bright wrappings to reveal a doll, a toy camera, a clockwork kitten that danced, or a box of crayons. Enchanted, she wanted to play with everything at once.

'Steady on there, Holly,' Christopher reproved her mildly, as he tried to instil some sense of organisation into the proceedings. But Holly wasn't listening.

'Look, Daddy! Look, Daddy! I've got a tea-set for my dolls!' Her tiny fingers curled round the miniature china cups and saucers with infinite care and daintiness. Charlotte, watching, smiled at the distant memory of being given a doll's tea-set herself when she'd been small.

'Shall I put it up here for you, Holly, in case it gets broken?' she offered.

'I can do it.' Holly clambered to her feet, wading her way through the shoals of multi-coloured paper. Then she placed the tea-set in its box on the table.

Edmund was watching. 'It's obscene the amount of

presents children get these days,' he observed loudly. 'When I was a boy we had a couple of toys and a tangerine if we were lucky.' He sounded personally offended, as if he'd somehow been deeply deprived.

'This is a more materialistic age,' Carol pointed out, 'and I don't think it does children any harm to get presents, as long as they're brought up to appreciate what they're given.'

'When I was headmaster of Charlton, I noticed that it was the children who had been given lots of toys *instead* of love and attention from their parents, who became spoilt and unappreciative,' Neil remarked.

'Humph!' Edmund looked down his nose and then, stony faced, gathered up his own presents, which consisted of books, a tie and a bottle of Glenfiddich. 'I'm going to the study for a bit of peace and quiet,' he announced, rising.

'Oh, aren't you going to watch us all opening our presents?' Virginia asked.

He didn't reply, but trod heavily away without a backward glance.

David's mouth tightened. 'He could at least have put on a show of enjoying himself,' he said in a low voice.

'I think it's preferable he doesn't stay with us,' Christopher remarked, *sotto voce*, glaring balefully at his father's receding back view. 'Who wants a bad-tempered bugger like that around anyway?'

'Chris, please . . .' Virginia protested weakly.

Embarrassed, Charlotte pretended not to hear, and instead re-examined the beautiful scarf David had given her. It was long and narrow, to be worn wound round the neck with the ends trailing, and he'd chosen it for its varied shades of blue flowers on a navy background. Blue was her favourite colour, and she was deeply touched by the thoughtfulness that had gone into his choice.

'You really do like it?' she heard him whisper at that moment.

Smiling, she looked up into his face. 'I love it, sweetheart. It's perfect.' She'd given him a shirt, the best she could find in a swanky shop in Jermyn Street, and it had cost her more than she'd ever admit.

The stack of presents beneath the tree had diminished rapidly and now a tired silence fell on the group seated around it. Everyone felt satiated with too much food, too much wine, and an excess of keeping up cheerful demeanours when in fact they'd all have rather crawled away and been on their own. Virginia looked at the mess on the floor with a sort of hopeless despair, knowing Gladys and Ruby had gone back to their own homes in the village, and wouldn't be back until the next day. Charlotte, intercepting the look, rose briskly.

'Mrs Farrell, why don't David and I clear up in here and get tea for everyone? You've been rushing around all day and you must be exhausted.'

'Oh, my dear! Would you really . . . ? No, I can't possibly let you. No, really . . .' she protested.

'Nonsense. It's no trouble.' Charlotte started gathering up armfuls of paper.

With David's help, the hall was soon cleared, the floors once again a gleaming stretch of polished oak, the tree looking rather isolated in the corner, denuded of all the presents beneath it.

In the kitchen, Gladys and Ruby had left out plates of sandwiches and biscuits, sheltering under taut sheets of cling-film. Charlotte put on the kettle, glad to have something to do.

Carol and Neil wandered in with Virginia, and drew up chairs round the kitchen table, revived by the thought of cups of tea.

'Has anyone told Edmund that tea's ready?' Virginia asked suddenly, looking at her sons. Christopher was helping Holly to a cup of milk.

David shrugged. 'I suppose I'd better,' he volunteered, helping himself to a sandwich and ambling off, munching as he went.

Charlotte put the large teapot on the table in front of Virginia, and then slid into the seat beside Holly.

'Thank you, dear,' Virginia remarked absently.

When David came back, followed by his father, Charlotte noticed that David's attitude to Edmund seemed much friendlier. Perhaps they'd sorted out the problem about money that David had mentioned that morning.

'So who do you think will win the next election?' she heard him ask.

Engrossed in political talk, whilst the others chatted amongst themselves, Charlotte was at first unaware of a bell ringing. Virginia was the first to hear it, and she perked up her head on its long neck, like an elderly gazelle.

'That's the bell,' she announced. 'Chris, go and see who it is, will you, dear? I can't imagine who can be calling on Christmas afternoon!'

Christopher patted Holly. 'Eat up that sandwich, sweetheart.'

'Then can I have a biscuit?'

'Please, Daddy.'

'Please, Daddy.'

'Yes, you can, darling.'

As he left the kitchen, Holly gave Charlotte a conspiratorial smile. 'Do you think Daddy will let me have two?' she whispered, looking at her grandmother out of the corner of her eye to make sure she wasn't being overheard.

'It might mean another "please",' Charlotte teased.

Holly regarded this piece of information solemnly. Then she nodded slowly. 'I think it will.'

Impulsively, Charlotte put her arms round Holly and gave her a hug. She'd never particularly liked children and, although she presumed she'd have her own one day, they were not something she'd thought about much. It was only when her mother nagged about wanting grandchildren before she was too old to enjoy them, that Charlotte gave babies any serious thought. Holly, however, with her infectious giggle and trusting manner, was altering all that.

Charlotte heard voices coming along the corridor from the hall, Christopher and a woman's. She was laughing, a light, musical laugh that floated on the air.

'We're all in here,' he said, pushing the kitchen door open.

A woman stepped into the room, petite, exquisite, with shining black hair and large dark eyes. She was wearing a russet suede coat, fastened up to the neck with frogging, and high Russian-style boots.

For a moment there was a stunned silence. Then she strode swiftly forward, light on her feet, graceful in her movements. Her right hand was outstretched and in her left arm she held a large parcel.

'Mrs Farrell! Forgive me bursting in like this, but I heard

your granddaughter was staying with you for Christmas . . .
I can never resist children . . . And so I hope you will forgive
me for dropping in like this, with a little Christmas present
for her.' After she'd shaken Virginia's hand with grave
politeness, she turned and placed the parcel gently on Holly's
lap.

'There you are, darling. This is for you. I hope you like
it,' she said, smiling into the child's face.

Holly gazed up at the woman, open-mouthed; to
Charlotte's amusement, Christopher seemed equally
captivated.

'What do you say, Holly?' he coaxed.

'Thank you,' Holly replied obediently. Then she started
pulling the wrapping off her present.

Then Charlotte noticed Edmund's face, and Virginia's,
too. His was deep crimson, his eyes bloodshot and bulging,
while hers had turned a sickly shade of grey.

'Here, have my chair,' Neil said expansively, seemingly
unaware of the sudden tension in the atmosphere.

The woman sank, smiling, on to the seat, while she
watched Holly.

Suddenly Virginia seemed to pull herself together and
remember her role as hostess.

'Let me introduce everyone to you,' she said breathlessly.
'This is my sister and her husband, Carol and Neil
Whittaker, and Charlotte Taylor, who is David's girlfriend,
and our younger son, Christopher . . .' As usual her voice
drifted off into silence before starting up again.

'And this is a neighbour of ours, Olivia Middleton.'

The grass was crisp and whiskered with hoar frost beneath

Charlotte's feet. Overhead a robin sang with the full-throated joy of being alive. It was a relief to be out of the house, away from the oppressive atmosphere that had reached a climax the previous evening. Getting up early, she'd slipped down to the kitchen to make herself a cup of tea and found Gladys already at work, clearing away last night's dinner dishes. 'I have the kettle on already,' Gladys said cheerfully. 'I'll make you a cup.' Although it was Boxing Day, she'd come in as usual, leaving Ruby behind to mind her baby.

Thanking her, Charlotte drank the strong brew and then, wrapping up against the cold, set out for a walk. Skirting the wooded area at the bottom of the long lawn, she went through a gate and into the field beyond. A stream ran sluggishly on the far side, clogged with rushes and weeds. As she walked over to it and stood looking down into the water, she realised she was more relaxed than she'd been for the past three days. It was such a relief to be away from the Farrell family. For the first time since she'd met David, a shadow of foreboding about their future together had touched her. Not that she loved David any less, in fact she felt closer to him that she'd ever done, but the stress of staying at Chelwood Manor had awakened a wariness in her, and made her wonder if it would ever be possible for her to be a part of this family. It was the strain of getting caught up in their unhappiness that was so exhausting.

Last night the trouble had started when Christopher suggested Olivia Middleton stay on for dinner. Up to that point the undercurrent of tension had been there, but suddenly it burst wide in a display of naked jealousy and hatred that had left Charlotte appalled. Nothing like it had ever happened in her home. Now, in all its raw intensity, she had seen a family divided against itself. It had left her feeling deeply shocked.

Charlotte, guessing that Olivia Middleton might be the cause of Virginia's unhappiness and the reason for Edmund to go creeping out of the house at night, watched with horrified fascination as Christopher proceeded to flirt with her, persuading her to stay on for dinner and making a great deal of fuss of her in general. Did he realise, she wondered, that he was treading on his father's toes? Or was his behaviour purposely designed to humiliate Edmund in his own house?

'Of course you must stay,' Christopher said, sweeping away Olivia's rather feeble excuses. 'You can't be on your own on Christmas night, especially having brought over such a lovely present for Holly.'

Charlotte looked at her hosts covertly, watching fascinated as Edmund appeared torn between wanting Olivia to stay whilst pretending he didn't. Virginia, meanwhile, appeared to be held together by a network of fine wires that might snap from strain at any moment. Her hands shook and her head jerked like a puppet's. Charlotte had never felt so sorry for anyone in her life.

'I'm sure Olivia's got other things on, Chris,' Edmund boomed aggressively. He turned to her, baring large, ivory-coloured teeth.

Christopher was not to be put off. 'You're not doing anything, are you?' His fascination with this exotic neighbour was obvious.

'Well . . .' Olivia put her head on one side, her black hair resting on her shoulders like thin skeins of silk. She wore hardly any make-up, and this gave her a fresh, unspoilt look. For a split-second her eyes flickered to Edmund's face, and then back to Chris's. Without missing a beat, she spoke with serene composure. 'I'd love to stay.'

She never once, Charlotte realised, bothered to make eye-contact with Virginia. This was a man's woman, if ever she'd seen one; a woman who secretly despised her own sex and wasn't going to waste her time on them.

'Great!' Christopher was blatantly delighted, and at that moment Charlotte felt sure he couldn't be aware of his father's involvement with Olivia Middleton. But was David? Charlotte looked at him and couldn't be sure.

'Why don't you all go to the drawing room?' Virginia suddenly said, her smile fixed as if it had been painted on her face. 'I have to . . .' Helplessly, she looked round the kitchen as if she had no idea what she had to do.

'We'll help,' Charlotte had said sturdily, jumping to her feet. 'Come on, David. I'll load the dishwasher if you hand me the tea things.'

Now, as Charlotte continued her walk along the side of the stream, she could still picture in her mind's eye the bizarre group that had sat round the fire the previous evening. From tweedy Carol with her short grey hair, to glamorous Olivia who was wearing a burgundy red velvet skirt and a rash of diamonds on her chiffon blouse, they looked an ill-assorted group, as if they'd been hastily assembled at random for an experiment in human relations. Edmund couldn't take his eyes off Olivia, and neither could Christopher. Seemingly oblivious to his father's chagrin, Christopher continued to engage her in animated conversation, and soon she was laughing at his jokes, and ignoring Edmund altogether. David, on the other hand, had looked bored. After a while he had picked up a copy of *Country Life* and started reading it.

That left Neil, Carol and Virginia, who were making no attempt to compete in the badinage that flowed relentlessly between the others. They had talked stiltedly, turning from time to time to say something to Holly.

'Do you like all your presents?' Carol asked her at one point.

'I like my dolly!' she replied, clutching the very expensive baby doll Olivia Middleton had given her.

'What are you going to call her?' Charlotte asked. The doll must have cost a small fortune, for its face was beautifully moulded, and it was dressed in lace and lawn baby clothes, with silk booties and a gossamer wool shawl.

'Dolly.'

'Just Dolly? Wouldn't she like a real name, like you?'

'What sort of real name?' Holly asked.

Charlotte looked reflective. 'What about Anne? or Samantha? or Lily? or Gloria? Or how about Felicity?'

Holly's eyes lit up. 'Flissy! I'm going to call her Flissy.' Her smile as she cradled the doll was seraphic.

'Time for your bath, sweetheart,' Virginia announced.

'I want Daddy to bath me.'

Christopher looked over at her. 'Why not let Granny do it tonight?' It was obvious he didn't want to leave Olivia.

'I want you to,' Holly insisted.

'I bathed you last night. Go on, darling. Go with Granny. Perhaps she'll let you have a bubble bath,' Christopher coaxed.

'Yea-a-a-h!' Holly jumped up and down. 'A bubble bath!'

When they'd gone, Christopher turned to Olivia once

again. 'Do you ever go up to London?'

'Of course. At least once a week.' Then she laughed. 'Where else would I shop?'

He laughed too, but looked nonplussed. 'Aren't there any good shops in Devizes?'

Olivia shrugged, her bare shoulders gleaming through her transparent blouse. 'Not for clothes.'

'I don't know! You women!' Edmund, looking at her, spoke in a voice of such teasing intimacy that Christopher and David looked at him sharply.

'Well,' he blustered defensively, seeing their expressions, 'your mother's the same. Never has anything to wear.'

There was silence, until Carol observed in a self-righteous voice, 'I can't be bothered with clothes. They're a waste of money.'

Neil cleared his throat rather more loudly than was necessary. 'Did you move to Barrow recently, Mrs Middleton?' he asked Olivia.

Her voice was soft and whispery. 'I bought Magnolia Cottage a year ago.'

'You like it here?' Carol queried. 'Barrow's a small village.'

'I love it because it's quiet and peaceful.'

'You don't look the quiet and peaceful type.' Her dry smile prevented the remark from sounding rude.

Olivia laughed softly. 'Oh, I am, I assure you.' Then she turned pointedly to Christopher again. 'Where do you live in London?'

'Fulham. Holly lives with her mother in Islington.'

'You must miss her.'

Christopher nodded. Then Edmund rose from his chair,

heading for the drawing room door. 'How about some champagne?' he boomed. 'Give me a hand, will you, Chris?' It was more a command than a request.

'Can't David help? I've been on my feet all day with Holly, and I'm knackered.'

'Oh, I'll get it myself,' Edmund muttered crossly, leaving the room.

Olivia moved closer to Christopher. 'What do you do?' It was as if they were the only people in the room.

'I'm a quantity surveyor. Very boring, I'm afraid.'

'Not boring at all,' she smiled reassuringly.

Christopher grinned, running his hand over his beard. 'I wanted to be an architect, but I didn't do well enough at college.'

'You could have if you'd wanted to,' Carol interjected.

Olivia ignored her. 'I wanted to be an artist. I love painting. Of course, I only do it as a hobby. I'm not good enough to be a professional artist.'

Just as Charlotte was wondering when they'd stop indulging in self-deprecation as a means of attracting each other, Edmund hurried back into the room with two bottles of Moët.

'Here we are!' he said heartily.

'And it isn't even six-thirty yet,' Neil observed *sotto voce*.

Edmund spun round. 'What was that?'

'I said it isn't even six-thirty,' Neil repeated loudly. 'You don't usually serve drinks until after six-thirty.'

'So what? There's no law to say one can't have a drink earlier.' Red faced, he stripped the gold foil off the first bottle. When he'd filled the glasses he carried them round on a tray, politely offering Carol hers first. When he got to

Olivia, he stood and looked down at her, lingering a moment before moving on. The gesture did not go unnoticed.

'What the fuck do you mean?'

Charlotte, coming out of the dining room where she'd been clearing the last of the supper things, heard Christopher's voice coming from the study. Then she heard Edmund.

'How dare you behave like that!'

'Behave like what?' Christopher slurred his words and Charlotte's heart sank. She hadn't seen him drink any of the champagne or wine at dinner, yet he sounded drunk.

'You know perfectly well what I mean,' Edmund stormed. 'The way you threw yourself at Olivia Middleton. You embarrassed the poor woman, Chris. I won't have you behaving like this under my roof.' He was so angry he did not seem to notice Christopher's eyes were bloodshot and he was swaying as he stood challenging the older man.

'You're a vindictive old sod!' Christopher shouted, his words echoing round the kitchen. 'The trouble is you're fucking jealous!'

Charlotte retreated into the dining room again and put the tray of dirty glasses back on the table, feeling unable to go into the kitchen while the men battled it out.

Edmund had returned a few minutes earlier. He'd driven Olivia Middleton back to Magnolia Cottage, because it was after midnight, while Virginia had gone straight to her room. Carol and Neil had also gone up to bed. Furious at finding himself in a position where he was unable to stay for even a few minutes with Olivia, he'd come storming back, determined to have it out with Christopher.

'You're a waster! A bloody drug addict!' Charlotte heard him roar. 'You're no good to anyone! No wonder Linda left you!'

'At least I was faithful to her, for all my faults,' Christopher shot back.

'How dare you?' Edmund's voice was dangerously low now. 'How dare you talk to me like that.'

Charlotte hovered nervously. Should she just go to her room and leave the mess in the dining room? At that moment David appeared in the doorway on his way to the kitchen with the used coffee things.

'What are you doing, La?'

She indicated the shouting in the kitchen with a nod of her head. 'I can't very well barge in on that, can I?'

David listened for a moment, his head cocked. 'Oh God, are Dad and Chris at it again?' He plonked the coffee tray on the table beside hers. 'So what's new?' he sighed.

'You mean they often fight?'

'They sure do.'

'But I thought your father and Christopher got on well together. He's always sticking up for Chris, isn't he?'

'If you love someone more than anyone else in the world, it's not easy to forgive them when they persist in destroying themselves,' David said quietly.

There was a sudden crash from the kitchen. It sounded like crockery being thrown on the floor. She looked aghast at David.

' . . . And fuck you, too!' Christopher was yelling.

'Oh God, why does he have to drink so much?' David cried out.

'How can he be drunk? I never saw him drink anything!'

'He kept going upstairs to see if Holly was OK . . .'

'You mean . . . ?'

'Sure.' David sounded weary. 'He brings his own.' He paused, frowning. 'As I tried to tell Dad, he's never given up booze, although he pretends he has. I wish to hell he'd realise what he's doing to himself.'

David looked close to tears, and Charlotte's heart went out to him in sympathy. 'Oh, darling,' she said. 'I keep forgetting how badly it must affect you.' And it must hurt David terribly to feel his parents were more inclined to accept the assurances of an addict than believe the concerns of his brother.

Breakfast was about to start. Virginia, looking more harassed than ever, was trying to get everyone into the dining room, whilst looking after Holly who, over-tired from yesterday's excitements, was being decidedly truculent.

'I don't want breakfast!' she wailed, still clutching the doll Olivia had given her the previous evening.

'You must. Now, come along,' Carol admonished, taking her hand.

'Be a good girl, darling,' Virginia pleaded.

Holly glared at her balefully. 'My mummy doesn't make me have breakfast!'

'I'm sure she does.' Carol was standing for no nonsense. Virginia might be a push-over as far as the child was concerned, but she had no compunction about making Holly obey her.

Lifting the little girl onto the chair, she plonked a cereal bowl in front of her. 'You're having cornflakes,' she said firmly.

'I don't *want* cornflakes!' Holly turned and looked at Charlotte, her mouth drooping and her chin trembling. 'I don't want cornflakes,' she repeated, piteously.

'Where's Christopher?' Neil asked, helping himself to coffee.

'Where you'd expect him to be!' Edmund replied grimly. 'Still in bed.'

Hurriedly Charlotte moved to intervene. She leaned over and put an arm round Holly's shoulders. 'If I make you some toast and jam, will you eat it?' she asked softly.

Holly nodded, blinking away tears. 'Strawberry jam.'

'OK. Strawberry jam it is.'

Christopher appeared an hour later, red eyed and subdued. He and his father ignored each other. Charlotte tried to lighten the atmosphere.

'If your daughter goes missing one day,' she said to Christopher smiling, 'you'll know I've kidnapped her.'

His mouth twitched ironically. 'I often wish I could,' he said, and Charlotte immediately regretted the crassness of the remark.

For the rest of the day, Charlotte stayed with Holly. David had told her he'd got some more business to sort out with his father, and had closeted himself in the study with Edmund, while Carol and Neil had taken themselves off after lunch for a walk through Barrow. Virginia, saying her head was splitting, had retired upstairs for a rest.

'What would you like to do?' Charlotte asked, as Holly looked at all her Christmas presents again.

'Give Flissy a bath,' she said without hesitation.

'We'll have to take off all her beautiful clothes.'

'Yes.'

'OK. Where shall we wash her?'

'In a bowl, like Mummy washes Ben.'

'Who's Ben?'

'My baby brother.' Holly spoke proudly. Then she thought deeply for a moment before announcing, 'Now I've got a baby, too.'

Edmund, having said that Mackie was in need of a good walk, was striding angrily down the drive. His fury at not having been able to stay – even for a short while – with Olivia the previous night, was only equalled by his anger that Christopher had flirted so outrageously with her.

Pulling in his stomach, he quickened his pace as he glanced at his watch. It was just after five o'clock; he could spend an hour with her now without causing suspicion. An hour of heaven which would soothe his ruffled feelings and quell his fears that she might wish for someone younger. At the end of the drive he turned left and made his way across the fields, round the outskirts of Barrow, his sense of anticipation growing with every step. How stupid to think a ne'er-do-well like Chris, stinking of whisky and full of bullshit, could attract Olivia more than he did! It was laughable, really. He had so much more to offer for one thing. Wealth – and he wasn't mean with his gifts – culture, good conversation and, most valuable of all, experience.

Magnolia Cottage was an ugly Victorian house, built of bricks the colour of ox blood and set behind high speckled laurel bushes. When Edmund had first met Olivia, he couldn't imagine what had possessed her to buy such a hideous place. Surely, he thought, she'd have been more attracted to a charming house with pretty chimney-pots and a porch and shutters on the window? Once inside he realised, though, that the large gloomy rooms made a magnificent gothic background to her dramatic taste. Carved furniture, dark walls and rich hangings all contributed to a glamour that was more mysterious than obvious. The rooms were dimly lit even during the day, the sunshine filtered through tall palms placed on low tables in the window. Olivia did not believe in bright lights.

Edmund rang the doorbell and heard it clank a long way away. Mackie waited expectantly by his side, grinning hugely, his pink tongue lolling.

She seemed to be taking a long time to answer the door, and he was about to press the brass bell again when Olivia opened it and stood staring at him.

'I didn't expect you this afternoon,' she said breathlessly. Then, from out of the shadows of the hall behind her, Christopher emerged.

Chapter Five

'Thank God that's that!' Neil said, closing his suitcase. 'Another Christmas over and next year we'll be in our own home.'

'Hush! They'll hear you.' Carol, stuffing a pair of shoes into her zip-up bag, gave him a warning glance. They were in their room at Chelwood Manor, getting ready to leave, and for the first time in four days they felt quite light-hearted.

'It has been hellish, though, hasn't it?' Neil remarked, lowering his voice. 'Virginia's been more of a nervous wreck than usual, and Edmund's impossible.'

'Christopher upset him.'

'*Everything* upsets him.'

'Do you think he's having an affair with that woman?'

'Of course I do. Don't you?'

Carol paused before agreeing reluctantly. 'Poor Virginia. She doesn't realise what's going on, thank goodness.'

'I think she does.'

'Do you?' Carol's brow became furrowed as if she had a sudden pain. 'Oh, God, what can we do? Edmund really is a sod.'

'He'll never leave Virginia, though. I'd say this Olivia whatever-her-name-is will be just a passing fancy. Nothing to worry about.'

Carol looked at her husband with mock severity. '*You'd* better not start having fancies, passing or otherwise, or you'll find yourself getting thwacked around the head with a golf club!'

Neil chuckled. Now that they were going home, Carol was becoming her usual jolly self again, her state of discontent evaporating.

'No risk of that,' he replied comfortably. 'I value our golf clubs too much.'

'So I should hope,' she rejoined, smiling. Then she was struck by a thought. She lowered her voice again.

'I wouldn't be surprised if Chris doesn't take her away from Edmund, judging by the fight they had last night.'

The piquancy of the situation amused Neil. 'May the best man win.'

'That's horrid!'

'You must admit she's more Chris's age, and he hasn't got a girlfriend right now, has he?'

'Virginia told me he hasn't had a serious relationship since he broke up with Linda,' Carol confided.

Neil carried their luggage to the bedroom door. 'Are you coming? I'll put these in the car and then we can go.'

She glanced round the room for the last time. 'Yes, I think we've got everything.' Cheerfully they walked down the stairs. It would be nice to stop on the way for a ploughman's lunch at a country pub, Carol decided. To be going home was cause for a little celebration.

Charlotte and David were already loading up her car while Virginia watched them, her face pale and sad as her family got ready to depart. Then Edmund strolled out of the house, hands dug moodily in his trouser pockets.

'You're all off, then?' he remarked to no one in particular. Then he looked at the assembled company. 'Where're Chris and Holly?'

'I don't know, dear,' Virginia replied vaguely.

'Aren't they supposed to be leaving too? I thought David and Charlotte could drop them off at the station.'

David looked puzzled. 'I didn't think they were leaving until this afternoon?'

'That means *I'll* have to take them to the station, since your mother refuses to drive these days,' Edmund grumbled.

'That won't kill you,' Carol said, feeling able to speak her mind now that she was about to leave.

Edmund shrugged and gave a mirthless smile. 'It would just seem more sensible. I would have thought that, as David will be driving right past the station, he should take them, but of course I could be mistaken,' he added sarcastically. 'But I don't want Chris and Holly to leave before they have to.'

Christopher, emerging from the house holding Holly's hand, looked at his father stony-faced. 'I wouldn't dream of inconveniencing you by expecting you to take us to the station.' Then he turned to his mother with a smile. 'We'll call for a taxi, Mum. It's no hassle.'

'I want to stay,' Holly announced, clutching Flissy under one arm. She'd added scarlet ribbons from the Christmas wrapping to the doll's wardrobe, in a broad sash round its middle and another round its neck. 'Daddy, we don't have to go yet, do we?'

'We're staying a little while longer, but we do have to go this afternoon, or Mummy will wonder where you are,' Christopher replied.

Holly left her father's side and went to tug Virginia's skirt.

'We're staying for a bit,' she said triumphantly.

'I know you are, sweetheart.' Virginia bent to hug her. 'Gladys is cooking your favourite lunch.'

'Cheesy-toast?'

Virginia nodded. Gratified, Holly turned to her father. 'We're having cheesy-toast for lunch.'

Charlotte came up to them, grinning. 'Now there's a young lady who knows her own mind! I have a feeling she'll go far.'

Christopher's bearded face softened. 'It's been lovely getting to know you, Charlotte. Maybe we can all get together in town one of these days?'

She hesitated. She knew David and his brother didn't get on well, but on the other hand she couldn't bear not to see Holly again. *What the hell*, she thought, *I can see them on my own. And eventually Chris and David might learn to like each other,* she mused. Turning back to Christopher she said, 'Give me a ring. I'm in the book. Perhaps you could bring Holly to tea?'

'Great!' He kissed her on the cheek. 'Have a safe journey.'

Everyone was saying goodbye now, and for a moment Virginia clung to David as if she couldn't bear to let him go.

'Good luck with your promotion, darling,' she said. 'Let me know as soon as you hear.'

'I will, Mum.' Then he shook hands with his father, who was still standing watching the proceedings with a sour expression. 'Thanks for everything, Dad.'

'Don't spend it all at once.'

David laughed awkwardly. 'Let's go,' he said to Charlotte. Slamming the car door, he revved the engine. The car shot off down the drive, scattering gravel in its wake. Charlotte looked back; her last glimpse of the family was of Edmund glaring arrogantly at them, while all the others clustered together. Holly, waving cheerfully, had a broad grin on her little face as she hugged her doll.

Christopher moved closer to his mother, away from the others.

'Cheer up, Mum.'

Virginia's eyes were wistful. 'I wish you all lived nearer.'

'I know.' His smile was understanding. 'I was wondering if I could bring Holly down again in a few weeks' time?'

Her face lit up with delight. 'Of course, Chris! You can come any time you like. Any time,' she said fervently.

'Thanks.'

'Are we coming again?' Holly piped up loudly.

Virginia nodded. 'Yes, darling.'

Then it was the turn of Carol and Neil to say goodbye, and suddenly the atmosphere became as it should have been over Christmas. There was a feeling of genuine goodwill as they kissed each other, while Mackie barked with excitement and the wind blew Holly's blonde curls around her head.

'Have a safe journey,' Virginia called out as the car moved away.

Carol waved. 'Take care of yourself.'

'You're looking very pleased with life, Chris,' Linda observed later that day as they sat in her living room with Holly on her lap.

'Actually, Christmas was absolute fucking hell.'

She shot him a warning glance.

'Holly,' she said, hugging her daughter, 'why don't you go and see what Ben's doing? Show him your beautiful new doll.'

'It's a baby not a doll,' Holly insisted. 'It's Flissy.'

'Well, show Flissy to Ben.' Then Linda turned to Christopher. 'D'you want a cup of tea?'

'Thanks. Is Denzil home?'

'He'll be back soon. He's gone to the supermarket; we've nearly run out of disposable nappies for Ben.' As she spoke, she went through to the kitchen, which was across the hall from the living room. Christopher ambled after her.

'So what was wrong?' Linda asked.

'Things are bad at home.'

Linda looked at him as she filled the kettle. 'In what way?'

'The old man's having an affair.'

'Who with, for God's sake? That doesn't sound like him. A bully he may be, but a philanderer? Are you sure, Chris?'

Christopher nodded, seating himself at the kitchen table while she got out some biscuits and put them on a plate. 'Mum's in more of a state than usual, and he's like a bear with a sore head. If it hadn't been that Holly was having fun, I'd have come straight back home.'

'But who is she?' Linda looked intrigued. 'The one he's having an affair with?'

'A neighbour. Moved into Magnolia Cottage last year. She's very beautiful, too.'

Linda's eyebrows shot up. 'Seems you're a bit attracted to her yourself?' Her tone was teasing.

'That's the problem.' He sounded morose. 'She came

over, unexpectedly, on Christmas afternoon, and she and I hit it off immediately. That's when Dad went crazy; at least he did when she'd gone. We fought over her the next day, too.'

'Oh, Chris!' Linda spoke to him like an indulgent mother; she was grinning. 'What's going to happen now?'

'What I'd really like to do is take Holly home again in a couple of weeks, just for the weekend.'

'But why? If it was such hell? So that you can see this woman again?'

Christopher looked at his ex-wife keenly. 'You're not jealous, are you?'

She smiled with genuine warmth, though her voice was filled with mock severity. 'Why the hell should I be jealous? It was I who left you, remember? Anyway, I've got Denzil now.'

'I just wondered. I've never really stopped loving you, you know.'

'Don't, Chris,' she said gently. 'It's no good going over the past again. Actually, I think you deserve a little happiness. The problems we had should have been handled differently, and I daresay if we'd both been older, and more experienced, things would have been different.'

'I'm not blaming you for leaving, Linda.'

'I know. It's just that I should have got professional help or counselling or something, instead of yelling at you all the time. I thought you were weak. And a fool.' She shook her head as she reached for the teapot and dropped two teabags into it. 'I didn't understand about addiction at the time.'

'At least I never touch the stuff these days.' He sounded

humbled. 'You had a rotten deal, Linda. I nearly killed both of us.'

'That's all in the past, Chris. Tell me more about your lady friend.' As she spoke she unhooked two mugs from the dresser shelf and put them on the table in front of him. 'What's her name?'

'Olivia Middleton.'

'Ah!' She grinned. 'Fancy stuff? Sounds like Janet Reger underwear and pearls.'

He nodded, laughing now. 'You're right.'

'So you want to go back to Chelwood to consolidate your position?' she asked teasingly. 'And take Holly as an excuse for being there?'

'Exactly. I'm going to take her out next time she comes to London, but she told me it wouldn't be during January because she's got builders in the house.' He paused, taking a deep breath. 'But quite apart from that, I'd like to see more of Holly. We've grown so close over Christmas. I want to be able to take her to the zoo. And to spend the odd day at my flat. I'd like to be able to drive her into the country for a picnic when it's fine; couldn't you relent a little on the conditions?'

'I'm not trying to be difficult, Chris. I'm really not. It's just that I feel she's *safe* at Chelwood; just in case you do drugs again or get drunk, like you used to. I'm terrified of Holly being exposed to a situation where you're incapable. Especially if you're driving.'

He tried to suppress the rising memory of being drunk every evening at Chelwood. Even though it wasn't until Holly was in bed, he knew Linda would be furious. Supposing his parents were to mention that to her?

'Perhaps,' Linda ventured, looking at his downcast face, 'if this Olivia turns out to be someone you form a relationship with, you can take Holly out together?'

'She gave Holly that doll.'

'I like her taste,' Linda admitted. 'So what are your chances, Chris?'

'She was very encouraging. I spent yesterday afternoon with her, and we got along really well, talking about so many things that interest both of us; and then of course Dad turns up! I thought he was going to explode when he saw me there.'

'What was *his* excuse for visiting her?'

'He said he was passing, while walking Mackie, and thought he'd thank her again for giving Holly a doll.'

They both laughed. 'Oh, really!' Linda scoffed. 'Does your mother realise what's going on?'

'I think she does. She seemed delighted when I invited myself back. I have a feeling she'd really like me to score one over the old man.'

Carol and Neil sat by the fire, enjoying being back in their own home once more. Neil had his favourite brand of whisky by his elbow, and it was still only six o'clock. Carol was looking forward to some of her favourite television programmes.

'I'm worried about Virginia,' Carol said to her husband. 'She'll have a nervous breakdown if she stays in that house with Edmund much longer.'

'Forgive me saying this, dear, but Virginia is capable of having a nervous breakdown anywhere! I'm sure she'll be fine now that Christmas is, thank God, over. It was too much for her. Christopher and Edmund fighting all the time.'

'I know.' Carol stretched her strong stocky legs towards the fire. 'How are we going to get rid of this Olivia Middleton, though?'

'*We* are not going to do anything!' Neil said firmly. 'You must stop worrying about Virginia.'

'It's because she's five years younger than me. I always had to look after her when we were small. She was always the highly strung one.'

'You can say that again.'

'Oh, Neil, do be more understanding.'

'I can't stand helpless women. That's why I married you. You're strong. Capable. Independent. If you'd been married to Edmund you'd have stood up to him, instead of becoming a servile wreck like her.'

Carol was torn between being flattered and having a sense of loyalty towards her sister. 'You could pour me another gin and tonic,' she said instead.

'Very well, my dear.'

They sat for a while, sipping their drinks in companionable silence, letting the stress of the past few days slide away. Carol realised Neil was right. There was little they could do to help Virginia, if she refused to help herself.

David spent their first night back in London at Charlotte's flat, also experiencing a sense of release which was something akin to being let out of prison.

'Never again,' he swore, hugging Charlotte as she prepared an omelette for their supper. 'I'm sorry I dragged you through all that hell, sweetheart. Still, at least Dad gave me enough money to get some decent clothes. Will you come shopping with me tomorrow?'

She hugged him back, happy they were on their own again. He'd told her about his father's gift on the way home; only she knew what lectures David had had to endure to get it. 'Are you going to spend the whole five hundred pounds on clothes?' she asked.

He stepped back and looked at her. 'Yes, I thought I would. I desperately need some new suits and shirts. What chance do I have of promotion if I don't look the part?'

'But you've already been put up for promotion, haven't you?'

'Yes. Well, sort of. I mean, I think I'm going to be offered the job that's going in the sales department, but of course it isn't confirmed yet.'

Charlotte didn't pursue the subject. David never seemed to have any money. She knew he owed rent, his share of the telephone at his flat; his credit cards were also all over the limit. His lack of responsibility where money was concerned worried her at times. She'd been brought up to consider her financial obligations and to learn to budget.

'What's the matter, darling?' he asked.

Charlotte shook her head and busied herself with opening a bottle of wine. 'I was just thinking it might be better to pay off some of the money you owe. You could get one good suit at the January sales next week, and use the rest to settle your debts.'

He grabbed the bottle from her. 'No, I'd rather get a decent wardrobe. Now where's the opener?'

She handed him the corkscrew. 'Anyway,' he added, 'when I get promoted I'll be getting a bigger salary; then

I'll be in a position to get financially straight. OK?'

'That's true,' she agreed peaceably. The last thing she wanted was a fight, and she knew how touchy he could get about money.

Back home in Barrow, Olivia was promising Edmund that there was no reason, no reason whatever, for him to be jealous of Christopher.

'Don't be silly, darling,' she said soothingly, stroking the back of his neck as they lay entwined on her drawing-room sofa. 'There's no one like you, and I don't know what I'd do without you.'

From the silky hollow of her neck, Edmund mumbled that he'd die without her.

'You've brought me alive, darling, just when I thought I'd never be happy again,' he whispered, after they'd made love.

Olivia held him close, enveloping him in clouds of white chiffon and Claude Montana perfume. In contrast, Edmund lay inert and heavy in thick cavalry-twill trousers and Viyella shirt. It struck her how lacking in dignity men were when they made love. They humped, sweating, grovelling like desperate dogs, intent on unloading their rampant burden, driven on by their own excitement, while she lay, accepting, cool, acquiescent, detached, reminding herself that at the end of the line she could be mistress of Chelwood Manor and a very rich woman. Edmund had a great deal more money than people realised and, in a moment of weakness or bravado – she wasn't sure which – he'd told her just how much he was worth. The trouble, she reflected, was that he didn't like parting with it. That was why he was reluctant to get rid of Virginia. Over and over again he told Olivia how much it would cost.

'You're so wonderful, my love,' she crooned softly, sure that she could get him to change his mind in time. As far as his son was concerned, she'd have to be careful. The thought of getting Christopher into bed was intriguing; would he be like his father? Only younger? Less creased and wrinkled, with a flat stomach and firm thighs? She'd half a mind to encourage him, just for the experience. It was a long time since she'd had a lover under fifty, because the younger ones weren't rich. Both her ex-husbands had been in their sixties.

Edmund raised his head and looked into her eyes. She immediately softened her expression, smiling enticingly up at him.

'You're so wonderful . . . more wonderful than I could have dreamed . . .' Her voice drifted away, emotionally.

'Oh, God, Olivia. You drive me crazy. I'm getting a hard-on again! Oh, what you do to me,' he groaned.

'Give it to me, sweetheart,' she urged. 'Give it to me again!' Her breath rose and fell, and her slim hands slid down to his bulky hips.

Edmund was unaware of the phone ringing in the hall, but Olivia heard it. Christopher had promised to call her at this time. She let it ring. Eventually it stopped. She smiled to herself as she feigned another orgasm. She had no doubts that Christopher would try again later.

Chapter Six

'Come in, darlings! It's so good to see you!' Margaret Taylor embraced Charlotte and David as they arrived for dinner on New Year's Eve. Tall and pretty, with stylishly cut tawny-blonde hair and a slim figure, she looked much younger than her age, with an unlined face and a healthily glowing skin.

'Daddy's getting a bottle out of the fridge,' she announced, leading the way into the drawing room. 'Now, tell me all about Christmas.'

The drawing room had a comfortable, lived-in look, with books and magazines piled up on tables beside deeply cushioned chairs, and dark coral walls which set off their eclectic collection of paintings to dazzling effect. Charlotte looked around, noting the familiar objects with delight. She'd lived all her life in this eighteenth-century house overlooking the Thames in Chelsea, and it had been a wrench to leave home and get herself a flat three years ago. But, gently and lovingly, her parents had nudged her from the nest, knowing she'd benefit in the long run from having her own place.

They'd been right, of course; Charlotte had learned to overcome her shyness and forge ahead on her own. She glanced at David as he sat on the sofa beside her mother, and reflected that she was the luckiest girl alive. Everything had worked out perfectly. Her bid to succeed hadn't only brought her a job she loved, but the most marvellous man.

She watched, smiling, as Margaret regaled David in her animated way about lunching at the Savoy on Christmas Day, and a rush of affection and gratitude towards her mother made her say impetuously: 'I'm so glad you had such a good time, Mummy. You're always cooking for everyone else, you deserve to be taken out occasionally!'

Margaret was touched by her daughter's words. 'Oh, La, you are sweet. It was a lovely treat, but I do enjoy thinking up new dishes, you know. And the books sell like hot cakes!'

'Because they tell you how to make hot cakes, I suppose!' David remarked, laughing.

At that moment Colin Taylor came bounding into the room, a small, dynamic man, bursting with energy. His chubby face was wreathed in smiles.

'La!' he exclaimed, rushing over to hug her. 'How's it going? Are you well? Oh, it's lovely to see you again! Did you have a wonderful Christmas?' Then he turned and shook David by the hand. 'How are you, old chap? Let's have a drink, shall we?'

This is what Christmas day should have been like, Charlotte thought, proud of her parents. The difference in the atmosphere between her home and David's was incredible. Where fear and friction stalked hand-in-hand with bitter resentment in one family, openness, goodwill and deep affection abounded in the other.

'So, did you have a good time down in Wiltshire?' Colin asked breezily as he handed out glasses of champagne.

Charlotte and her mother exchanged secret knowing looks.

'Great,' David replied heartily. 'It was fun, wasn't it, La?'

'Great,' she echoed loyally, guessing he didn't want Margaret and Colin to know about the dissent in his family.

'The countryside can be so pretty, with snow and everything, at this time of year,' Margaret observed diplomatically.

Charlotte smiled gratefully. 'Yes. Chelwood Manor is beautiful, too, with lovely gardens. And they had the most wonderfully decorated tree in the hall.'

There was a pause, and Colin's bright eyes darted to his wife and daughter in turn, reading the undercurrent of atmosphere, but too tactful to say anything.

'So what's on the menu tonight, Margaret?' he asked instead, in a jovial voice. 'What *pièce de résistance* have you dreamed up for us to partake of?'

'Wouldn't you rather have a surprise?' she asked.

'Oh, yes please,' said Charlotte. Her mother loved to dish up her new concoctions for the family, getting them to guess the ingredients, and then asking for their comments which she jotted down in a notebook.

Susan, who was four years younger than Charlotte and still living at home, appeared at that moment. Without a pang of jealousy, Charlotte thought how pretty she looked. Enviably slim, with fair hair like Margaret's, she had high cheekbones, a heart-shaped face, and large grey eyes fringed with thick dark lashes. She was also beautifully dressed, wearing an Antonia design in black velvet trimmed with black braid. As secretary to Antonia Bonel, a Mayfair dress designer, she'd been given clothes to go with the job. Antonia insisted that all her staff be beautifully dressed if they were likely to be in contact with her rich clients, and it was one of the perks of an otherwise underpaid job. Charlotte grinned at her sister approvingly, wishing she exuded the glamour of a successful working girl but knowing she somehow just missed it.

'Hi there!' The sisters greeted each other with little shrieks of delight. Then Susan flung herself at David, giving him a smacking kiss on each cheek.

'Hi, David! We missed you both at Christmas. Did you have a marvellous time? I bet you did!'

Charlotte giggled. 'How's life with you, Susie?'

'Fantastic! We had a great time here, didn't we, Mum?' Susan patted her mother's arm. 'Then Alex took me to the ballet on Boxing Night and we had dinner afterwards at the Ivy. Oh, it was all wonderful.'

'Who's Alex?' Charlotte inquired. Susan seemed to have a new boyfriend every few weeks.

Susan beamed enthusiastically. 'He's a disc jockey with Central Radio. Hey!' Her long hair swung silkily about her shoulders as she turned to look at David. 'I must introduce you two. You might be able to get him to plug Flight Records on his programme!'

David nodded thoughtfully. 'Let's wait until I'm running the sales department. I'll be in a stronger position then.'

Margaret's face lit up. 'You're going to be head of sales? How wonderful, David! Many congratulations! When did all this happen?'

'I'll be taking over quite shortly, I hope.'

Charlotte added, 'He's been buying new clothes—'

'Not just because I'm being promoted,' he interrupted, laughing.

'But I thought it was because—'

Again he cut her off in mid-sentence. 'I don't just buy new clothes to wear to work.'

'No, of course not.' She looked away, blushing at the snub.

'Who's for more champagne? Got to drink up before we sample the culinary delights your mother has prepared for us tonight,' Colin said, going round with the bottle again. His smile was fixed this time.

Charlotte suddenly had the uneasy feeling that they'd brought an element of the Chelwood Manor discord back to London with them. Usually, there were never these awkward moments in her home, when ugly silences had to be retrieved by forced remarks; when what was said seemed to be open to misinterpretation and misunderstanding.

'I'm just going to nip into the kitchen to do the finishing touches,' Margaret announced. 'I'll call you when dinner's ready.'

'Want any help, Mummy?' Charlotte asked.

'What! And spoil my lovely surprises?' Margaret laughed. 'No way, sweetheart! If you know what's coming it will spoil the whole effect.'

They started with tiny pancakes filled with chicken livers and sweetcorn.

'And . . . what else?' Margaret coaxed.

'Garlic?' Charlotte suggested.

'That's a safe bet,' Susan remarked. 'I think there's also sage, and maybe chilli?'

'Black pepper of course,' Colin remarked, chewing thoughtfully. 'Your mother puts black pepper in everything.

111

I also detect red wine . . . and maybe a little onion?'

Margaret nodded, delighted. 'You've got it! Plus soured cream, a touch of sugar and a sprinkling of paprika.'

'It's very nice,' Colin observed appreciatively.

'Thank you, darling. I thought of doing the next book just on starters. What do you think?'

'I think it'll bring in a nice fat cheque from your publishers,' Colin commented with relish. 'Have you got a title? How about *Simple Starters*?'

'What about *Satisfying Starters*?' Charlotte suggested.

'*Scrumptious Starters* is better,' said David.

'It could be *Simply Scrumptious Starters*,' Susan added.

At ten minutes to twelve, Colin produced more champagne and they all braced themselves for the reverberating chimes of Big Ben on the television. Suddenly, the others were all hugging and kissing each other, and chinking glasses, while Charlotte and Susan laughed with happiness and Margaret grew misty-eyed as she held Colin's hand. And as the boom of the great clock struck twelve, David raised his glass, 'To vast riches and a glittering future,' he said loudly, then added, almost as an afterthought, 'for all of us . . .'

'Lousy bastard!' David raged. Charlotte had never seen him so angry. 'I've got a good mind to go straight to the chairman of Flight to tell him what's happened.'

'Oh, sweetheart,' she commiserated. She hated to see him upset, beside himself with fury, his mouth tugging down at the corners. 'Perhaps they'll give you promotion later on in the year?'

It was a week after the dinner at her parents'. He'd arrived at her flat shortly after she'd got back from work, and one look at his face told her how deeply disappointed and angry he was.

'It's not fair!' he exploded. 'It's jobs for the boys, that's what it is! Don Gabriel wanted to get his boyfriend into the company and he's given him the job I wanted! He'd promised me I'd be moved to the sales department after Christmas, and now he brings this jerk in, out of nowhere!'

'That is unfair,' Charlotte agreed. 'Don Gabriel is the managing director of Flight, isn't he? Does he really have the power to bring in an outsider for a key position like head of sales?'

'Whether he does or not, he's bloody well gone and done it!' He thumped the arm of the sofa with his fist.

'And he'd really promised you the job?'

He looked at her, eyes smouldering and heavy lidded with resentment. 'Of course,' he said after a moment. 'God, and to think I know things about him and his private life that would ruin him if they got out.' He laughed harshly and without amusement. 'One word from me to the chairman and he'd be history!'

'But you wouldn't, would you?'

David shrugged. 'Oh, of course I wouldn't. None of them are worth it. I'm going to hand in my resignation tomorrow. I don't have to sit back and allow myself to be treated like this. Who the fuck does Don Gabriel think he is, anyway?'

'Is there any way you can sidestep him and still get promotion?'

'No. He's made sure he's in the seat of power. He even hires and fires the fucking *cleaners* . . . !'

'Darling, I'm so sorry.' She thought about the five

hundred pounds he'd blown on new clothes because he'd been so sure he'd get the post as head of sales. He'd also counted on receiving a much larger salary so that he could get himself out of debt.

'I wish there was something I could do,' she said wretchedly.

David grimaced. 'Oh, I'll find something else, don't worry. With my experience and know-how, I'll soon find a good job. I'm not going back into accountancy, though; that's for sure.'

'Do you hate it so much?'

'There's no future in it,' he replied flatly.

Charlotte didn't pursue the matter, offering him instead a drink followed by an omelette *fines herbes*. 'If I'd known you were coming I'd have got in some chops,' she explained.

'An omelette will do fine, darling,' he murmured, gazing fretfully into space. When she went to the kitchen she could still hear him pacing up and down the sitting room in silent anguish. She felt sick with disappointment for him, and promised herself she would do everything in her power to help him secure the job he wanted.

'When are you coming up to London?' Christopher asked, telephone receiver cupped in his hand as he talked. It was nine o'clock at night, the best time to phone Olivia, for at that hour she was certain to be alone.

'Maybe next Wednesday.'

'Can we meet?'

'I'd like that.'

'Where are you staying?'

'I hadn't planned to stay; I thought I'd just go up for the day.'

'Do stay, Olivia. I'd like to take you out to dinner, otherwise I'll hardly see you at all.'

There was silence on the line and he could imagine her twisting a strand of her black hair round and round her finger, the way she did when she was thinking.

'I don't know . . .'

'Oh, please.' This would be her third visit to London since they'd met at Christmas; Christopher was falling more deeply in love with her every time he saw her. Meanwhile she remained friendly but elusive, saying she no longer saw much of his father, but that she was not yet ready to start a new relationship.

'I'm glad you're not seeing Dad,' Christopher affirmed. 'For Mum's sake, as well as my own,' he added shyly. He wasn't much good at wooing women and he knew it. He was too blunt and too direct for the games most people played; would Olivia have preferred it if he *did* play games? Life was too short in his opinion. He'd never played hard-to-get or I-don't-really-care-anyway tactics with Linda, or she with him. For as long as they'd been together they'd been totally direct with each other. In his opinion it saved time and avoided misunderstandings.

'I suppose I could spend the night in town,' Olivia was saying thoughtfully. 'I could book a room at Blakes.'

'You could also stay with me.'

'I think not, Chris. You know I don't want to rush into anything so soon after . . . well, so soon.'

'OK.' He tried to curb his patience.

'Come to Blakes about seven. We can dine there.'

He winced. He didn't have the sort of money that would run to dining somewhere as expensive as that.

'I'll come at seven, but I know a marvellous Russian restaurant in Fulham where we can have dinner,' he said firmly. 'They make the best blinis in town.' They also don't cost an arm and a leg, he thought to himself.

'I'll see you on Wednesday, then.'

'Yes.' Christopher longed to say more but he was afraid of frightening her away. She sounded so cool and collected on the phone, as if she didn't really care whether she saw him again or not. For a moment, a niggling doubt that she might still be having an affair with his father entered his mind, but then he dismissed it. His father was old and married. It stood to reason that she'd prefer a younger lover, someone nearer her own age, who was single. Christopher was without conceit, but he did consider himself a better choice than Edmund for a woman in her thirties.

'What will you be doing during the day?' Christopher asked, wanting to keep her talking as long as possible so he could listen to her soft, whispery voice.

'I've got a fitting with my dressmaker. I'm having my hair done, and I've got various bits of shopping to do. Why?'

'I just wondered. Will you be up in time for lunch?'

'I'm not sure.' Olivia sounded vague, as if she didn't want to be committed to any more arrangements. 'I must go now.'

'I'll see you Wednesday, at seven.'

'Yes.'

'Look after yourself.'

There was a chuckle. 'I always do. Goodbye, Chris.'

'Goodbye, Olivia.'

When he'd hung up, Christopher sat contemplating the enchanting creature who now dominated his thoughts. Was it her unavailability that was so intriguing? That elusive facet of her personality that had got him hooked from the beginning? He wished he knew what made her tick, what games she played. After a while he went to bed, too mesmerised even to want a drink. Next Wednesday. He could hardly wait. He felt completely bewitched.

'Your phone's been engaged for *hours*!' Edmund whispered in agitation. 'Who have you been talking to, for God's sake?'

Olivia's voice was soothing. 'I haven't been talking to anyone, sweetheart . . .'

'Your line's been busy,' he said accusingly. He was so distraught he forgot to keep his voice lowered; he was sure anyway that Virginia was asleep upstairs.

'I know.' She spoke with patience. 'So stupid of me! I hadn't realised I'd knocked the receiver off its cradle when I turned down my bed. One of the pillows must have knocked it sideways. I only discovered it a few minutes ago.'

'It should have whistled. If you leave the receiver off, it whistles, so you know what's happened.'

'Oh!' There was a pause. 'Maybe it did. I haven't been in the room. I was watching something on television downstairs.'

'What were you watching?' Edmund couldn't keep the suspicion out of his voice, no matter how hard he tried. He was obsessed by Olivia, feeling her presence like a great dark angel, no matter where he went or what he did, and the thought of her talking for hours to someone else . . . another man . . . Christopher . . . ! He clenched his fists and closed his eyes in despair. How was he going to prevent her leaving him? The thought tortured his guts and induced a kind of mental frenzy. He couldn't endure life without her. She had reawakened the torpor that being married to Virginia had induced, and now making love to Olivia had become like an addictive drug that kept him in a permanent state of longing.

'I watched *Newsnight*,' she replied calmly, 'and then the arts programme afterwards was so fascinating that I could hardly tear myself away.'

Edmund grunted. 'I was worried about you.'

'Darling, there's no need to be.'

'I don't think you should be living alone at Magnolia Cottage. I don't think it's safe.'

'From burglars, you mean?'

'Or worse,' he said cryptically. 'That's why we got an alarm. You read such terrible things in the newspapers these days. No one's safe. I hope you lock all the doors at night.'

'Yes, and I set my alarm, too . . .' She paused. 'What's brought this on, Edmund?'

'I care so much about you, Olivia.' He sounded hurt. 'I'm terrified something might happen to you. I want to be with you, darling,' he went on, anxiously. 'All the time, and keep you safe, so that nothing and no one can hurt you.'

She sounded amused. 'Nothing's going to happen to me, Edmund.'

'We're living in terrible times, sweetheart. A woman is no longer safe, anywhere.'

'Oh, dear, you are getting morbid!' she said lightly. 'Do you want to move into Magnolia Cottage so you can protect me?'

'Don't tease.' His tone was stern. Finding her phone engaged for so long had unnerved him more than he'd realised.

'Are you coming to see me tomorrow?' she whispered.

'Yes. It'll have to be in the afternoon, while Virginia is having her hair done. About two o'clock.'

'I'm going up to London on Wednesday.'

'Do you have to?'

'Yes, I've a lot of shopping to do, Edmund, and I've got several appointments. In fact, I thought I might stay for the night and come back on Thursday.'

He felt himself turn cold. Suspicion uncoiled itself like a serpent in his mind.

'That'll be nice. Will you be seeing anyone?' He forced himself to speak calmly.

'My mother, probably.' Again, the coolness of her tone maddened him almost to the point of making a reckless promise about their future together.

When he finally said goodbye and hung up, he realised he felt more depressed than he could ever have imagined. It was with a heavy heart that he went upstairs and climbed into bed beside Virginia.

David's mood of discontent and disappointment lasted several weeks, during which Charlotte found it hard to get close to him. She desperately wanted him to realise he had her full support whatever, but he seemed withdrawn, in a world of his own, with a slow fuse of anger burning away inside him.

'You'll find another job where your talent will be appreciated,' she assured him several times, but he still seemed too angry to take comfort from her encouragement.

He blamed Don Gabriel for double-crossing him by promising him a job and then giving it to someone else, and nothing appeared to alleviate his bitterness.

In desperation, Charlotte finally phoned her father. He had a high position in a finance company in the City, and she was sure he'd help David find a job.

'Is there anything in your company, Dad?' she asked, after he'd told her times were difficult and unemployment high.

'There's nothing here, my pet. Has David actually left Flight Records?'

'Not yet, but he wants to. They've treated him so badly and I feel so sorry for him. He has to find something else.'

Colin Taylor sighed. 'My advice, in the present financial climate, would be to tell him to stick with it for a while. Jobs don't grow on trees these days, you know.'

'But he's so unhappy, Dad. He was really looking forward to this promotion, which would have meant a much bigger salary, and now he's stuck in the accounts department, which he hates.'

'If he hates accounts, then he shouldn't try and join a finance company, sweetheart. What does he really want to do with his life?' Colin had years of experience in interviewing and training young men who wanted to enter the money market, and he knew it took a certain type who really enjoyed the life.

Charlotte hesitated, at a loss. 'I'm not really sure if he does have a burning ambition to do anything particular,' she admitted at last. 'He wants something interesting, of course, where he gets to meet people, and he wants to earn a lot of money.'

'Ummm,' Colin murmured. 'I wish I could help, sweetheart, but we are in the middle of a recession, and my advice to David would be to stay put for the time being.'

'Oh, dear, I do so want to help him.'

'He won't like you so much if you do,' her father pointed out wisely. 'Let him find his own way, La. Men are proud, you know. As it is, you probably already do too much for him for his own good.'

'No, I don't! What do you mean?'

'Don't you cook dinner for him several nights a week? Don't you spend all your money on the food and the wine? Don't you go Dutch when you do go to a restaurant?'

Feeling annoyed, Charlotte wished she hadn't told her family so much about her relationship with David. 'He'd do the same for me,' she said, more angrily than she'd intended. At least she hadn't told her parents that David was also in debt, or that she'd offered to help him with his rent and electric bill.

'I'm sure he would,' Colin agreed soothingly. 'Why don't you suggest that he stays with Flight Records, at least until he finds something else?'

'Yes, OK.'

'If I hear of anything, I'll let you know.'

'Thanks, Dad.' Charlotte hung up thoughtfully, wondering what she could do. If only David's parents were more understanding. It did seem unfair that they'd given so much more to Christopher than they had David.

As Charlotte spent the morning with Myra, planning the working schedule and costings of doing up a house in Holland Park for a rich Italian businessman, her mind kept straying back to David and wondering what she could do to help him.

'You're being too maternal,' Myra Grant told her good-humouredly, when she explained what was on her mind. 'How old is he, for God's sake?'

'Twenty-eight.'

'So why should you worry about him?'

'Everyone needs a supporting hand from time to time,' Charlotte said reasonably.

Myra pouted, her voluptuous mouth at odds with the steely look in her eyes. It wasn't that she didn't like men, she just thought the majority of them were rather hopeless.

'Let him find a job for himself, and if he doesn't, he's just going to have to go on social security, isn't he? I think he's crazy if he leaves Flight Records!'

'He doesn't feel he can stay now.'

'Balls!' said Myra sturdily. 'So he was passed over in favour of someone's boyfriend? Happens all the time.'

Charlotte smiled at Myra's abrasive manner. She knew she didn't mean to be unkind, just that she didn't really understand the situation. Charlotte made up her mind that, when he came round to her flat tonight, she would cook his favourite dinner, and have the champagne he so adored chilled and ready. She might even splurge out on fresh asparagus from Harrods, which was wildly expensive because it was out of season, but which he loved, especially with her home-made hollandaise sauce.

'You could have anyone you want,' Myra said suddenly, breaking into her thoughts.

Charlotte looked up from the estimates she was studying. 'What?'

'I said, you could have anyone you want. You don't have to stick with David, you know. All you lack is confidence,

Charlotte. That's why you're hanging on to David, isn't it? You're afraid you won't find anyone else.'

'Myra!' Charlotte was shocked. 'But I love him!' she blurted out, vehemently.

'I know you do, and in my opinion you're wasting your time.' In spite of her words, Myra's tone was conciliatory. 'Believe me, Charlotte, I know about men like David.'

'What do you mean?' Tears smarted behind Charlotte's eyes. Myra had never spoken to her like this before.

'He's a loser, La. You can sense it a mile off.'

Charlotte flung her pen down on the desk. 'That's a terrible thing to say! How can you talk like that? We're in love, Myra. I hope to marry him one day! Of course he's not a loser.'

Myra leaned back in her swivel chair, and regarded Charlotte with sympathy. 'Listen, my dear. I'm ten years older than you. I've been around. You're an attractive young woman, who doesn't have to saddle herself with someone like David. I promise you, because I know all the signs, that, if you marry him, you'll be supporting David, financially and figuratively, for the rest of your life! Let him sort himself out, for God's sake. You're not his *mother*!'

Charlotte looked at her angrily. 'It's because his mother is so hopeless that someone has to care. Someone has to look after him.'

Myra remained cool. 'Why?' she asked blandly.

'What do you mean, why? Don't you feel protective towards anyone? Hasn't there ever been anyone you'd lay down your life for?' she demanded heatedly.

Myra nodded. 'Yes, there has, Charlotte. And that's why I'm telling you all this. When I was twenty, I was very like you. I, too, fell in love with an attractive man who swept me off my feet, was wonderful in bed, and finally managed to charm off me my money, my time, my energy, and finally my flat, because I took out a second mortgage to help him start his own business. And guess what?' Her voice took on a bitter edge. 'Surprise! Surprise! He went off with his new secretary!'

Now Charlotte could understand the source of Myra's bitterness. She softened her tone, and said gently, 'That's awful, Myra, but it's not like that with David and me. He's never asked me for anything! It's I who suggest I cook dinner at home, and it's I who said we should go Dutch in restaurants. After all, thanks to you, I am earning a decent salary.'

'And he's never protested, of course?'

Charlotte felt annoyed again. What business was it of hers anyway? Just because she was fast approaching forty and still unmarried, there was no need for her to take out her resentment on Charlotte. 'How can you talk about him like this?' she asked. 'You're not respecting my feelings. I love him, Myra, and he loves me. He's going through a bad patch, and I fully intend to support him through it, as any decent partner would.'

Myra looked back at her, sadly. 'Oh, he's always going to need your support, La,' she said softly. 'I don't doubt that for a moment.'

'Well, I did it!' David's expression was jubilant. 'I told that cunt, Don Gabriel, just where he could stick his fucking job!'

Charlotte felt the blood drain away from her face. She

leaned against the sink, where she was washing salad for their dinner.

'You've actually resigned?'

'Yup! Got any champagne in the fridge?'

She nodded silently.

'So now I'm free as a bird!' In high spirits he took two glasses out of the cupboard, and eased the cork out of the bottle with a gentle *pop*.

'What are you going to do next?'

'Find another job.'

'What in? Another recording company?'

'I haven't made up my mind yet.' His tone was casual. Then he grinned. 'It was worth everything to see Don's face today when I told him what I thought of him; him and his faggoty boyfriend!'

'Was that wise?'

'What do you mean? He's double-crossed me!'

'He might have recommended you for another job, or given you a reference.'

'Oh, fuck that for a *chanson comique*!' He handed her some champagne. 'Here's to freedom!' he said gaily. 'To independence! To having a bit of fun!'

As she sipped her drink, she wondered what he was going to do for money, but his mood was catching, and when, after they'd had dinner, he whisked her into the bedroom with another bottle of wine, she felt her doubts slipping away. It was stupid to worry. Of course he'd get another job, and probably a much better one. Of course he was going to carve a successful career for himself in the future! Hell, he was only twenty-eight.

Holding David close, her naked body moulded to his,

she knew that, no matter what happened, she would stand by him for ever. He was her life now. Somehow she would help him find a job, look after him until he was back on his feet. '*For Richer, For Poorer . . .*' The words of the wedding service came back to her, reminding her of the meaning of love. Carried away on a euphoric wave of passion, she promised she would always be there for him.

'I love you so much,' she whispered. 'Everything will work out OK, sweetheart.'

David sighed and pulled her closer. Charlotte drifted off to sleep in his arms.

The next morning she awoke with a splitting headache, reality setting in when David announced he didn't intend to go to the office of Flight, but was staying at home instead.

'What? Not go to work?' she asked, closing her eyes as the throbbing beat a tattoo behind her eyes. Why had she drunk so much wine last night, she asked herself?

'Why should I?' he demanded, stretching comfortably on the bed beside her. 'I fancy a nice day, lounging around, not being at everybody's beck and call. Christ, I've worked so hard for that bloody company! I deserve a break after the way they've treated me.'

Charlotte rolled on to her side, wishing she could take the day off, too. It was something she'd never done since she'd started working for Myra. Even when she'd had a heavy cold with bronchitis last winter, she'd turned up at the design studio every day, without fail.

'I tell you what I'll do,' David said, sliding out of bed. 'I'm going to bring you breakfast on a tray.'

She opened her eyes, surprised. He never did anything

domesticated as a rule, not even make the coffee after dinner.

'You will?'

'Yup. It's what you need. Coffee, grilled bacon, toast and honey.'

Charlotte groaned, holding her head.

'Bacon is the best thing if you've got a hangover,' he assured her. 'It restores the fat to your system which has been destroyed by the alcohol.'

'You don't say.'

He grinned. 'Truly. I promise you.' He turned to leave the room. 'Don't go away.'

A minute later he was back with a glass of chilled mineral water and a couple of aspirins. His nudity, as he stood before her, disturbed her, although she felt ill.

'Go back to sleep until I bring you breakfast,' he said gently. Then he stroked her cheek with his cupped hand. 'Poor baby! Why don't you take the day off?'

She shook her head, instantly regretting the movement.

'I can't remember what I'm doing today,' she said, trying to visualise the page in her appointments book. 'I'm sure I've got a hundred things to do. Oh, God, I wish I hadn't drunk so much.'

David took her hand, squeezing it in both of his. 'Lie still, sweetheart. Surely I can call Myra and say you're ill? You must have a day off sometimes.'

'We're very busy, I know that. Pass me my diary, will you, David?'

'Not until you've had something to eat.' He kissed her mouth, softly and gently. 'Can you think of anything nicer than breakfast, followed by staying in bed all day, with me beside you?'

She gazed up at him. It was, of course, the most blissful suggestion she'd ever heard. Smiling, she returned his kiss.

'Could you ring Myra for me? Say I've got 'flu?'

His hands stroked her arms, the fingers warm and firm. 'Leave it to me.'

'Say you think I'll be all right by tomorrow.'

'Are you sure? You wouldn't like the week off?'

'Oh, quite sure!' She sounded shocked. 'Perhaps you'd better not say 'flu; say I've eaten something that's disagreed with me. That sounds more plausible.'

'OK, darling. I'll fix it, don't worry.' He nuzzled her tenderly before tucking the duvet round her shoulders.

She dozed, hearing in the background the clink of crockery, while the fragrant aroma of sizzling bacon permeated the air. Life was wonderful when David was happy: he was kind, compassionate and deeply loving. Somehow, Charlotte reflected, half dreaming, she was going to have to find a way of making him happy all the time.

Chapter Seven

'David says there's no future in the wine trade,' Charlotte told Christopher when he brought Holly to tea at her place a few weeks later. 'He was offered quite a decent job with a firm of wine importers, but he said it wouldn't lead anywhere. It was a dead-end job.'

Christopher smoothed his beard thoughtfully. 'That's what he's said about every job he's ever gone after. I don't know what he expects from life; to start near the top I suppose, with a guarantee he'll end up as chairman. I wish he'd get real.'

'That's not true,' she protested. 'He's merely ambitious, and I admire anyone who wants to get on in life. He deserves to get a good job with his talents.'

'It's not your problem.'

'It is, in a way, Chris. What affects him affects me.'

Holly, absorbed in playing with samples of fabric and braid that Charlotte had left on a table to take to show a client, brought over a piece of dark blue velvet.

'Can I have this for Flissy? To keep her warm?' she asked.

Charlotte smiled. The doll Olivia Middleton had given Holly for Christmas still seemed to be her favourite toy, and she'd brought it with her today. Charlotte lifted Holly on to her knee and ran her fingers through the golden curls that hung down her back.

'I have a problem, Holly.'

Holly looked up into her face with the expression of a child whose trust has never been betrayed.

'Can't I have it?'

'You see, it doesn't belong to me. That's why I can't give it to you.'

Holly nodded sadly, in understanding.

'On the other hand, I do have something else you might like for Flissy.'

Holly's face lit up instantly.

Charlotte rose and, taking Holly's hand, led her to the bedroom. Holly's eyes were round as she looked at the richly swagged canopy over the bed.

'Do you sleep in that?' she asked wonderingly.

'Yes, that's my bed. Now, how would this do for Flissy?' From a drawer she withdrew a gauzy wool scarf, coloured in soft, rainbow hues. She grinned as she heard Holly's gasp of delight.

'Will this keep Flissy warm?' she asked.

'Yes.' Holly beamed hugely, her cheeks pink with pleasure.

'Good. Let's go back and have tea. I bought some chocolate biscuits, just for you.'

Holly arched fine blonde eyebrows. 'Mummy says I'm not allowed to have chocolate biscuits until I've had bread and butter.'

'Well now, isn't that lucky, because I've made some Bovril sandwiches to start with.'

When they returned to the living room, Christopher was looking through her portfolio of designs.

'Did you do all these?' he asked, impressed.

'Yes. Myra is letting me do more and more on my own. Those are designs for the interior of a flat in Belgravia. The owner's stinking rich, so I've been able to go to town. The kitchen alone is going to cost over thirty thousand pounds.'

'Good Lord, that's quite something, isn't it?'

'Yes, it's a big job. Work has already started. I have to be on the site every morning by eight, checking everything's going according to plan. Luckily, Myra has her own team of builders and plumbers and decorators, so they know what they're doing.'

'You've got a great sense of colour,' Christopher observed. 'I like the way you've designed the hall, with yellow walls and a black and white marble floor.'

'What makes it is having all the pictures framed in black,' she explained, pointing to her sketch which showed walls hung with a collection of engravings. 'And the narrow black and gold border fixed just above the dado rail.'

'You're very clever. You should start up on your own, you know.'

Charlotte flushed with pleasure. 'Do you think so? I'd like to, when I've had more experience.'

He looked at her keenly. 'Don't underestimate yourself, Charlotte. You've got talent. You should be putting your energy into a creative outlet, not . . .' His voice trailed off, as if he weren't sure whether to continue.

'Not what, Chris?'

He shrugged. 'You're so busy caring for my brother, you're not leaving yourself enough time or space to concentrate on your work.'

'That's rubbish,' she exclaimed, outraged at his interference.

'But you've got to think of yourself, too. You ought to meet Linda, my ex-wife. She'll tell you not to make a doormat of yourself to any man.' He laughed ruefully. 'She sure told me where to get off.'

'If I may say so,' she said crisply, 'the situation between David and me is quite different to the situation between you and Linda. I love David and we have a wonderful relationship. I hope we have a great future together.'

Christopher looked at her understandingly, his large hand absently stroking Holly's back as she sat on the sofa beside him, wrapping Flissy in the scarf.

'I know, La. This is not the moment to kick a man when he's down, but don't let it drift on for too long. I know David. Once he finds someone who's prepared to look after him, he won't lift a finger to help himself. That's why Mum and Dad have had to be tough with him. No doubt he's told you I'm the favourite? Well, it's bullshit!' he added bluntly.

For a moment she regretted inviting him over to tea. She'd been longing to see Holly again, but she hadn't been prepared to sit and listen to Chris insulting David, and now she wished he'd go.

'I'm lucky to have someone in my life like David,' she observed coolly.

Christopher looked at her closely again. 'I wish you didn't have such low self-esteem. You're a very striking looking girl, La. Put on a bit more make-up and you'd be really pretty.'

At that moment, Holly, who had been silently but effectively working her way through a plate of chocolate biscuits, spoke up in a piping voice.

'Mummy's pretty, isn't she, Daddy?'

Christopher hugged her, kissing her cheek. 'Mummy's very pretty,' he agreed.

'Am I going to be pretty?'

'You, my sweetheart, are going to be the prettiest girl in the world.'

'You certainly are,' Charlotte agreed, smiling.

Holly didn't miss a beat. 'Have you any more chocolate biscuits?'

'For you, sweetheart, anything!' In a short space of time, the child had got under her skin, capturing her heart with her roguish smile and cheerful disposition.

'I wish she was mine,' she admitted as she brought the biscuit tin back from the kitchen.

Christopher nodded. 'Olivia says the same.'

'She hasn't any children of her own, has she?' Charlotte was glad they'd changed the topic of conversation away from David.

'No, she's unable to have any. When she comes to London she always buys something for Holly; a dress or a toy. She'd make a very good mother.'

'You're seeing a lot of her, are you?'

'As much as I can. I haven't felt like this for a long time, La. But she's being cautious about getting in too deep. She's only recently broken up with my father, you know.' He looked away, embarrassed.

'That must be a relief for your mother.'

'I'm not sure Mum ever knew exactly what was going on.' He looked at Holly. 'When Olivia and I really get it together, we might be able to have a visitor for the odd weekend, which would be nice.' He silently indicated his little girl.

David arrived home a few minutes later, letting himself into the flat with his own key. He looked at first surprised and then disgruntled to see Christopher sprawled comfortably on the sofa. Charlotte was sure she'd told David she'd invited him to bring Holly to tea, but he appeared to have forgotten.

'What's going on?' he asked suspiciously.

'We're having tea,' Charlotte replied unnecessarily. 'I'll go and make a fresh pot. You'd like another cup, wouldn't you, Christopher?'

'Thanks. Can Holly have a drop more orange juice?'

'Of course.' Charlotte rose and went to the kitchen.

David followed her. 'What's Chris doing here?' he asked in a low voice.

'I told you I'd asked him to bring Holly to tea,' she replied.

'I'd forgotten.' He opened and shut the doors of the kitchen units, as if looking for something.

'Is there anything I can get you, David?'

He shook his head. 'I suppose you didn't remember to get in any shortbread, did you?'

'Oh!' Her hand flew to her mouth. 'Oh, sweetheart! I forgot!'

'Not to worry.' He looked so tired and dispirited, she wanted to put her arms around him.

'Are they staying long?' he asked in a low voice, so as not to be overheard.

'I don't think so. I just thought it might be a good chance for you and Chris to get together . . . away from your parents, you know,' she explained, as she refilled the teapot.

'Well, thanks very much!' said a sarcastic voice in the doorway. They both spun round, startled. Christopher was standing there looking angry.

134

'Thanks for trying to reconcile us to each other, but let me tell you, you haven't a cat's chance in hell, La. David and I have nothing in common.'

Charlotte looked at him, startled, taken aback by his manner. David's face hardened.

'Anyway, it's time we went,' Christopher continued. 'I have to get Holly back to Linda's.'

'I'm surprised you're allowed out with her in the first place,' David remarked.

'And what exactly do you mean by that?' Christopher looked him squarely in the face.

'Doesn't Linda realise you're a secret drinker? That you're never really sober? That your pretence of drinking non-alcoholic stuff is a complete sham?'

'You know I never touch the stuff when I'm with Holly.' His face had gone red with anger.

David spoke scathingly. 'You can't last five minutes without a drink.'

'That's not true!' cried Christopher, enraged. 'Who the fuck do you think you are, accusing me of all that shit when you bloody well know it's not true! What makes you think you're so fucking perfect, anyway?'

Charlotte had never seen anger like it. In a few seconds, Christopher's eyes had become bloodshot. He seemed incandescent with fury. If he'd been an older man, she'd have sworn he was about to have a stroke.

'You've been trouble since you were a teenager, Chris!'

'I was out of my skull and didn't know what I was doing, but that's all over now,' Chris retorted.

'You'll never change. You've been out of your skull for

135

the past eight years. I don't think Linda should let you anywhere near Holly.'

With a bound Christopher was across the kitchen, delivering a punch that smacked David hard in the face. Taken off guard, David stumbled and fell, hitting his shoulder against the kitchen table as he went down with a yell of pain. Appalled, Charlotte watched as Christopher continued to hit him, fists flaying.

'Stop it!' she shouted. 'For God's sake, stop it, Chris!'

She tried to grab the back of Christopher's hair, hoping that by twisting it she could hurt him enough to force him to let go but, in spite of his bulk, he was too quick for her, dodging his head every time she got near him. He seemed to have gone completely crazy and, as David got to his feet, Christopher pushed him down again, punching him about the head and chest. Blood was running down David's face from a cut above one eye, and from his mouth.

Then a piercing cry, shrill and terrified, filled the kitchen. It sent an icy shiver through Charlotte and caused the brothers to stop in mid-blow. They all turned to look at the doorway. Holly was standing there, her face bleached white. She was shaking violently and, as the tears rolled down her cheeks, she clutched herself in dismay.

'I wet myself, Daddy!' she sobbed.

For a moment Christopher stood rock still, then a look of deep distress filled his face and, picking Holly up, he held her gently in his arms.

'Oh, my baby. My baby,' he whispered brokenly. Tears glistened in his eyelashes. He rocked her to and fro. 'Don't be frightened, sweetheart. It's all right. It's all right. Daddy was just being silly.'

'You're a fucking lunatic!' David stormed, pushing past to go to the bathroom. 'Get me some ice, La. I think my jaw's broken.'

In shock, Charlotte went to the fridge and got out the tray of ice. Holly was still crying, her face buried in Christopher's neck.

David was leaning over the hand-basin in the bathroom, spitting and groaning. Grabbing his face-flannel, Charlotte put a handful of ice-cubes in the middle, tucked the ends over, and then held it gently to his jaw.

'That bastard's hurt me really badly. Some of my teeth are loose,' he muttered. The basin was streaked with blood and saliva and he had difficulty talking.

'Oh God . . .' Charlotte was filled with dismay. 'Hold the ice to your face, David. I'll call for a cab to take us to St Stephen's hospital. You should be X-rayed.'

What went wrong? she asked herself as she dialled the number of the mini-cab company. How could having Christopher and his little girl to tea have turned out so disastrously? She'd only wanted them to be friends. But one thing was certain. It was unlikely she'd be able to have Holly to the flat again, and for that she felt regret.

As soon as she'd booked a cab, she hurried to the bedroom to get her coat. She found Christopher on his knees in front of Holly, removing her wet socks as she sat on the dressing-table stool.

'I'm so sorry, Charlotte,' he murmured without looking up. 'I don't know what the hell came over me. I'm really sorry.'

'You've hurt David badly, you know. I'm going to have to take him to the hospital,' she said angrily.

'Oh, shit.' Christopher shook his head, distressed that what had been a lovely afternoon had turned out so disastrously. Holly was still trembling, her head was bowed over her doll.

'Can I have dry socks, Daddy?' she whispered.

'I'm afraid not, my pet. You'll have to wait until you get home.'

'Here are some dry pants for her,' said Charlotte, handing him a pair of her smallest briefs.

'Thanks.' His expression was dejected and she could guess he was thinking that Linda wouldn't allow him to take Holly out on his own again. And he was probably right. He'd told her about the 'conditions' imposed by his ex-wife; now they started to make sense.

'Bye bye, Holly.' She bent and put her arms around the little girl. 'Look after Flissy.'

Holly nodded, but didn't look up.

Chris rose, rubbing his face with both hands, as if wanting to obliterate something. Then he leaned forward and to her surprise, kissed her gently on the cheek.

'I can't tell you how sorry I am,' he said with sincerity. Then he paused before adding: 'You're too good for either of us, you know.'

David's jaw wasn't broken, but he was suffering from severe bruising, a gash above one eye, and his teeth had cut into the inside of his mouth. The hospital told him to go home and rinse with hot salty water and take a couple of aspirins if his face continued to hurt.

'I'm going to phone Linda when I get home,' he grunted through swollen lips, as they returned to the flat in a taxi.

138

Charlotte remained silent, sickened by the whole thing. The sight of Chris attacking like that filled her with disgust, and if she felt shocked by what had happened, she couldn't bear to think how terrified Holly must have been.

'Chris is crazy! He ought to be locked up!' David murmured ruefully. 'I think he's on drugs again. Linda must be told because he shouldn't be allowed out in that condition with Holly. He was trying to kill me, you know. I could see it in his eyes.'

Charlotte could understand his bitterness.

When they got back, Chris and Holly had gone. The tea things had been washed and put away and, for the first time, the flat had a sad, deserted air.

'Why don't you have a nice hot bath while I get supper?' she suggested. 'I could give you yours on a tray in bed.'

David shot her a grateful look. 'That would be nice.'

'OK, sweetheart.' She kissed him on the cheek but he winced and drew sharply away.

'Be careful! My face's agony.'

'Poor darling.'

Later, as she lay beside him, he took her hand and held it tightly.

'I'm sorry about what happened earlier,' he said. 'I should have warned you that Chris is inclined to flip from time to time. I should've stopped you asking him to bring Holly to tea.'

Charlotte looked at him. His eyes were watching her tenderly.

'It's all right, sweetheart,' she said instantly. 'I'm just so sorry it worked out so badly. I had hoped, in time, you might become friends; like Susie and me.'

David shook his head. 'I know it was stupid of me to bring up the subject of drinking but that wasn't enough reason for him to try and kill me, was it?'

'God, no!' She sighed. 'I wish none of it had happened. It's so tragic for Holly, too.'

During the next few days, Charlotte thought constantly about Holly, wondering what was happening to her and how badly she might have been affected by Chris's behaviour. David had told Charlotte to 'stay out of it'. Reluctantly she'd agreed, although she longed to ring Chris and ask how Holly was. But one evening, while David was playing squash, she went to see her parents. She confided her worries to them.

'What a sad situation,' Margaret remarked. 'And how awful for David's parents.'

'You're wise to stay out of it, La,' Colin advised. 'It's their family problem, not yours. If the two brothers don't see eye to eye, there's nothing you can do about it.'

'I know.' She nodded in agreement. 'The trouble is, I *am* practically one of the family. At least that's how I feel.'

Margaret looked questioningly at her daughter. 'Does this mean you and David might get married, darling?'

'Hang on there, pet,' Colin chided. 'La's only known him for two minutes.'

'Over four months,' Charlotte said proudly. Four months of heaven, she thought. Four months of having someone wonderful in her life, when she never thought it would happen. Someone who cared for her and, most of all, needed her. She beamed at her parents happily. 'I'll marry him tomorrow if he asks me.'

'Has he found a new job yet?' Colin asked practically.

'He's got several interviews coming up. I know he'll get something good.'

'Meanwhile, is it fun having him stay at the flat?' Margaret asked. At first she'd been a bit shocked at the idea of Charlotte living with someone, but when Colin reminded her that their daughter was twenty-six and that times had changed, she realised it was at least a good way of finding out if they were really suited.

Charlotte looked enthusiastic. 'It's wonderful, Mum. The only blot on the horizon is David's worry over Christopher.' She paused thoughtfully before adding, 'Of course it probably doesn't help matters that he's in love with his father's mistress.'

'*What?*' Margaret looked appalled. 'Their father has a mistress? You never told us!'

'How could I? David is always with me when I come to see you. I'm not sure he wants it known.'

'How did you find this out?'

'It was obvious to me, anyway, over Christmas.'

'What's she like?' Her mother was fascinated.

'She's very beautiful,' Charlotte admitted. 'Small, dark, sort of vulnerable and fragile looking. She arrived unexpectedly on Christmas Day with a present for Holly. I have a feeling she was trying to embarrass Edmund into leaving Virginia.'

Margaret looked stunned. 'What on earth did Virginia do?'

Charlotte shrugged. 'She sort of carried on doing the hostess bit. I'm not sure she realises what's going on.'

'Of course she must realise.'

'She may only think Olivia and Edmund are flirting.'

'I'd know if your father was having an affair! I can't believe *she* doesn't.'

'Edmund visits her, as far as I can gather, very late at night, after Virginia's gone to bed.'

Margaret closed her eyes for a moment, as if she could imagine Virginia's pain. 'What an absolutely awful situation.'

'Well it's not us, so cheer up and have another drink,' said Colin sturdily.

'Thank you, darling.' Margaret smiled at him lovingly. 'Make mine strong. With all the shocks La's giving us, I need it.'

As Colin took her glass he bent down and kissed his wife swiftly on the lips.

Watching, Charlotte hoped that, in time, she and David would have as long and lasting a relationship as her parents.

The next few weeks were strained, as David continued to job-hunt, always coming home announcing, 'There was no future in what they offered me.' It was his favourite phrase, and whilst Charlotte understood what he meant, and that he was right to plan long-term, she still felt that in the short-term he should take what he could. The bank had forbidden him to issue any more cheques until he cleared his overdraft, and the credit companies had asked for the return of his cards. His ex-flatmates had also started threatening him, through a solicitor, for what he owed in back rent, telephone and electricity.

As diplomatically as she could, Charlotte paid all the bills and bought all their food, and at least twice a week managed to give him some money by asking him to do some shopping for her and then purposefully forgetting to ask for the change. For her it was the happiest time she could remember: it was so reassuring to have David depend on her; every day he thrilled her by telling her he didn't know what he'd do without her. Far from grudging the money it cost to support him, she revelled in being able to give him the help he so badly needed.

'I'll pay you back, I promise,' he kept saying, but she silenced him with her kisses. It was the first time in her life that anyone had depended on her for anything, and she felt intoxicated by this new-found power of being able to make another human being happy.

With renewed energy and the spirit of benevolence filling her every hour, she whizzed through the day as if inspired.

Myra thought she was mad.

'What's got into you?' she demanded one lunchtime as they stopped for a break.

'Nothing's got into me,' Charlotte replied, laughing.

'But you're killing yourself! Every spare second you're shopping for food, or rushing home to iron David's shirts, or thinking up ways to keep him amused.'

'This is a bad time for him,' she said curtly. 'I'm only being supportive.'

'You're keeping him,' said Myra firmly.

'He'd do the same for me if I needed help.'

Myra didn't reply, but her thin, immaculately made-up face looked disapproving.

'Why don't you like him, Myra?'

'I don't dislike him, La. I think he's very attractive, very sexy and very charming.'

'So why are you always criticising him?' Charlotte demanded.

'It's you I'm criticising, not him.'

'We've had this conversation before, haven't we?' There were times when Myra made her really angry with her cool, calculating opinions.

Myra looked amused. 'I wouldn't be a good friend to you if I only said the things you wanted to hear,' she replied lightly. 'Now finish your coffee. We've got an afternoon's hard work in front of us, seeing how the new central-heating system is working at that wretched mansion in Belgrave Square. If I have one more word of complaint from Rag-Tag or whatever he calls himself . . .'

Charlotte burst out laughing, despite herself. 'You mean Raggity-Tag, and let me remind you he's number one in the pop charts this week with "Sugar Susie". He's our richest client.'

Her boss groaned theatrically. 'Whatever! He's the rudest man I've ever come across, and the scruffiest, and it's only because he's given me the most enormous budget to do up his gin palace that I'm even agreeing to cross his threshold!'

A week later, David came home looking jubilant. He had a bunch of pink roses in one hand and a bottle of champagne in the other. As soon as Charlotte saw him she knew something had happened.

'I've got a great job!' he announced excitedly. 'It's the one I had an interview for last week and they asked me to go back this afternoon . . . and I got it!' He looked so happy her heart melted with relief.

'That's fantastic, sweetheart,' she exclaimed.

'Isn't it wonderful? Oh, La, it's such a relief. I'll be in the money again, and then I can start repaying you for all you've done for me.'

Touched, she slipped her arm through his. Together they went into the living room and sat on the sofa.

'Tell me all about it.'

He grinned with satisfaction. 'It's with an electronic company. I've been put in the sales division, which is what I like best, and after a couple of weeks' training session, learning about their products, I'll be travelling a lot. The pay's very good, much more than I got at Flight, and they have excellent bonus schemes . . .'

'Travelling?' Charlotte cut in. Her heart sank. 'Where will you be travelling to? Will it mean you'll be away a lot?'

'A certain amount. They've given me certain areas, including Wales . . .'

'Oh, in *England*!' She sighed with relief. 'I thought you meant abroad. How are you going to get around?'

His smile of satisfaction deepened. 'They're giving me a company car, and of course an expense account. I'll have to stay in hotels some nights, and go to restaurants. Isn't it fantastic?'

'Yes. Fantastic,' she said, trying to sound pleased, although a lot of the joy had drained out of her. Now she'd become accustomed to their being together all the time, it was going to be strange – not to mention lonely – if he was going to be away a lot.

'What's wrong?' he asked intuitively, lifting her chin with his fingertips and looking into her eyes.

'I'm going to miss you when you're away,' she said in a small voice.

145

He pulled her closer. 'Silly girl. It'll probably only be for the odd night. A lot of the time I'll be able to come back to London at the end of the day.'

'You will?'

'You don't think I can do without you for long, do you, sweetheart? Of course I'll come home at night, just as often as I can.' His kiss was warm and reassuring.

'I'm so proud of you,' she whispered.

'And I love you, dear heart.' It was the first time he'd called her that and she loved it. Everything was going to be all right now. She was sure of it. Like a lot of couples, they'd been through a sticky patch, but now he'd got a job, everything would be fine again.

'I want to make love to you,' he said, his eyes hot.

Charlotte smiled at him, almost shyly. It was the first time in weeks that she'd heard that note of yearning in his voice, and it made her feel breathless.

The job proved to be harder work than either David or Charlotte had expected. He was away three, sometimes four nights a week and, although Charlotte was glad for him that he was working again, she nevertheless missed him, finding her evenings long and lonely once again.

'You should get out and about and make more friends,' Myra advised briskly one day. 'In the past few months you've shut yourself away with David, and neglected everyone else.'

'There never seems to be time: the days go by so quickly. When David's home I like to be alone with him as much as possible. I don't even get to see Mum and Dad and Susie that often,' Charlotte replied.

'Friends are more important than lovers,' Myra told her severely. 'Friends are for ever.'

'So is David!' she protested. She was fed up with Myra's opinions. 'Maybe, if we get married, we'll feel like socialising more, but I don't want to go out without him now.'

'Ah, true love,' Myra mocked gently. 'God, how often I've been there, and back again. Just don't give up on everyone else, La. You're an attractive young woman, so don't go staying in every night on your own, waiting for your knight in shining armour to come riding home. Have a bit of fun while the cat's away!'

'Myra, you're incorrigible,' Charlotte forced a laugh, 'and I absolutely refuse to take your advice. I think it stinks!'

The phone was ringing when Charlotte got back to her flat at six o'clock that evening. She'd left the office earlier than usual, because she'd got to draw a design for a sun room in a house on the outskirts of London, and she found it more peaceful at home.

'It's me,' she heard David say when she answered it.

'Hi, sweetheart! Where are you?'

'I'm up in Derby, but I'm leaving in a few minutes, so I should be home by eight o'clock, eight-thirty latest.'

'That's terrific. I'll have dinner ready.' He'd left London early that morning and she hadn't been sure when he'd be back. 'Have you had a good day?'

'Yes. Really good. I've got lots of orders, but thank God the weekend starts tomorrow. I'm knackered.' He sounded it, too, she thought.

'We can be nice and quiet,' she assured him. 'There's

147

nothing planned, so you can crash out.'

'Good.'

'It'll be wonderful to see you again. You've no idea how much I miss you when you're on these trips.'

By the time he got back, the fragrance of roasting lamb permeated the air, mingling with the scent of rosemary. He sniffed appreciatively before taking Charlotte into his arms.

'It's so good to be back. God, I'm getting sick of being away so much. How are you, dear heart?'

She gazed up at him, taking in the contours of his face and the pale blue of his eyes.

'Happy to see you,' she said simply.

'I'm absolutely starved! When will dinner be ready?' His boyish grin made her melt, as it always did.

'Five minutes?' she replied, leading him into the living room. The table was laid for two there, with flowers and candles and a bottle of wine.

David looked down at her. There was a wealth of tenderness and regard in his expression.

'You've taken so much trouble. Where would I be without you, my little angel?'

Chapter Eight

David was standing in the middle of the living room with the phone in his hand, when Charlotte came through from the bathroom. They'd finished dinner a little while ago and had planned to have an early night.

'What's the matter?'

David stared down at the carpet, looking perturbed.

'That was my mother on the line.'

'Oh! I never heard the phone ring. What did she want?' She tied the sash of her cream woollen dressing-gown and ran her fingers through her damp hair.

'She was in a helluva state. Chris went down to stay with them yesterday. She says he and Dad are having a terrible fight.'

'What? Right now?'

'That's what she said. She sounded really freaked out.'

'Oh, my God, David.' She could just imagine the scene. Father and son roaring at each other in that big gloomy house, just as they'd done on Christmas night.

'What's it about?' she asked.

'Olivia Middleton. Apparently she's been carrying on with both of them, and Chris found out. Mum sounded really scared. She said Chris had gone berserk and was threatening to kill Dad.'

'Is she calling the police? Why doesn't she call them?'

'I suggested that, but she hung up while I was talking.'

'What else did she say?'

'That was all. I heard sounds in the background and then she put down the receiver. Perhaps she didn't want them to know she was phoning me.'

Charlotte sank weakly into an armchair.

'Oh, this is awful, David. What are you going to do?'

His hands made a gesture of helplessness. 'What the hell can I do? I'm here, and they're down in Wiltshire.'

'Why don't you ring her back? Make sure she's all right?'

He nodded. 'I will. Good idea.' He dialled the number as he talked. 'Poor old Mum, she always gets in a state when Chris goes on the rampage. It's happened before.' He held the receiver to his ear for a moment, then put it down again.

'The line's busy. Perhaps she's decided to phone the police after all. I'll try again in a minute.'

'Why is Chris staying at Chelwood? If he wanted to be with Olivia, why didn't he stay with her?'

'If you've ever lived in a village, you'd know the answer to that! They know which brand of toothpaste you're going to change to before you know yourself.'

'So what about your father and Olivia? Doesn't the village know about them?'

'They may guess, but I don't think he's blatant about it. Chris is a fool, though. He should stick to seeing that woman in London.' He closed his eyes wearily. 'This is all I need after the long week I've had.'

'Would you like some coffee?'

He nodded silently, and reached for the phone. 'I'll try again.'

When she returned to the living room ten minutes later, he was asleep, the phone on the floor beside his chair. He stirred as she placed the coffee on the table beside him.

'Any luck?' she asked.

He shook his head. 'The line's still busy. I'll phone Mum in the morning. All I want to do is go to bed.' He gazed up at her with a rueful smile.

'Sorry I'm such a dead loss tonight, sweetheart. I promise I'll make it up to you in the morning.'

Charlotte caught his proffered hand in hers. 'I'll hold you to that,' she replied, grinning.

They were still asleep when the front doorbell rang early the next morning.

'I'll get it,' said Charlotte, rolling on to her side and getting out of bed. It was Saturday and when she saw the hands of her bedside clock were at eight-thirty, she felt a stab of irritation. Who on earth could it be at this hour?

Two uniformed policemen stood on the doorstep, their expressions implacable.

'Is Mr David Farrell at home, please?'

Charlotte was thrown for a moment.

'Yes,' she said uncertainly. 'What's it about?'

'We'd rather talk to Mr Farrell, if you don't mind,' the elder one said politely.

'OK. I'll get him.' She hurried up the stairs to her flat and shook David's shoulder urgently. 'It's the police,' she whispered. 'They want to talk to you.'

'What?' He opened his eyes sleepily. Then he was suddenly fully awake, as if he'd remembered something.

'*Shit!*'

'What is it?'

'I couldn't find a meter last night, so I parked the car outside. I meant to move it before we went to bed! Damn and blast! I suppose they've towed it away.' He clambered out of bed, and struggled into his dressing gown, hurried down the stairs to the main street door, clutching his car keys.

Fully awake by now, Charlotte decided not to go back to bed. Slipping into the bathroom, she turned on the shower, then stepped under the refreshingly cool stream, feeling the tiny needles of water splash on her shoulders while the gentle roar cut off the outside world. She never heard the shout from the downstairs hall, nor saw David leaping back upstairs, to struggle into his clothes. It wasn't until the bathroom door flew open and she saw him standing there, looking at her in a strange way, that she realised something was wrong.

'David?' Hurriedly she turned off the shower and reached for a towel. 'What's happened?'

For a long moment he seemed unable to speak. As if he were struggling with some terrible inner conflict, his mouth worked silently before he covered his face with his hands.

Frightened, she put her hand on his arm.

'For God's sake, David. What is it?'

'My family.' His voice was muffled, seemed to come from a long way away.

'What about your family?'

He rocked his head silently from side to side.

'Your *family*?' Suddenly she remembered the fight the previous night. 'Oh, my God, what's happened?'

'Oh, Jesus! Oh Jesus! Oh *Jesus*!' With his hands still

covering his face, he collapsed on to his knees, crouching on the bathroom floor at her feet.

Appalled, she dropped to her haunches, and put her hands on either side of his head. How silky his hair feels, she thought irrelevantly as she stroked it.

'Tell me what's happened, David.'

'I should have done something,' he moaned. 'Oh, God, I should have been there.'

She tried to take him into her arms, but he pushed her away. Sobbing, he kept repeating: 'It's not true! Jesus Christ, it can't be true!'

Charlotte felt herself quivering, feeling sick, hoping she was not going to faint. With a tremendous effort she tried to get David to his feet, but he was too overwrought, too weakened by shock and grief, and her strength was not great enough to support him.

At last she summoned up her courage, and spoke.

'Is your father hurt?'

There was a long pause, and then David said brokenly, 'Christopher.'

'What about him? Is he . . . ?' she couldn't bring herself to say it.

'Christopher,' David repeated. Charlotte felt herself spinning dizzily, frightened now by what he meant.

'I must go, right away.' Gripping the side of the bath, he pulled himself to his feet. He looked terrible.

'Go where?'

'To Chelwood.' He staggered into the little hall, where the morning sunshine fell slanting through the window on to a vase of daffodils, their scent sharp and bitter.

'How will you get there?' Charlotte couldn't get her

153

mind to work. Her brain felt like marshmallow. She seemed to be wading knee-deep in treacle. Struggling to get a grip on herself, she rushed into the bedroom, pulling on jeans, a sweater, a warm jacket and her brown leather boots.

'It's OK,' said David, coming into the room. 'You needn't come. I'll take my car. I can be there in . . .' his voice broke.

'Of course I'll come with you. I can drive.' She grabbed her handbag, checking her money and keys.

'No. I'll drive.' In silence he put on his shoes. Did up the laces. Picked up his warm winter coat.

If only I knew what had happened, she thought, looking at his shut-in face. That Christopher was badly hurt – dead even – now seemed a certainty, but how in God's name had it happened? Had Edmund killed him?

Without a backward glance, David strode out of the flat. Two minutes later they were in his company car, his foot hard down on the accelerator. His grip on the steering wheel was fierce, his profile grim as he stared at the road ahead. Then he put a tape in the cassette, and turned the volume up so that conversation was impossible. Charlotte, sitting tensely beside him, realised he wasn't even aware of her presence.

Carol and Neil Whittaker also had a visit from the local police early that morning. Briefly outlining the 'incident' at Chelwood Manor, they were requested to drive to Barrow, to meet the detective inspector in charge of the case, so they could fill him in with background details of the Farrell family.

'Mrs Gladys Scovell, who lives in the village near

Chelwood Manor informed us of your whereabouts and your relationship to Mrs Virginia Farrell,' the young constable told the Whittakers.

Shocked, Carol and Neil looked at each other, unable at first to take in what had happened.

'We'd better pack an overnight bag,' Carol said at last.

Neil longed for a strong whisky and soda, but knew he mustn't because he was just about to drive. There'd be time for a drink to steady his nerves when he got there. Instead he went round the house, making sure the windows and doors were locked, while Carol, too stunned to cry, stuffed night clothes and sponge-bags into a hold-all. Ten minutes later they were on the road heading for Barrow.

The village of Barrow, set at the bottom of a hill in a lush valley ten miles south of Devizes, had one village store, a chemist, two antique shops, a butcher and three pubs. Dominating the village green was a Norman church of historic distinction, which attracted passing tourists. The people of Barrow were a close community, with their church fêtes and cricket matches and whist drives, but on this particular Saturday morning, something had happened that had driven from their minds all thoughts of their usual activities.

They were clustered together in groups, experiencing a camaraderie reminiscent of the days of the Second World War. Conversation was subdued and whispery. All they could talk about was what had happened up at the Big House.

Chelwood Manor was always referred to as the Big House by the people of Barrow. Set out of sight behind a high brick wall, it had the feel of grand isolation, set in many acres of lush countryside. In fact the house itself stood only fifty yards from the nearest row of cottages and shops, screened by tall elms as well as the old ivy-covered wall. The previous owner, whom not many could remember because his executors had sold the property to the Farrell family nearly thirty years ago, had been the Earl of Stanton. His coat-of-arms was still wrought in the iron gates at the entrance to the drive, and the church bore memorial plaques to several members of the Stanton family, who had been buried in a private plot in the graveyard.

Virginia Farrell was liked by the villagers, who regarded her with a mixture of affection and pity. Edmund was not popular. He was thought to be a bully, and too mean to give his wife a decent housekeeping allowance. Gladys and Ruby were able to embellish these rumours with first-hand knowledge of what life was like up at the Big House, and on this morning they were being freely quoted.

Then there were the sons. Him who was on drugs, they whispered. Him who was a bad lot. And the other; never could stick to any job for longer than five minutes.

As David drove down the one main street towards Chelwood, two hours after they'd left London, going as fast as he dared, Charlotte, sitting beside him, had the uncomfortable feeling that they were the centre of attention. People were grabbing each other's arms, pointing at the car, staring with morbid fascination as they swept past. David did not seem to notice. Eyes still intent on the road, he took the right-hand bend beyond the church, and then had to brake sharply. A cordon had been flung across the road that led to Chelwood, and beyond it they could see police cars parked on the grass verge. As the car drew to a standstill, a policeman came over.

'I'm afraid no one's allowed to come this way, sir,' he informed them politely. He was a fresh-faced lad, and Charlotte was struck by his youth. There was still the peachy bloom of a schoolboy on his cheeks.

'I'm David Farrell.'

A startled look flitted across the policeman's eyes for a moment, then it was gone.

'Of course, sir. Please go ahead,' he said, untying the plastic ribbon at one side.

The car slid forward. In two minutes they'd be at Chelwood.

Charlotte took a deep breath. She glanced at David's profile. He looked composed, but there was something forbidding in his expression.

The drive was filled with more police cars, a large police van which was fitted like a mobile office, and two ambulances. Groups of uniformed men and women stood around, but they stopped to stare when David drew up and parked his car opposite the three-pillared front entrance.

Charlotte clambered out, stiff and shaky. She looked around, remembering arriving here on Christmas Eve. Was it only three months since they'd last been here? Clinging to the door of the car, she wondered why there were so many police.

David had got out on his side, his blond good looks diminished by the misery that now engulfed him. Almost immediately, a tall man who had been talking on a mobile phone came towards them. He had grey hair which just showed under his peak cap, and his face, though grave, was nonetheless sympathetic.

'Mr David Farrell?' he inquired. Again Charlotte noticed the hushed tones. Were the police trained to talk in a particular way under certain circumstances?

'Yes, I'm David Farrell.'

'My name is Grindley, sir. Detective Inspector Tom Grindley.' He signalled to another officer to join them. 'This is Deputy Chief Constable Ron Franklin. He was the first officer to arrive at the scene, and he and I will be working together, in conjunction with other officers from the local constabulary.'

David nodded mutely.

Tom Grindley looked enquiringly at Charlotte, who had moved to David's side.

'You are Miss . . . ?'

'This is my girlfriend, Charlotte Taylor,' said David.

Charlotte saw Tom Grindley eye her closely. She raised her chin and looked back at him. Where David was concerned, she knew she could be strong. He needed her at this moment more than he had ever needed her before, and she knew she would not let him down.

Tom Grindley held her gaze for a moment before turning back to David.

'The police photographer is in the house at the moment, sir. The forensic team have arrived also, although I'm not sure, in the circumstances, that they will have much to do.'

'I want to see for myself what happened,' David announced. His words came out in a nervous rush, and he was gripping Charlotte's hand so tightly her fingers felt as if they were being crushed.

Grindley looked doubtful. 'I'm sure you'd rather wait until we've sorted things out a bit,' he said carefully.

'No.' David shook his head adamantly. 'I'm not going to believe what's happened unless I see it. I'm not going to be able to accept it. I could also do with a drink,' he added desperately.

'I'll see what I can do, sir.' Then he walked off briskly in the direction of the entrance to the house.

The deputy chief constable indicated the police van.

'Why don't we sit in there for a few minutes, sir? It'll be warmer, and I'd also like you to give me a few details. We need to know something of the background to what's happened here.'

'OK.' As they walked across the drive, David looked up at the house, as if he expected to see someone looking out of one of the windows.

The van was fitted with a table, bench seating, and a lot of radio equipment. Charlotte climbed in first, followed by David who took a seat beside her. Franklin followed, sitting opposite them and pulling a large ruled pad of paper towards him on the table. He looked pale and unfriendly, but when he spoke his voice was kind.

'I just need to take down a few details, sir. For our records. It won't take long.'

'What do you want to know?'

'Your full name, sir?'

'David Ashley James Farrell.'

'And your address?'

'I'm living with Charlotte at the moment; Flat 3, 4b Onslow Gardens. That's in London.'

'Your age, Mr Farrell?'

'Twenty-eight.'

'Occupation?'

'I work for an electronics company: P.N.G. Links.'

Ron Franklin wrote everything down with careful precision.

'And your position in the company, sir?'

David hesitated for a moment; Charlotte knew him well enough to guess he'd tried to make his job more important than it actually was. She squeezed his hand understandingly.

'I'm a rep for the company,' he admitted in a quiet voice.

Ron Franklin wrote that down too, before turning to Charlotte to ask her the same list of questions.

Just as she'd finished giving him all her details, Detective Inspector Tom Grindley appeared, accompanied by a police constable, carrying a bottle of brandy and two glasses.

'We found this in the kitchen,' Tom Grindley said, indicating the brandy. 'Put it on the table, will you, constable?'

'Thanks.' David reached for the glasses and, taking the bottle, started to pour himself a drink.

'Do you want one, La?' he asked as an afterthought.

She shook her head. 'I want to know what happened,' she said to Tom Grindley. 'I gather from what David's told me that his brother Christopher is dead?' As she spoke, the impact of what was happening hit her, and belated tears rushed to her eyes. It was as if her emotions had been frozen, blocked by shock; but now that she'd mentioned Christopher's name, it was like being hit over the head by an emotional mallet.

Was it her imagination, or did Tom Grindley look at her strangely? She dabbed her eyes with a screwed-up tissue she found in the pocket of her overcoat, and for a moment her heart leapt. Perhaps Christopher was all right after all?

The memory of his genial bearded face filled her mind, and then she remembered the darker side, the black rage she'd seen exposed that day in her kitchen. But, please God, she prayed, let him be all right.

'Yes. Mr Christopher Farrell is dead,' the detective inspector told her formally, dashing her hopes.

'He committed suicide.' David spoke suddenly in a harsh voice.

Charlotte's hand flew to her mouth. *Suicide?* It was the last thing she expected. Suicide because he and his father had fallen out over a woman? The tears flowed down her cheeks. Christopher must have been terribly unhappy to have killed himself over a woman.

Suddenly Tom Grindley looked tired. 'If that was all that's happened, there wouldn't be so many of us here.'

Wondering what he meant, Charlotte retreated into a shell of shock and misery again while, through her jumbled thoughts, she heard him question David.

'When did you last have contact with your brother, and the other members of your family, sir?' he asked.

David seemed to pull himself together with a super-human strength, his only sign of emotion being the shaking hand that reached again for the brandy bottle.

'As a matter of fact, I spoke to my mother on the phone last night,' he said.

'What time would that be?'

'What time did Mum phone, Charlotte?' David asked, turning to her. 'Was it around nine? Nine-thirty?'

'I think it was nearer ten o'clock,' she replied numbly. 'We'd finished dinner, and I'd had a shower.'

David nodded. 'Yes. You're right. I suppose it might

have been getting on for ten o'clock.'

'How did your mother seem? What did she say?'

'She was in a tizz. My father and Christopher were fighting. They both had the same girlfriend, you see, and Chris had found out. Mum said Christopher had gone berserk. She said he was threatening to kill my father. Isn't that right, Charlotte?' Again David turned to her, needing her support.

She nodded gently, slipping her arm through his. 'That's what you told me,' she agreed.

Tom Grindley leaned forward, and Charlotte noticed Chief Constable Ron Franklin was still writing down everything that was being said.

'What did you say to your mother, Mr Farrell?'

'Well . . . I didn't get a chance to say anything, really. As soon as she'd told me what was happening, she hung up.'

'Just like that? Without saying goodbye?'

David nodded wretchedly.

'What did you do then?'

'I called back. Several times. Didn't I, La?'

Charlotte nodded. 'The line was busy. In the end we went to bed. David was exhausted as he'd been on the road all day. There didn't seem much we could do, anyway, from London.'

Tom Grindley eyed her with interest before turning back to David.

'What exactly did your mother say?'

David repeated the conversation again, adding, 'Christopher has been unstable since he was seventeen. None of this surprises me.'

'It doesn't?' The detective inspector raised his eyebrows. 'You didn't take this call last night from your mother too seriously then? Has she made a similar call to you, in the past, involving your brother?'

'Not exactly. We're used to Christopher blowing up from time to time, I suppose.' Once again he turned to Charlotte. 'He did it in your flat not long ago, didn't he?'

For a fleeting moment, Charlotte felt surprised at David comparing Christopher's outburst in her kitchen with a rage that ended in him taking his own life.

'He did lose his temper, but it was over very quickly and then he was sorry,' she said, feeling tearful again. What on earth had possessed him to kill himself? she wondered. Had his father pushed him too far? Perhaps he felt he was about to lose Olivia?

'You'll be required to formally identify the bodies, sir,' she heard Tom Grindley say. 'Are you sure you wish to do it in situ? I really wouldn't advise it, you know.'

Charlotte looked at Grindley and then she looked at David, the blood draining from her head with such suddenness she thought she was going to faint.

'Bodies?' she breathed. At that moment she realised something more fearful, more terrible than she could ever have imagined had happened at Chelwood Manor last night.

David turned to look at her, his eyes expressionless, his voice flat.

'I tried to tell you this morning, but I couldn't. Before Chris committed suicide, he shot both my mother and father.'

Chapter Nine

Carol and Neil arrived just as David and Charlotte stepped out of the police van. Before the car had even stopped, Carol opened the door and, as Neil braked, she clambered out and rushed towards David, arms outstretched.

'My poor boy,' she said, pulling him towards her. 'This is a terrible tragedy. How are you bearing up?' She gripped his shoulders and looked searchingly into his face.

David hung his head for a moment, his arms hanging slackly by his side. 'I've got to identify them,' he said.

'Can't Neil do that for you?' She turned to her husband, 'Neil . . . ? You can identify Virginia . . .' her voice, usually so brisk, broke.

'No, I have to do it,' David said quickly. 'I have to see what happened, how Christopher did it.' He was still holding Charlotte's hand in a fast grip, as she stood close to his side.

'What? You have to go into the house and . . . and see what's happened?' Neil asked falteringly.

David nodded and then, with a glance of confirmation to Tom Grindley, he strode off in the direction of the front door, dragging Charlotte with him.

'You can't take her in, too,' cried Carol, appalled. 'We'll look after her.'

'I'm all right, really,' Charlotte said, faintly. All she could think of was that, no matter how dreadful she felt, David needed her.

'Oh, my God,' said Carol. 'Surely, David . . . let Neil go with you instead.'

David ignored her and, turning to the detective inspector, said tersely, 'Where do we begin?'

'In the hall, sir.'

In grim procession, Grindley leading the way, they entered the house, passing the police constable who guarded the entrance. Charlotte looked around. It was bleak and cheerless without the beautiful Christmas tree that had stood in the corner last time she'd been here. A burly policeman, his shirtsleeves rolled up, was examining a window-frame. His beefy hands were encased in tiny white gloves, and she realised he must be from the forensic department as, with a delicate movement, he brushed the windowsill with a silvery powder.

Then she gasped. The body of Edmund Farrell lay at the bottom of the stairs. For a moment it looked as if he'd slipped and fallen. Lying on his side, with his head resting on his arm and his legs spread out, he might have been sleeping. For a wild moment Charlotte wondered if he was really dead; she almost expected the dark eyes to fly open and the bellowing voice to shout abuse at them, cursing them for letting this happen.

When she moved closer, pulled forward by David still gripping her hand, she saw the dark, almost black stain that welled through his thick beige sweater, and the pool of blood that had spread under him.

'He's been shot twice in the chest,' Grindley explained

in a normal voice. Charlotte thought how inured he must have become to violent death.

David just stood rock still, mesmerised by the sight of his father lying there. As if in a trance, he gazed and said nothing.

Grindley continued: 'The victim was shot at point-blank range by a 12-shot .22 automatic. Time of death hasn't been exactly verified yet. Presumably he was shot shortly after you spoke to your mother at around ten o'clock, or a little later.'

David nodded.

'Poor Gladys,' he said suddenly.

Charlotte looked at him, wondering why he'd mentioned Gladys. But the detective inspector knew.

'That would be Mrs Gladys Scovell? Who comes in every day to work for your parents?' He shook his head. 'Nasty shock for her this morning when she arrived.'

'Didn't she have her daughter, Ruby, with her?' David asked.

'Not as far as we were able to gather, sir. She was in shock by the time we got here, but I'll have to question her later on today. No doubt she'll tell us more. I don't think she knew Mrs Farrell had also been shot.'

'She didn't go upstairs, then?'

'Apparently not.' Grindley looked down at Edmund again. 'Are you able to formally confirm that this is the body of Mr Edmund Farrell, sir?'

'Yes, I am.' David's voice was so low Charlotte could barely hear his reply. She moved closer, gripping his hand.

'Are you all right, miss?' Grindley turned to her in concern. Charlotte was battling with faintness and nausea, but she was determined to stick with David until the ordeal was over.

'Why don't you sit down for a moment, miss? Would you like a glass of water, perhaps?' His tone was fatherly and Charlotte gave him a wobbly smile.

'I'll be OK.'

'There's really no need for you to go through this, you know. Why don't you have a rest in the police van?'

'No, really,' she protested, but all the time she was wondering why David had insisted on this macabre tour of the house? Surely bodies were usually identified in a mortuary?

Tom Grindley said no more, but he continued to keep a watchful eye on her as they walked up the wide staircase to the first floor. When they reached the landing, Charlotte glanced along the corridor to where she'd slept at Christmas. Looking back, it was like a dream now, or a far-distant memory. Had she really spent three days with this doomed family? Had she seen them quarrelling? Felt the tension in the atmosphere? Been witness to their coming destruction without an inkling of what was to happen? It seemed unbelievable that a mother, father and son had died in this house only last night, and yet she'd had no premonition of it.

Guided by Grindley, they were walking towards Virginia and Edmund's bedroom now. At that moment the police photographer emerged, tripod in one hand, large camera case in the other.

'All done?' Grindley asked briskly.

'Yes,' he replied. 'I'll get back to the station now.'

What a terrible job, Charlotte reflected, photographing

dead bodies all the time. He, like Grindley, must have become inured to gory sights, and she wondered why anyone should choose such a career. She watched him scuttle down the stairs, and then she heard David give a moan of anguish and, turning, she followed his gaze into his parents' bedroom.

Nothing had prepared her for the sight that met her eyes. With her face half blown away, Virginia Farrell lay slumped sideways on the side of the big double bed that dominated the room. Her shoulder and the part of her head that was still intact leaned against the padded headboard, her blood mingling with the rose-pattered chintz so artfully it could almost have been designed so. Virginia's legs hung lifelessly to the floor, her feet still encased in neat navy-blue shoes. By her side rested the phone, the receiver still gripped in her hand.

'Jesus Christ!' David started to breathe rapidly. 'She must have been shot while I was talking to her! She . . . she didn't hang up, she was . . . Oh, my God!' He averted his face and, turning, staggered back into the corridor.

'I'm sorry!' he gasped, overcome. 'I'm sorry!'

Charlotte slipped her arm round his waist, and he leaned against her heavily. She felt stronger now than when she'd first seen Edmund's body, and she knew it was because at that moment David was the weaker of the two of them. He took a handkerchief from his pocket and dabbed his upper lip.

'I'm sorry . . .' he repeated, wretchedly.

'Take your time, sir,' Tom Grindley said kindly. 'We'll proceed whenever you're ready. In your own time.'

David broke away from Charlotte and, raising both hands,

leaned against the passage wall, his face buried in his arms. The silence was broken by his sobs, great dry heart-rending sobs that were torn from his lungs. Charlotte put her arm round his shoulders.

'David . . . David,' she whispered, gripping one of his clenched hands. 'Hold on to me, darling.'

'Mum . . .' he gasped convulsively. 'Oh, Mum . . . !'

'I know. I know, sweetheart.' She pressed herself to his side, wanting to warm and comfort the man who had suddenly become a child crying for his lost mother. She glanced at the detective inspector, who was standing a few feet away, his face averted.

'Could you get someone to bring David some more brandy?' she begged.

Grindley nodded, and gave instructions to the chief constable who was still making notes.

'I'll be all right,' David muttered, his voice muffled by his arms. 'Just give me a minute.'

Charlotte stroked his hair, and wondered if she'd ever get the sight of Virginia's face erased from her mind. It seemed to dominate her line of vision, although she was in the passage outside the bedroom now. It was everywhere she looked, filling her mind, her thoughts, her spirit. For the rest of her life she would see the bloodied hole, spiked with shattered bones and teeth, and the one remaining eye staring at her as if at any minute it might blink.

David straightened up, wiping his face with his handkerchief.

'Let's get this over,' he said, looking towards his mother's bedroom.

'We just need you to formally tell us, sir, that the victim is indeed your mother,' the detective inspector said.

David nodded. 'Yes, it is.'

'Let's go back downstairs, sir. You might like to sit in the study and rest for a few minutes before we proceed to the kitchen.'

'The kitchen?' David asked in a hollow voice.

'Yes, sir. It is in the kitchen that you brother took his own life.'

Olivia, waking late, wondered why there were no comforting sounds coming from the kitchen, which was under her bedroom at Magnolia Cottage. Mabel always arrived at nine-thirty, and her first task each morning was to get Olivia's breakfast tray ready and bring it up to her at ten o'clock. The sounds of china being gently chinked, and taps running and cupboard doors being opened and closed, made Olivia feel secure and looked after. It reminded her of when she'd been a child. Her granny, with whom she'd lived, was always in the kitchen preparing little treats and special dishes with which to indulge her; Olivia had always loved being spoiled. By the time she was fifteen it had become a way of life, a necessity to her survival. She needed to have people pandering to her wishes, giving her little presents, putting themselves out for her.

Edmund was so good at that. His gifts of jewellery and trinkets, expensive perfume and chocolates, and all the other things he gave her meant so much. Especially as she came to realise he was renowned for his meanness. Everyone knew he hardly gave his wife any money for housekeeping, and that Virginia had to ask every time she wanted anything new.

Olivia smiled to herself. Edmund was putty in her hands, agreeing to her every whim, never grudging a penny if she wanted something special. He was the most generous man she'd ever known, unlike her two previous husbands, who had been rich, but who had deprived her of what she considered were the essentials in life.

Then there was Christopher. Her smile deepened. He hadn't the money to be generous, but he gave of himself in the most marvellous way, drawing her out and encouraging her to talk about herself, so that in the end he succeeded in making her feel clever. Edmund she needed. Christopher she loved. It had happened so suddenly, almost from the moment she'd set eyes on him at Chelwood on Christmas Day, and now she tried to share herself between the two. It needed careful handling. Edmund would go crazy if he thought she'd seen Christopher, and Christopher would go berserk if he thought she was still seeing his father. But it worked. It had to. She needed the feeling of being protected by Edmund, as if she were a little girl again, and she needed to feel like a woman, intelligent and sensuous, as she did with Christopher.

Glancing at her art-deco diamond wristwatch, a present from Edmund, she saw it was nearly ten-fifteen. The silence in Magnolia Cottage was now oppressive and made her uneasy. Getting out of her cream-satin-swathed bed, she went to the top of the stairs and called down.

'Mabel? Are you there?'

Somehow she hadn't expected an answer. The silence was solid, almost palpable. Looking up Mabel's number, she got back into bed and dialled her cottage. She hung up after five minutes. Somehow she'd known that too would be empty. Yet where was Mabel? And her husband, who was a retired electrician and stayed at home all day? And her married son and his wife, who lived with them?

Olivia got dressed, driven on by a presentiment that something was wrong. This was not a case, she was sure, of her cleaning woman letting her down for some trivial reason.

As she had no friends in Barrow, she decided to walk to the village shop where they always knew what was going on. Not that she felt a great need to be told now.

Olivia thought about her grandmother again, only this time it was not in connection with the lovely little treats she'd given her, but because she also knew she'd inherited a talent from the old lady she didn't much care to possess. It was the gift of second sight. As if she'd already been told, she knew she'd never see Edmund and Christopher again.

David sipped his brandy slowly, sitting in the study for a few minutes in order to recover. Beside him on the sofa, Charlotte sat holding his hand, whilst in the two armchairs flanking the fireplace, Carol and Neil drank from Edmund's decanter of whisky, stunned into silence. There was no cheering blaze in the grate today as there'd been when they last sat together in the room over Christmas; no briskly polite conversation, no anticipation of the next exquisitely cooked meal by Gladys.

Tom Grindley was asking David to tell him everything he could about Christopher. Although Charlotte had heard it all before, she still found it a heart-breaking tale of a young man, who had been seduced into taking drugs when he was seventeen, and whose life had been ruined as a result.

'What did he take?' Grindley asked.

173

'Amphetamines, cannabis, cocaine, heroin, LSD; you name it, he took it,' David replied. 'He even tried to grow magic mushrooms in the garden, but Dad found out.'

'Then he was hospitalised?'

David nodded. 'He was drinking by that time as well. Then when he came off drugs he drank very heavily instead. He tried to hide it from us, but we all knew he was drinking. That's right, isn't it, La?' Once again he turned to her for support.

'Yes,' she admitted. She glanced up at the detective inspector, who was walking around the room, looking at the books and ornaments and occasionally picking something up to examine it.

'Christopher was such a nice man,' she said sadly. 'It seems such a dreadful waste. He adored his little girl, he was a kind, thoughtful person. Whatever happened to make him do a thing like this?'

'We know what happened,' David cut in. 'Mum told me on the phone last night before . . .' He was unable to continue.

Charlotte tried to picture the scene. Virginia up in her bedroom, phoning David in London, because she was so frightened of Edmund and Christopher downstairs, yelling at each other. What had she expected David to do? Call the police for her? Intervene on the phone in an effort to persuade his father and Chris to stop? Or had she thought David might phone Olivia and ask her to rush over and put a stop to their deadly rivalry? For deadly rivalry it undoubtedly had been.

Edmund must have been coming down the stairs when Christopher, incensed and jealous of his father, had raised the .22 automatic and fired. He must have taken the gun, loaded it and then gone into the hall, where he challenged his father. What did he say? 'Stay away from Olivia or I'll kill you?' And what would the cold, arrogant Edmund have replied?

Whatever he'd said, Christopher had then shot him twice according to the police. A moment later he would have heard his mother's screams coming from her bedroom upstairs. She'd have realised what had happened. She had to be silenced. He would have rushed up the stairs, two at a time, gun in hand and, bursting into her room, shot her at point-blank range as she sat on the side of the bed, phoning David.

Charlotte covered her face with her hands, seeing it all as clearly as if she'd seen it on film. The blood spraying around the room, the shattering silence that would follow the loud blast.

It was no wonder he went downstairs; no doubt he had had several stiff drinks in the kitchen before deciding he must end his own life. What else could he do? Faced with the murder of his parents, he had no option.

'I think I'd like a drink,' Charlotte murmured weakly.

'Here, have mine,' David said immediately, handing her his glass which still had some brandy in it. 'Poor darling. You shouldn't have come. This is terrible for you.'

'I'll be all right,' she said bravely.

Tom Grindley spoke again, addressing himself to David once more.

'You mentioned a clinic where your brother went. Had he been back recently, do you know?'

'I've no idea. I think it unlikely.'

'In your opinion, was he back on drugs again?'

David shrugged. 'I don't know. He might have been.'

The detective inspector cleared his throat. 'Mr Farrell, do you feel able to identify your brother now? I'm sure you'll agree the sooner we can get this business cleared up, the better.'

'Yes. Sure. Let's get it over and done with.' David rose slowly, as if all his joints hurt. Charlotte stood up, too.

'You wait here,' he said to her.

She shook her head. 'I'll be better if I come with you. Reality is never quite as bad as imagination. If I see exactly what has happened I'll be able to cope, otherwise . . .' She broke off, shuddering.

'Are you going back to London after that?' Carol asked suddenly. It was the first time she'd spoken, and David turned to her, startled, as if he'd forgotten she and Neil were sitting there.

'I've no idea,' he replied, bewildered. 'Probably not. On the other hand, what do we have to stay for?' He looked at Charlotte, expecting her to say something.

'The house will have to be locked up, when . . . when everyone's gone,' Carol pointed out practically.

'I think we'd like you all to stay in the vicinity,' Tom Grindley said. 'We shall need further statements from all of you, and there are still a lot of loose ends to tie up, although I think we can say that this is a fairly open-and-shut case.'

'I don't want to stay in this house,' Charlotte said with unusual firmness. 'Anywhere, but not here.'

'Don't worry. We'll go to a hotel,' David assured her.

'Are you ready then, sir?' the detective inspector asked. 'Are you sure about this, Miss Taylor?'

Charlotte clenched her teeth. 'I'm sure.' Taking David's

hand, she followed Grindley across the passage and into the kitchen.

Gladys lay back in the chair, wishing the feeling of weakness would leave her. Her family filled her cottage, making endless cups of strong, sweet tea, all crowding round her, wanting to hear every detail of what she'd found that morning when she'd arrived at Chelwood Manor. They'd rushed over immediately after the police had sent her home in one of their cars, tumbling out of their own cottages in Barrow, hurrying up their garden paths and along the street to find out what had happened.

Nothing like this had ever occurred before in any of their lives, and all of them, with the exception of Gladys, felt a sense of importance at being tenuously linked with such a sensation. It was a feeling shared by most of the inhabitants of Barrow. As the news spread, and with it the realisation that their village would now be famous the width and length of Great Britain, people hovered outside their houses, or gathered in the courtyard of the largest pub, parading for the benefit of the watching media and themselves eyeing the chroniclers as they descended in a motley collection of vehicles. Television camera crews, photographers and journalists were arriving every few minutes, laden with equipment, eager for an angle. By the evening, the village no one had ever heard of would be a celebrated landmark. It would attract the morbid sightseer from miles around, and the country lanes would become blocked with traffic as people craned their necks out of car windows to get a glimpse of the old manor house where it had all happened.

'We must watch the one o'clock news on the telly,' said Ruby, who had stayed at home that morning instead of accompanying her mother to work, because her baby wasn't well.

'I'm not going to speak to no reporters,' murmured Gladys, putting down her third cup of tea. 'The police told me not to, and I don't want to, neither.'

Her sister Mabel, living the nearest, had been one of the first to rush over as soon as she saw Gladys climbing out of the police car.

'Whatever's up?' she had asked, alarmed.

'I must sit down,' said Gladys, feeling ill. The shock of going into the kitchen and finding young Mr Farrell lying on the floor with a gun in his hand had nearly made her heart stop with fright. When she'd gone through to the hall and found his father lying in a pool of blood, her legs had given way beneath her as all the strength had drained out of them, while black spots danced before her eyes and a clammy chill made her clothes stick to her back.

Gladys had looked up the stairs then, wondering about Mrs Farrell. It was as if something dreadful lurked on the darkened landing, waiting for her. She couldn't go any further. With a cry of panic, she somehow got herself into the study, where she grabbed the phone and dialled 999. Then she sat huddled, trembling and sick, not daring to move and yet afraid to stay.

'How long did the police take to come?' Mabel asked.

Gladys shook her head. 'It seemed like a long time. Then I sees the car coming up the drive. I don't know how I got from the study to the front door, having to pass Mr Farrell lying there, but I was that relieved! Nice they was to me, too. Made me sit down again while I told them as how I'd found Christopher first, and then his dad. Asked me if I'd been upstairs, they did, and when I said I'd been too afraid, one of them nips up, like, and when he comes back down, he's as white as a sheet.'

'He'd found Mrs Farrell, then?'

'Yes.'

'What happened then, Ma?' Ruby asked, as all the aunts and uncles and nephews and nieces crowded round, eager to hear the story first hand, wanting to know, and relive in their own imagination, every terrible detail.

'They asks me my name, and where I lives, and I tells them I comes every day to the manor, and that my daughter is usually with me. Then they asks me if anything happened yesterday.'

'What sort of thing?' asked Mabel.

'A fight between Christopher and his mum and dad, and I says not that I knows of.' Gladys closed her eyes, sick at heart.

'Well, there's nothing I can tell the police because I didn't go to work yesterday, on account of Larry being ill,' Ruby remarked.

'The police are coming to see me later and they want me to make a statement, but I'm not to talk to no one else,' said Gladys. 'If any of them newspaper reporters come here, tell them as I'm not well.'

'Poor Mum.' Ruby sounded sympathetic as she rubbed her mother's cold hand between her own. 'Why don't you lie down for a bit? Have a kip?'

'I don't rightly knows as I could, love,' Gladys replied. 'I feel real poorly.'

'I'll fetch Dr Burns to see you,' said Mabel, jumping to her feet, glad of something to do. 'He'll give you something.'

'What can he do? There's this . . . this hollow in the middle of my chest, and I don't know if it'll ever be filled up again.' Gladys wept now. 'I feel that terrible . . . and to think that only yesterday afternoon . . . !'

Suddenly her eyes widened and she went rigid, her hands gripping the arms of her chair.

'What is it, Mum?' Ruby asked, alarmed.

'O-o-h-h-h-h!' A long desperate cry filled the room and the panic that emanated from Gladys could be felt by the others.

'Glad!' Mabel demanded shrilly. 'What's up? What on earth's the matter, for pity's sakes?'

'I'd . . . *forgotten*!' wailed Gladys.

Ruby went cold. She'd forgotten too. What had happened this morning had destroyed coherent thought, wiped out recent memory, reduced her, as it had her mother, to numbness. The most they could take in was that Edmund and Virginia Farrell had been shot, and it looked as if their son Christopher had done it before killing himself.

'Oh . . . my . . . God.' Ruby paused between each word as her eyes met her mother's.

Gladys covered her face with her hand.

'Oh, no, no!' she sobbed. 'He couldn't have! He couldn't have!'

Ruby's hand was clapped over her mouth as if she didn't dare voice what they'd both remembered. It was too terrible, too unthinkable to contemplate.

'Oh, please God, no!' Gladys was crying loudly. 'It was so quiet upstairs . . . I never thought . . .'

Mabel gripped Ruby by the arm, alarmed.

'*What is it?*' she hissed frantically.

Ruby dropped her hand from her mouth.

'It's Holly,' she said brokenly. 'Holly was staying at Chelwood, too. Her Dad brought her down yesterday.'

It was too much. Seeing Edmund and Virginia lying dead had been sickening enough, something Charlotte knew she would never forget. But now, faced with the body of Christopher, his hand still gripping the rifle as it lay across his stomach, she realised that this was a much more tragic sight. She felt overwhelmed with grief and a sense of loss. Chris had been more than a friend; he'd also been David's brother, Holly's father and Olivia's lover; his death was going to be felt keenly by them all.

'Oh, God,' she heard David say.

Christopher was lying on his back on the kitchen floor. He'd shot himself in the neck and a great pool of blood had spread on to the terracotta tiles like a crimson lake. The force of the bullet had forced his head to one side, but his expression surprised Charlotte, for he looked so peaceful, as if he were asleep. It was his hands, though, that made her want to cry most of all. They looked such gentle, innocent hands, and yet they were holding a rifle.

Moving away from David and the others, Charlotte sank on to a kitchen chair and wept as if her heart would break. Now, at last, the full enormity of what had happened seared her mind, robbing her of the last shreds of self-control. She wept for the man she only knew slightly, but had liked so much; the devoted father who would have given his life for Holly. She wept, too, for Edmund and Virginia, whose

181

delight at the birth of their younger son must have turned to horror as they realised what he was going to do. And she wept, most of all, for the waste of a young life, a man not yet thirty who had seemed to value his existence but who had nevertheless ended up courting his own self-destruction.

'Why don't you take her outside?' she heard Tom Grindley say to the deputy chief constable.

Charlotte felt someone take her arm, help her to her feet, and lead her away out of the house and into the front drive, where the cold wind chilled the tears on her cheeks and made her catch her breath. They suggested she rest in one of the ambulances and they offered her sal volatile.

'No, just a glass of water, please,' she said weakly.

All around her the activity had stepped up, as first Edmund's body then Virginia's, and finally Christopher's were taken from the house in body bags and carried to an ambulance.

She chose to sit in David's car. She wondered when they'd be able to get away from this dreadful place, with the sight of broken bodies and the smell of blood and the knowledge that some wild, tortured element had been let loose last night, causing havoc which would have far-reaching effects on those who were left behind.

Then David came out of the house with Tom Grindley, talking in the shadows of the strange three-pillared porch, before they made their way over to her.

'We've done everything we can for the moment,' David said, reaching into the car to grip her shoulder in a comforting gesture. 'Carol and Neil are going to find an hotel where they can stay. Shall we do the same?'

Charlotte looked up into his face, drawn and strained

but with the colour being whipped back into his cheeks by the sharp wind. She nodded, afraid if she spoke she'd burst into tears again.

'There's nothing around here, but there's an hotel called the Court not far away. We might be able to get into that.'

What she really wanted was to get back to London, but knew there was no way she could leave now. If David had to remain, then she would stay, too.

'All right,' she replied. 'When can we go to this hotel?' The desire to get away from Chelwood was obsessive. She never wanted to see this brooding house again, nor go anywhere near the blood-splattered rooms. Childishly, all she longed for was home, her childhood home, where her mother would welcome her with a big hug and her father would pat her on the back and tell her she was 'his girl'.

At that moment, a police sergeant hurried over to speak to the detective inspector. His face was flushed and he was breathing heavily.

'Sir?'

Tom Grindley looked at him. 'What is it?'

'We've had a call from the lady cleaner, Mrs Gladys Scovell.'

'She's at her home, isn't she?'

'Yes, sir.'

'What did she want?'

Charlotte noticed the police sergeant's jaw was clenching and unclenching, and his mouth was stiff as if his lips were frozen. He gulped before speaking.

'It seems, sir, she forgot to mention, because she was so shocked, that a little girl was also staying in the house . . . !'

Charlotte's thin scream of anguish made the men turn to

look at her as she sat huddled in the passenger seat of the car.

'Not Holly!' she cried, wrenching the door open. 'Oh, please God, not Holly, too!'

David had gone white, his eyes staring blankly.

'*Holly?*' He spoke as if he doubted the man was speaking the truth. 'Holly? Here?'

'Mrs Scovell said she always came with her father, when he stayed here, sir.'

Tom Grindley looked as if he'd just aged ten years. He spoke to David.

'Who did this child belong to? How old was she?'

While David answered, Charlotte thought: *They're talking about her in the past tense already.*

'When was the child last seen?' Grindley asked the sergeant. 'Did Mrs Scovell tell you that?' he added with irony.

'Yes, sir. She says she last saw the little girl when she left here, shortly before five o'clock. She was apparently playing in the study.'

Linda always played the radio quietly in the mornings while Ben had his nap and she pottered around the house. It was quiet and peaceful at this hour, and on a Saturday particularly so. Many of the residents of Mulberry Avenue went away for the weekend, and those who hadn't had piled into their cars and gone shopping shortly after breakfast. On this particular morning, Linda had decided that several of her house plants needed repotting. Denzil was out, their au pair, Magda, was doing the ironing, and so she set to work. She had a way with plants. They grew and flourished in her care as she watered and fed them regularly; she even had a 'sick bay' in the bedroom window for plants that her neighbours had thrown out with the rubbish when they'd stopped flowering.

Selecting a large terracotta pot in which to replant a pale pink begonia, she only vaguely heard the newscaster announce a newsflash, was still only half listening when the word 'Barrow' filtered through to her consciousness, causing her to stop and listen.

A moment later as she heard the words, ' . . . parents were shot dead' and then ' . . . their son was found in the kitchen having apparently killed himself', she knew with the most terrible clarity they were talking about Chris and Virginia and Edmund. 'There were no signs of a break-in,' the announcer continued, 'and it is thought to be a domestic incident, involving no outsiders.'

And? screamed a voice in Linda's head, as the weather forecast started. *And* . . . who else had been shot? What had happened to Holly? Why was there no mention of Holly? Surely Chris couldn't have harmed their little girl? Could he?

At that moment, as if reacting to his mother's distress, Ben awoke in his nursery next door and started bawling.

'Magda!' Linda shouted down the stairs. 'Magda!'

A dark-haired girl of nineteen appeared in the hall below.

'Yes, Mrs Blake?' She was Polish, quietly spoken and devoted to Ben.

'Can you get Ben up for me, please? He's crying and . . . something's happened, Magda, I've got to make a phone call.' Linda tried to keep her voice steady but the look of panic in her eyes betrayed her. She rushed back into her bedroom and dialled the Wiltshire phone number of her ex-in-laws, which she still knew by heart, even though she'd had no contact with them for over two years.

Her mind was spinning dizzily in circles of disbelief. She was beginning to doubt her own sense. Had she really heard right? Could Chris possibly have shot Virginia and Edmund before shooting himself? No, surely not. It must have been another family they were referring to. In a moment, she'd hear the phone at Chelwood Manor ringing, and one of them would answer, Edmund most likely, and Linda would say, 'Oh, I just heard this dreadful thing on the radio about a family . . . no, no, of course I didn't think it was you, but they said Barrow, and so I just thought I'd give you a ring . . .' And they'd all have a little laugh, filled with relief that of course it wasn't any of them . . .

The line gave the busy signal. She replaced the receiver with forced patience, wiping her eyes with the back of her hand, wondering how many minutes she should give it before she tried again. The words she'd heard kept repeating themselves over and over in her mind as if they were on a loop. Surely, if there'd been a small child involved, the announcer would have said so? The thought brought her a few seconds' comfort, but when she dialled Chelwood again and the line was still busy, she knew instinctively that her worst fears had been realised. A moment later she heard Denzil's key in the front door lock. Flinging herself down the short flight of stairs to the hall, she told him what she'd heard on the radio.

'I've got to get to Chelwood, Denzil,' she said, distraught.

Chapter Ten

The police swarmed into the house like drones entering a hive, some scouring the ground floor and cellars, others going up to the first floor and the attic. They'd searched the house initially, but no one had been looking for a small child. Now, with the hunt renewed, there was an almost manic feverishness in the atmosphere.

Charlotte and Carol sat waiting in David's car, while Neil and David stood helplessly in the drive, advised by Grindley to stay out of the house for the time being.

'Our chaps will find her,' he said, compassion in his voice.

'Yes, but what are they going to find?' Neil muttered, as Grindley strode off.

David didn't answer, but bit his bottom lip furiously, scuffing the gravel of the drive with his feet.

'This is a nightmare, isn't it, old boy?' Neil observed sympathetically.

'You can say that again.'

'You mustn't blame yourself, you know. There was nothing you could have done. Virginia should have phoned the police, not you, last night.'

Charlotte felt an overwhelming sense of dread. The car window was open, and she could hear the voices of the policemen as they searched the house, shouting to each other. Several times she heard: 'Nothing here,' as they progressed from room to room, but at any moment she expected someone to call out: 'Found her.' Then her worst fears would be realised.

'Perhaps she's not in the house at all,' Carol remarked hopefully.

'But where could she be?'

Carol shrugged, unable to answer.

Grindley came striding over from one of the police cars; he'd been talking on a phone. Charlotte's heart leapt with optimism. There was an urgency in his step as he walked purposefully towards the house. Charlotte got out of the car and followed him to the pillared portico.

'Is Holly all right?' she asked.

Grindley glanced fleetingly at her, saw the flicker of expectation in her eyes, then shook his head.

'I've just spoken to the mother. I'm afraid the little girl was definitely here yesterday. She wasn't due to go back to London until tomorrow.'

'I was afraid of that,' said Carol, joining them. 'Linda never comes here now. I didn't for a moment think she'd have fetched Holly yesterday evening.'

Charlotte stood looking bleakly at the lawn which ran down the side of the house, remembering Christmas Day, when the air had been filled with the sound of Holly's joyous laughter as she played with her new ball. Her sturdy little legs in red tights had scampered over that grass. Her small pink hands had clutched the ball to her chest, and she'd giggled at her own efforts to throw it.

Deputy Chief Constable Ron Franklin emerged from the house.

'There's no sign of her in there,' he informed Grindley. 'We've gone over the place with a toothcomb. Her clothes and a few toys are in one of the bedrooms. She must be around somewhere.'

Grindley nodded. 'Order the men to search the grounds. Start close to the house and fan outwards. I want every shrub and bush examined, and if nothing turns up, spread out to the woods at the bottom of the lawn and the surrounding fields.'

Overhearing, Carol gasped. 'You mean she may have been in the garden all night? In these freezing conditions?'

'Perhaps she ran away?' Charlotte suggested. 'In spite of the cold she'd probably have been safer out of that house that in it.'

'D'you think so?' David looked appalled.

'We need volunteers,' Grindley said to Franklin. 'Recruit helpers from the village to help search the grounds. I myself am not convinced she's out there. I want you to get the men to go over this house once again, but this time I want you to look in every nook and cranny; taking the place apart. She's got to be somewhere.'

'Yes, sir.'

'It's possible she's been hidden. You should be searching for –' he paused, averting his face from the family who stood there listening – 'searching for a bundle of some sort,' he added in a low voice.

Franklin nodded. 'Will do, sir.'

David stepped forward, his face white, sweat glistening on his upper lip.

'I'll start looking in the garden. I know all the places where a child might hide. Chris and I used to play hide and seek all the time when we were small.'

'David.' Charlotte grabbed his hand. Tears smarted her eyes and her voice was choked. 'They don't think she's hiding anywhere. Not of her own accord, I mean. They think she may have been . . .' But she couldn't finish the sentence.

'I'm still going to look round the garden,' he said stubbornly.

Carol looked at David curiously. 'Why do you think she's still . . . well, alive?'

'It's just that if Chris could leave the bodies of Mum and Dad lying around like that, why would he try and hide Holly?'

'Unless,' Neil said slowly and painfully, 'he shot Holly first, before everything got out of hand, and he hid her body somewhere.'

'That doesn't make sense. Chris wouldn't have hurt Holly in a million years. He loved her more than anything else on earth,' Charlotte protested.

'I agree,' Carol affirmed. 'For all his faults, he did adore that child.'

Tom Grindley looked from one to the other, his expression unconvinced. 'Then, let's get searching again,' he said with forced cheerfulness.

'I'll go round the garden,' said David, before anyone could stop him. Charlotte watched as he strode off, his shoulders hunched up near his ears, his hands deep in his pockets.

'Maybe she ran away to someone's house,' Carol suggested, 'although she'd surely have been frightened of going out in the dark.'

'Umm.' Grindley looked thoughtful.

'You'd have thought,' he said, 'that if she'd run to someone's house she'd have gone to Gladys Scovell's cottage. After all, it's only down the lane, and presumably she knew her grandmother's domestic help?'

Charlotte felt crushed. Grindley was probably right. And yet ... She turned away from him, unable to speak. If anything had happened to Holly ...

A young policeman, pink cheeked and with eyes that betrayed his shock at the events of the day, came hurrying out of the house.

'Excuse me, miss. You are Charlotte Taylor?'

Charlotte turned to him, startled.

'Yes,' she replied uncertainly.

'There's a phone call for you, miss.'

'Are you sure? No one knows I'm here.'

'The lady said she was your mother.'

Charlotte hurried into the house, carefully avoiding looking at the bottom of the stairs. The carpet and gleaming wooden floor were stained dark with Edmund's blood, and the police photographer was still taking pictures from various angles of the chalk marks that had outlined the body.

Glancing around, Charlotte saw a mobile phone lying on the table in the centre of the hall, where Virginia usually arranged newspapers and copies of *Country Life*. The policeman cried out in warning, but too late. She had already grabbed it, and found it splashed with blood. A little trickle ran between her fingers and she dropped the instrument with a cry of horror.

'Forensic haven't finished in here yet,' the constable said in agitation. 'We mustn't touch anything. Your mother's on the extension in the study, miss.'

Feeling nauseated, Charlotte wiped her hand with her tear-sodden tissue. 'Oh, my God.'

'Are you all right, miss?' he asked anxiously.

She nodded numbly and, on shaking legs, went to the study.

'Hello? Mum?' she said weakly, picking up the old-fashioned instrument on Edmund's desk.

'For God's sake, what's going on?'

'How did you know I was here?'

'I was watching the news on SKY Television and I heard what had happened. When there was no reply from your flat, I guessed you might have gone down to Wiltshire with David. La, is it true? That both David's parents and his brother have been shot?' Margaret Taylor sounded as if she couldn't believe what she'd heard.

'It's true, Mummy. It's so awful, I can't tell you. And now Holly's gone missing.' Charlotte gave a sob.

'Oh, my God,' Margaret said slowly. 'Oh, Charlotte!'

As Charlotte told her mother what had happened, she could hear the police thumping about upstairs.

'They're searching for Holly again. They think her body may have been hidden somewhere in the house or the grounds.'

'You mean . . . ? You don't think . . . ? Oh, La, surely not!'

'She was here yesterday. She wasn't due to go back to London until tomorrow. I'm just . . . h-hoping she's run away,' Charlotte sobbed.

'Oh, darling.' Margaret's voice was gentle.

'Oh, Mummy, she must have been so frightened! I can't bear to think how scared she must have been, with Chris running amok with a gun, in the middle of the night, shooting . . .' She couldn't continue.

'Sweetheart, do you have to stay down there? Surely you and David won't be needed once they've found Holly?'

'I don't know. I can't think. It's so terrible for David. Imagine having your whole family wiped out like this! I don't know what we're going to do, Mummy. David's aunt and uncle are here and there's talk of us staying the night in some local hotel. I'll have to stay if David does.'

'Of course. Oh, sweetheart, I'm so sorry. Give David a big hug from me and take care of yourself, La. Let me know about Holly.'

'Yes, I will. And I'll let you know where we're staying.' Charlotte gave a deep, sobbing sigh. 'You know, I can't believe any of this is happening!'

It was lunchtime and there was still no sign of Holly. Only one ambulance waited in the drive now, alongside the police vans and cars. The ambulance crew sat inside, resigned to the knowledge that, sooner or later, they too would have to carry one more gruesome burden to the police mortuary.

Charlotte, sitting in the study with Carol and Neil, was aware of the cautious sympathy of the police. They were tiptoeing around the house, speaking in hushed voices now, as if they were afraid of disturbing the family. Now that the second search for Holly had been fruitless, the frantic thumping and shouting had stopped as suddenly as it had begun. Instead they acted as if Chelwood was a hospital, where the sick lay in various stages of decline.

'Are you sure you don't want a drink, Charlotte?' Neil

asked, rising to refill his glass from the whisky bottle. His face was flushed, and he was slowly but steadily getting drunk.

'No, thanks,' Charlotte replied. 'Water's fine. Anything else will make my headache worse.'

'No sign of David, yet. I wonder where he's got to?' Carol observed. Neil had given her a strong gin and tonic and she, too, was a little drunk.

'I expect he's still searching the garden and the woods for Holly,' said Charlotte.

Neil stood, feet apart, back to the empty cold grate.

'No news is good news, they always say,' he remarked, swaying slightly.

'But where can she be?'

None of them answered the question. None of them dared. They, and the whole village of Barrow, were keyed up, desperate to know what had happened to four-year-old Holly Farrell.

The strain of waiting was driving Charlotte crazy. Waiting and not knowing. Waiting, and wondering with dread what they would discover when they did find Holly.

Detective Inspector Tom Grindley was faced with the task of making his initial report on the incident to his superior, Detective Chief Superintendent Alex Osborne, head of the CID for the county. The body of the four-year-old child had not yet been found, but at this moment that was not the issue. It was obvious to Grindley that this whole case was a straightforward domestic incident. There was no evidence of a break-in, nothing had been stolen and, according to the evidence of the elder son, David Farrell, his brother had a record of drug and alcohol abuse, which at times had caused him to become violent and behave irrationally. As far as he was concerned it was an open-and-shut case, and there was no cause to look further afield for a suspect. Christopher Farrell was as guilty of killing his family, before committing suicide, as if he'd left a written confession.

When he got through to his chief, he was brief and to the point.

'It's a "domestic", sir. No outsiders involved,' he told him.

Detective Chief Superintendent Alex Osborne, who was in the middle of lunch at his home fifteen miles away, grunted with relief. Murders committed by unknown persons meant a great deal of work, which could drag on for months, if not years. To have a case which could be sewn up in a matter of hours was his idea of a perfect crime. Especially on a Saturday afternoon.

'Good show, Grindley,' he barked down the phone. 'Keep me posted if there are any further developments.'

'I will, sir. There's still the little girl to find, but I'm sure we'll find her body within the next few hours. She can't be far.'

'Nasty business, Grindley.'

'Very nasty, sir. But at least it's straightforward.'

'Well done. I'll see your report on Monday?'

'Yes, sir.'

When he'd hung up, Alex Osborne returned to the dining room and resumed his seat opposite his wife. She had cooked him his favourite dish; steak and kidney pudding, which she'd served up with sprouts and mashed potatoes.

'Very nice, my dear,' he remarked approvingly. 'There's

nothing like a good steak and kidney pud.' He gave a satisfied smile. Then he glanced out of the window. It was a dull, cold day, but it was dry, and only the faintest breeze stirred the branches of the trees.

'I think I'll go to the club for a round of golf after lunch,' he observed at length.

His wife looked up. Her usually placid blue eyes looked startled. 'What about the shootings over at Barrow? It's on all the news! Shouldn't you go there?'

'No need.' Alex Osborne looked complacent. 'Had a word with Grindley just now. It's a straightforward "domestic". He'll have the whole thing wrapped up by Monday.'

'I see.' Mrs Osborne was a quiet woman, not given to arguing with her husband. 'Will you be back in time for tea?'

'I shouldn't think so. I'll have a noggin at the club and be home around six-thirty.' He looked out of the window again. 'It'll do me good to play golf today. I could do with a breath of fresh air.'

At two o'clock, a call came through from the mortuary for Grindley.

'What is it?' he asked, curtly. It had been a long day and a harrowing one, but he couldn't go off duty until Holly's body was found. A sense of desperation and frustration was beginning to get him down.

'We've found a key in the pocket of the trousers of the younger man, Christopher Farrell,' the mortuary attendant told him.

'What sort of key?'

196

'It's quite small. Plain. Not very heavy.'

'Could it be a front door key?'

'No, I don't think so.'

'Has it got the maker's name on it? Banham? Yale? Chubb?'

'No. Nothing. It's not that sort of key, Inspector. It's more like a key for an inside door, or a cupboard.'

There was a long pause, and when Grindley answered, his voice was filled with suppressed emotion. 'Have it sent over to me, at Chelwood Manor, right away, will you?'

Linda sat rigidly in the passenger seat of their Volvo estate. Denzil was at the wheel beside her. Every now and again he placed his strong capable hand over one of her clenched fists, but she seemed oblivious to everything except the road that stretched ahead. Teeth clenched so that her jaw ached, she remained tensely silent, nerves straining, heart beating jerkily in her rib cage. Only one thought filled her head: *let Holly be all right.*

It would be another forty minutes or so before they arrived in Barrow, although Denzil drove swiftly and assuredly. Ben slept in the back, strapped into his clip-on child's seat, oblivious of the trauma surrounding him.

'We'll be there soon,' Denzil remarked comfortingly.

For answer Linda closed her eyes, as if she was in physical pain.

'Would you like the radio on, darling?' he asked. 'There might be some news . . .'

Linda shook her head violently, and her breath caught in a sob. As long as she heard nothing, she could harbour hope. She could continue to tell herself that Holly *must* be all right, safe in someone's cottage, or unharmed in the woods at the bottom of the lawn.

Her first reaction had been one of total disbelief when a later newsflash had suggested that Chris could have killed his daughter along with his father and mother.

'*Kill Holly?*' she'd cried out incredulously. 'Never! Never!'

Denzil had remained silent, wanting only to soothe and comfort her and, above all, drive her down to Wiltshire as quickly as he could. But his own heart was heavy. He feared the worst. If Christopher had gone berserk with a gun – and Denzil thought he was capable of it – why should he have stopped at his parents? Only God knew what had triggered the horror that had led to the murder of Virginia and Edmund Farrell, but if someone had it in their power to shoot their parents before shooting themselves, what inhibiting force would prevent them from killing their own child, too? Holly had to be dead, in his opinion, otherwise they would have found her hours ago.

On the outskirts of Barrow, the media had grown in strength, blocking the lanes with their mobile radio and film unit vans, filling the forecourt of the largest pub with their cars.

Photographers, hung about with cameras and telephoto lenses, were scurrying along the pavements in the direction of Chelwood Manor, jostling each other, their equipment jiggling around as they hurried. A television crew, sound and camera linked together by wires, pelted past on heavy feet, accompanied by a well-known news presenter clutching a clipboard. Others, men and women, some talking into mobile phones as they ran, dodged those laden with heavy and awkward equipment, and sprinted ahead.

'Dear God!' gasped Linda, in panic. 'What's happening? What are they all doing?'

Denzil wound down the car window, guessing what had happened. Then he heard one of the journalists shout over their shoulder to another. The words seemed to freeze his blood.

'Yeah. They've found something. Heard it on the police radio.'

The key was quite slim and made of a dull grey metal. It looked old and worn, and might possibly, Grindley thought, have been antique. Not large enough to have fitted any of the inside door locks, he started looking around to see what it might fit.

'Of course there's nothing to say it belongs here at all,' Deputy Chief Constable Ron Franklin told him. 'The deceased might always have carried it in his pocket; it could fit something in London.'

'Thanks, Franklin. That's just what I needed to hear.'

'I'm sorry, sir, but we don't know it comes from anything in this house, do we?'

'No, but we're soon going to bloody well find out,' Grindley snapped in exasperation. 'Let's ask the family first if they've ever seen it before.'

'It looks sort of familiar,' Carol said, but her voice was filled with doubt. 'I'm not sure.'

Neither David nor Neil had any idea where it belonged.

'It could fit anything from a large tea caddy to a desk,' Neil said vaguely.

Suddenly, Charlotte felt a prickling sensation creep up the back of her neck.

'Could I look at it more closely?' she asked Grindley. 'I have a feeling I've seen it before.' Then she shook her head. 'No. It's not mine. I thought it belonged to a desk I have at my flat, but it's the wrong shape. And yet it's somehow familiar. I'm *sure* I've seen it before.'

'What? Down here?' Carol asked. 'When you were staying for Christmas?'

'Yes.' Charlotte turned the key over and over in her palm.

'Well, I've no idea what it belongs to,' David remarked. He looked tired and strained, his face pinched from cold after his long fruitless search in the grounds for Holly. He had dark circles, like bruises, under his eyes.

'Wait a minute!' Charlotte jumped to her feet. 'I'm sure . . . I'm sure . . . *Yes! I know!* I know where it comes from! Oh, my God, we may be too late!'

Carol and Neil had risen too, galvanised from their alcoholic torpor by her sudden excitement.

'What is it?' Carol asked, almost fearfully.

'The wooden chest in the bedroom I slept in . . . the wooden blanket box! I remember going to get a blanket from it because I was cold one night. I'm sure this is the key that locks it!'

Grindley and Franklin didn't wait to hear any more. Grabbing the key from Charlotte's hand, they dashed out of the room and up the wide staircase to the first-floor landing, taking the steps two at a time. Running after them, although her legs felt as if they'd turned to lead, Charlotte followed. Behind her, David pounded up the stairs, too.

Grindley suddenly swung round, facing Charlotte. 'Which room is it in?'

'This way.' She ran on ahead, past Virginia's bedroom,

where mercifully someone had shut the door, to the end of the corridor.

'In here,' she panted, opening the door and rushing in.

The eighteenth-century carved blanket box stood at the foot of the bed. Charlotte remembered how much she'd admired it, thinking of a client of Myra's who would pay anything for it. She pointed to it now, and Grindley's expression was thunderous.

'This chest?' He turned to Franklin who was looking abashed. 'Why wasn't this forced open when we searched in here? I gave strict instructions that everything was to be thoroughly examined.' As he spoke he inserted the key into the lock. It turned as easily and smoothly as silk. Charlotte, gripping the footrail of the bed, felt hot, dizzy, as though she was going to faint. She wanted to shut her eyes, but couldn't bear to.

The lid opened creakily. She hardly dared look. The atmosphere in the bedroom was electric as she and David, Grindley and Franklin, Carol and Neil and several policemen crowded round, watching.

'Jesus Christ!' It was Tom Grindley who spoke first. Then there was a whimper. Charlotte peered down into the deep wooden chest, and there, curled up on a blue blanket, clutching Flissy to her chest, was Holly, flushed and hot, her blonde hair dark with sweat as it clung to her forehead and neck, her eyes swollen and sleepy. She looked up into Grindley's face as he bent over to lift her out; her chin trembled and her mouth drooped at the corners.

'Come along, little lady,' he said with great gentleness. 'Out you come.'

Holly fought him off, small feet in red shoes kicking,

arms flailing. A bellow rose from her throat.

'There, there,' he said soothingly. 'I'm just going to lift you out. You're all right, now.'

She screamed louder, wriggling so that he could not get a hold on her, arching her back as she lashed out at him with arms and legs.

'Come on, Holly,' Carol said, trying to speak in a normal voice, although she was blinking rapidly with the first tears she'd shed that day.

'No! No!' shrieked Holly. Terror filled her eyes. Petrified, she alternately shrunk back or struck out whenever Grindley or Franklin came close to her.

Then she saw Charlotte. Her screams ceased as abruptly as they'd started. She sat upright on the folded blanket and sobbed pitifully, covering her eyes with one of her hands in a posture that was heartbreakingly mature.

Charlotte dropped to her haunches and looked over the side of the chest.

'Hello, Holly darling,' she said in a low voice.

'I . . . I . . . I want my Daddy,' Holly sobbed.

'I know, sweetheart, but Mummy will be here very soon.'

'Mummy?' Her face was awash with tears, the fair eyelashes stuck together. 'Is Mummy coming?' she asked in a trembling voice.

'Yes, sweetheart. Will you let me lift you out of there?'

Holly nodded slowly, once more clutching her doll which she'd cast aside when she'd fought off Grindley and Franklin.

'That's right, bring Flissy with you,' Charlotte said, gathering the little girl into her arms. As she stood up, she held Holly close, loving her in that moment as if she'd been

202

her own child. Her innocence seemed highlighted by the terrible ordeal she must have been through; there was something deeply touching about the way she clung round Charlotte's neck now, with Flissy wedged between them.

'Would you like a drink?' Charlotte asked softly.

Holly nodded. 'Where's Daddy?'

'He's . . . he's not here right now, but Mummy soon will be,' Charlotte added hurriedly, fighting back her own tears.

They hurried in procession down the stairs. Charlotte was thankful to see a couple of policemen holding a sheet over the bloodstained floor so Holly would not see it.

'How did you get into the chest, Holly?' David asked, as Charlotte carried her into the study. Her ordeal seemed to have affected him deeply.

Holly looked round the room, cowering in fear at seeing so many strangers. The ambulance unit waited to examine her. Several policemen hovered uncertainly, looking at her with a mixture of curiosity and disbelief. They had all been so sure she was dead, yet here she was, sitting on Charlotte's lap, clutching her doll.

'Drink,' she whispered.

'I'll get her some water,' Carol said, brisk once again, glad to have something to do.

'How are you feeling, love?' asked one of the ambulance men, dropping on to his knees before her and taking her hand.

Holly pulled away, and pressed herself against Charlotte.

'I think she's all right,' Charlotte said quietly. 'Very hot, but she doesn't seem to have any injuries.'

'She's probably very dehydrated. It's lucky she didn't suffocate,' he replied. 'Let her sip the water slowly. We'll take a look at her when she's more settled.'

'There are probably cracks in that old chest which would have let the air in,' said Carol, coming back with a glass of water.

David looked anxiously at Holly. Charlotte gave him a reassuring smile.

'She's going to be all right, sweetheart. Don't worry.'

'But how the hell did she get in there? And why was the key in Chris's pocket?'

'The main thing is she's alive and well.'

David spoke quietly to Holly. 'Can you tell us what happened, Holly?' he asked.

Holly turned away from him, refusing to talk. Grindley had drawn up a chair facing Charlotte, and for the first time that day he looked relaxed.

'We won't rush things,' he remarked, smiling at Holly. 'Let's go easy. She must have been locked in that chest for – ' he paused, looking down at his wristwatch to calculate – 'for twenty hours or more. Obviously what she has to say will be of vital importance, but she's been deeply traumatised; we'll take it at her pace.'

Charlotte nodded, kissing the top of Holly's head. The little girl smelled of dried urine and sweat, but otherwise she seemed unharmed; physically, anyway. Charlotte felt weak with relief. 'Are you all right, sweetheart?' she whispered, remembering how Holly had been on Christmas Day, her face ecstatic as she opened her presents. 'Would you like something to eat?'

Holly shook her head.

'What happened, Holly?' David persisted, gently but firmly, as he perched on the arm of a nearby chair. 'How did you get into the chest?'

Holly didn't answer.

'Well?'

Grindley signalled to him with a warning look not to continue.

'Take your time, Holly,' he said kindly. 'There's no hurry.'

'At least you had Flissy with you,' Charlotte said.

But Holly remained silent. She sipped the water while Charlotte held the glass, but refused to talk.

'Is Flissy the name of your dolly?' Grindley asked.

'You got her for Christmas, didn't you?' Carol asked encouragingly.

'Did you hear anything last night, Holly?'

Holly shrank even further back into Charlotte's arms; her mouth was set in stubborn lines. She kept looking down at her doll; nothing they said could break her silence.

'She's in shock,' Charlotte heard one of the ambulance crew mutter to another. 'Better leave her until her mother arrives.'

Charlotte kissed Holly again. 'Mummy will be here any minute now,' she said reassuringly. 'Won't that be nice?'

Grindley got to his feet, slowly and painfully as if his joints ached.

'I think I hear a car arriving now,' he said, going into the hall.

Chapter Eleven

Holly sat curled up on Linda's lap, refusing to speak. It was early evening and they'd all taken rooms at the Court Hotel, an old-fashioned and comfortable establishment six miles south of Barrow, where they could stay the night. The detective inspector had said he would be at the hotel at ten o'clock the next morning to question them all further.

The owners of the Court, Peter and Daphne Phillips, made their own private sitting room available so that the family would not be disturbed by the other guests. They'd also stationed their head gardener at the entrance to prevent the press, who had followed them from Chelwood, from pestering them.

Meanwhile, Holly was refusing to say anything. Her small mouth was stubbornly clamped shut, and the most she would do, in answer to Linda's questions, was to shake her head.

'She's in shock,' Carol kept saying. 'She may have seen what happened before she was locked in the chest.'

Neil looked worried. 'Don't you think you should get a doctor to look at her, Linda? She's obviously traumatised.' He watched Holly, sitting hunched and pale on her mother's knee, still clutching her beloved doll.

Linda shook her head. In spite of her exhaustion she was calm now, and fiercely protective of her daughter.

'She's been checked over by the ambulance crew,' she pointed out. 'There's nothing wrong with her physically and, as for being traumatised, that's not surprising. It will take time before she gets over her ordeal. I think peace and quiet is what she needs. As soon as she's had her supper I'll give her a warm bath and put her to bed.'

Holly, hearing, grabbed the lapel of Linda's jacket and held on to it tightly.

'It's all right, sweetheart,' said Linda, understandingly. 'I promise I won't leave you. Not for a moment. You can sleep in my bed tonight, would you like that?'

Still Holly said nothing, but her grip relaxed.

'Is there anything I can get either of you?' Charlotte asked. She felt more a part of the family now than she'd ever done. And she'd liked Linda from the moment she'd set eyes on her, rushing into the study at Chelwood, so relieved that Holly was alive she'd burst into tears. An exchange of looks between the two women at that moment had cemented an instant friendship. Holly was the bond they shared, and as Linda took the little girl into her arms, she realised that it had been Charlotte who'd been comforting her. Linda's gratitude showed in her response to Charlotte now.

'Thanks, love. Could you ask if her supper's nearly ready? I ordered a boiled egg and it seems a long time in coming.'

'Of course,' Charlotte replied. Denzil was putting Ben to bed in the family room they'd booked for the four of them, and she could see how much Linda depended on him. 'I won't be a moment.'

'Thanks. I want to get Holly off to bed, but she must eat something first.'

Charlotte hurried to the hotel's receptionist, and was told a waitress would be bringing Holly's supper within a few minutes.

'Is there anything else, madam?' The woman was eyeing her with undisguised curiosity. It wasn't every day a multiple murder took place in this peaceful part of the world.

'Not for the time being,' Charlotte said, 'but we're expecting my boyfriend, David Farrell, to arrive any moment. Could you tell him where we are?' David had remained behind at Chelwood Manor, to lock up under the supervision of the detective inspector. She'd wanted to stay behind with him, but he'd urged her to go ahead.

'I'll join you as soon as I can,' he'd said, his voice flat with weariness. 'I want to stay and find out who's going to clear up all . . . all this mess,' he added falteringly.

Then Denzil, dear dependable Denzil, had gone up to collect Holly's things from her room before they'd set off for the Court. Charlotte could see why Linda had married him. He bore a marked resemblance to Christopher. That is, Charlotte corrected herself, the Christopher she knew and liked. Not the wild, uncontrollable creature she'd had a glimpse of in her flat that day; not the Christopher who had killed his family in a frenzy; but an altogether quieter, more relaxed person, with a gentle sense of humour and a very kind nature.

As Charlotte returned to the hotel sitting room, accompanied by a waitress with Holly's tray, she found the others arguing. Linda sounded heated.

'I just know Chris didn't do it! They've got it all wrong.'

Carol answered carefully, aware that Holly's eyes were watchful and that she was listening to everything that was being said, 'I don't think there's any doubt about it, I'm afraid.'

'It's an open-and-shut case, Linda,' Neil agreed. 'Who else could it have been? Who else had a motive? I think you'll find Edmund and Chris had a fight over you-know-who – and things got out of hand . . .'

'I don't agree!' Linda said vehemently. As she spoke she deftly cracked open Holly's egg and started spreading butter on fingers of toast. 'We'll discuss it later,' she continued pointedly, 'but I know he would never do a thing like that.'

There was an awkward silence. Everyone had something to say, their own theories to put forward, but none could air them while Holly was there. Linda spooned the egg into her mouth, while Neil went off to order more drinks.

'All right, my sweetheart?' Linda asked Holly. 'Now, how about some lovely toast?'

But the little girl refused to eat any more and, tucking her doll tightly under her arm, leaned back with her eyes shut. A few minutes later she was fast asleep.

'I think I'll let her lie on the sofa for the time being,' Linda said, as she gently laid Holly among the cushions. 'There's no point in waking her up now in order to put her to bed.'

'Put this over her,' said Carol, offering her beige, hand-knitted cardigan. With Holly tucked up, sleeping soundly, the others relaxed. Within a few minutes Denzil joined them, reporting Ben to be settled for the night, too. Then David arrived.

'Are you OK, darling?' Charlotte asked, concerned. He looked terrible, red-eyed and hollow cheeked. He nodded briefly, but did not reply.

'Why don't we ask if we can have something to eat in here?' Denzil suggested. 'I don't suppose any of us wants to sit in the restaurant and be stared at.'

'Good idea,' Linda agreed.

'Not that I'm hungry,' Carol remarked, 'but I suppose we should eat something.'

Neil suggested sandwiches and coffee, and more drinks. While he went to arrange it, and David sat slumped holding Charlotte's hand, Linda returned to what she'd been saying earlier. She addressed herself to David initially.

'I don't believe it was Chris who did this,' she began. 'I can't even imagine why the police think it was him.'

David looked surprised. 'But, Linda, you only arrived on the scene this afternoon. Charlotte and I have been there since half-past ten this morning. We saw what had happened. Of course it was Chris, for God's sake, he still had the gun in his hand! He'd shot himself in the neck . . .'

Carol turned away with a gesture of horror.

'I'm sorry, Aunt Carol,' he continued, 'but it's absurd for Linda to think anyone else *could* have done it. You heard the police? There was no sign of anyone breaking and entering. Nothing has been stolen. Dad and Chris must have had a fight about that woman in the village . . .'

'I know all about Olivia Middleton,' Linda cut in. 'Chris told me all about her, and I'm certain he wasn't jealous of his father because, as he told me, he had no need to be. It was Chris she loved and he knew it. He loved her, too. And when you think of it, he had everything to live for; he actually had a future for the first time in ages.'

'I wonder if the police have talked to Olivia?' Charlotte

asked suddenly. 'My God, I suppose she knows what's happened?'

'She must know. The whole village is in chaos,' Carol said in a matter-of-fact voice. 'She'd have to be deaf and blind not to know.'

Linda looked at her curiously. 'Didn't you like her, Carol?'

Carol sniffed. 'How could I like a woman who went off with my sister's husband! And, not satisfied with that, then went off with her son!'

'I met her once, briefly,' said Linda slowly. 'She and Chris came to pick up Holly one afternoon, to take her to the zoo.'

The others waited.

'I rather liked her,' Linda continued. 'I feel very sorry for her now. I must try to get over to see her tomorrow. At least we've got each other: I gather she has no one.'

'I don't suppose she'll be alone for long,' Carol retorted.

Linda ignored the remark, and turned to David again. 'You don't believe Chris shot your parents and then committed suicide, do you?'

'Whether I believe it or not is immaterial; it happened,' he replied in broken tones.

'David's right,' Charlotte said.

Denzil came back into the room at that moment and, hearing David's words, asked, 'Have the police confirmed it?'

'Yes,' David replied, and Charlotte nodded to Linda, as if to confirm what David said was true.

'It seems to me there are a hundred unexplained factors and loose ends that don't add up,' Linda argued crisply.

'What about Holly? Why was she locked in a chest? It's a miracle she didn't suffocate.'

The others looked at her in silence, unable to suggest any explanation.

David spread his hands in a gesture of helplessness. 'Look, Mum phoned me and *told* me what was happening. I wish to God I'd realised how serious the row was, but being in London, I doubt I could've got here in time . . .' He trailed off, clearly distressed and Charlotte squeezed his hand reassuringly.

'And the police are really satisfied with that theory?' Linda persisted.

'It's fact, not theory,' Neil interjected. 'If David hadn't had that call from Virginia, then the case might be open to doubt, but knowing how Chris was capable of flaring up, it seems to me to be quite straightforward.'

Linda looked at them all, and her expression was candid. 'I'm sorry, but I don't believe it for a second,' she said bluntly.

The room was silent and they all looked at her.

'Why are you upsetting David like this?' Charlotte asked.

'And why are you defending Chris, dear?' Carol added. 'Because he was Holly's father? That's understandable, I suppose.'

Linda blinked. Her eyes were wet with tears, although her voice remained steady. 'It's not just because he was Holly's father. I still cared about him.' She turned to Denzil with a watery smile. 'Denzil has been married before, he understands that, just because you're divorced from someone, you don't necessarily stop caring for them. But, more importantly, I knew Chris better than anyone. All his faults.

All his weaknesses. We remained close, you know, even after we parted. He would never kill Virginia and Edmund, and he would never take his own life. For one thing, he loved Holly too much to do anything to hurt her.'

'Oh, come on, Linda,' David protested. 'I was fond of Chris, we all were, but both Charlotte and I have seen him fly into a terrible rage over nothing! Tell Linda about that time in your flat, La,' he urged.

Charlotte repeated what had happened.

Linda listened carefully. Then she nodded.

'Yes, that's typical of Chris,' she agreed. 'Temper exploding. A rush of adrenaline, fisticuffs! Yes, that was Chris all right. But not what happened at Chelwood. That was quite different.'

'In what way?' Neil asked. 'Neither Virginia or Edmund would have been a match for him if he'd become violent. This time he just happened to have a gun in his hand. What's the difference?'

'There's all the difference in the world!' Linda flashed back. 'If Chris had got into a fight with his father, he might have knocked him down, hit him a few times, but he'd never have laid a hand on Virginia. Never. No matter how high he was on drugs when we were married, he never hit me; he'd never touch a woman.'

'Whose gun was it anyway?' Denzil asked.

'It was Edmund's,' Neil said. 'I recognised it at once.'

'That's another thing,' Linda continued, doggedly. 'When Chris lost his temper it was over in a flash. By the time he'd gone to the gun room yesterday, unlocked the cupboard, taken the gun out, then loaded it, he'd have calmed down. He did become violent at times, but never for more than a few moments, and then it was all over. These murders seem too meditated for him.'

'That's all very well,' said Neil argumentatively, 'but the police think otherwise, and I must say, so do I.'

David spoke gently now. 'I know it's a terrible shock, Linda. It's a shock for us all, and it's especially bad for you because he was Holly's father, but I'm afraid we're going to have to face facts.'

Linda covered her face with her hands. Denzil put his arm around her and pulled her towards him.

'It's hard for her to accept,' he said softly.

Linda looked up and she was crying openly now.

'It's impossible for me to accept! I do not believe Chris did it!'

'Perhaps the post mortems will reveal something,' Charlotte remarked. She understood Linda's wanting to defend Chris, but she was upsetting the others. David, in particular, had had a gruelling day and looked close to collapse.

'What's there to be revealed?' he demanded. 'Mum and Dad were shot at point-blank range and Chris held the gun to his . . .' He buried his face in his hands.

'Please,' said Carol, troubled, and addressing Linda. 'Do we have to go into all this again? We're all very upset and tired.'

Neil plonked his empty glass down on the table. 'The sooner we get the inquest over the better. Then everything can be buttoned up and we can all try to get back to normal.'

'I still think the police have jumped to the wrong conclusions,' persisted Linda.

'Things may look different tomorrow, when Holly tells

us what happened,' said Charlotte, looking over at the sleeping child.

Linda said nothing, but reached out to stroke Holly's wayward blonde curls.

'Poor baby,' she whispered, almost to herself. 'She must have been so frightened.'

As Charlotte got dressed the next morning, she watched the eight o'clock news on breakfast television. David, showering in the adjoining bathroom, rushed through, a towel slung round his hips.

It was the lead story, and as the commentator described what had happened, they watched a shaky aerial shot of Chelwood Manor, filmed from a helicopter. It showed the activity in the drive, with the police cars, vans and ambulances resembling Dinky toys. Uniformed figures hurried to and fro. An exterior shot of the three-pillared entrance followed, with Grindley talking to another police officer, and then suddenly the screen was filled with Chris's face, smiling and genial. Charlotte gave a little cry of shock. He looked so well and happy in the picture, it was hard to realise he was now dead. She recognised it as a photograph that had stood on Edmund's desk, and she wondered how the film crew had got hold of it. A moment later, shots of Virginia and Edmund flashed on to the screen, old-fashioned, grainy black-and-white photographs taken a long time ago.

'Oh, David . . . !' she said brokenly, putting her arm round his waist. He was watching the television as if he couldn't believe what he was seeing, his hand covering his mouth.

' . . . It is thought Virginia and Edmund Farrell's twenty-six-year-old son, Christopher Farrell, shot his parents following a dispute, before shooting himself,' said the commentator in a flat, expressionless voice.

Grindley's face, grave and full of self-importance, filled the screen next.

'We are not looking for any other suspect,' he confirmed.

'What about the little girl, Holly Farrell, who was found locked in a chest?' asked the interviewer, his back to the camera as he thrust a microphone under the nose of the detective inspector.

'Well, the little girl hasn't told us anything yet, but we are not expecting the facts to change, even when she is able to talk. Someone locked her in the chest, most likely for her own protection, and the important thing is she's safe and well.'

'Have you any idea who could have locked her up like that? Might she not have suffocated?'

Grindley nodded. 'Yes, indeed. At the present time I am unable to comment on that, but I hope to make a statement within the next forty-eight hours.'

'But you're pretty confident it might have been her father?'

The interviewer, Charlotte thought, was like a dog worrying a bone.

'I cannot confirm that at this stage.'

Charlotte looked at David. 'Is that true, d'you think?'

'I suppose it's possible,' David said slowly.

'We'd better go down and have breakfast,' Charlotte observed. 'Grindley will be here at ten.'

When they arrived in the downstairs hall of the Court,

there was a collection of newspapers on a table by the reception desk. David strode straight over to them and picked one of them up.

'Take a look at that!' He sounded appalled. The headline was bold and black: THE ONLY SURVIVOR. Below it was a photograph of Holly being carried out of Chelwood Manor, the previous afternoon, in Linda's arms. There were also pictures of David, looking drawn and upset, and of Charlotte wiping her eyes with a handkerchief.

'Oh, my God!' she exclaimed. In lurid terms, she read of the 'massacre' of the family, the 'bloodstained interior of a luxury mansion', and how 'when four-year-old Holly finally talks, she may reveal all'.

There was a commotion in the driveway of the Court at that moment, a couple of flashes from press cameras, and then she saw a crowd of reporters and photographers trying to get past the two gardeners who were guarding the entrance.

David grabbed her hand, dragging her out of sight down a corridor that led to the hotel lounge. At that moment, the owner, Peter Phillips, appeared. He looked harassed.

'I've set aside a room for you all at the back of the hotel. We usually use it for conferences. It will give you a modicum of privacy.' He glanced towards the drive through the glass entrance door.

'I'm going to ring the police to see if we can't get the press to leave you alone.'

'Thanks,' said David gratefully.

Linda and Denzil joined them a few minutes later. She looked as if she hadn't slept. Holly was in her arms, clinging round her neck. Denzil followed with Ben.

'Did you have a bad night?' Charlotte asked as they took their place round a table in a corner set for breakfast. It was rather like sitting in isolation in an aircraft hangar, Charlotte thought, looking around the big and bare conference room, the pale green walls seeming to echo every sound.

'Never slept a wink,' Linda replied, smiling wanly.

'How did you sleep, Holly?' Charlotte asked, coaxingly. 'Flissy looks well!'

Holly looked back at her with a faint smile, but said nothing. Charlotte looked inquiringly at Linda, who shook her head.

'Not a dicky-bird,' Linda replied. 'I'm beginning to think it may take some time. I think if we go home today and get back to normal as quickly as possible, it will help.'

Charlotte nodded, understanding.

Carol and Neil appeared and, in silence, two waiters served breakfast. No one had anything left to say. The previous day had left them bankrupt of words and numbed of feeling. A curious calm had descended on them all, and Charlotte found it momentarily peaceful. It was a respite from the horror and grief of the previous day and she wondered how long it would last.

Death had never touched her before. This new experience left her feeling strange; stranded on unfamiliar territory, wondering when the ground would crack wide beneath her feet again, wondering when feeling would return to her atrophied emotions. To her surprise she'd slept better than she could have hoped and, when she'd first awoken, she hadn't been able to remember where she was. Only David by her side had been a recognisable factor. Then memories of yesterday had come crowding back. She'd expected a rush

219

of emotion to return to overwhelm her, but instead she'd felt nothing. Curiously light without the burden of grief and horror, she felt she could cope with whatever the day might bring.

Detective Inspector Tom Grindley arrived just before ten, accompanied by Ron Franklin. Charlotte wondered if they worked in tandem, like those detectives in television plays who always have a sidekick.

'How's everyone today?' he asked briskly, looking round the breakfast table. A variety of murmurs responded to his greeting.

'I'd like to talk to each of you individually, and I'd like to start with you, Mrs Blake,' he said to Linda. 'And Holly,' he added pointedly.

Charlotte and David, Carol, Neil and Denzil decided to go back to their rooms rather than wait in the public lounge.

'Franklin will come and fetch you when you're needed,' Grindley informed them. 'This is not going to take long, and then you'll all be free to go.'

When they were alone, he turned back to Linda, his expression hopeful. 'Has Holly been talking about her experience yet?'

Linda shook her head. 'No. She's not talking at all, not about anything. I'm really worried about her.'

Grindley's manner was reassuring. 'This is not unusual in small children after they've had a severe shock. The important thing is not to try to push her too hard. I'll get a police doctor to come right over to have a look at her. I think his advice will be to treat her normally until the shock gradually wears off. It might take a bit of time, though. We don't know how much she saw.'

Linda nodded. 'Can I take her back to London today? I realise she's a vital link in your discovering what happened, but I think the sooner she's home, the quicker she will recover.'

'I agree. And she's not that vital a link. I mean, basically, we know what happened. Of course, it's important for us to know who locked her in the chest, but we have our own theories: I doubt that whatever Holly has to say will change anything.'

'But you're assuming it was my ex-husband who did the shooting, and I'm sure it wasn't.' Linda sounded heated. 'I was married to him for several years, Inspector; I knew that man through and through. He would never do a thing like this.'

Grindley observed her gravely, his head cocked to one side. What he saw before him was a motherly-looking young woman, low on glamour but high on common sense. She spoke with utter conviction, too, and although she sounded angry, she was far from being hysterical.

'Tell me what you really think happened,' he suggested, more to humour her than anything else. Even the most sensible people, in his experience, could have a blind spot towards those they were fond of.

'I think someone with a grudge against the family killed them,' Linda replied. 'Probably someone they knew, which would explain why there wasn't a forced entry. Not many people liked Edmund Farrell, you know. I believe he'd made enemies in the business world before he retired. For all we know, that person, not wishing to harm an innocent child, may have hidden Holly in the chest himself.'

'And then planted the key on Christopher Farrell?'

Grindley shook his head, almost amused. 'I don't think that's likely, Mrs Blake. That would leave this person open to being identified by Holly.'

'It's only a theory,' Linda admitted, 'but all I know is, it wasn't Chris. I'd stake my life on it.'

'Let's hope that will not be necessary,' Grindley remarked with an attempt at dry humour.

Charlotte was the last one to be subjected to Grindley's questioning.

'I didn't know them very well,' she said, candidly. 'Chris I knew better than his parents, but I've only been going out with David for four months.'

Grindley pressed on. 'Did you speak to Mrs Farrell when she phoned the other evening?'

'No. I was in the shower at the time.'

'But you were in the room when David Farrell phoned her back a few minutes later?'

'Yes, I was, but the line was busy, so he never got through.'

'So the first you knew about the incident was when the police called at your flat the next morning, to inform Mr Farrell what had happened?'

'Yes.'

'Right. I'm sorry I've had to go through this again, Miss Taylor, but I don't think we shall be troubling you any more.'

'Have you talked to Olivia Middleton? She lives in Barrow?' Charlotte asked curiously.

'As a matter of fact, I'm seeing her this afternoon. Why do you ask?'

'She was friends with both Edmund Farrell and Chris; she might know something,' Charlotte suggested. She didn't want to meddle in the affairs of David's family, but she had a gut feeling that Olivia might be able to throw some light on what had happened.

'Wasn't she somewhat more than a friend?'

Charlotte looked away. What she did not want to do was discuss the sex lives of David's father and brother.

'Possibly,' she said, guardedly. 'I've only met her once but Chris seemed very fond of her.'

'Quite so.' Grindley rose, bringing their meeting to an end. The others – with the exception of Denzil and Ben – came back into the conference room. Holly clung to Linda's hand. She'd refused to speak to Grindley when he'd seen her earlier; now she buried her face in her mother's skirt.

'It's all right, darling,' Linda said reassuringly.

'We'll leave her alone for the time being, I'm sure she'll open up soon,' Grindley remarked, purposely keeping his distance from her. 'I'm just off to take a statement from Gladys Scovell.'

'How is Gladys bearing up?' Carol asked.

'She's still very shocked.'

'So many people are shocked by what's happened,' Ron Franklin volunteered, speaking for the first time. 'Nothing like this has ever happened in Barrow.'

'Nothing has *ever* happened in Barrow,' Neil said dryly. His consumption of whisky the previous evening had left him with a crushing hangover, and all he wanted to do now was to get off home.

Mabel arrived at the usual time at Magnolia Cottage, agog to find out how Olivia was bearing up. To her surprise she found her already dressed, and sitting at her writing table

in the drawing room. Her make-up was meticulously applied
and her hair caught back with a black velvet bow; only
swollen eyelids betrayed a sleepless night spent in tears.

'Can I get your breakfast, Mrs Middleton?' Mabel
inquired.

'Only coffee today, thank you,' Olivia replied without
looking up as she continued to write.

'Not even a bit of toast?'

'No, thank you.'

'Shall I leave something for your luncheon, then?'

'Nothing, thank you, Mabel.' She glanced up. Her mouth
was set in a taut line, her dark eyes unblinking.

'I shall be leaving for London this afternoon.'

'Very well. Will you be back tomorrow, then?'

'I'm not coming back at all, Mabel.'

The older woman's jaw dropped. Her eyes widened.
'What, never?'

'That's right. I'm selling the house. My lawyer will see
to everything. I'll give you a cheque for what I owe you.'
Olivia's voice was expressionless.

'Then you won't be wanting me no more, Mrs
Middleton?'

'I'm afraid not.'

'We'll be sorry to see you go.' Mabel looked around at
the sombre room she had dusted and polished every day for
the past year. 'Where will you be going, then? To live in
London?'

'I'm not sure yet.' Olivia had picked up her pen again. It
was a sign of dismissal from her presence. Then she
remembered something.

'A police officer is coming to see me, to discuss . . .' For the first time her voice faltered. Then she seemed to pull herself together. 'He'll be here at noon. Will you please show him in? Then you can get off home.'

'Yes, Mrs Middleton.'

Mabel returned to the kitchen, where she made herself a cup of tea. She'd do a quick wipe round before she left. No use killing herself if the house was going to be left empty. It wasn't until she went up to the bedroom that the impact of what Olivia had told her sank in. In the middle of the floor a dozen suitcases were neatly stacked. The hanging cupboards and shelves had been emptied, and all the bottles of perfume on the dressing-table removed. The room had a stripped, desolate air, more as if the occupant had died than was planning to go away.

Mabel made the bed with its oyster-satin hangings for the last time. She was going to miss coming here. It had been a real eye-opener, seeing how someone like Olivia Middleton lived. When she'd first gone to work at Magnolia Cottage, she'd had that much to tell her friends in the village, she was forever being invited in for cups of tea so she could describe what it was like. Those dark heavy brocade and velvet hangings! That long sofa, covered in black satin, with a whole leopard skin thrown over it, casual-like; the exotic paintings, the perfumed candles, the light from the windows blocked out by great plants . . . There was something so seductive about the place that it was no wonder Edmund crept over under cover of darkness, to where the fragile black and white occupant awaited his arrival like a spider in her web. But then there was the young Mr Farrell, too! Mabel shook her head as she ran a duster over the bare dressing-table.

What goes around, comes around, Mabel reflected. Those who are up to no good perish in the end, she thought darkly.

At noon the front door bell rang, and Mabel went to let in Grindley and Franklin. She'd met them the previous evening when they'd gone to interview Gladys.

'This way, sir,' she said civilly, although she thought they were a pair of fools. Where was their common sense? How come they were going around questioning people, unable to see what was right under their noses?

'It's like the police have drawn a sketch,' she told Gladys, 'but they're letting someone else fill in the colours.'

'Yes, Christopher Farrell was here yesterday,' Olivia told Grindley.

Franklin was writing everything down on his pad.

'Was he on his own?' Grindley asked.

'Yes.'

'Where was his little girl, Holly, then?'

'She was with her grandmother. Mrs Farrell was going to show Holly how to make fairy cakes, Chris told me, and then there was something on television she thought Holly would enjoy.'

Grindley knew all about Olivia Middleton's having an affair with both the father and son; for someone who'd been so recently, doubly bereaved, she was being incredibly calm.

'How did Christopher Farrell seem?'

'Perfectly all right,' Olivia replied. 'He was well and very happy. We'd made plans for later on this week . . .' For the first time she faltered and, blinking rather rapidly, she pressed her lips together.

'When did you last see Edmund Farrell?' Grindley continued.

'Three days ago,' she replied immediately. 'He came over to see me after dinner.'

'He was on his own, too, I presume?' Grindley tried to keep the edge of sarcasm out of his voice.

Olivia raised her chin and looked directly at him. Her dark eyes were filled with pain. 'I'm not going to bother denying I was having an affair with both men. I expect half the village has told you about it. Yes, Edmund came on his own, and he stayed until after midnight.'

'Tell me, Mrs Middleton, are you still married? Is there a Mr Middleton around, who perhaps might take objection to your personal life?'

'There is a Mr Middleton around,' she admitted. 'But he lives in Monte Carlo with the nineteen-year-old secretary he ran off with whilst married to me. I think it's highly unlikely he'd be interested in what I do these days.'

Grindley glanced at Franklin to make sure he was getting it all down.

'Anyway,' Olivia continued smoothly, 'according to the news this morning, you don't suspect anyone of the shooting. You seem to think it was Christopher Farrell.'

'And you don't, Mrs Middleton?' he continued swiftly.

Olivia looked long and hard at him again. Finally she spoke. 'He was capable of it,' she agreed. 'Chris could get into a terrible rage.'

'Have you ever seen him get into one of these rages?'

She nodded. 'It was stupid, really. We were stuck in a traffic jam in London, and someone tried to edge in to get ahead of us. Chris went mad.'

'Have you any idea what the fight could have been about the other evening?'

'Do we know Chris and his father were fighting?' she asked curiously.

'Yes, Mrs Middleton. I gather they might have been fighting over you. Is that possible?'

She pursed her lips and looked down at the papers on her desk. 'Maybe Edmund had cause to be jealous,' she said at length, 'but Christopher didn't. He should have known that.'

'Where were you on Friday evening, around five-thirty?'

'I was here.'

Grindley's brows furrowed, and there was a perceptible pause. 'At around five-thirty?' he repeated.

'Yes. He came to tea and he didn't leave here until after six.'

Franklin continued to scribble frantically.

Grindley had one more question. 'You fully intended to continue your affair with both men? Even if it caused trouble between them?'

She flushed then, and looked away. 'Yes,' she replied simply.

'Is there anything else you'd like to tell me?'

'There's nothing more to tell. I'm leaving here. Going away for good. You won't need to see me again, will you?'

She looked so thin and vulnerable, but then Grindley remembered she was capable of being ruthless enough in her love affairs, and he asked gruffly, 'Where will you be going?'

'London to begin with. After that, I don't really know. I'm putting this house on the market and my lawyer will be

228

handling everything. I can give you his name and you can always get hold of me through him.' As she spoke, she reached for pen and paper and started to write.

Chapter Twelve

Charlotte and David returned one week later to Barrow for the joint funerals of Edmund, Virginia and Christopher. Held in the little Norman church by the village green, friends and relatives came from far and wide to pay their last respects. None was prepared, though, for the hordes of newsmen and photographers who had been camping outside the church since dawn. Like a re-run of the day of the shooting, television crews and the journalists jostled each other for the best position, regardless of the feelings of the congregation.

'It's disgusting,' Carol commented, her skin pale and puffy-looking against the unbecoming black of her coat and hat. She and Neil were sharing the first car in the funeral cortège with David and Charlotte, and they all felt a sense of shock when they saw they were to be the target of dozens of camera lenses.

In the second car, Linda and Denzil shared the same feelings.

'I do think we should be allowed a little privacy,' Linda said angrily. 'What do they want? Pictures of us all weeping? Well, I for one am not going to give them that satisfaction.'

Denzil squeezed her hand. 'Good girl.'

'I suppose they're hoping to get pictures of Holly. That

would really make their day, wouldn't it?' she added bitterly.

'You were right to leave her and Ben with your mother.'

Linda nodded. 'Nothing would have induced me to let her go through this circus.' As their car slowed down, the photographers pressed closer, cameras thrust forward; a hundred rainbow-hued probing eyes, shutters blinking, clicked away like distant gunfire.

'God, will I be glad when this is over,' Linda remarked in heartfelt tones.

'I suppose we have to go to the cremation after this service?'

She looked at Denzil, thankful for his presence. 'I'm afraid so, love. This is something I have to do. For me. For Holly. And because, in spite of the inquest, I'm still damn certain Chris didn't do it.'

'I know, sweetheart.' Denzil didn't argue because he didn't want to upset her more than was necessary. She'd been so devastated when the inquest had found Chris guilty of the murder of his parents, that she'd sworn to prove his innocence, no matter how long it took.

'I owe it to Holly, if not to Chris himself,' she told him.

Denzil wasn't so sure, although he didn't say so. David, Carol and Neil were convinced it was Chris, and so were the police. Common sense told Denzil it couldn't really be anyone else. When he'd talked about it with the others, Charlotte had put his own feelings into words

'Why should it *not* be Chris?' she'd asked.

At the time he'd replied: 'Because Linda doesn't want it to be.' That was the crux of it, as far as he was concerned. As Holly's mother and Christopher's ex-wife, Linda didn't want to face the facts. She wanted the memory of Chris to be untarnished. She wanted Holly to grow up remembering her father with pride. Denzil held Linda's hand tighter. In spite of his inner reservations, he had vowed to help her in whatever she did to try and prove Christopher's innocence. For Holly's sake as well as Linda's.

Charlotte and David, with Carol and Neil, took their places in the front pew on the left of the aisle, while Linda and Denzil sat on the opposite side with some cousins of Edmund. Subdued organ music filled the air with a melancholy atmosphere as the congregation stared at the three coffins placed in a row. On each pale oak coffin, identical sprays of spring flowers reposed, their bright colours in contrast to the old grey stone walls of the church.

Charlotte, her hand in David's, felt his despair. As the choir sang 'Lead Us, Heavenly Father, Lead Us', David wept. Biting back her own tears, she swore to do everything in her power to comfort him; one day she'd make him happy again. His loss was devastating, but he still had her, and she would always be with him. This past week had drawn them even closer together. Somehow, she promised herself, in the years that lie ahead, I will try and make up to him for all he has lost.

The cremation, in Devizes, was attended only by the immediate family. Afterwards they joined the rest of the mourners at the Court Hotel for a ritual gathering, which David had organised with Neil's help.

Charlotte didn't know anyone. Distant relatives and old friends of the Farrells greeted each other with a mixture of sadness and curiosity. The air was filled with muted exclamations of horror as the more knowledgeable told the less well informed the details of what had happened. David was immediately surrounded by a bevy of elderly ladies, each trying to outdo the other in expressing their sympathy; Charlotte was proud to see how dignified and courteous he was. Then she overheard two elderly gentlemen, of military bearing, gossiping as they downed their whisky and sodas.

'I suppose he'll give up work altogether now,' one of them remarked. 'Ever since he's been a boy, David has hated work in any shape or form.'

Charlotte edged nearer.

The second one spoke. 'Trouble is, Virginia spoilt him. He thinks the world owes him a living. I remember Edmund telling me so.'

The first one spoke again. 'No doubt she over-compensated when Christopher was born. Edmund told me it didn't stop David from being jealous, though.'

'How much does he stand to inherit now?'

Charlotte stood immobilised, feeling astounded. Out of the corner of her eye she could see the first old gentleman cast his eyes to the ceiling as he did a mental calculation.

'If he sells Chelwood and everything in it, he could probably get over a million. Edmund also had a great deal of money in stocks and shares. All in all, he'll inherit around two million.'

'Not bad, considering where he came from! Come on, old chap, let's go to the bar to get another drink.'

Together they shambled off and Charlotte looked after them, wide eyed. David inherit two million? Reeling with shock herself, she wondered if David, in the midst of his own horror and grief, had stopped to realise what his parents' death would mean for him: that he would now inherit his father's entire fortune, and Chelwood Manor, too. And what had the old man meant by, 'Not bad considering where he came from?' Was that a snobbish allusion to Edmund having been a self-made man? She glanced over at their stooping back-views as they got their glasses refilled, and felt deep anger. What a horrid thing to say at a time like this, she reflected. How spiteful, and how unfair to David.

Linda and Denzil came over to her at that moment. Denzil held an extra glass of champagne in his hand which he gave to her.

'Have this, Charlotte. You look as if you need it,' he said.

She took the proffered glass gratefully.

'Are you all right, love?' Linda inquired, her kind eyes searching Charlotte's face with compassion. 'You must have had a terrible week holding David together; he's heartbroken, isn't he?'

'It has been tough,' Charlotte admitted. 'I hope once today is over, we can get back to some form of normality.'

'I've just heard,' Denzil said, 'that the police are going to clean up Chelwood. Burn the stained carpets and everything, and send in a band of cleaners to scrub the place from top to bottom. They've been liaising with Neil, to spare David's feelings.'

Charlotte shuddered. 'God, what an awful job! I wondered who's going to do it?'

'Is David going to live at Chelwood, then?' Linda inquired.

'Oh, I hope not!' Charlotte exclaimed, appalled. 'I never want to set foot in that place again!'

'Neither do I,' Linda agreed. 'I never liked the house in

the first place. It always had a sinister atmosphere; but I put that down to the occupants,' she added dryly.

'The police are certainly being very helpful,' Denzil remarked. 'I heard they only released the bodies as soon as this in order to spare all our feelings, and so that we could get the funeral over and done with. That's why they've ordered the house to be cleaned up too. I must say it does make one regard them as more human, doesn't it?'

'Did they say when the pathologist's report would be through?' Charlotte asked.

'In a couple of weeks, I gather,' Denzil replied.

'I'd like to know what they say about the case,' said Linda.

Charlotte looked at her in surprise. 'What do you mean? It will only tell where they were shot, and what injuries were sustained; it won't alter the verdict at the inquest, will it?'

Linda's jaw hardened. 'I don't know,' she said dully. 'All I know is that Chris didn't do it. If I'd thought he was capable of that, do you suppose I'd have let Holly go down to Chelwood with him? I know I imposed conditions, but I never minded him taking her down to stay with her grandparents. I thought Chelwood was the safest place for her to *be*, if she wasn't with *me*!' Her voice had risen, and several people stopped talking to turn and look at her.

Denzil took her arm. 'Easy there, love,' he said gently.

Her eyes shone with angry tears, and Charlotte looked at her uneasily. Linda was usually so calm and controlled.

'Has Holly spoken about what happened yet?' she asked tentatively.

Linda shook her head. 'She's talking again, though not

much, but whenever I mention Chris, or Chelwood, she clams up. Refuses to say a word.'

'She's been examined by a child psychiatrist and a counsellor, but they can't get anything out of her either,' Denzil affirmed.

'Can they guess when she'll start talking about it?' Charlotte said, wondering if Holly had blocked out her experience so entirely that she remembered nothing of it.

Denzil shrugged. 'Frankly, they've no idea. They say that one day something will click in her head, a mental door will open, and then she'll tell us what she saw. Until then, there's nothing we can do.'

'Poor Holly.' Charlotte thought of the merry little girl she had first known, and how the tragedy had changed her.

At that moment they were joined by Carol who, having got the sadness of the funeral and cremation over, was now tucking into champagne and rather enjoying seeing so many of her old friends.

She looked around the crowded conference room and spoke conspiratorially. 'I half wondered if she'd turn up today.'

'Who?' Linda inquired.

'You know. The woman in the village. It wouldn't have surprised me, I'll never forget her nerve in turning up on Christmas Day.' Carol turned to Charlotte for support. 'Brazen, wasn't it?'

'It was . . . unfortunate,' Charlotte agreed.

'I presume you're talking about Olivia Middleton?' Linda looked levelly at Carol. 'I don't suppose she had the gall to come here today.'

'Do we know where she's gone?' Denzil inquired. 'Neil

237

told me she'd left Magnolia Cottage.'

'Nobody seems to know where she's fled to,' retorted Carol.

Linda and Denzil started moving away. 'Charlotte, are you coming to the bar to get another drink?' Denzil asked, offering her an excuse to escape from Carol.

'Oh! Oh, yes. Thanks.'

'I must find Neil, anyway,' Carol announced. 'We ought to be getting home. It's quite a drive and we've had a long day. No doubt I'll be seeing you again, Charlotte?'

'Yes. Of course.'

Linda and Denzil too had decided to head back home to London.

'My mother is looking after Holly and Ben,' Linda explained, 'but I'll call you, La. We must get together.' She hugged Charlotte affectionately and kissed her on both cheeks. 'You've been a brick, caring for David ever since this nightmare started. It must be awful for you, finding yourself in the middle of somebody else's family drama. And thank you again for being so sweet to Holly.'

Charlotte's eyes started to prick. 'I love Holly,' she said simply.

'Doesn't everyone?' said Denzil, with understanding. 'She got right under my skin before I even noticed her mother!' he teased, putting his arm round Linda's waist.

They laughed, a welcome reaction to Denzil's skilful defusing of the moment. Then he looked serious again. 'Take care of yourself, La,' he said.

People began to drift away; there was a distinct feeling of relief that this dreaded day was over at last, and everyone could now go back to their own homes, and their own lives to pick up the threads of their existence again. Everyone, that is, except the immediate family.

For a moment, Charlotte felt envy. The strain of the past week had left her feeling so drained that she longed to crawl away to some dark, quiet place where she could rest. When would life ever get back to normal for her and David? She remembered the conversation she'd overheard and for a moment she felt a shudder of unease, before she recovered herself. She had David, and together they would overcome any difficulties in the future.

Everyone had gone, and only David was left, standing by the bar, talking to two young men and a tall girl in her twenties.

'Come and join us,' he called out when he saw Charlotte standing uncertainly watching them.

'Meet Andrew Newton, Trevor Newton and their gorgeous sister, Natalie Newton. This is La. Charlotte Taylor!' he said by way of introduction. 'They're cousins of mine, La. Through my mother. Isn't that right?' He turned and looked at the others, and she realised he was drunk. 'They're second cousins, once removed,' he continued. 'Although I never understand the "removed" bit!'

'Hello,' said Charlotte politely. The men were tall, well dressed, with charming though bland faces and stupid eyes. Natalie was altogether different, stylish with long blonde hair showing under a large black fedora, and an avaricious expression. She eyed Charlotte from top to toe before dragging her black cashmere and fox-fur cape around her. Her eyes were unfriendly and she said nothing.

Charlotte, who suddenly felt very dowdy, looked appealingly at David.

'Shall we go?'

'David said he'd give us a lift,' Natalie drawled. 'We've got to get back to town and we were afraid we'd have to take a train.'

Charlotte looked at her squarely. 'How did you get here?' she asked bluntly.

Natalie raised finely plucked eyebrows. 'We came over from Newbury, in the Roller, with our parents, but they had to go back home.'

'Ish no problem,' David cut in hurriedly, his words slurred.

Charlotte looked doubtful. 'I think I'd better drive, then. I've only had one drink. Can I have the car keys, please, David?'

'Shertainly not,' he replied, giggling suddenly.

'I must drive,' Charlotte contradicted him firmly. 'With your job, you can't afford to lose your licence.'

'Oh, fuck the job!' he chortled. 'They can go stuff themselves!'

The journey back to London was like a bad dream. Charlotte, at the wheel, drove David's car with skill, but as it grew dark it also started to rain, and David got irritable because she wouldn't go faster.

'It's not safe,' Charlotte protested. 'Besides, there is such a thing as a speed limit.'

David, who had insisted in clambering into the back of the car with Natalie and Trevor, while Andrew sat in the front with Charlotte, continued to give instructions whilst waving a half-filled bottle of champagne he'd taken with him when they'd left the Court Hotel.

'Get into the outside lane, for God's sake, or we'll be here all night,' he shouted at one point.

Charlotte gritted her teeth, trying to make allowances for his behaviour. It was obviously a reaction to what he'd been through, but she wished to God they were alone. It would have been easier then to reason with him. As it was, Natalie and Trevor were giggling on either side of him, at some joke they chose to keep private and, from time to time, grabbing the bottle and taking a swig from it.

'I'm doing my best, sweetheart,' she replied, keeping her tone light. 'Why don't you have a snooze?'

'A *snooze*?' David laughed uproariously.

'What do you think he is, a baby?' Natalie laughed. 'Are you taking over as his mummy?'

The bad taste of her remark nauseated Charlotte.

'No,' she replied evenly, 'I'm not, but I think he needs peace and quiet after what he's just been through.'

'Ohhh! She does look after you, doesn't she? How sweet!' Natalie cooed.

Charlotte put her foot down hard on the accelerator and overtook a line of heavy vehicles. All she had to do now was to think of a way of getting rid of this bunch of morons as soon as they got into London.

David dozed, the bottle, now empty, resting between his thighs, his head back and his mouth partly open. The others had quietened down too and, under her cape of cashmere and fur, Natalie slept with her head on David's shoulder. As they swished along the A4, past Chiswick, David awoke and, sitting up, leaned forward and put his hand on Charlotte's shoulder.

'All right, my little angel?' he asked softly. He'd sobered up and there was a note of apology in his voice.

'Yes, I'm fine.'

'Sorry I got so pissed. This has to have been the worst day of my life.'

'I know, sweetheart. Let's have a really early night, and then it will be over,' Charlotte replied understandingly.

'Whose talking about an early night?' murmured a female voice from the rear seat. 'What a frightfully boring idea! We must all go out to dinner.'

'I think not,' said Charlotte, loudly and firmly. 'David and I have had a long day and now we're tired, and all we want to do is go to bed.'

'I don't think I want to know about your private lives!' Natalie trilled suggestively.

Charlotte ignored the remark.

'What's the time?' Andrew asked, peering at his wristwatch by the light of the dashboard. 'God, it's only half-past six!'

'Half-past six!' Natalie exclaimed. 'My dear, the night hasn't even begun yet!'

'I do rather fancy going out to dinner, you know,' David said thoughtfully. 'What do you say, La? You don't want to cook, and it would do us good to have a decent meal, wouldn't it? I've only had a slice of toast and a couple of sandwiches all day.'

'We *must* go out! How about the Connaught?' Natalie suggested.

Charlotte blinked. The Connaught, she'd heard, was so

expensive that even her father only used it for special clients.

David sounded more cheerful than he'd done all week. 'Let's pick up some wine at the off-licence on the corner, then we'll go back to our place, have a few drinks, and then go and dine somewhere.'

'Yeah!' the others chorused.

Charlotte's heart sank. Was this terrible day never to be over? Was she now to share this evening, when all she wanted to do was curl up in bed beside David, with these hellish cousins who were determined to have a good time?

Detective Inspector Tom Grindley watched as the chief constable turned the key in the heavy front door lock of Chelwood Manor before handing it to him.

'All done, sir. The place is as clean as a whistle. You'd never know anything had happened in there, now,' Franklin replied.

'What did you do with the bedding and the carpets?'

'The lads had a bonfire, sir, at the bottom of the garden.'

'Best thing.'

'Then we got in a firm of cleaners, sir. They scrubbed the place from top to toe. If the family want to move back in, you'd never know anything had happened.'

'What family, Franklin?' Grindley ribbed him mildly. 'There's only David Farrell left. He owns this pile, now, I suppose.'

'And the best of bleedin' luck to him, too, sir. I wouldn't have this gloomy old place if it were given to me on a platter.'

'Then how lucky for you it hasn't been,' observed his superior, dryly.

'D'you think David Farrell will want to live here, sir? After everything that's happened?'

Grindley shrugged. 'I doubt it. He looks too like a towny to want to be stuck in a place like this.'

'He'll get a good price for it, that's for sure.'

'It's a marked house, Franklin. Not everyone wants to buy a place where a crime has been committed. Leaves a nasty atmosphere, you know.'

Ron Franklin nodded sagely. 'You're right.'

'Let's be off, then. I'll post these keys to David Farrell. Apart from the formality of waiting for the pathologist's report, that just about wraps everything up.'

Linda phoned Charlotte two days after the funeral.

'How are you doing, love?' she asked, sounding calm and cheerful again.

'I'm OK,' Charlotte replied, without much conviction.

'How's David?'

'Not yet recovered from the funeral. We had the most hellish evening in living memory, too, with some cousins of his. They wanted a lift back to London, and then they insisted we go out to dinner and drink a lot of champagne . . . God, it was *ghastly*!' Charlotte spoke with such feeling that Linda gave a sympathetic chuckle.

'Poor you! It wasn't by any chance the Newtons, was it?' she asked.

'Yes,' Charlotte confirmed.

Linda's chuckle was deeper and richer. 'They're a nightmare family! Related to Virginia. They were always coming over to Chelwood when I was first married to Chris. Natalie was after him at one point. The girl's a slut.'

Charlotte recalled how she'd been all over David. Her heart pounded uncomfortably.

'She . . . she is quite attractive though, isn't she?' she said nervously.

'She's so dangerous she's safe,' Linda replied, confidently. 'She goes after men with such blatancy that everyone picks up the danger signals – including men. And they run for their lives! Subtle she is not!'

Charlotte laughed, reassured by Linda's attitude.

'Listen,' Linda continued, 'let's fix a date for lunch. Can you get away from work long enough to come here?'

'Yes, I'd love that. I'm longing to see Holly again, too.'

Linda laughed, 'I think she wants to see you! We're having a major tussle at the moment over the woollen scarf you gave her for her doll. I want to wash it, but apparently Flissy will die of cold if she's parted from it for ten seconds.'

'Tell her I'll bring a spare wrap for Flissy. We can't have Flissy catching a cold.'

'Holly's such a spoiled little girl,' Linda crowed indulgently. 'She'll love you for ever!'

'That's rather what I counted on!' Charlotte responded.

They fixed to meet two days later. When Charlotte arrived at the elegant little house in Islington, she was greeted by Holly in a tiny tartan kilt and a red polo-necked sweater. She had Flissy tucked expertly under one arm as she came running across the hall, but she stopped stock-still as soon as she saw Charlotte.

'Hello, Holly darling,' Charlotte said softly, dropping on to her haunches.

'Hello.' Suddenly the little girl looked shy.

'May I pick you up and kiss you?' Charlotte asked.

For answer, Holly opened her arms wide, smiled broadly, and flung herself at Charlotte.

'Hello, sweetheart,' Charlotte exclaimed, hugging her close. She smelt of baby shampoo and her cheeks were smooth and soft. 'How are you, darling? And how's Flissy?'

Linda, watching, grinned. 'Come and have a glass of wine, La.'

'Sounds great.' Carrying Holly, she followed Linda into the long, low, comfortably furnished drawing room. French windows at one end led on to a garden with a small lawn, at the far end of which was a swing and a climbing frame.

'Oh, what a lovely house,' Charlotte looked around appreciatively.

'I don't know about lovely,' Linda replied cheerfully. 'I should think, compared to the houses you do up, it's a complete shambles! Nothing matches anything. The furniture is a mish-mash from my mother's house and Denzil's family. It's only got one thing going for it, and that's comfort.' As she talked, she opened a bottle of chilled white wine and poured some into two glasses.

'You're not in a rush, are you?'

'Mercifully, Myra, my boss, is at a design exhibition in Manchester for two days, so although I've got a lot of work on, as long as it gets done, it doesn't matter when.'

'Great.' Linda, in cream trousers and a long, rose-coloured sweater, dropped into an armchair. 'We're only having pasta and salad, so let's relax for a while.'

Charlotte sat in a large, comfortable chair opposite and sipped her wine. She'd only been in the house five minutes, and yet already the tranquillity of the place was giving her a feeling of calmness.

As they chatted, Holly played on the sofa, wrapping and unwrapping her doll in the babies' blanket Charlotte had stopped off to buy on the way. She looked well and bright eyed, Charlotte thought, but every now and then she would stop to look at first her mother and then Charlotte, as if she were listening intently to what they were saying. Once Linda paused in the middle of describing her plans for the garden when the spring came and, smiling gently, asked, 'What is it, Holly?'

Holly shook her head and she didn't reply.

'Was there something you wanted to say, sweetheart?' Linda persisted gently.

But the little girl bent her head over her doll again, rearranging its blanket.

Charlotte and Linda exchanged knowing looks, but continued to talk about the garden. A few minutes later, the au pair, Magda, appeared in the doorway.

'Your luncheon's ready, Holly. Ben's already in his high chair.'

'I don't want lunch,' Holly said quietly.

'But it's your favourite!' Magda sounded enthusiastic. 'It's fish fingers!' Her Polish accent was pronounced.

'With ketchup?' Holly's blonde eyebrows were raised hopefully.

'Yes, we have the ketchup.'

Without further protest, Holly slid off the sofa taking Flissy with her. When she trotted out of the room, Linda rose and took a chair nearer to where Charlotte was sitting.

'She's being marvellous, but there's definitely something on her mind, and she won't talk about what happened at all,' she said in a low voice.

'She's obviously blocking it off, poor little thing.'

'The child counsellor she's seeing says we mustn't rush her; on the other hand, if she appears to want to talk, we must be there to encourage her.' Linda sounded worried. 'God knows how long it will take and, until she does talk, we're never going to get to the bottom of the matter.'

'Do you think she saw it all happen?' Charlotte sounded appalled. She was still having terrible dreams herself, seeing the bodies of Edmund, Virginia and Chris, lying in pools of blood. She couldn't bear to imagine what such an experience would do to the mind of a small child.

'We don't know,' Linda sighed. 'All I want to do is clear Chris's name.'

There was silence as Charlotte took another sip of wine. Whilst she could understand Linda's feelings, and her wish to have any stigma removed from Holly's father, it seemed impossible that anyone else could have done the shooting.

'It's going to take David a long time to get over this,' Charlotte remarked, sipping her wine. 'He's absolutely broken hearted, I'm afraid.'

Linda's expression was candid as she eyed Charlotte carefully, watching her reaction. 'David and I have never been friends, I'm afraid,' she admitted. 'But I can see he must be very upset, especially about his parents. He wasn't close to Chris, though. As you probably realised at Christmas, he was always jealous of him.'

'He feels Chris was the favourite,' Charlotte said, hotly. 'I think he's right, too. The Farrells did seem to do far more for Chris than they ever did for David.'

'That's not true, La. Edmund and Virginia bent over backwards to make sure they didn't favour one more than

248

the other. I know that for a fact. Virginia, especially, worked very hard at treating them both the same. It may look as if Chris got more from them, but that was because he had a bad problem, and needed sorting out.'

Charlotte felt angry. 'I don't think you understand what it was like for David. He was put in the humiliating position of having to ask for money every time he needed anything. He hated doing it.' She shook her head at the memory of David having to justify himself so thoroughly to his father at Christmas; and his father ensuring that everyone knew how generous he'd been.

'You mentioned, the other day on the phone, that David was thinking of selling Chelwood.'

'Yes. He doesn't want to live there, and I don't blame him.' Charlotte shuddered. 'I hope I never even have to see that house again.'

'It won't be all his to sell, of course,' Linda said tentatively.

'Oh, I think it will. There were only the two sons, weren't there?'

Linda bit her lip, looking down into her glass, as if not sure whether to say any more or not.

'What is it?' Charlotte asked, intuitively.

'I'm afraid David could be in for a bit of a shock,' Linda admitted. 'Virginia told me, when Chris and I got divorced, that both she and Edmund had changed their Wills. They added in a codicil that says that, if anything were to happen to Chris – and remember at that point he was quite likely to overdose on one drug or another – his share of the family fortune was to go to Holly.'

Charlotte's face lit up with delighted surprise. 'Oh, that's very fair, isn't it, Linda? I'm so glad they did that. It'll be a nice little nest-egg for her when she's older, won't it?'

'Spoilt brat!' Linda smiled indulgently. Then she grew serious again. 'I'm not sure how David's going to take it, though, when he finds out. If he imagines he's going to get everything, he's going to be very disappointed.'

Charlotte, thinking about it, wondered for a moment if she might be right. Certainly David had been expecting to inherit the entire estate. But then, the inheritance was huge; she was sure he wouldn't begrudge Holly her share in it.

'I'd let the lawyers tell him, if I were you,' Linda advised, watching the doubtful expression on Charlotte's face.

'Yes, I will,' Charlotte said slowly.

Linda was thoughtful. 'I suppose it might strengthen his feelings that Chris was the favourite,' she admitted sadly. It was as if she was thinking aloud. 'I know Virginia really tried to make no difference between them, but I suppose, in the end, nothing can equal one's love for one's own child.'

Charlotte felt herself turn cold. She looked into Linda's kindly face, and saw the dawning horror in her expression.

'Oh, Charlotte!' Her hand flew to her mouth. 'Oh, my God, I thought you knew? Oh, I'm so sorry. I should never have said anything.'

'What are you talking about, Linda?' Charlotte's voice was cold.

Linda closed her eyes for a moment, and took a deep breath.

'You didn't know?' she asked. 'Virginia and Edmund thought they couldn't have children, so they adopted David. Two years later they had a baby of their own: Chris. It's funny how that often happens, isn't it?'

Chapter Thirteen

Charlotte felt stunned as she hurried away from Linda's house after lunch. She needed to be on her own for a while to think about what Linda had said. Bracing herself against a stinging March wind, she started walking in the direction of Camden Town, barely aware of the traffic roaring by, or the people she passed on the pavement. Her emotions were mixed but mostly, at this moment, confused and hurt. Why had David never told her he had been adopted? Was he so ashamed of the fact that he didn't even want her to know? Did he regard it as a personal failure?

She'd always been aware of his need to appear cleverer than he was, and richer, and more successful; that was why he'd boasted about Flight Records giving him promotion. She'd always found it rather a touching quality, that he wanted to impress her. Now, Charlotte knew the reason for his boasting. His feelings of inadequacy, especially compared to Chris, must run deep. All along he'd been feeling inferior to everyone else because he wasn't the Farrells' own son. No wonder he resented Chris and had talked of him as the favourite. No wonder he hated Chelwood and all it stood for.

Poor David. The little boy must have felt shocked when he'd been told he was adopted; the teenager must have tried to outshine the real son of the house in his endeavour to be better at everything; now the man was still bitter and resentful, even though that younger 'brother' was now dead.

And yet it had been Chris who'd turned into the black sheep of the family, not David. Surely that reversal of their expected roles must have made David feel better? She felt totally bemused: this new revelation had made David seem a different person, no longer the son of Edmund and Virginia, but a stranger. Was he a stranger to himself, too?

The wind grew colder, the sky darker, as Charlotte walked on deep in thought, knowing she was vaguely heading in the direction of home. She wouldn't say anything to David yet. Let the dust settle on this present tragedy before she prised open the secret he had kept so well. Let things get back to normal – or as near normal as possible – before she tried to get him to talk about his origins.

Then Charlotte remembered what Linda had said about the Will. That was likely to add to David's sense of being hard done by, even though it was right that Holly should inherit her father's share.

It was beginning to get dark, one of those bleak winter afternoons when melancholy seems to hang brooding in the air. She glanced at her wristwatch. It was nearly four o'clock. She had reached Bayswater. On impulse, she hailed a taxi and gave the driver her parents' address. The desire to talk to her mother was strong. Margaret had a wonderful knack of listening and saying little, but at the same time conveying total understanding and sympathy. Right now, the burden of knowledge that had come to Charlotte today was too much to bear alone. If she couldn't talk to David about it, at least she could talk to her mother. And her advice on how to handle the situation would be invaluable.

Charlotte found Margaret working in the professionally equipped kitchen of the Cheyne Walk house. Wearing an apron patterned with little pink piglets, she announced she was experimenting with different ways of cooking plantain for a magazine article she'd been asked to write.

'Come and have a cup of coffee while you talk to me,' she said, after she'd hugged Charlotte in welcome. 'It's so good to see you, sweetheart. How's everything? Tell me what's happening.'

Margaret Taylor's manner was like a soothing balm to Charlotte's troubled spirits. Sitting at the scrubbed kitchen table, surrounded by the paraphernalia of cooking, with the delicious smell of grilled red mullet wrapped in vine leaves filling the air, Charlotte sipped some freshly made coffee and repeated to her mother what Linda had told her.

'Adopted?' Margaret looked up from cutting the plantain into short lengths. Her expression was astounded. 'And he never told you?'

'That's what hurts, Mum. It's as if he didn't trust me. What am I going to say? Should I let on that I know?'

Margaret shook her head. 'I wouldn't, if I were you. After all, it's not that important as far as the two of you are concerned. I mean, it doesn't alter your relationship, does it?' She popped the pieces of plantain into a saucepan of boiling water, adding a sprinkling of salt. Then she looked up at the big electric clock on the wall.

'I'll give those ten minutes,' she murmured, more to herself than Charlotte.

'I suppose you're right,' Charlotte said doubtfully, 'but I

don't like the idea of there being a secret between us. I always thought we knew everything there was to know about each other, and suddenly I find I'm living with someone . . . well, someone quite different.'

'In what way, darling? He's still David, isn't he? He's the same person you were living with before you knew he was adopted?' As she spoke, she started scrubbing some sweet potatoes in the sink.

'You know what I mean, though, don't you, Mum? I feel some of the trust has gone,' she added miserably. 'How *can* he be the person I thought he was, when Virginia and Edmund weren't even his parents? For a start, genetically he's not related to the Farrells at all. But that's not what I mind. What I feel so bad about is the fact he hid it from me.'

Margaret turned to look at her daughter, and her eyes were sympathetic.

'That's the real problem, isn't it?'

'Yes. Why should he do that? Does he think I'd turn against him if I found out he came from a very different sort of background to the Farrells'? Does he think I care about that sort of snobbish rubbish?'

'I don't think that was his reason, La. He must know you too well for that. I think you'll find he himself couldn't accept he'd been adopted. Maybe he couldn't come to terms with the fact he wasn't the elder son of a well-to-do family.'

Charlotte sipped her coffee. She realised what her mother had said was the most likely explanation.

'Oh, Mum . . . he must feel awful to act like that,' she said at last.

Margaret nodded. 'I'm afraid that's probably true. If he's

254

really feeling that inadequate, then he needs to be given a feeling of self-worth. Hang on a second, sweetheart, while I make a note of this.' Dropping the sweet potatoes into a second pan of boiling water, she grabbed a large notepad that lay on the kitchen table.

'Boil those for fifteen minutes,' she said aloud, as she scribbled frantically, 'then peel and cut into slices, add the peeled plantain, sprinkle with oil, salt and pepper and grill until golden brown.'

Charlotte smiled. 'I shall be inviting myself to dinner at this rate. It sounds delicious.'

Her mother looked up, pleased. 'Oh, *do*, darling. What a good idea! Wait until you taste those plantains, especially when I top them off with a dash of Angostura bitters and a squeeze of lime.'

'Oh, Mum! It's too much! Can I really stay? Can I leave a message on the answering machine for David to join me here?'

'Brilliant idea! Let's spoil him tonight. Daddy can open some nice wine, and we can start with mushrooms stuffed with *foie gras*, and I'll whip up some tiny apple and quince tartlets.'

'How come I feel better already?' Charlotte demanded. 'There's *nothing* as comforting as food . . . and I'm getting so fat.'

Margaret's eyes swept over her. 'No you're not, La.'

'There speaks a loyal mother.'

'You can still eat well and eat slimmingly, you know.'

Charlotte's eyes widened. 'Why don't you write a cookery book that's full of slimming recipes? You could make a fortune.'

'Well, it's an idea. It cuts out all my favourite things, though. Cream, butter, chocolate . . .'

'Don't talk to me about chocolate!' Charlotte groaned, rising. She'd put on a bright red skirt with a navy blue jacket for going to lunch with Linda and, as she paraded up and down the kitchen, she patted her hips and thighs.

'Look, Mum. Fat! Cellulite! I'm . . . I'm getting really *chubby*!' she exclaimed. 'It's all this comfort eating I've been doing lately; it's ruining whatever there was of my shape.'

Margaret laughed. 'It'll soon drop off, sweetheart. Stop eating sugar and fatty things and take some exercise; you won't recognise yourself in a few weeks.'

Charlotte looked serious again. 'I wish I knew what was going to happen.'

'In what way?'

'Every way. David wants to give up work . . . At least he said he did, but that was when he thought he was going to inherit everything from his family. Oh, I do so want him to be happy, Mum. I wish he'd suggest we get married,' she added.

'Would that change things, La?'

'I honestly think it would.' She sounded positive. 'I think it would make him more secure, for one thing. Especially now I know about this adoption business.'

Margaret didn't reply, but busied herself draining the plantains.

'I love him so much, Mum, and he's been incredibly brave over this whole ghastly business. I'd have cracked up completely if it had been you and Daddy and Susie who had died. I just don't know how he's managed to control himself.'

She shuddered. 'It really has been hell.'

'The worst is over now, isn't it?'

'Yes. There is still the pathologist's report to come, which is due any day now, but everyone says that's a pure formality in this case.'

David arrived just as Colin was opening a bottle of Tattinger.

'Well timed, old chap!' he said, greeting David with his firm handshake. 'Come on in. Glad you could make it.'

Charlotte rushed forward to kiss David. 'Hi, sweetheart! Had a good day?'

'Yeah, fine, thanks.' He kissed her lightly on the lips, then slipped his arm around her waist.

'It's good to see you,' said Margaret, with sincerity. It was the first time she'd seen him since the shooting, and her manner was warmly maternal. 'You've had a terrible time, my dear, and I'm so sorry.'

'Thank you, Margaret,' he said simply. 'I couldn't have got through it without La.'

Margaret's smile embraced them both. 'I'm sure you were there for each other. Now come and sit down and have a drink. Dinner won't be long.'

Charlotte made no mention of having lunched with Linda, and she was thankful that David seemed to have forgotten. He'd been looking at cars all afternoon, and he was full of talk about the various models he'd seen. After dinner he continued discussing the finer points of a Renault as opposed to a Citroën with Colin, while Charlotte helped her mother clear away.

'Is he buying a new car?' Margaret whispered.

Charlotte shrugged. 'It's the first I've heard of it.'

'His company provide him with one, don't they?'

'Yes.'

'You've still got your Peugeot, haven't you?' As she spoke, Margaret blew out the candles on the dining-room table.

'Yes, I've got my good old banger. Men just get interested in cars for no particular reason, don't they? I expect he did it to take his mind off everything. I don't suppose he's actually going to buy one. When's Susie coming back?' Charlotte asked. 'I wish she'd been here tonight.'

'You know Susie!' Margaret laughed. 'She's gone to the theatre straight from work, and then she and her friends were going out to supper afterwards.'

At ten o'clock, David got to his feet and announced it was time they were going home.

'There's something I have to show you, La,' he said importantly.

'What is it?'

'Just some . . . some papers.' It was obvious he wasn't going to say any more.

Charlotte's heart sank. It must be the Will. He must have heard from the lawyers earlier today, and now he wanted to tell her all about it.

'OK.' She kept her tone light. Then she hugged her mother and father.

'Thanks for a wonderful dinner,' she said. David echoed her sentiments.

'Splendid evening. You must let me take you both out to dinner one night,' he said expansively.

Margaret reached out and her hand touched his cheek. 'That's very sweet of you, David. Now take care of yourself.'

When they got into the street, David gripped Charlotte's arm and hurried her along the pavement to where he'd parked his car.

'What's this all about?' she asked.

He chuckled, and she realised he seemed to be genuinely happy. 'Wait and see,' he replied with a mischievous smile.

Cheered up by his good mood, she snuggled down in the car beside him, feeling more relaxed than she'd done for days. If he was content, then so was she.

David went ahead of her to unlock the front door and turn on the lights, then he led her into the drawing room. She looked around, expecting to see an official-looking document lying on the coffee table or her desk.

David watched her. 'What are you looking for?'

Charlotte felt herself blushing. 'Er, you said you had something to show me . . . I thought it must be your parents' Will,' she blurted out, unable to lie to him.

He threw back his head and laughed. 'Oh, *that*! It hasn't come through from the solicitors yet, but there's no hurry. I know what's in it, anyway. I get everything. Lock, stock and barrel!'

Charlotte sat down slowly. For a moment she stared at the carpet, stunned by what he'd said. Who was right? David or Linda? It seemed more likely that Chris's share of the estate would go to his daughter, but David spoke with such confidence. Perhaps he had some information that Linda didn't possess.

'So . . . what were you going to show me?' she asked lamely.

David went over to her desk and, with a flourish, brought over a stack of travel brochures.

'What are those?'

'What do you think? We're going to travel!' Like an enthusiastic schoolboy, he dropped on to the sofa and scattered the literature on the floor in front of him, spreading the brochures out like a fan.

'Where do you fancy?' he said excitedly. 'India? The Gulf of Mexico? Russia? Tai-Wan?'

Charlotte blinked. 'When?'

'When?' he repeated. 'Whenever we like, of course. I was wondering if we couldn't take in several countries, while we're at it? If we went to Hong Kong, we could go on to Japan, and from there we could always fly to Australia.'

'Hey! Hang on a moment!' She awoke to the fact he was in earnest; that he was really planning a grand tour.

'What's the matter?' She could detect the first signs of his getting irritated.

'Well, David, it's a lovely idea, but firstly I only get two weeks off in the summer and a week in the winter; and secondly, there's no way I can afford to take a trip like this.'

'I'm going to pay for it! I'm going to pay for us to do it in style, too. We'll go club class all the way, and we'll stay at the best hotels. If one's going to do something, one might as well do it properly.'

'But there's work!' she protested.

'Not for me there isn't, sweetheart!' David said glibly. 'Not any more. I'm quitting at the end of the week.'

Charlotte felt the blood drain away from her face and her heart took a dive. 'You haven't really, have you?' she asked in a low voice. 'You haven't resigned?'

He nodded. 'Of course I have! Why should I go on working in that grotty company, having to be out on the road every day of the week, when I could be seeing the world?'

'But I can't give up work,' she said quietly.

David looked at her puzzled. 'For heaven's sake, why not? You're twenty-six, you've no ties, and you've never been anywhere! If you don't get out of the rut you're in now, you never will.'

'I'm not in a rut,' she protested, stung by his words. 'I love my work and I want to start my own interior design company in due course. Anyway, I'd be letting Myra down if I left her, now.'

'Surely coming with me is more important?'

'That doesn't come into it,' she said, suddenly panicked that she might lose him if she didn't go with him. 'I can't just chuck in my job and go off round the world like that!' she protested.

'And why not?'

Charlotte looked at him unhappily. 'I can't afford to give up work, and I don't particularly want to. I love what I do.'

He looked at her sullenly. 'You can do as you like, but I'm going to travel. If you don't want to come with me, and let me pay for you to have a marvellous time, then I suppose there's nothing I can do to make you change your mind.'

Distressed, she rose and went and sat beside him on the sofa. 'Don't be like this, David. You're making me miserable. Of course I'd like to go abroad with you and visit wonderful places, but I can't walk out on Myra. Anyway, I have to earn my living. I have a mortgage for one thing. I have my whole future as an interior designer to think of.'

He didn't answer.

'Why don't we go somewhere exciting for two weeks in the summer?' she suggested.

'It's not what I want.' His tone was flat.

'What exactly do you want, David?' she asked softly.

Those hot blue eyes that excited her so turned back to the cover of one of the brochures. It showed a picture of a sandy cove, golden in the sunshine, with tall palm trees and a shady parasol under which a couple lay reading. In the distance the sea was as blue as sapphires.

'What I want, Charlotte, is to get away, visit wonderful places and live a life of luxury. And I never want to have to work again.'

Charlotte put her arms around his shoulders and hugged him. 'Everyone has that daydream,' she said, smiling indulgently.

'Yes, but I mean to make it a reality, whether you come with me or not.' There was something wistful in the way he spoke that touched her deeply.

'Is David there?'

Charlotte instantly recognised Neil's voice on the telephone.

'I'm afraid he's out,' she replied. David had left after breakfast, refusing to say where he was going or what he was going to do.

'Do you know when he'll be back, Charlotte?' Neil's tones were clipped and businesslike, his manner brisk.

'He'll be back for dinner tonight,' she said. 'Can I give him a message?'

'Ummm.' Neil hummed and hawed, undecided. 'We've heard from the solicitors about Edmund and Virginia's Wills and, as I'm one of the executors, I thought I'd better have a word with him.'

'Yes. Right. I see.' Charlotte wondered what she was supposed to say. She didn't want him to know Linda had already told her the contents of the Wills, as that would make Linda seem indiscreet.

'D'you know when David will be going down to Chelwood again?' Neil asked, breaking her thoughts.

'I've no idea. Why?'

'Well, he's going to have to visit the place sooner or later. Virginia has bequeathed various personal items to Carol, so as soon as probate has been declared, Carol will want to pick them up.'

'Yes, I see.' Even Neil and Carol, Charlotte reflected, are out for the pickings.

'So can you tell David I rang?' Neil continued.

'Yes, of course. I don't think he's been sent copies of the Wills, though. I'm not sure he knows what they say.'

'No matter,' Neil replied breezily. 'He'll be hearing from the lawyer in a day or so, but tell him not to expect any money for a long time. It takes ages for everything to be sorted out.'

Charlotte's heart sank. She had no experience of inheritances, but she did know that David was hoping to receive the money he'd been left straight away. Perhaps now he'd cancel his grandiose travelling plans, although it was already too late to prevent him giving up his job.

'I'll tell him,' she said with forced brightness, trying to keep her worry out of her voice. 'I'll get him to ring you this evening.'

'Thank you, Charlotte. Are you keeping well?'

'I'm fine, thank you.'

'And David? How is he bearing up?'

Charlotte remembered David the previous evening, excitedly making plans as he shuffled through the travel brochures, having spent the afternoon looking at expensive new cars.

'David's OK.'

'Glad to hear it. It's knocked poor old Carol for six, I'm afraid. Virginia was her last living relative and so it's been a great shock. Take a bit of getting over.'

'I can imagine. Will you give her my love and I'll ask David to phone you tonight.' She was anxious to get off to work and it was already after nine. 'I have to go now, Neil, but we'll talk soon,' she added.

'Very well, m'dear.'

When Charlotte arrived at the design studio, Myra was on the phone, struggling with a pile of work. She looked tired and harassed and Charlotte realised that her having so much time off had really put an added burden on her employer.

'Sorry I'm late,' she mouthed, as she hung her coat on an art-deco coatstand. Myra had bought it for a client, who had then decided she didn't want it.

Myra nodded in acknowledgement, and continued describing some wallpaper. 'Imagine a pale Prussian blue,' she was saying, 'with a design of creamy and rust-coloured tulips; you know those lovely ragged-looking tulips the old Dutch masters used to paint in still lifes? I think it would look fantastic in the bedroom, and if we festooned the four-poster in shades of cream and rust, with maybe some blue piping to edge the hangings . . .'

Charlotte smiled to herself, seeing the room in her mind's eye, marvelling at how inspiring Myra's descriptions could be. When her boss hung up, Charlotte grinned across the desk at her.

'Sounds good enough to eat!'

Myra shrugged. 'Thank God that woman doesn't argue. She's happy to go along with all my suggestions; she didn't even balk when I said I thought she ought to have the dining room painted ink blue, with white grosgrain curtains and a glass table! It's going to be sensational, with white candles and flowers, and chairs upholstered in dark blue.'

'Who is this accommodating client?'

Myra consulted her notes. 'The Comtessa de Castelliano. Spanish I think. Stinking rich and socially ambitious. Wants a swish setting for entertaining.'

'Nice work if you can get it,' Charlotte agreed.

'Charlotte.' There was something in Myra's tone that made Charlotte look up from the mail she was going through.

'What is it?' she replied, wondering why she had a sudden tight feeling in her chest.

'How are things going?'

'OK. Why?'

'I mean, is the worst over?' Myra seemed to be picking her words carefully. 'You've had a dreadful few weeks and I've quite understood about your needing time off, but can we get back to normal now, do you think? There's a lot of work on the schedule and we're getting behind.'

'I'm so sorry, Myra. Of course I won't be needing any more time off. I'll work late, if necessary, for the rest of the week to catch up. I'll come in on Saturday, too, if you'd like.'

Myra threw up her hands in mock horror. 'No, no!' she said hurriedly. 'If you come in then *I'll* have to come in, and I'd planned to go to the country Friday night.'

Charlotte laughed. 'I am sorry my life has been so chaotic recently.'

'My dear, La, I'm not blaming you. The circumstances you've found yourself in have been unique! Who ever heard of a whole family being wiped out like that! God!' She shook her head in disbelief. 'It will take David a long time to get over it, won't it?'

'I think it will,' Charlotte said thoughtfully. 'Right now he wants to travel around the world.'

Myra raised her eyebrows, but said nothing.

'In fact,' Charlotte continued, 'we had an argument last night, because he wanted me to give up work, too, so that I could go with him! I told him it was impossible, of course,' she added quickly, as she saw Myra's expression of growing dismay.

Myra leaned back in her swivel chair. 'Will you mind if he takes off for a while?'

'No, I can understand his wanting to get away from everything for a while,' Charlotte replied with honesty. 'Especially as his parents – Virginia and Edmund, I mean – kept him so short of money.' Too late she realised her slip.

Myra's eyes narrowed. 'Why did you hesitate? Virginia and Edmund *were* his parents, weren't they?'

'Oh, God, Myra, you mustn't let on!' Charlotte begged. 'I'm not supposed to know myself. Linda let it out the other day.'

'Let what out? What's the mystery?'

'Promise you won't say anything? I don't think David wants anyone to know.'

'For God's sake, La! Of course I won't say a word; what the hell is it?'

'David was adopted by the Farrells when he was born. He's not their real son.'

'Is that all?' Myra looked astonished. 'I thought you were going to say something terrible! Lots of children are adopted; it's not a disgrace, nor does it mean they have to have hang-ups.'

'I know.' Charlotte nodded. 'But David feels badly about it, I guess. That's why he's always been jealous of Chris and called him the favourite.'

'And you mean you've been going out with him, *living* with him, for God's sake, all these months, and he never told you?' Myra asked, scandalised.

Charlotte blushed. 'It's no big deal,' she said lamely.

'That's right. It isn't. So why has he made such a secret of it?' Then something occurred to her. 'I suppose he *knows*?'

'Oh, he must do.'

'Perhaps he doesn't. Perhaps his brother told Linda, and she just presumes everyone knows,' Myra reasoned. 'In which case, as my American clients would say, you're mixed up in one helluva dysfunctioning family, sweetheart!'

267

Chapter Fourteen

When Charlotte returned home from work that evening, she found the place deserted; the bed still rumpled from the previous night and the sink filled with dirty dishes. There was no sign of David. The first thing she did was to straighten up the flat. Her mother sometimes laughed at her for being so fussy, but she'd worked hard to make the rooms look attractive and she couldn't help feeling irritated when David left a mess. It was the only snag in an otherwise perfect relationship.

Gathering up his discarded shoes, sweater and squash racket from the living-room floor, she threw out all the old newspapers he'd left scattered around, straightened the books on the coffee table, and plumped up the cushions which had somehow ended up at one end of the sofa. In the bathroom she found a heap of damp towels on the floor, his shaving things scattered everywhere, and the soap, slimy and soggy, lurking by the plug hole.

Now for the bedroom, she thought, with exasperated indulgence. Half an hour later, she looked around with satisfaction. The rooms looked, as her mother always teasingly said, as if she were expecting a photographer from *House & Garden*.

When the front door bell rang a few minutes later, she

hurried to answer it, thinking it must be David. He was always forgetting his key. To her surprise she found herself looking at a young woman she had never seen before. About the same age as Charlotte, there was something bold about her expression; she exuded a confidence that almost amounted to arrogance. Thin and neatly dressed, she wore no make-up and her dark hair hung limply to her shoulders.

'Is David in?' she asked before Charlotte had time to say anything.

'No, I'm afraid he's out. Can I help you?'

'When will he be back?' She stepped into the hallway, almost pushing past Charlotte. 'I don't mind waiting.' Her eyes were like shiny buttons, probing and darting, examining Charlotte from head to foot.

'I'm not sure,' Charlotte said hurriedly. The young woman made her feel unaccountably uneasy, and she didn't want to encourage her to wait. There was something threatening about her that Charlotte didn't like.

'Can I give David a message?' she asked politely.

'No. I have to see him. You're Charlotte Taylor, aren't you?'

'How did you know?'

The young woman shrugged, thin shoulders hunched. 'I've seen your pictures in the papers. I'll wait until David gets back,' she announced.

'It may not be for some time . . .' Charlotte began.

'That's OK. I'm in no hurry.'

With the young woman standing her ground, Charlotte felt obliged to lead the way into the living room, wishing she'd never answered the door. Who the hell was this girl, anyway? And what did she want?

270

Without speaking, the young woman followed her, dumping her large shoulder bag on the sofa before groping in her pockets for a packet of Silk Cut. Still without a word, she lit a cigarette, blew out the smoke with satisfaction, and then sat down.

'Nice place you've got here,' she remarked, her greedy eyes taking in everything.

Suddenly Charlotte felt nervous. Maybe she'd been a fool to let this strange girl into her flat.

'What's your name?' she asked, and 'How do you know David?' Charlotte's tone was brusque: she only had her word for it that she did know him.

'My name's Connie.' There was umbrage in her voice now. 'I've known him for years. You've had quite a bit of excitement recently, haven't you?' she continued, dragging deeply on her cigarette. 'I've been glued to the newspapers!'

'You're with Flight Records, are you?' Charlotte inquired, desperate to find out who this girl was and what she wanted.

Connie threw back her head and gave a short laugh. 'Christ, no! Why should I be with Flight? They're not a bad company, though. I begged David not to leave, because even if the accounts department isn't very glamorous, it is a steady job. But no, he'd got it into his head that Don Gabriel didn't like him, and that was that.'

Shrugging, she tapped the ash from her cigarette into an ornamental Rockingham bowl that Charlotte's grandmother had given her.

Charlotte hardly knew how to contain her annoyance. This young woman seemed to know David far too well for her liking, and yet she'd never heard him mention anyone called Connie.

'Still, it's irrelevant now,' she continued. 'I don't suppose David will need to work. His parents left quite a fortune, didn't they?'

So that was it! Charlotte straightened up. This young woman, whoever she was, had read in the newspapers that David's parents had died. The media had stressed how rich they had been, and had referred to Edmund as a 'self-made millionaire'. She'd come round to see if she could get a handout! The thought infuriated Charlotte, and she knew it would make David angry, too. How dare this girl come to her flat trying to con some money out of him?

Charlotte said in a firm voice, 'I think it would be better if you left. I'm not sure when David will be home, and he'll be tired.'

Connie settled deeper into the sofa. 'I don't know what your problem is, but I'm not going anywhere. I know David will be happy to see me. It's been a little while since we last met.'

A cold hand seemed to reach out and touch the core of Charlotte's heart. This woman's presence was menacing.

'Will you leave, please? I've nothing to say to you, and I'd be grateful if you'd go.' She glared at Connie, who was trying to outstare her.

'You obviously don't know who I am,' Connie said with a sly smile.

Charlotte felt her head buzzing, and her throat contract. For a moment her gaze faltered before she raised her chin again, determined not to lose the upper hand.

'I don't *care* who you are. I'm asking you to leave my flat.'

They continued to look at each other, and then the silence

was broken as Charlotte heard David's key in the lock. She smiled with relief.

'Here *is* David. I'm sure he'll ask you to leave, too.'

Connie's expression was both triumphant and patronising.

'I wouldn't bet on it. David and I have been lovers for years. I think, in fact, he'll be quite interested in what I have to say.'

Linda, having tucked Holly up in bed for the night, returned to the drawing room, where Denzil was enjoying his usual evening playtime with Ben. They were both lying on their stomachs on the floor, with a handful of brightly coloured bricks between them, and each time Denzil formed the bricks into a pyramid, Ben knocked them down, spluttering with laughter as he did so. Linda watched them for a moment, standing quietly in the doorway so as not to disturb them, but then Ben saw her, and he gave an extra loud gurgle.

Denzil looked up, pleased to see her. 'Everything all right, love?'

Linda nodded. 'How was your day?'

'OK.' He kissed her with swift tenderness on the lips as she sat down on the floor beside him.

'How has Holly been today?'

Linda looked thoughtful. 'I found her playing with her doll, and I'm sure she was re-enacting what happened to her at Chelwood.'

Denzil sat bolt upright, instantly alert. 'What did she do?'

'She kept putting Flissy in the top drawer, over there.' Linda indicated a small antique chest of drawers which stood against the wall, opposite the fireplace. 'It wasn't so much what she was doing as what she was saying.'

Denzil watched her intently. Linda had suffered so much from what had happened to Holly, and he could see she was still affected by it, identifying with her daughter's ordeal.

'She was saying things like: "Daddy won't let anything happen to you," and, "I'm putting you here to keep you safe," ' Linda replied.

'Then what happened?' Denzil asked.

'At one point, she said, "Don't worry, sweetheart. Daddy won't let him hurt you." ' Linda turned stricken eyes to Denzil and her lips trembled. 'I believe Chris put her in that oak chest for her own safety.'

'And then pocketed the key.'

'Yes. You see what this means, don't you? Chris wouldn't have done that if he'd been shooting his parents, would he? And if Holly's remembering right, he obviously refers to someone else being responsible,' Linda concluded triumphantly.

Denzil was more cautious. 'Holly could have been re-enacting a scene with her doll of how she'd have *liked* things to happen. She adored Chris, didn't she? She'd never want to put him in a bad light, even in her own little play fantasies.'

'No . . .' Linda paused thoughtfully. 'But I'm sure Holly was remembering rather than inventing, taking over the role of her father, with herself as the doll.'

'OK, assuming you're right, who was Chris trying to protect her from?'

They looked at each other in silence.

'Another man in Olivia Middleton's life?' Denzil

suggested. 'That seems the most likely, doesn't it? Someone, maybe an ex-lover or husband, who had a vendetta against both Chris and Edmund?'

'And he killed Virginia too, because she'd be able to identify him?' Linda added.

'Yes.' Denzil's tone became more positive. 'And when Chris realised what was happening, he locked Holly up for her own protection.'

'I don't think Chris thought anything would happen to him. I think he popped Holly into the chest, intending to go back and let her out shortly afterwards, because he'd realise she could only survive in that limited space for a certain length of time. He'd also realise that, if anything happened to him, no one would know where she was.'

'Which is what *did* nearly happen,' Denzil said. 'We'd never have found her if the key hadn't been discovered in Chris's pocket.'

'I think I should get hold of Detective Inspector Grindley right away,' she said eagerly.

'It's not much to go on,' Denzil warned her.

'It's a start though, isn't it? It opens up the case again. He wanted me to let him know the moment Holly started talking about what happened.'

Denzil lay on his side on the hearth rug, propping himself up on one elbow as he built another pyramid for Ben.

'OK, give him a ring. And why don't you encourage Holly to take her "game" with her doll a stage further? Why not get her a few more dolls? Maybe some of those boy dolls . . . ?'

'That's how they get children who have been abused to tell what happened, isn't it?' Linda said reflectively. 'The child psychologist told me we should encourage her to talk or act out what happened.'

He nodded. 'It will help her to get it out of her system. It might also reveal exactly what really happened.'

Linda bit her lip and her eyes were suddenly bright. 'Poor little scrap,' she said sorrowfully. 'Whoever *is* responsible for putting her through all this should be put away for ever. Oh, Denzil . . . I'm so afraid it may have done her permanent damage! Who knows what's going on in that little head?'

He reached out and took her hand. 'The more we can encourage her to talk, the better, love. Get her to tell it like a story,' he urged. 'She's obviously already made a start. What she needs now is to be given the confidence and courage to go all the way. To open that door fully and let it all come out.'

'I know.' Linda gave him a watery smile as she wiped her eyes. 'Will you help me, Denzil? You're so wise . . . and Holly loves you. She might open up to you even more than to me.'

The grip of his hand tightened. 'I'll do anything you want, sweetheart. Get some more dolls tomorrow and we'll take it from there. In the meantime, give Grindley a ring and let him know she's begun to talk.'

'I will. Oh, Denzil, God knows what I'd do without you. You've been a tower of strength since it happened. I am grateful, you know.' Linda, who was usually so strong and calm, leaned her weight against him, for once the vulnerable one.

He nuzzled her, sliding his arm around her.

'Shall I tell you something?' he asked earnestly.

'What is it?'

'I have to say that, at first – like the police and everyone else – I thought it was Chris who had done the shooting.'

She looked at him with pained eyes. 'And now?'

'I don't any more. As you said, it would have been out of character for him to kill in cold blood, and most certainly with Holly around.'

'He just wouldn't have done it,' she said firmly.

'I know. The more I think about it, the more convinced I am that you're right.' He paused, thinking back. 'I suppose, in the heat of the moment, it was easier to pin it on Chris than to look further. On the other hand, if it *wasn't* Chris, why did Virginia phone David and say Chris and Edmund were having a terrible fight?'

'I've thought about that. I believe they did have a fight; it's only to be expected, isn't it, if they discovered Olivia Middleton was sleeping with both of them? But I think that's all that did happen between them. I think someone else must have been responsible for the killings,' Linda explained.

'So, apart from believing Chris didn't murder his parents, you don't think he committed suicide either?'

'What? Having put Holly in a chest where she could have suffocated? No, never in a million years. Someone else was in that house that evening, I'm sure.'

David stood in the living-room doorway, his face grey with shock.

'Connie?' He sounded as if he could scarcely believe it.

'Hi, there!' She greeted him with a smile before getting up and going and standing in front of him.

He glanced nervously from Connie to Charlotte and then back to Connie again.

'What are you doing here?' he croaked.

'What d'you think? I came to see you.'

He flushed then, an angry red stain suffusing his face, making the veins in his temples rise like worms beneath the surface of the skin, making his eyes a hotter blue than ever.

'*But I told you . . .*' he began furiously. Then, as if Charlotte's presence had suddenly sunk in, he moved swiftly to her side and put his arms around her.

'It's all right,' he said urgently, looking into Charlotte's face. 'You've got to believe me; it's all right.'

Charlotte stood rigid, not responding, all the pain in the world crushing her heart.

David turned to glare at Connie. 'What the fuck do you want? I told you I didn't want to see you again.'

Connie smirked. 'I don't particularly want to see you again either,' she retorted, cheekily, 'but I thought we ought to talk.'

David frowned, puzzled. 'Talk?'

'Yeah. Remember? Things you told me?' She cocked her head on one side and, watching her, Charlotte thought how cunning she looked, like a bird watching its prey before it pounces.

A shaft of fear seemed to pierce David's eyes, and then it was gone again, but not before Connie had seen it. She nodded, knowingly.

'Exactly! Shall we go to the pub for a drink . . . on our own?'

David seemed to rally and pull himself together. He glanced nervously in Charlotte's direction before speaking.

'You're talking a lot of nonsense, Connie,' he snapped.

'Nonsense, is it? And I was about to offer you my congratulations.'

Desperation gave Charlotte the courage to speak.

'What's going on, David?'

'Nothing for you to worry about, La.'

'I don't believe you.' Her voice quavered. 'Who is this woman? What does she want?'

'My name happens to be Connie,' the young woman said angrily.

David looked pleadingly at Charlotte. 'I've told you, this has nothing to do with us. Nothing at all. It's true I used to go out with Connie, but that was before I met you.'

'If you believe that you'll believe anything!' Connie flashed bitterly. 'We were together until he left Flight. Go on, David, tell her! We were together until you moved in here, weren't we?'

That was in January, Charlotte thought. *January!* So all through October, November, December, and Christmas, when he was pretending she was the only person in his life, he was still seeing Connie.

Charlotte felt herself sliding to the bottom of the blackest pit in the world, as despair confiscated her emotions and misery filled her horizon. Sick with anguish, she slumped into a chair, unable to speak.

'You're a bloody liar!' David was shouting at Connie. 'I may have *seen* you, but we were finished a long time ago, and you know it.'

'Have it your own way,' she said, not caring. 'Other things you told me interest me much more.'

'I don't know what you're talking about!' he raged. He turned to Charlotte. 'Don't believe a word she says! She just came here to make trouble; she's jealous!'

Charlotte sat mute, too shocked to speak.

'Oh, come on, let's go to the pub,' Connie said impatiently. 'We have to talk.' She struggled into her coat again, and grabbed her bag.

David looked hesitant, undecided whether to go or not.

'Come on,' Connie urged.

Dropping on to his haunches in front of Charlotte, he took her hands and held them tightly in his.

'Listen, sweetheart. I'll be gone half an hour; that's all. Don't worry. This has nothing to do with you and me. Let me settle this matter, and then I'll be right back. OK?' He spoke softly and reassuringly, as if she were a child.

Charlotte didn't answer, but continued to look at him with dumb misery. She had no words to say. Her world had crashed about her, and although David appeared to want to pick up the pieces, she knew that it would be hard to mend the broken hopes and shattered dreams that now lay before her.

'I shan't be long, I promise,' he was whispering now, while Connie stood waiting impatiently.

They left her sitting there, the front door banging after them. The silence of the flat seemed like a vacuum filled with emptiness. Heartbreak comes slowly, with small cracks at first, she thought, and then in little pieces.

Detective Inspector Grindley had received the report from the pathologist that morning. As expected, it was straightforward and to the point, and he skimmed it briefly. Mr Edmund Farrell, aged sixty-six; two bullets embedded in the centre of his chest, one piercing his aorta, shot from point-blank range, by a .22 automatic rifle. Death had been instantaneous. Stomach contents . . . Grindley skipped the details and read on: Mrs Virginia Farrell, aged sixty-two, killed by a single bullet from not more than three yards away. The bullet entered her skull through her left eye, shattering the cranium, cheek and jaw bones, teeth, and three vertebrae in the neck. Death instantaneous. Again, Grindley skipped the details and went on to read the report of Mr Christopher Farrell. Aged twenty-six. Two bullets in the neck, fired by the same rifle that had killed the other two. One bullet skimmed the surface of the neck, missing the jugular by a fraction, and causing minor injury; second bullet entered the skull through the larynx and travelled on to penetrate the cranium. Death instantaneous.

Grindley laid the document down on his desk with relief. It was as he had supposed, and now the case could be closed. The most sensational murder of the year had been solved on the day it had happened; he could now put his final report to his superior, Detective Chief Superintendent Alex Osborne, head of the CID for the county. The luckiest stroke of all, of course, had been finding the child alive. It had made him look a hero in the eyes of the media; even his wife had seemed proud of him that day.

Getting up, he strolled out of his office and walked down the brightly lit but barren corridor of the police station, until he came to a door at the far end. Ron Franklin was sitting at his desk, which was piled high with papers. He rose when Grindley came into the room.

'Morning, Franklin. Here's the pathologist's report on the Chelwood Manor murders. We can close the case now. File these papers for me, will you?'

'She's a trouble maker!' David shouted. 'Couldn't you see

that for yourself, La? OK, so I slept with her a few times before you and I met but *that was all*!'

Charlotte watched David, desperate to believe every word he said, but nevertheless still shattered by what had happened. He'd returned from the pub, alone, after an hour, and now he was trying to persuade her that Connie had no motive except to try to borrow some money from him.

'I could see it was the money she was interested in,' Charlotte admitted, 'but it was more than that, David. From what she said you've been seeing her recently. Certainly since Christmas. She knew all about you and Don Gabriel.'

David flushed, and poured himself a second glass of wine. 'Oh, I may have run into her, but not for more than a couple of minutes. Why are you believing her and not me? Don't you trust me?'

'Of course I trust you,' she said swiftly, wanting to trust him more than anything, 'but there was something wrong . . . the way she talked . . .' Her voice drifted off. She felt puzzled herself by Connie's manner, but she couldn't quite put her finger on what was behind it.

'The girl's crazy!' he said angrily. 'I don't know why you let her in in the first place. I finished with her ages ago; she's nothing but trouble.'

'But why should she say you were having an affair until you left Flight, if it wasn't true?' Charlotte argued. She felt stricken, desolate. She wanted to believe David, and yet Connie had sounded so plausible.

'I told you she's a liar!' David stomped around her living room, filled with indignation. 'How can you possibly believe her?' he added incredulously.

Charlotte felt the tears rising again, stinging her eyes, making her feel choked.

She wasn't sure why she believed Connie, but in her heart, she had to admit she did.

'What did she say when you got to the pub?'

David shrugged, finished the last drop of wine in his glass. 'Nothing much. She wanted money. I told her I couldn't give her any. Damn cheek asking me in the first place, just because of what she'd read in the newspapers. I sent her on her way, I can tell you. We won't be hearing from her again.'

'How can you be sure?' Charlotte sniffed, unconvinced.

'I told her to get lost.'

Charlotte drew a deep, sobbing breath and dried her eyes. If she went on questioning him, she instinctively knew she'd only make matters worse.

'Come here, little angel,' David said, dropping on to the sofa beside her. 'Cheer up. There's no need to be miserable, sweetheart. That girl means nothing to me. Nothing at all. She never did. It was just one of those things and I sort of drifted into it without really meaning to. I promise you, though, that I never slept with her once I'd met you. I'd never cheat on you, La. You do believe that, don't you?'

His eyes were so penetrating, so fiercely earnest, that Charlotte felt herself grow weak, dissolving with relief . . . and with gratitude. *Thank you, God, for letting me keep him,* she thought, as David put his arms around her. *Never let him want anyone else. He is everything I have ever wanted . . .* She clung round his neck, crying with reaction. Soothingly he stroked her back and held her close. His reassurance was tender and gentle.

283

'It's all right,' he kept saying softly. 'Don't be upset, sweetheart. We'll never hear from that girl again. She's right out of our lives now.'

Gradually, Charlotte's shock and misery subsided. Maybe, she reflected, I've grown up in this moment and come to realise that love isn't an idealised romantic interlude that happens somewhere between childhood and old age, but something that has to be worked at. Something that required compromises and adjustments and, most of all, trust. If she didn't believe David now, their love was dead. Finished and over. She *had* to trust him if they were going to go forward together. She raised a tearstained face to his.

'Are you sure you'll never see her again?'

'Quite sure. It's you I love, La. Only you.'

They were the words she wanted to hear.

'You won't go back to her?' she asked, still needing reassurance.

'Not in a million years. Not in two million years. I don't know what I was doing with her in the first place.' His cheek was warm against hers, his arms strong about her.

Charlotte gave a watery smile. 'I love you.'

He kissed her fervently, as if he were aware of her deep hurt.

'Not as much as I love you, my little angel,' he whispered. 'Let's go to bed. Let's put this horrible evening behind us, and we'll never talk about it again.'

'All right.' His hands were on her breasts now, cupping them gently, his thumbs rotating on her nipples with a light touch. She pressed herself closer. It was not enough that he desired her now; she wanted David to make her feel she

284

was truly his, and that he'd never look at another woman again.

'My little angel,' he whispered again as he undressed her slowly, kissing her shoulders and the inside of her wrists and elbows; smoothing with a feathery touch her stomach and the insides of her thighs.

'I love you,' she whispered back, looking into his hot blue eyes, committing herself to him for now, for the future, for ever.

That night his love-making was tender and compassionate, as if he wanted to heal the hurt she'd suffered earlier, as if he wanted to assuage the pain Connie's arrival had caused.

'I adore you . . .' he said a hundred times, and in the end Charlotte believed him. He *was* truly hers and always would be.

It was only later, much later, as she lay awake while David slept soundly beside her, that she realised the appearance of Connie had made her forget to ask him about the contents of the long brown envelope that had arrived that morning.

Chapter Fifteen

Grindley had never heard of the woman.

'Who?' he asked the sergeant, who had come into his office to inform him there was someone to see him.

'Westcott, sir. A Miss Westcott.'

Grindley shook his head. 'Did she say what she wanted?'

'Only that she got your name from the newspapers, in connection with the Chelwood Manor murders.'

'Is she a journalist?' Grindley had a love-hate relationship with the press. They could be useful when he wanted to get over a point about a case, but damned intrusive when he didn't.

'I asked her, sir, but she said she was just a member of the public who had some information for you.' The sergeant paused, wondering what the hell he'd say to Miss Westcott if Grindley refused to see her. 'She's quite insistent, sir. She's come down from London. I said you were probably busy, but she said she'd wait.'

'Oh, God,' Grindley groaned. 'I hope she's not some crank. I suppose you'd better say I'll see her, but tell her I can only spare a few minutes as I've got to go out.'

'Yes, sir.'

A minute later a young woman in her twenties was shown into the room. Neatly dressed in a beige pleated skirt and navy blue blazer, her hair was taken back in a ponytail and her face was serious. Grindley rose and tried out his rusty smile.

'Good morning, Miss Westcott. Do take a seat.' Her handshake was limp, he noticed. And rather clammy.

She sat opposite him, and leaned forward with a purposeful air. 'I got your name from the newspapers,' she began without preamble.

'So I gather. What can I do for you, Miss Westcott?' He looked across the desk at her. He'd had experience of both men and women who became obsessed with what they thought was 'vital information', and they all had the same fanatical gleam in the eyes, the same intense way of talking. It was usually quicker to hear them out and promise to 'look into' the matter, than to refuse to take them seriously.

'You were in charge of the Chelwood Manor massacre, weren't you?' She pinned him down with her direct manner, demanding a straight answer to her question.

Grindley raised his eyebrows at the description. 'Yes, I was in charge,' he agreed.

'And at the inquest it was found that the younger Farrell son, Christopher, had shot his parents before committing suicide.'

'That's correct. What is your interest in this case, Miss Westcott?'

'It wasn't Christopher Farrell who did it.'

Grindley pressed the tips of his fingers together. 'I see,' he replied calmly. 'On what do you base your assumption?'

'Because I know he had nothing to do with it. He was as much a victim of murder as his mother and father.'

'And you know who *did* commit the murders?' he asked ingenuously.

'No . . . But I know who arranged for the family to be murdered.'

'Ah-h-h!' he said again, drawing out the exclamation with a knowing inflection.

There was a pause, and then she turned on him angrily. 'You're not taking me seriously, are you? You think I'm making it up. Well, I'm not. My own life is in danger because of what I know. I've been threatened. If it gets out I've been here today I'll probably end up like the others!' Her voice had risen, and Grindley's heart sank.

'If you've any information concerning the murders I'd be very grateful to hear it.' Grindley tried to sound sincere, but he didn't find it easy.

Miss Westcott took a deep breath, like a diver about to plunge into the water. 'They were killed by a hit-man, hired to carry out the shootings.'

'Go on.'

'He was paid nine thousand pounds. Three thousand a head. It was all planned months ago.'

'I see.' Grindley spoke carefully. 'Do you know who this hit-man is?'

She shook her head. 'I've no idea. There must be known criminals who do this sort of thing. It's up to you to find him.'

'Of course we can try, but it would help a great deal if you could tell us who hired him? Can you do that, Miss Westcott?'

'Of course! That's the point of my visit, Inspector. It was David Farrell who hired a hit-man, and I should know because I'm his ex-girlfriend, Connie Westcott.'

The long buff envelope lay on the kitchen table, torn open at one end. Charlotte regarded it nervously, longing to have a look at the document inside, but not daring. David must now know that he was only inheriting half his parents' fortune, and she wondered how he'd taken it. One thing was certain; he'd see it as yet another sign that Edmund and Virginia had cared more for Christopher than for him. For a moment Charlotte longed to turn the clock back to those happy times when she'd first met David; those months they'd spent getting to know each other before they'd gone to Chelwood for Christmas. Those early days had been a divine voyage of discovery, when all at once her dreams had seemed to be coming true. Then they'd gone to Chelwood and, bit by bit, the dream had seemed to be crumbling, falling apart. She was distracted from these morbid thoughts by David breezing in, with a bottle of wine and two dressed crab, beautifully packed in a chilled box.

'I picked them up at Harrods,' he said kissing her. 'I just fancied crab for dinner.'

'My God, how extravagant!' she said, before she could stop herself.

Immediately, he made a grimace. 'Oh, for Christ's sake, La! You're always such a wet blanket. What's the matter with you? You used to be fun and now you're sounding like my mother.'

She winced, remembering how he'd referred to Virginia's nagging.

'I'm not,' she retorted, hurt. 'I just don't want to see you getting into debt.' Involuntarily she glanced at the envelope, but David had his back to her as he put the wine in the fridge.

'Why should I get into debt? Things are looking up for the first time in my life, so don't go spoiling everything!' He spoke lightly, almost jokingly, but his words stung her and she turned away.

'Have you seen this?' David picked up the envelope and flapped it in front of her.

'No.'

'Didn't you read it?' he asked, surprised.

'Of course I didn't read it,' she retorted, thankful now she'd resisted that temptation. 'What is it?'

'Oh, come on, La!'

She braced herself and spoke up. 'I suppose it's your parents' Wills?' To her surprise he threw back his head and laughed.

'God! You're keener to get your hands on their money than I am!' Then he shook his head. 'No, it's not the Wills. These are the deeds to Chelwood.'

'You haven't had the Wills yet? Then you don't know what's in them?'

'Oh, I know what's in them,' he replied amused. 'The old firm of family solicitors will be forwarding them to me any day now, but in the meantime, I asked them to send me these deeds. I want to go through them before I put Chelwood on the market.'

Averting her eyes, Charlotte put the dressed crab on two plates. Something inside her was festering and bubbling, about to explode if she didn't give it release; but how could she? In some ways she wished Linda hadn't told her about the adoption and the changes in the Farrells' Wills. To have been ignorant of these facts would have made her present situation so much less stressful.

In silence they went through to the living room. While David poured the wine, Charlotte laid the table.

He was the first to speak. 'I wonder how long probate on Chelwood is going to take?'

'I think it usually takes months,' she replied, a part of her hoping that was the case. The longer it took, the further away was the day when he would want to start travelling, forcing her to a decision about whether to go with him or be left behind. It was a moment she dreaded. She did not share his restlessness, his desire to be anywhere but where he was at that moment; she did not crave an exciting lifestyle or a desire to escape from reality. Mundane though it might be, Charlotte realised she was happy with the way her career was going, content with her beautiful flat, glad to be near her friends and family. Perhaps, she reflected silently, I have a greater sense of belonging, because of the way I was brought up. Her parents had given her a sense of security, too, obviously denied David by his adopted family.

'What are you thinking about, La?'

She started from her reverie, and blushed. 'Nothing really.'

'You're not still worrying about Connie, are you?'

Momentarily, she had forgotten the existence of Connie, and his words brought the memory of her back. Her whole life these days seemed to be pervaded with anxiety about one thing or another; she felt like a rat in a trap, trying to escape, but finding each exit led to another source of worry.

'I wasn't thinking about Connie.'

'What then?'

'I feel panicked about *everything*,' she said candidly. 'I used to be so . . . well, so complacent, nothing fazed me; but these days I feel the top of my head is going to blow off.'

He looked at her sympathetically. 'You've been through a helluva lot, with my family dramas!'

'Maybe.' She hung her head, knowing that was only a part of the trouble. Her real fear and apprehensiveness lay in wondering what was going to happen between herself and David in the long run. There was an edge of danger in their relationship that hadn't been there at the beginning, a sense of dread that she was unable to rationalise.

'It's all over, though.'

She looked up at him. His expression was gentle and tender.

'What's all over?'

'The deaths . . . the funerals . . . the newspapers hounding us. People forget very quickly. It's all over, La. Nothing more can happen now.'

'You don't think so?'

David shook his head. 'It's history. We can get on with the rest of our lives now, thank God.'

'Charlotte, is that you?' It was Linda on the phone, sounding excited and rather agitated. It was eleven o'clock the next morning and she'd called Charlotte at the design studio.

'Hi, Linda! How are things?'

'Listen. I've got to talk to you. Something's happened that I think proves Chris had nothing to do with the shootings.'

'What is it?'

'Holly's telling us what went on at Chelwood . . . at least,

293

she's not actually talking about it, but we got her some dolls and she's been play-acting the most terrifying scenario with them.'

'You're not serious?' Charlotte's heart skipped a beat as Linda's words brought back to her the hideous scenes she'd witnessed in the old house.

'I am, La. But I'd like to talk to you about it before I go to the police, just in case I'm letting my imagination run away with me.'

'OK. When shall we meet?'

'Can you come over at lunchtime? It will be easier to show you what Holly is doing with her dolls than to explain.'

'Yes. I can't stay for long; I'm very busy at work, but I can come at twelve-thirty for an hour.'

'Perfect! I really think we're going to get the truth soon.'

Charlotte took a taxi to Mulberry Avenue. Myra was in Birmingham working on the designs for a new hotel, and Charlotte had left the studio in the hands of their secretary.

Linda greeted her with barely concealed excitement.

'Come in, love,' she said. Then she lowered her voice conspiratorially. 'Holly's playing with her dolls now. We'll sit down and have a quiet drink while we watch her, but don't let on you're interested in what she's doing. The moment she thinks she's being observed, she stops.'

Charlotte nodded in understanding. At that moment, Holly came running into the hall, with Flissy as usual under her arm.

'Hello, sweetheart!' said Charlotte. 'How lovely to see you!'

'Yes,' said Holly, smiling shyly.

'And how is Flissy?'

'Very well.'

'Very well, *thank you*,' Linda prompted gently.

'Yes.' Holly grinned broadly.

Charlotte laughed. 'Well, Flissy certainly looks in the pink!'

Linda led the way into the long, comfortable drawing room, and Charlotte followed with Holly. Ben was already sitting on the floor, playing with a toy truck.

'I do love this room,' Charlotte remarked, looking around appreciatively. While Linda opened a bottle of wine, she went to the french windows and looked at the garden. Early spring flowers were coming into bloom, and the neat little lawn was a pale shade of emerald in the milky noon sunlight.

'Come and look at my daffodils,' Linda said suddenly, leading Charlotte out through the windows. Half-way down the narrow gravel path she turned to her, whispering, 'Let me explain something. It will make it easier for you to understand what Holly's doing. She has a doll in a sailor suit, which she calls "grandpa". There's also a doll in a crinoline; it's an old one of mine actually. That's the one she refers to as "grandma".'

Charlotte nodded, understanding, while something chilly seemed to crawl up her spine.

'Then there's another doll, a boy dressed like a fireman; he's known as "daddy". There's also the fairy we usually put on the top of the Christmas tree, a gaudy-looking creature in silver tinsel and tulle.'

'Who is that meant to be?' Charlotte asked, intrigued.

Linda's smile was wry. 'Olivia. Holly calls her "Livvy".'

'And does Flissy play a part in this game?'

'Oh, yes.' There was pain in Linda's eyes now. 'Flissy

is Holly herself. She's inseparable from that doll, and I think she identifies with it. Let's go back. Take a seat on the sofa, and I'll give you a drink. And remember, appear to pay no attention to Holly. We'll try and carry on a normal conversation, but watch; watch and listen. I think you'll be amazed.'

In silence they returned to the drawing room, where the children were each playing in a little world of their own. Ben was blowing bubbles as he spun the wheels of his truck, and Holly, with her back to them, was playing in front of the antique chest of drawers that stood against the wall near the door. There were carved upright chairs on either side of the chest, and the various dolls were strewn around her, with the exception of Flissy who, Charlotte noticed, was on Holly's lap. Handing her a glass of wine, Linda sat down beside Charlotte, and under the cover of inane murmuring, they started to watch. Nothing much happened for a little while but then Charlotte watched, intrigued as Holly talked to Flissy, asking her if she'd like a bath. 'Grandpa's changing his clothes,' she informed the doll. 'D'you want to change your clothes?' Then she spun round and picked up the 'granny' doll and the 'grandpa' doll, made them roar at each other, with unintelligible words.

'Grandma's angry!' Holly whispered to the doll. 'Grandpa's angry, too!'

Transfixed, Charlotte knew with a dreadful sense of inevitability, that something dreadful was going to happen. Knew also that there was nothing she could do to stop Holly throwing the 'grandpa' doll violently on to the floor where it landed in a heap, arms and legs awry. Charlotte jumped involuntarily. It was all she could do to suppress the cry that sprang to her lips. Then Holly grabbed Flissy and, with heartbreaking tenderness, held her to her chest.

'Don't be frightened!' she whispered.

There was a pause and Charlotte hardly dare breathe. Holly was so absorbed in her play and oblivious of them, that to have disturbed her would have been like waking someone who was sleep-walking.

'Got to get away . . .' Holly said suddenly, lifting Flissy with little jerky movements. 'Got to get away . . . Let's hide!' The voice was whispery.

Appalled, Charlotte watched with stricken eyes. Beside her, Linda gave her a little nudge, and nodded silently. There was a fearful ring of reality about this game of Holly's, an aping of grown-up behaviour and speech, a reflection of what it seemed Holly had observed.

'Got to hide . . .' Holly repeated urgently.

The atmosphere in the room was tense, and even Ben had grown quiet, sucking thoughtfully on a red wooden brick.

'Who's that?' Holly asked suddenly, whispering again. 'Who's that?'

Charlotte froze, and beside her she could feel Linda grow rigid. Her fingers, interlaced, clenched like bird's claws, the nails digging into her skin. As if in agony she watched her small daughter as she clapped her hands loudly, shouting 'Bang! Bang!' She was still then, as if listening, and then she spoke again.

'Where's Daddy?' she asked in a breathless whisper, as she clutched her doll. 'Where's Daddy?' She rocked Flissy silently, sadly. Then she exclaimed: 'There's Daddy!'

Then she opened the top drawer, pushed Flissy down into it, and slammed it shut again.

'Ssh . . .' she whispered, sitting down again. 'Daddy says you must keep very quiet.'

Charlotte looked at the small back view, dressed today in a flowered skirt and a white T-shirt. The little plump elbows and the silvery-blonde curls seemed to be trembling. She wanted to gather Holly up in her arms and hold her close and try to help her forget all that had happened, but she knew she couldn't. There was more to be exorcised from her baby mind, and it would be a long time, if ever, before the horror would be completely erased.

Holly sat playing with the tawdry skirt of the Christmas tree fairy for several minutes, and then, as if she'd suddenly remembered something, she jumped to her feet, yanked open the drawer, and lifted out Flissy. Cradling the doll in her arms, she sat crooning softly, in a sad little voice.

The tears were streaming down Charlotte's face now and when she looked, she saw Linda was crying also.

'Let's go into the garden again,' Linda suggested in a choked voice. They hurried from the room before Holly could see their distress.

'Oh, Linda, I don't think I can bear it,' Charlotte wept. 'What that child has been through!'

Linda nodded and blew her nose. 'I know. I've spoken to her counsellor, who is a children's psychotherapist, and she said I was to let Holly play with those dolls as often as she likes. Apparently the more she acts out what she saw, the better. It's a way of getting it out of her system, at least until she starts to talk about it.'

Charlotte felt the pain of that day like a raw wound. Holly's play-acting had brought everything to the surface again. But it also posed more questions than it answered.

'My God,' she gasped, as realisation dawned, 'that means Edmund was shot *before* Chris got back from visiting Olivia!'

'Exactly! I believe Virginia and Holly were upstairs when Edmund was shot. His body was found at the bottom of the staircase, wasn't it?'

Charlotte nodded, knowing she'd never be able to forget the sight of Edmund lying soaked in his own blood, but with such a peaceful expression on his face he might have been asleep.

'Maybe Edmund was upstairs too, and heard something? He could have been shot as he went downstairs to investigate,' Linda said thoughtfully.

'I suppose that's possible . . .'

'And supposing Chris came back at that moment and disturbed whoever had shot Edmund? They might have already shot Virginia, too!'

The two women looked at each other in horror.

'Maybe they were both shot in front of Holly . . . !' said Charlotte. If that had happened, Holly could be scarred for life. The sight of Edmund lying dead had been bad enough, but Virginia, with half her face blown away, was infinitely worse.

Linda looked pale and drawn. Her hand was shaking as she tried to smooth the lines from her forehead.

'I think the last thing Chris did, before he died, was to protect Holly by locking her in that chest. That's why he put the key in his pocket. If he was killed, he'd know the key would be found on his body, whereas if he'd left it in the lock, no one would know where she was hidden.' Her voice trailed off sombrely. 'He always said he loved her so much he'd be willing to give his life for her, and that's exactly what I believe he did.'

'Oh, Linda!' Charlotte was bereft of words, imagining the scene; an intruder running amok with a gun, killing first Edmund and then perhaps shooting or at least threatening Virginia, while Chris dragged Holly into the spare room and hid her in the blanket chest.

'I wonder why Chris was shot in the kitchen, and not upstairs?' Charlotte asked suddenly.

'Maybe he went downstairs again, in order to draw the murderer away from where Holly was hidden,' Linda suggested.

'And then he was shot in cold blood and the gun placed in his hands so it would look as if he'd killed his family?'

'God, I wish I knew.' Linda sounded weary and sickened by what had happened. 'How are we going to prove all this, La? There are no witnesses, except possibly Holly, and I can't expect her to get up in a court of law and give an account of what she saw.'

Charlotte nodded. In a way she would feel glad if it could be proved that Chris was innocent, but a new disquiet now filled her mind, leaving her troubled, although she couldn't pinpoint its cause.

'What happens next?' she asked.

'I'm going to contact the detective in Barrow. I think he should reopen the case, and I'd like to know what the pathologist's report said.'

'So would I. If Chris didn't do it, who did?'

Linda looked at her candidly. 'To be frank, La, I don't give a damn. All I want to do is clear Chris's name, for Holly's sake as much as anything, and I'm not going to rest until I've succeeded.'

They went back into the house when Magda called out that lunch was ready. Because of the children, their conversation now became general.

'I went to the zoo!' Holly announced, round eyed.

'That must have been fun,' Charlotte said encouragingly.

'I had a ride on a donkey.' She scooped some shepherd's pie on to her spoon and jammed it into her mouth. 'And I saw . . . and I saw a lion!' she added, as she chewed. 'He went Gr-r-r-r-r!'

'My goodness!' Charlotte pretended to be startled. 'That was exciting.'

Holly nodded, blonde curls bobbing. 'Have you been to the zoo?'

'Not since I was a little girl.'

Again the round blue eyes gazed into hers. 'Was there a zoo then?'

When everyone laughed, Holly looked pleased, and laughed too, with the fat chuckle Charlotte so loved.

'I just adore that child,' Charlotte told Linda, as they had a quick cup of coffee before she returned to work. 'You're so lucky to have such beautiful children.'

Linda smiled. 'I know. I'm really blessed. I don't know what I'd do without either of them. Children are the greatest boon in life.'

Charlotte nodded. 'I hope, one day, I have children. To me, family life is the most important thing of all.'

'It is. That's why I gave up work when I had Ben. Luckily Denzil earns enough to keep the wolf from the door, but even if he didn't, I think I'd rather go without things than miss a moment of being with Holly and Ben. You come from a close family, don't you, La?'

'Very close, and it's wonderful. Tell me, Linda, I've been meaning to ask you; does David actually know he's adopted?'

'Good heavens, d'you mean he hasn't mentioned it to you yet?'

'He hasn't said a word. It occurred to me that perhaps Chris knew and that's why you know, but no one had told David?' Charlotte explained.

'No, David knows all right. I believe he was told right from the start. All the usual stuff about being "special" and "chosen", you know. I gather Edmund and Virginia were really good in the way they handled it. I wonder why David's never mentioned it?'

Charlotte looked thoughtful. 'I think it's probably to do with feeling rejected by his own mother.'

'That's sad, because it shows a sense of insecurity,' said Linda. Then she smiled. 'I'm sure you're giving him that sense of belonging he so badly needs, La. He's very lucky to have you.'

Charlotte looked pleased, but surprised. 'I think I'm the lucky one,' she remarked.

As soon as Connie Westcott left, Detective Inspector Grindley called the Deputy Chief Constable into his office.

'Take a seat, Franklin. Something has come up. I don't think we need take it seriously, but as Chelwood Manor is on your patch, I thought you ought to know that I've had a young woman in here just now, accusing David Farrell of hiring a hit-man to carry out the shootings.'

Ron Franklin's jaw hung slack as his mouth opened in astonishment.

'She never!'

'She even went so far as to say nine thousand pounds was paid out; three thousand a head, as she so charmingly put it,' Grindley continued.

'No!'

'The motive was apparently a lifelong grudge held against the family by David Farrell who, incidentally, is an adopted son. He was also after the money.'

'He never!'

Grindley looked pained. 'Franklin, could you not be a little bit more coherent? Ask a few pertinent questions, perhaps? Instead of sitting there, oohing and aahing?'

Franklin pulled himself together and shut his mouth firmly. 'I was expressing surprise, sir.'

'Well, if you ask me, I think her story's a load of crap! This young woman is an ex-girlfriend of David Farrell. If anyone has a grudge, it's her. They've split up, and I think she wants to get back at him.'

Franklin nodded, still too surprised to say much. Nothing as dramatic as the Chelwood case had ever happened to him since he'd joined the police force, and he found it both macabre and exciting.

'Well . . . !' It was a remark, not a question, and he shook his head wonderingly.

'Well, what, Franklin?' barked Grindley. Connie Westcott had rattled him. He didn't like aggressive women, and he felt annoyed that a case that had been so neatly wrapped up could now be under question.

'Well . . . er, that's that, isn't it, sir? You said we needn't take this information seriously, and I agree. Does she have any evidence to go on?'

'Not a shred. I asked her if she knew who the hit-man

303

was, but she had no idea. I think she made the whole thing up, just to make trouble.'

'You do hear of people employing hit-men, though, sir.'

'Franklin, you've been watching too much television! This is not Chicago.'

'So you don't think we should pull him in for questioning, sir?'

Grindley didn't hesitate in his answer. 'Good Lord, no. Waste of his time, and worse, a waste of police time, too.'

Charlotte didn't tell David about her lunch with Linda. She couldn't see the point. Why remind him of that dreadful day, just as he appeared to be coming to terms with the loss of his family? Especially as Holly's play acting with her dolls was far from conclusive.

It was then that she realised that, ever since Christmas, little secrets had started to develop between them, many of them emanating from her. Was she trying to protect him from hurt and anger; or was she really protecting herself?

Chapter Sixteen

'Who the hell gave permission for the funerals to go ahead and the bodies to be cremated?' Grindley stormed.

Franklin spoke in the tones of someone who knows he's about to have his head bitten off.

'It was Detective Chief Superintendent Alex Osborne, sir. The family asked for permission, and as you were on a week's leave, right after the Chelwood murders, it was referred to him.'

Grindley swore under his breath. When the head of the county CID gave permission of that sort, there was little he could say. Or do. At least not in front of Franklin.

'Well, I hope to God the path. lab. can give us a more detailed report. We need it now. Those bodies should never have been cremated.'

'But the case had been closed, sir,' Franklin protested. 'You told me yourself that—'

'I would not have sanctioned the funerals,' Grindley said firmly, 'let alone cremations. Has all the evidence at the scene of the crime been destroyed, too?'

'Yes, sir.'

'I suppose it was the chief superintendent who also gave permission for the house to be cleaned up? And the bedding and carpets chucked on the bonfire?'

'The case *had* been closed, sir,' Franklin repeated.

Franklin didn't know why he was protecting Alex Osborne so fiercely from Grindley's wrath, except that it had been Grindley who had dismissed the incident as a straightforward 'domestic' in the first place. It didn't seem fair that the head of the local CID was about to be made a scapegoat.

Grindley sat at his desk in a quiet state of panic. He'd paid little attention to Connie Westcott's account of what had happened, but he'd been unable to ignore Mrs Linda Blake when she'd phoned him the next day. As she'd described Holly's game, he'd felt his blood pressure rise. If he'd got the case wrong, he could kiss his promotion goodbye.

'It's clear her father's not the killer,' Linda had told him. 'I think someone else must have got into Chelwood and shot Edmund Farrell before Christopher got back from visiting Olivia Middleton.'

When Grindley heard those words, his heart gave a lurch, and for a dreadful moment he wondered if Connie Westcott had been telling the truth, after all. Yet he'd been so *sure* the younger son had committed the murders before killing himself.

'So sure,' he repeated to himself under his breath. But supposing he'd been wrong . . . ?

'Bring me the original path. report, Franklin. I'd like to go through it again while we wait for what will hopefully be a more detailed one, that is if they've kept more detailed notes on file.'

'Yes, sir.'

While the chief constable fetched the report, Grindley

went through in his mind the broad details of the case again. *Why* had he been so sure Chris Farrell had been guilty? Had he overlooked something vital? Jumped to too obvious a conclusion? Or been led up the garden path by someone else . . . ?

'Here we are, sir,' said Franklin, coming back into the office and laying the report on the desk.

'Thanks.' Grindley scanned the typed pages. 'What do we have here? Three murders that took place on the night of 28 February. And they were all still alive when the cleaning woman left at five-thirty.'

'That's right, sir. She said the little girl was watching television with her grandmother in the study.'

'Did we ask her which door she left by?' Grindley asked suddenly.

'Yes, sir. The back door. She never used the front entrance herself. She said she and her daughter walked down the drive of Chelwood Manor to go home, and that she didn't see anyone in the drive or in the garden either.'

'Did she say what the family were doing at that time? Apart from Mrs Farrell and Holly? Where was Edmund Farrell, for instance?'

'Upstairs, changing his trousers. Apparently he'd got mud on them from working in the garden, and he'd gone to change into clean clothes. At that time, Mr Christopher Farrell was still out.'

'With Olivia Middleton, at Magnolia Cottage,' Grindley affirmed from memory.

'Yes, sir.'

Grindley leaned forward, his thick fingers interlaced on the desk in front of him. He looked tense.

'It could be,' he said slowly, 'depending on the exact timing, *that Edmund and Virginia Farrell were already dead when Christopher returned home.*'

Franklin looked startled. 'Does the path. report indicate Christopher died later than the others?' Then his brow cleared. 'But it would, of course, anyway, sir. He might have committed suicide *hours* later. We don't know they all died within a short time of each other.'

'I don't think that's what I mean, Franklin.' Grindley gazed into space, as if he were wrestling with a monumental riddle.

Franklin picked up his copy of the report, and read something that had caught his eye.

'It says here, sir, that Christopher Farrell shot himself twice. I wonder why twice?'

'The first shot hadn't killed him, so he had to pull the trigger again. It's obvious, Franklin.'

'Edmund Farrell was also shot twice. In the chest,' Franklin continued. 'But Virginia Farrell was killed by a single bullet entering just above her left eye . . .' His voice trailed off, remembering how she'd looked, slumped against the bedhead.

'What I don't understand is why no one heard five shots being fired?'

'Perhaps the wind was blowing in the wrong direction that day, sir.'

Grindley looked at him sternly. 'Don't try and be funny, Franklin.'

Franklin looked pained. 'I wasn't, sir,' he said stiffly. 'It's the only explanation. There wasn't a silencer on the gun, and as Chelwood is only fifty yards from the nearest

308

buildings on the outskirts of Barrow, the sound of gun-fire must have been carried in the opposite direction.'

'All right, all right,' Grindley grumbled. 'I want copies of all the statements we took, from the family, from the village people, everyone, because someone, I'm sure, is lying.'

'Yes, sir.'

'I want the pathologist to give me more details, too. It's a tragedy all the bodies have been cremated.'

'I think it was done for humanitarian reasons, sir. To spare the family the ordeal of having to hang around, waiting for the funerals.' Franklin's eyes were earnest. When his own mother had died the previous year, he hadn't been able to settle to anything until after the cremation.

Grindley looked at him scathingly. 'I *know* why it was done, Franklin. You don't have to labour the point.' Worry was making him tetchy. He had the most horrible feeling that a major question mark now hung over the case. And if he'd got it wrong . . . ? Misinformed the head of the local CID . . . ? Which in turn had led to the destruction of further evidence . . . ? He thought with growing horror about the cremations, and the bonfire which had consumed the carpets and bedding . . . There was no evidence left of the incident, except the original findings of the pathologist.

'I particularly want to read David Farrell's statement again,' he told Franklin.

'You think he may have had something to do with it, after all, sir? He has an alibi.'

'Just get me the statement and stop arguing,' Grindley snapped.

A week later, as Charlotte was getting ready to go to work,

David received a phone call from Detective Inspector Grindley. At first she didn't realise who David was talking to, but she could tell from his expression and terse, monosyllabic remarks that he was angry. Finally she heard him say: 'I can't think why you need to see me again.' There was a pause, and then, 'OK, I suppose I'll have to.'

When he hung up she looked at him anxiously. 'Who were you talking to?'

'That detective fellow from Barrow. You're not going to believe this, but he wants me to go all the way down there so he can ask me some more bloody questions.'

'Why, for God's sake?'

'I don't know. As if I haven't been through enough!' There was a note of despair in his voice.

'But what can you tell them that they don't already know? You've made a statement. We've all made statements. Why have you got to go back?' she sounded bewildered.

'Grindley said something new has turned up.' He looked at Charlotte, hot blue eyes tinged with worry. 'I bet it's Connie! She'll have made up some story to get me into trouble, just because I dumped her for you.'

'But what could she say?' Charlotte reasoned, trying to keep a grip on her emotions.

David ran his hand through his hair, pressing the crown of his head for a moment. He shut his eyes as if he were concentrating. 'I've no idea,' he replied at last. 'Connie's capable of anything.'

'Shall I come with you tomorrow? I can ask Myra if . . .'

'No. It's OK. I'll drive down and come straight back. I'll have to use your car, now I've handed the other one back to P.N.G. Links.'

'That's OK.'

'God, what a bore!'

'Poor sweetheart.'

'I sometimes feel this nightmare is never going to end, don't you?' he observed. 'All I want to do is sell Chelwood, and then get the hell out of this wretched country and go off around the world.'

Charlotte averted her face, hiding from him how much his words depressed her. It was obvious he had plans that, unless she gave up all that was dear to her, she couldn't share in. Suddenly, it seemed as if they wanted quite different things.

Her thoughts were interrupted by the thud of mail being thrust through her letter-box.

'I'll get it,' David said.

With hands that now shook, Charlotte applied a little lip gloss, looking at herself in the dressing-table mirror, seeing the fear in her eyes. Suddenly, the flat was quiet, filled with an oppressive heavy silence, like the calm before a storm. Then she heard it.

'What the . . . ?' David's voice echoed through the rooms. Charlotte turned cold.

'What's this? How *dare* they do this to me!' he exclaimed, coming into the bedroom. His face was red. 'Listen to this! They've left half the estate to Chris, to be passed on to Holly in the event of his death!'

'Oh, David!'

'Can you believe it?' he exclaimed. 'Half of *everything* goes to Holly! And they *promised* me that I'd get everything because Chris would only spend it on fucking drugs!'

'Oh, I'm sorry, sweetheart,' she murmured, sitting on

the edge of the bed and reaching for his hand.

David squeezed her hand tightly, his eyes glazed with a hurt expression.

'Didn't I always say Chris was the favourite! How bloody right I was!' He hurled the documents across the room.

Charlotte looked at him, wishing he hadn't taken it so badly. Nevertheless, she couldn't share his view that the Will was unfair.

'But I suppose, if anything had happened to you,' she pointed out, 'your parents would have wanted the money to go to any children you might have had.'

He didn't answer, but stared sadly into space.

'Why have you never told me you were adopted, David?' she asked impulsively.

Too late she realised it was the worst thing she could have said, especially at this moment. David turned on her, his expression livid. 'What's that got to do with you?'

She blanched, stunned by the force of his anger. 'It . . . it has nothing to do with me,' she stammered, 'but I wanted to know why you've never told me. I thought we told each other everything. That there were no secrets between us.'

'Why should I tell you? It's my business, nobody else's.'

'But I thought I was different . . .' Her eyes appealed to him to understand the hurt she felt, but he wasn't listening.

'Virginia was always going on about my being "specially chosen",' he continued, 'but that was rubbish! Two years ago they changed their Wills. Virginia told me then that Chris couldn't be trusted with money, that he'd squander it on drugs and drink, and she was right. It was then she told me I'd get everything.'

'Why would she say that if it wasn't true?'

David shrugged. 'Anything for the sake of peace, that was her motto. She'd always promise me what I wanted in order to keep me quiet.'

Charlotte remained silent, remembering how nervous and highly strung Virginia had been, like a violin string that is stretched too tautly. Her life must have been a hellish balancing act between the men of her family. To please Edmund must have sometimes meant going against her sons; to please them must have meant flying in the face of her husband's rage. Charlotte felt sure that, in moments of stress, Virginia would have succumbed to promising anything.

'Perhaps you shouldn't have believed her,' Charlotte said quietly.

David shot her a look. 'Don't tell me what I should or should not have done with my family,' he retorted. 'How did you find out about this adoption business anyway?'

It was an effort to talk now. She felt weighed down by the situation.

'One of your family told me,' she said lamely, not wanting to identify Linda as the source. She remembered Linda saying that she and David had never really got on.

'I bet it was Chris,' David said. 'He was very conscious of being the real son of the house.'

Suddenly his anger evaporated as if spent.

'Oh, God! I knew they never really cared for me. It was all a sham, an act to impress other people. As soon as Chris was born, their very own son, they lost interest in me. I was a nuisance from then on, but there was nothing they could do; they were stuck with me for life.'

Charlotte went to him then and put her arms around him. 'Sweetheart, I'm sure they loved you. Linda said they treated

313

you and Chris in exactly the same way; they loved both of you. It wasn't just an act.'

'Linda? So it was Linda who told you I was adopted. Jesus, I wish she'd mind her own business. She's always disliked me.'

Charlotte nodded silently, knowing it was true.

Suddenly he got up and started pacing the room, enlightenment filling his face.

'It's her, of course! Why didn't I think of that before?' he exclaimed.

'What are you talking about?'

'I bet Linda's behind the change in the Wills. It would be just like her.'

'David . . . I've got to go to work,' Charlotte said in desperation. She hated leaving him in this mood, but it was already after nine and Myra would be doing her nut if she was late again.

'OK!' he said curtly.

'Will you be all right?'

He nodded, sinking back on to the bed again. 'I'm just terribly saddened,' he said. 'I never thought it would end like this.'

She leaned forward to kiss him. 'Never mind, darling. Money isn't everything.'

He grunted. 'What a ridiculous platitude *that* is!'

'Good health and love are more important.'

'You're such a bloody romantic, La,' he said, but not unkindly.

'I'll see you tonight.'

'Let's go out somewhere, La. An exciting restaurant. I'm getting bored with home cooking.'

As her vision cleared she saw two reporters and a photographer at the bottom of the doorsteps.

'Leave me alone,' she said angrily. She pushed open the heavy door and hurried into the communal hall, slamming it behind her. The experience had left her jarred and rattled. How dare they pounce on her like that? It was a gross intrusion of her privacy, and she deeply resented being the object of media interest just because she was David's girlfriend. It told her one thing though. David obviously hadn't returned from Barrow yet. The flat, as she expected, was empty, with a deserted air that was melancholy. She'd left the rooms impeccably tidy that morning, and now they mocked her with their orderliness.

Her heart cried out for David to return. This emptiness, this dreadful stillness, was a type of loneliness she'd never experienced before. For a moment she felt like running out of the flat and going home to her parents. Then she scolded herself for being so babyish. She was a grown woman of twenty-six, who had her own flat, a good job, and in due course would have her own business. Nevertheless, she continued to pace around the living room, wishing she still smoked, wondering whether to open a bottle of wine, asking herself again and again, what in God's name is happening?

When the phone rang, she rushed to answer it, feeling sick with apprehension. It was Neil.

'I say, Charlotte, what's this about David being arrested?' he asked anxiously. 'A reporter from one of the tabloids phoned and tried to get something out of Carol, but we didn't know what he was talking about. What's going on?'

'It's awful,' Charlotte replied, her voice shaky. As briefly as she could, she outlined what had happened. 'He's being

She knew if they went out she'd have to pay. Having given up his job, David was running into financial difficulties again.

'I'll bring in something really nice,' she suggested. 'It'll be much cheaper than going out. I'll see you tonight, darling.' There was sympathy in her voice.

'Have a good day, sweetheart,' he replied, and he gave her a hug as she turned to leave the room. 'Where would I be without you, little angel?'

When Charlotte arrived at the design studio there was a message to ring Linda. She dialled the number and, as soon as they'd exchanged greetings, Charlotte told her about Grindley wanting to see David again.

'So I gather,' Linda said knowledgeably.

'How did you know? Has he asked to see you again, too?' Charlotte asked.

'Not at the moment, but he says he'll want to see Holly in due course. When I told him about her playing with her dolls, he was sceptical at first, but now I think he believes Chris is innocent.'

'My God, that's wonderful,' Charlotte exclaimed. 'Is he reopening the case?'

'I think he might,' Linda replied cautiously. 'Apparently he's finding out if the department that carried out the post mortems have any further details on file. Anything in their notes that might be useful. I wanted to talk to you about Connie Westcott.'

An icy dart flew into Charlotte's heart. 'What about Connie?'

'Apparently she's been down to Barrow to see the

detective inspector with her own version of what happened. I don't think he took her too seriously at first, but now he's not so sure.'

'What can she know?' Charlotte demanded, feeling suddenly unaccountably nervous. 'She turned up at the flat the other day, because she'd read all about it in the newspapers. David said she wanted money.'

'Did he give her any?'

'No. Of course not!'

'Well, the detective inspector thinks she was blackmailing him.'

'My God!' Charlotte felt stunned. 'What a ridiculous idea! Why should she want to do that?'

There was a long pause before Linda answered, and when she spoke it was cautiously. 'Obviously, Connie must think David knows more about it than he's admitted.'

'What do you mean?' Charlotte asked angrily. 'What can David possibly know? He's as much in the dark as any of us! How can anyone possibly suggest otherwise! For goodness sake, Linda, that's a terrible thing to say.'

'Well, I don't know, love. Something's going on.' Linda sounded weary. 'I just hope it's proved that Chris is innocent.'

'Even if he *is* innocent,' Charlotte retorted, angrier than ever, 'it doesn't mean David knows what happened.'

'He might be protecting someone.'

'Like who?' Charlotte said incredulously. 'Who could he be protecting, for God's sake?'

'What time did you say Virginia phoned David that night?'

'You know, around ten o'clock,' she said impatiently.

Linda's tone was flat. 'She couldn't have done, from what the Inspector is now saying.'

'But she did! I distinctly remember. We'd had dinner and I was in the shower. Anyway, does the exact time matter? I don't get the significance of this, Linda.'

'Virginia couldn't have phoned David at ten o'clock, because she'd already been dead for nearly four hours.'

Charlotte sat at her desk feeling sick to her stomach. A yawning abyss of fear stretched before her, and with it a deep feeling of anger. What was Linda trying to do, for God's sake? she asked herself. While she understood Linda's wish to prove Chris innocent, she felt bitter at the way she was trying to make out David had anything to do with the murders. Unable to concentrate, she continued to sit at her desk, tormented by questions to which she could find no answer. She regretted now that she hadn't accompanied David to Barrow this morning. In desperation she finally phoned her mother. If she didn't talk to someone, she'd burst.

'What's the problem, darling?' Margaret asked immediately. She could tell by Charlotte's voice that she was overwrought.

'I'm worried, Mum!' Then she told her mother about Connie's visit, and David being called down to Barrow to be questioned, and Holly with her dolls, almost certainly proving Edmund had been shot while Chris was still visiting Olivia.

'Oh, sweetheart, this is awful for you. Why do they want to see David?' Margaret asked. 'What are they going on, for heaven's sake?'

'He thinks his ex-girlfriend is getting back at him for ending their relationship,' Charlotte said miserably, ' and she's been making mischief with the police.'

'But what could she have said?'

'God knows, but coupled with Holly's version of what happened, they're obviously reopening the case. I'm so worried, Mum.'

'Why are you worried?' Margaret Taylor asked, 'Neither you nor David have anything to hide,' she reasoned.

'I know. I just feel very nervous. Meeting this old girlfriend really shook me up.'

'David is bound to have had several girlfriends before he met you; a good-looking chap like him can't be expected to lead a celibate life at his age. Forget about the past, La. The fact that he loves you now is what matters.'

Margaret's good sense was like a balm to her daughter's troubled spirit.

'Yes. I know,' she replied, feeling calmer.

'What exactly are you worried about?'

'Linda just told me Virginia was killed around six-thirty, according to the more detailed post mortem, but she didn't phone David until ten o'clock.'

There was a shocked silence on the line. When Margaret spoke again she sounded as if she was trying to keep her voice steady.

'So what are they suggesting, La?'

'I don't *know*, Mum. That's what is such hell.'

'Are you suggesting that someone has set him up?' her mother said, appalled.

'I don't know! What scares me is Connie may have cooked up something out of revenge when he told her he couldn't let her have any money. What happens if the police believe her?'

'Darling, I do think you're letting your imagination run away with you,' Margaret remonstrated gently. 'Why don't you calm down and, when David gets back tonight, talk it through with him? Wouldn't that be the most sensible thing?'

'I suppose so.'

When Charlotte hung up she tried to get on with her work, but her concentration had gone, and all she could think about was Connie, wondering how much she'd meant to David, and what could she have told the police that might be detrimental to him. It would all be lies, of course, malicious lies to damage his reputation and get him into trouble. Nevertheless she felt deeply uneasy. And why the hell did the police want to see David again today?

By half-past ten that evening, Charlotte was seriously worried. She'd expected David to be back in London hours ago; the drive from Devizes didn't usually take more than a couple of hours, providing you avoided the rush-hour, so what on earth could have happened?

When the phone rang at ten forty-five, she grabbed it with relief. It would be David telling her he'd be home shortly.

'Hi!' she said, greeting him in her usual familiar way.

'Hel-lo!' said a strange voice. 'Is that Charlotte Taylor?' The man's tone was chummy, as if he were an old friend.

'Yes, I'm Charlotte Taylor. Who is that?'

'Oh, great, Charlotte. Listen, this is Harold Spicer. I'm on the *Daily Globe*. Tell me, how do you feel about your boyfriend being held overnight at the Barrow police station for questioning?'

Charlotte tried desperately to stay calm. 'What are you talking about?' Her heart was pounding.

'You didn't know? The police want to find out a bit more about the murder of his family a few weeks ago. I'm surprised he hasn't been in touch with you.' The reporter's voice was as casual as if he'd asked her if she'd heard the latest weather forecast.

'I don't know what you're talking about!' said Charlotte. 'What newspaper did you say you were from? How did you get hold of this ridiculous idea? David merely went to Barrow to discuss his family's deaths with the detective inspector who was in charge of the case.'

'Never heard the phrase "helping the police with their inquiries"? That's the polite way of saying they have their suspicions, but can't prove anything yet! So, what's your reaction now?'

'My immediate reaction is to tell you to go to hell!' Charlotte exclaimed, banging down the receiver.

She was trembling all over. What in God's name was happening? Her heart ached in fear and she was filled with anguish. The idea of David having to spend the night in a police cell was horrifying. He was an innocent man. They had no right to lock him up. Surely they didn't suspect him of having anything to do with the killings? Round and round went the jumbled thoughts in her mind until she could stand it no longer. With shaking fingers she dialled Linda's number, too nervous to ring the police direct. Linda usually knew what was going on because she was in almost daily contact with the detective inspector, reporting on anything Holly might have done or said.

'I'm sorry to phone so late, Denzil,' Charlotte apologised,

'but can I speak to Linda, please?'

'She's in the bath,' Denzil replied. 'What's the matter, Charlotte?'

Briefly she told him what the reporter had said. 'I'm terribly worried, Denzil. Why should they be holding David overnight?'

Denzil sounded concerned. 'I don't know, La. As they're pretty sure now it wasn't Chris, I suppose they don't want to let a stone go unturned. It doesn't mean they suspect David of anything, I'm sure,' he added comfortingly.

Charlotte, her mind spinning so that she felt it was going out of control, tried to grapple with the reality of what was happening. The situation was reaching nightmarish new depths, and for the first time she felt really frightened.

'Hang on, La,' Denzil was saying. 'Linda's here. Maybe she knows something. My brother and I have been out all evening at a business dinner, so I haven't heard the latest.'

'Thanks.' Charlotte sank on to her bed, her legs suddenly too weak to support her.

'La, love.' Linda's sensible voice came on the line. 'Are you all right?'

Charlotte repeated what the reporter had told her.

'Don't worry too much,' Linda replied, although she didn't sound too convincing. 'Maybe we're *all* going to be questioned again. They're probably keeping David at the police station because they ran out of time and they'll finish questioning him in the morning.'

'Is that usual?'

'Wait there a moment, love. I'll ask Randal, Denzil's brother. He's a lawyer.'

There was a pause, and Charlotte could hear them talking.

When Linda came back on the line, it was as if she'd been warned to be careful what she said.

'Randal says it all depends, but they can't hold him for long unless they can find positive evidence against him.'

'Well, that's all right then,' said Charlotte in relief. No evidence existed because David was totally innocent. Linda's words had comforted her, but nevertheless she was appalled that the police should even think David would know anything.

'It seems,' Linda continued, 'that Edmund was shot first, and they now know he died at approximately six-thirty, which puts Chris in the clear as they've found a witness who saw him leave Magnolia Cottage at seven o'clock.'

'And Virginia . . . ?' Every time Charlotte thought of her, she was assailed by the terrible memory of how she'd looked in death.

'Apparently she was shot at six forty-five.'

'So Chris definitely couldn't have shot her either?'

'That's what it looks like.'

'Oh, God, Linda, I feel more confused than ever. Why would someone want to kill them?'

Linda drew in a deep breath. 'There is always the possibility a hit-man was hired to do it,' she said quietly.

'*What?*' Charlotte felt aghast, all coherent thoughts tumbling down like a long row of dominoes. 'What an extraordinary idea! Who would do such a thing?'

'That, love, is the sixty-four-thousand-dollar question. They're going to try questioning Holly in a day or so. I hate the idea of her being forced to tell what happened, but the child counsellor will do the questioning, with the police listening in, so any harmful effects will be minimised. I'm told, in fact, that Holly won't start to really get over her ordeal until she *does* talk.'

'Poor baby,' Charlotte sympathised.

'I know, but it has to be done.'

'I'm sorry to have disturbed you at this time of night, Linda,' Charlotte apologised again, 'and thank you for telling me what's going on. I've probably been letting my imagination run away with me.'

'You've been through a helluva lot, La. God knows, this isn't even your family, and yet you've had to bear the most intolerable circumstances. I'm sure David will be back tomorrow, with nothing more wrong with him than a stinking bad mood!' Linda chuckled richly.

Charlotte gave a little laugh, too. 'I'm sure you're right. I mean, why would they want to keep him?'

Chapter Seventeen

Tom Grindley lay staring at the ceiling of his bedroom, wondering whether or not he should get up and make himself a hot drink. It was four o'clock in the morning; soon a chill spring dawn would melt the darkness away and another day would have begun. Beside him his wife lay fast asleep, untroubled by worry and stress, her most demanding chore, he reflected with envy, being to look after him.

After several more minutes of indecision, he made up his mind. He couldn't lie here another second, tormented by the doubts and suspicions that now surrounded the Chelwood murders. Sliding from under the duvet, he grabbed his dressing-gown from the hook on the back of the bedroom door, and then went down to the kitchen.

Filling up the electric kettle, he switched it on, before taking the telephone message pad and pencil from the dresser and going to sit at the kitchen table. The case was bugging him. Six hours of questioning David Farrell had revealed nothing new, and yet he was now as sure as hell that Connie Westcott had been speaking the truth. The question was, could he prove it?

For a long moment he stared at the blank page of the notepad, trying to get his thoughts into some sort of order. Then, in his small, precise handwriting, he wrote PROS on the top left-hand side of the page, and CONS on the right. If he could list all the reasons why he believed David Farrell was guilty, and then list the reasons for presuming him innocent, he might be able to unravel the conflicting thoughts that were charging about in his head.

He started with the PROS. According to Connie Westcott, David Farrell had told her he was planning to hire a mercenary to kill his parents and brother, because he had a lifelong grudge against them and he wanted their money. On the other side of the page Grindley scribbled, 'He could have been boasting to make himself look big.' Under it he added, 'She could have invented the story out of revenge for being dumped.'

The kettle boiled and he rose to make himself a cup of tea. Sleep was out of the question. His mind was too alert and he felt too jangled to relax. What was the next PRO? It was an inside job. That much seemed definite. Edmund Farrell's own .22 rifle had been used, having been taken from a cupboard in the gun room where he normally kept it. Only Edmund and Christopher's fingerprints were on the gun; though Grindley had to admit, with a stab of deep concern, that most of the rifle had been wiped clean. Certainly David's fingerprints, taken for the first time yesterday, did not show, but then he didn't expect them to. David had spent the day in Derby, and the firm he'd visited in the hopes of getting a large order for P.N.G. Links had provided a perfectly good alibi. The next question was: *Had* David hired a hit-man? And if so, who was he?

Grindley sighed deeply and gazed out of the kitchen window to a garden bathed in cold blue, the trees etched black against a dull sky.

There was something wrong about this whole case, but for the life of him he couldn't think what it was. For all he knew he could be on a wild-goose chase, but he had this gut feeling that David Farrell was more deeply involved than he was admitting. And then, like a stroke of inspiration, something came back to him. When he'd taken David round the house to identify the bodies, they'd talked about Gladys Scovell being the person who had made the discovery. Grindley had explained that at first, she'd only discovered Edmund's body in the hall. How come David had asked: 'She didn't go upstairs, then?' How, at that stage, Grindley asked himself, had David known his mother's body was upstairs unless he was somehow involved?

Whatever the outcome, Grindley knew with a feeling of dread that he'd screwed up. He could lay some of the blame on Alex Osborne, the head of the CID, who'd gone off to play golf on the day of the murder, happy to believe it was a 'domestic' incident, but Osborne would no doubt protest that Grindley had misinformed him in the first place, led him to believe it was all buttoned up. Grindley had talked airily of an open-and-shut case that day, and now he cringed as he recalled how confident he'd been of his diagnosis.

Three hours later he was back at his desk in the police station, the file marked CHELWOOD INCIDENT before him. He'd have one last crack at David Farrell, and he'd get Franklin to be present, but if they couldn't break him, they'd have to let him go. So far they had insufficient evidence and, with growing horror, Grindley realised just how profoundly he'd believed David's original statement. It had all seemed to fit together at the time; but now, with hindsight, it all seemed a little too neat.

When he summoned Franklin into his office a few minutes later, they discussed the case briefly before getting the constable on duty to bring David from the cell where he'd been held overnight.

'The point we've got to try and pin him down on,' Grindley declared, 'is over the timing of the call he says he received from his mother on the night in question.'

Franklin nodded.

'In my opinion, he's lying. His mother *couldn't* have phoned him around ten o'clock.'

'But his girlfriend, Charlotte Taylor verified it, didn't she? We have a statement from her saying that when she came out of the shower, he'd just hung up from talking to his mother.'

'Yes, but did she say she actually heard him talking? Maybe he only pretended his mother had phoned. Maybe, when he rang back, he only pretended to be ringing back. Charlotte Taylor only had his word for it that the line was busy, hadn't she?'

Franklin looked startled. 'I hadn't thought of that.'

Grindley remained silent, taking the credit for this piece of deduction. He didn't mention that, when he'd told Linda Blake the exact times of deaths, it was she who'd pointed out that if the killings had taken place early in the evening, David couldn't possibly have spoken to his mother at ten o'clock.

'OK, Franklin,' he said. 'Let's get on with it. Get him brought in! I want to get to the bottom of this case if it's the last thing I do.'

Charlotte awoke early. As she surfaced over the grey rim of

consciousness, she became aware of a feeling of dread she couldn't at first recognise. Something had happened; something terrible. Then she remembered. For a moment she shut her eyes tightly, as if to block out the images that filled her mind, but they wouldn't go away: David was being held for questioning, and nothing either Linda or Denzil had said on the phone last night had done anything to alleviate her worry. She looked at her bedside clock; it was only half-past five. She must try and go back to sleep, even if only for a couple of hours. Breathing deeply and slowly, she tried to concentrate her mind on something else, something pleasant and inconsequential: the fabrics she'd selected to show a client for her bedroom curtains; the tender shade of green she'd chosen for another client's bathroom; the vibrant red for a basement dining room; but it was no good. Her thudding heart brought her sharply to the surface again. Sleep was impossible. Sleep would only, at best, produce fragmented nightmares and dark horrors; it would be better to get up and face whatever the day had to bring.

Myra found Charlotte already hard at work when she arrived at the design studio shortly after nine o'clock.

'How's it going, La?' she asked. Then she looked at her more closely. 'You look dreadful. Anything wrong?'

Charlotte gave a wry smile, and nodded. 'Yes. Very wrong. I'm worried sick, actually.'

Myra seated herself at her desk, an immaculate figure, in spite of the early hour, in a sharp navy blue and emerald green suit, her dark hair swept back into a chignon.

'La, what's happened?'

'David was asked to go down to Barrow yesterday by the detective who was in charge of the case. We imagined it

329

was a routine thing, but they've held him overnight for questioning.'

Myra's eyes widened. 'Why?'

'Your guess is as good as mine. I was given the information by a reporter for the *Globe*, who rang me late last night to ask how I felt about it.'

'Oh, for God's sake! I hope you told him to get lost?'

'Yes. What worries me is why they think David might know something. What could he know? I think his ex-girlfriend has been making trouble. If she's out to get him, God knows what she may have been saying.'

'I get the picture, La, but I'm sure you're worrying unnecessarily. The police have to look into every angle, even if it does sound implausible. They probably want to check out her story. See if there's anything to it.'

'What, all day yesterday? And then keep him overnight?' Charlotte queried. 'Surely they wouldn't take wild accusations from a stranger as seriously as that, would they?'

'I think they would,' Myra affirmed. 'Why don't you give them a ring and ask what's happening?'

'I'm scared, Myra. It's like going to the doctor's. I've always been nervous of people in an official capacity.'

'That's because you're shy. Shall I ring for you?'

Charlotte was grateful. 'Would you really?'

A few moments later, Myra was through to the duty officer.

'Good morning,' she said brightly. 'This is Myra Grant, a friend of Charlotte Taylor. Can you give me any information concerning her boyfriend, David Farrell, who I believe is being held for questioning in connection with the murders at Chelwood Manor?'

There was a pause, then she spoke again.

'Have you any idea when you will finish questioning him? I see. Well, thanks very much.' Then she hung up and looked across her desk at Charlotte.

'Not very helpful I'm afraid,' she said grimly.

'What did they say?'

Myra shrugged. 'They were noncommittal. Refused to confirm the name of the man they are questioning. They wouldn't say when they'll release him, either.'

'Oh, Myra! This is awful.' Charlotte's hands started to shake and her eyes brimmed with tears. 'What shall I do? What do they want with him? Perhaps I should get a solicitor. What do you think?'

'I think you should wait until he's either released or charged.'

'*Charged?*' Charlotte looked appalled. 'But charged with *what*? He didn't kill his family! What are you suggesting, Myra? Oh, God!' Her voice caught in a sob. She had risen from her chair, and was wandering distractedly around the office.

'Listen, La,' Myra said at last. 'There's nothing you can do for the moment. No doubt David will get back to London as soon as he can, and then you can talk the whole thing through with him. In the meanwhile, try and keep calm, and let's get on with some work. It's the best therapy in the world, you know. Otherwise you're just going to sit there brooding and feeling like topping yourself!' The way she spoke always amused Charlotte.

'You're right,' she replied, calming down. 'I'll make us both a cup of strong coffee, and I'll get on with ordering those bathroom fittings for the Rutland Gate property. I'm sorry to be such a pain.'

Myra grinned. 'Everything will work out OK, you'll see,' she said.

'I hope to God you're right.'

There was no word from David all day. Charlotte left a message on her answer-phone, asking him to call her when he got back, but she heard nothing. She tried to concentrate on work, but it was a day when she was stuck in the design studio, instead of going out to meet clients or visit sites, and that made it more difficult. All she could think about was David, wondering what was happening to him. If only she'd gone down to Wiltshire with him, she reflected, then at least she'd know what was going on. Common sense told her there was nothing to worry about; of course he'd be home presently, laughing about being grilled. But another part of her felt again that cold, creeping uneasiness.

At five o'clock she left the office and hurried home. For a moment, as she inserted her key into the street door, she allowed herself the fantasy of believing David was already home, lounging on the couch with pages of the *Evening Standard* strewn around him, and the television blaring. Then they would hug each other and kiss, and say what a dreadful day it had been, and how much they'd missed each other.

At that moment she was dazzled, blinded, startled, as a flashbulb from a press camera went off inches from her face. For a moment she couldn't see anything; she clung to the door-jamb for support.

'Any news on your boyfriend, Charlotte?' a voice asked her cheekily.

'When is he coming home, love?' demanded another.

questioned; he hasn't been arrested. "Helping the police with their inquiries" is, I believe, the phrase used. Of course the whole thing is a travesty. His old girlfriend, Connie, has obviously trumped up some wild accusation, and I suppose the police feel they have to check it out, but I think it's terribly unfair. David's already been through so much.'

'Connie Westcott, eh?' Neil remarked. 'Never did like the girl much. Never knew what David saw in her either.'

Charlotte's breath caught as her throat suddenly constricted.

'You knew her?' she asked before she could stop herself.

'Of course,' Neil replied. 'Carol and I were invited to the engagement party. She was after money; no doubt about that. I'm sorry if she's back in his life again. Sorry for you, too, m'dear. Let's hope she doesn't do too much damage, though I wouldn't put it past her.'

'Because she's out for revenge?'

'I wouldn't have thought revenge was her motive,' Neil said calmly. 'After all, she dumped him . . . for another young man.'

Charlotte's senses reeled. All along she'd presumed David had ended his relationship with Connie. To hear it was the other way around put an entirely different aspect on everything.

'I see,' she said slowly, although she didn't see at all. David *engaged* to Connie?

'I presume you knew all about her?' Neil continued, blandly. 'It was a great relief to the family when she left him.'

'No . . . I . . . er, I didn't know,' she replied, a feeling of unreality sweeping through her. Was this all really happening?

334

'When was this?' Her voice seemed to belong to someone else, far, far away.

'My dear, I'm most dreadfully sorry. I thought you knew all about it. I think they continued to see each other, but the engagement was actually broken off last autumn.'

Autumn, Charlotte thought dully. It must have happened just before she met him. But Neil had said they'd continued to see each other. What exactly did that mean? For a drink? For dinner? For quick sex? Tortured, her mind seemed trapped in an imaginary revolving door; round and round her thoughts kept going, always returning to the same spot: *does he still love her?* Why hadn't he told her about his engagement? Why had he implied that she'd been rejected by *him*? Tears stung her eyes.

'Are you still there, m'dear?' she heard Neil say.

'Yes, I'm here,' she said dully.

'Get David to call me when he gets back, will you? This is an unholy mess, and having these confounded reporters hanging around doesn't help.'

'I know. I was practically blinded by a flash-bulb when I got home a few minutes ago.'

'Get the police to move them on, if they're troublesome! They've got no business to be hounding you,' Neil blustered.

Charlotte smiled, in spite of her worry. Evidence of Neil's previous incarnation as a schoolmaster surfaced whenever he was annoyed.

'I'll be all right,' she assured him. 'I won't be going out again this evening.'

After she'd hung up, she decided to do something useful. Sitting around wasn't going to bring David back. Then she heard the outer door slam shut, followed by hurried footfalls

335

coming up the stairs to her flat. David's footsteps . . . ? Her heart squeezed in a nervous spasm and she felt the blood zing away from her head, leaving her giddy.

'Hello, little angel!'

Charlotte flew out of the living room. He was standing in the hallway; the man she loved and yet, for a fleeting moment, a stranger she didn't know at all.

He stood there, looking at her with his gorgeous blue eyes, and there was a smile on his face she didn't understand.

'Are you all right?' she asked, going to him, only wanting at that moment to put her arms around him.

'I'm fine. It's so good to be home again.' In response he held her close. She noticed a sour, stale smell and realised he hadn't washed or shaved.

'I'm bloody pissed off,' he added.

Charlotte drew back to look up at him. 'What on earth happened? I had a reporter ring me late last night; he told me you were being kept at the police station.'

Although his tone was grumbling, he looked quite relaxed. 'They wanted to go over everything again and again! All the same questions we had on the day it happened. Can you imagine? Christ, what a waste of time and money! Those country police are a bunch of fools. The whole thing was a farce . . .'

'But they believed you weren't involved and let you go?'

He moved away, looking at her strangely. 'Believed me?' he echoed. 'I was bloody well telling the *truth*! It wasn't a question of them believing me! I suppose that arsehole, Grindley, has to be seen to be doing something, but I wish it wasn't my time he wasted.'

'But how could it have taken so long?'

'They're so pedantic, that's why. They picked away at every little detail until I thought I would scream. God, it was a bore!'

Charlotte reached up to kiss him. 'At least you're home now. I expect you're hungry.' Now that he was back she forgot her anger and anxiety. His good spirits were catching and, more importantly, he seemed delighted to be back.

'I'm starving!' he replied, cheerfully. 'I could eat an ox!' As he spoke, he pulled off his tie and unbuttoned his shirt.

'God, it's good to be home!' he said again.

Charlotte smiled, looking with longing at his bare chest and arms as he peeled off his shirt. They didn't seem to make love so often now that they lived together, and she missed it. In some ways it was peaceful, she thought, the way married couples must be peaceful, but at times she longed for that first passion to return.

'Would you like a mixed grill?' she asked, knowing it was his favourite dish.

'You're a star.' And with that he sauntered off to the bathroom, humming a little tune.

Charlotte awoke with a start. She'd dreamed she was at Chelwood, in the study with Edmund, and he was telling her that David had been adopted.

'He's really the son of the devil . . .' Edmund was saying, and his voice was as soft and whispery as the rustling of leaves.

Shocked, and with her heart hammering, Charlotte rolled over in bed, seeing David's shape beside her in the dim light of dawn which filtered through her curtains. For a moment she lay looking at his shadowy form, curled up into a foetal position. He was facing away from her, and breathing so quietly and peacefully that she couldn't hear anything. Then she shut her eyes, and immediately the vision of Edmund, sinister and whispering, came back to her in all its vivid awfulness.

It was impossible to go back to sleep. Her mind was in turmoil, and there were so many unanswered questions in her life these days that she felt overwhelmed by a strange anxiety she'd never experienced before. What on earth had made her dream of Edmund?

For a long time, Charlotte lay looking at David's back view. She wondered how it was he could sleep so tranquilly when it was his family who had been murdered; while she, who had barely known them, should be suffering from such stress? Life was becoming a nightmare of uncertainties as far as she was concerned, and she was beginning to feel trapped by her own emotions. If she hadn't loved David so much, and needed him so deeply, she'd have walked away from the horror of the situation right now. Yet she couldn't turn her back on him. David slept on beside her, his face in repose. Gazing at him, Charlotte wondered how anyone could even imagine he had anything to do with the killings. Only Charlotte knew how deeply he had suffered when he'd seen Virginia with her face half blown away. Adopted or not, she'd been a mother to him for twenty-eight years, and it must have been terrible for him to have seen her struck down so violently.

Charlotte sighed, moved closer to him, and tried to forget her bad dream. David stirred, feeling the warmth of her body, and his eyelids flickered as he smiled drowsily.

'All right, little angel?' he murmured.

Charlotte didn't answer, but reached for his hand which lay relaxed on top of the covelet.

'Did you sleep well?' he asked, tightening his fingers around hers.

'So-so.'

'It's nice to be in a proper bed again.' His voice was luxuriously sleepy.

'It must have been awful for you,' she sympathised. 'I can't think of anything worse.'

He nodded slowly, eyes still shut. 'Stupid fuckers! The lot of them!'

There was a pause, and for a moment she thought he'd gone back to sleep. Then he spoke again, softly and dreamily. 'We must go abroad, La. Get the hell out of this wretched place and go somewhere hot where we can lie on the beach all day, and drink wine, and get a wonderful tan.'

It was almost as if he was talking to himself. She felt a cold little draught play around her heart. Somehow, she'd hoped he'd given up the idea of drifting around the sun-spots of the world.

'Where shall we go, little angel?' He sounded insistent.

'We don't have to decide right now, do we?' she hedged.

'We have to make plans, though.'

She didn't answer. The last thing she wanted at this early hour was a confrontation.

'I'm going to get up,' she announced suddenly, rolling out of bed.

David frowned. 'Why are you so restless?'

'There's a lot going on at the office,' she lied. 'I promised Myra I'd drop in at a house in Knightsbridge we're doing. The painters were behind schedule yesterday.'

'Why the hell can't Myra do it?' he grumbled.

'Because she's got another site to visit,' she said briefly.

Lying in a hot, fragrant bath a little while later, she tried to analyse her feelings. On the one hand she desperately needed David, and yet on the other a part of her wanted to get away from him, as she'd done just now. She didn't have to visit a property on her way in to work, so why had she pretended she did? What was she running away from? Why was she trying to escape the man she loved?

'There's a message for you to ring Linda,' Myra informed her when she arrived at the design studio. 'She sounded rather mysterious.'

Charlotte sank on to her desk chair and sighed.

'Trouble?' Myra inquired.

'I don't know . . . I feel jittery and exhausted. I don't know how much more I can take. Ever since the murders I've felt stressed, and the worst part is, it doesn't look like it's ever going to end!'

Myra nodded sympathetically. 'You haven't got over the original trauma yet, and just when you thought everything was cut and dried, it has started up all over again.'

'Exactly! It's like a nightmare that I can't wake up from. It's an awful thing to say, Myra, but I want to get away from it all; even David. I pretended to him that I had to visit a site on the way in this morning: isn't that terrible?' Charlotte sounded flat and weary.

'You'll be ill if you're not careful,' Myra warned. 'Why don't you take the rest of the week off? I'm sure I can manage.'

'That's sweet of you, but I'd rather work,' Charlotte

insisted. 'I have a feeling that work is the only thing that's keeping me sane at the moment.'

'OK, but take it easy. Surely you'll feel better when they finally do find out who committed the murders? To have that uncertainty hanging over you must be awful.'

Charlotte nodded. 'David says they're a bunch of fools down in Barrow. I'd better get on to Linda. Perhaps Holly has started talking.'

'That's the breakthrough you're waiting for, isn't it?'

'Yes. If she saw what happened it could clear up this mess once and for all. Poor little thing. In some ways I hope she's forgotten everything, but in other ways, whatever she can remember could be vital.'

Charlotte dialled Linda's number.

'Hi, Linda. I got your message to ring you.'

'Thanks, love. Listen, I've had another of my lengthy conversations with the detective inspector, about Holly.'

'Is she telling you anything yet?'

'Not a word, but he keeps ringing me in hopes. La, do you know what they questioned David about exactly?'

Charlotte paused, nonplussed, not sure what Linda was getting at.

'Well, no . . . he said they were asking him all the same questions they asked at the time. It was scandalous the way they kept him overnight. I mean, you'd think he'd something to do with it,' she added indignantly.

It was Linda who now remained silent for a long moment.

'What is it?' Charlotte asked, sensing there was something wrong. 'You surely can't believe . . . !'

'The detective let something slip when I talked to him late yesterday afternoon, after he'd released David.'

'What sort of thing?'

'He thinks David knows more than he's telling them. That's why—'

Charlotte exploded, cutting Linda off in mid-sentence.

'*What?* That's the biggest load of rubbish I've ever heard,' she expostulated. 'David's no more involved than I am!'

'I know . . . I know . . . I didn't say they thought David was responsible for what happened,' Linda said calmly. 'They merely think he *knows* something.'

'Why? Why should they think that?' Charlotte felt seriously alarmed now. 'It's that Connie woman, isn't it? She's been saying terrible things . . . Though God knows why.'

'She must be basing her accusations on something,' Linda reasoned.

'She's after money; Neil told me that. When David refused to give her any, the night she turned up at my place, I think she went straight to the police to make trouble.'

'So you think she was trying to blackmail him?' Linda asked slowly.

'Yes . . . no . . . I mean . . .' Charlotte paused, confused. If Connie was trying to blackmail David, that meant she knew something but would remain silent if he met her demands. But if . . .

'Oh, I don't know, Linda,' she wailed. 'I just don't bloody know any more!'

Chapter Eighteen

Neil arrived unannounced at Charlotte's flat a few days later. Surprised, she let him in. It was only half-past eight in the morning, and she wondered what on earth he wanted. 'I'm just about to leave for the office,' she explained. 'Have you come to see David?'

'Yes, if it's convenient,' Neil replied with elaborate politeness. He looked around her stylishly decorated living room as he spoke. 'Beautiful place you've got here.'

'Thank you.' Charlotte smiled, equally polite. She felt as if she and Neil had minor parts in some bizarre play. 'I'll tell him you're here. Would you like some coffee?'

'If it isn't too much trouble. I've just driven up from Newbury.'

'You must have had an early start.'

'Six-thirty. Early enough.' His smile was forced.

At that moment a lazy voice called out from the bedroom. 'Neil?'

'Yes, it's me. I've come to ask you a favour.'

As Charlotte hurried into the kitchen to get the coffee, David ambled into the living room, his hair rumpled, his face sleepy eyed. He was wearing boyish blue-and-white-striped pyjamas, and his bare feet made him look strangely vulnerable.

343

'Hi, Neil,' he said, yawning widely.

'Hello, old chap.'

'It's a bit early for a social call, isn't it?'

'Sorry about that, but this is the best time on the roads. Avoids the rush-hour, you know.'

Charlotte returned with a steaming cup of coffee, and set it down on the sofa-table in front of Neil.

'Sorry I can't stay, but I've got to meet an electrician at a flat in Lexham Gardens and I'm running late.'

'Of course. You run along, my dear.' Neil scrutinised her closely and a flicker of anxiety showed in his eyes.

'You've lost weight, Charlotte.'

She gazed at him in astonishment.

'Have I?' She looked down at herself. 'I don't feel any thinner.' Then she turned to the gilt-framed mirror that hung over the mantelshelf. Eye to eye with her own reflection, she thought her face looked pale and her eyes tired. But definitely not thinner.

'I think I only look as if I've lost weight because this suit has flattering lines,' she joked. 'The day I lose half a stone I'll hang a flag out of the window!'

'Take care of yourself, my dear. We can't have you getting ill; you've been through a lot lately, and you should take it easy for a while,' Neil reminded her kindly.

'That's what I'm always telling her,' David remarked, as he lounged along the length of the sofa, feet on a cushion. 'I want her to come travelling with me.'

Neil looked from one to the other, smiling politely.

Charlotte seized her briefcase and handbag. 'I really must be off. Goodbye, Neil. Give my love to Carol.'

'I will, my dear.'

Then she bent down to kiss David. 'See you later, love.'

He nodded silently. He was watching Neil curiously.

'What have you come for?' he asked.

'Ah, yes! In Virginia's Will there were several codicils . . . She wanted Carol to have some of her personal possessions; you know, books, and the tapestry rug she worked, and some clothes: things that mean a lot to Carol. I wonder if I could borrow the keys to Chelwood, so I can go and pick them up? I had a word with the family solicitor, and he said he had no objection, as long as you didn't mind.'

'What about probate? I was told I couldn't touch anything until probate had been agreed?'

'That applies to big items, like silver and paintings and furniture, and of course jewellery. Clothes and personal bits-and-bobs don't count.'

'I see.' David rose and stretched. 'I'm going to get myself some coffee; d'you want some more?'

'No thanks. This is fine.'

When David returned to the living room, Neil was examining some of Charlotte's drawings.

'She's a talented girl, isn't she?' he remarked.

'Ummm.'

Neil looked at a few more designs, then he turned back to David.

'So you don't mind if I borrow the keys for a couple of days?'

'I don't mind. Go right ahead. I'd go with you to help, but I don't think I can bear to go back to Chelwood right now, although I suppose I'll have to at some point.' As he spoke, he went over to Charlotte's desk, and withdrew the keys from one of the top drawers. 'Here you are.' He threw them skilfully for Neil to catch.

'Thanks.' The keys were cold and hard in Neil's hand. 'Is this the only set you've got?'

'Yup! Gladys has all the others, at the moment. She keeps an eye on the place. Let me have them back as soon as you've finished with them.'

'Of course, old chap. It's Carol, you know. She wants a few keepsakes of Virginia's. This has hit her very hard. Virginia was her last living relative, so it's been a great blow to lose her in this terrible way.'

'Yup,' said David again.

There was silence between the two men, as if neither knew what to say next.

'I'd better be off,' Neil remarked, pocketing the keys. 'Thanks, old chap. Good to see you. I'll return them before the end of the week.'

David padded on bare feet to the front door, to see Neil off.

'Thanks again,' Neil called out, as he hurried down the front door steps.

Neil drove swiftly away, pleased that his plan had worked so well. From Charlotte's flat he drove along the Old Brompton Road until he came to a café. It had a green and white striped blind over the window, and tubs of small box trees on either side of the entrance. Stopping outside he tooted his horn. Almost immediately, Carol came bustling out.

'You were quick,' she announced as she settled herself beside him. 'I'd barely finished my coffee.'

'David was still in bed. Charlotte let me in; she looks

346

very drawn and strained. Thinner, too, I thought, although she denied it.'

'Poor girl. I wouldn't like to be in her shoes.'

'And it's not over yet, not by a long shot,' Neil added grimly.

'I know. Did you actually see David? He didn't suspect anything, did he?'

'Not a thing . . . and why should he? Virginia did bequeath some bits and pieces to you, so it's not unnatural for us to want to collect them.'

'He believed you, then?'

'Oh, yes.'

Neil carefully overtook a lorry as they joined the Cromwell Road extension. Once clear he moved into the slower inside lane again.

'How long will it take us to get there?'

'If the traffic's light, we should do it in a couple of hours.'

For a while they drove on in companionable silence, each lost in their own thoughts, feeling no great need to talk. At last Carol asked in a troubled voice: 'We can't get into trouble by searching Chelwood, can we? I mean, we needn't tell anyone exactly what we're doing if they do find us there, need we? If we bump into Gladys or her daughter, we can tell them David gave us permission to collect some of Virginia's things.'

'Exactly. No harm in that. Besides, it's partly true.'

'Partly,' Carol echoed. Then she said, 'I'm not looking forward to this.'

Neil glanced at her and thought how she'd aged since the murders. The lines from her nose down to the outer edges of her mouth had deepened, and there were bruised-looking pouches under her eyes.

'You needn't come with me if you'd rather not, Carol. I can drop you off at the Court Hotel and pick you up afterwards.'

She shook her head. 'No, I'll come. It's the least I can do, however hard it is. I owe it to Virginia and I owe it to Christopher, too.'

In silence, they drove on. Somehow, somewhere in Chelwood Manor they were convinced they would find a clue to what had really happened. It was useless involving the police at this stage, they agreed, because they didn't have any concrete evidence to go on. Everything was supposition and guesswork, and yet Linda's conviction that Christopher hadn't been involved had galvanised them into action.

'What shall we do if we do find something that the police may have overlooked?' Carol asked.

'Inform them, of course.'

'Oh, God! It's going to be awful, isn't it?' she sighed. 'I don't know whether I hope we're successful or not.'

That same morning, Grindley had a call from the head of the CID for the district.

'What's going on?' Alex Osborne asked. He sounded deeply irritated. He himself had received a call from headquarters in London, demanding to know what the local police at Longley were playing at by pulling David Farrell in for further questioning.

'We're going to look like a bunch of fools if this case turns out not to have been a "domestic"!' he barked. 'You assured me it was an open-and-shut case, and that you'd sewn it all up. Now I'm being questioned about my part in the affair! I was asked why I went off to play golf on the day a major incident had taken place in my area. And why I authorised the cremations to go ahead, and the house to be cleaned!'

'I'm sorry, sir.'

'Has any new evidence come to light?'

'Not exactly . . .'

'Then what the hell's going on, man?'

'We had a tip-off, but it came from an unreliable source: David Farrell's ex-girlfriend, who may be seeking revenge. I thought it prudent, though, to question him again. There is also the child. She's still refusing to talk about what happened, but there are indications that both Mr and Mrs Farrell were shot whilst Christopher Farrell was still visiting his girlfriend in the village.'

'God Almighty!' Osborne exploded. 'You didn't take everything at face value, did you? I only left you in charge because you said it was a straightforward case! Now it looks as if a multiple murder has taken place, and we don't even know who committed it! This is a disgrace, Grindley! Your incompetence appalls me!'

Grindley felt the cold misery of failure flow over him as if someone had chucked a bucket of icy water in his face. He'd screwed up. Now he would always be remembered as the detective inspector who dismissed a multiple-murder case as a "domestic". He had taken everything on trust; from David Farrell's statement to Gladys Scovell's. At the time it had looked like a case that had solved itself, yet now he had a gut feeling that someone – perhaps David Farrell –

had painted the perfect outline of a picture, leaving him to fill in the colours. 'Painting by numbers' it was called in the world of art. 'A fucking cock-up' in police language.

Grindley pulled himself together. He still had his eye on promotion.

'These accusations may well be false,' he told Alex Osborne briskly. 'As yet I've no evidence which leads me to suppose that David Farrell had anything to do with the shootings. I'm merely making a few further inquiries to ascertain the facts,' he added with what he thought was dignity.

When he came off the line he sent for Franklin. There was an edge of panic in his voice as he issued hurried instructions.

'I want everyone questioned again about the Chelwood murders, and I mean everyone. Organise a house-to-house interrogation and find out exactly what everyone was doing on the evening in question. Find out if there were any strangers around, who was in the local pub that night, what sort of vehicles were in the car park. We may have to recall David Farrell again for further questioning, but leave him alone for the moment. I don't want him to know that we're suspicious.'

Franklin's jaw dropped. 'A house-to-house, sir?'

'That's correct. Leave no stone unturned. Meanwhile, I'm going to get on to Mrs Linda Blake again to see if the child's started to talk about her experience. That's what we need. A strong lead in the right direction.'

'Ironic, isn't it, sir, that we have what could be a prime witness, but she can't tell us a thing about it.'

'Bloody ironic,' Grindley commented dryly.

Alone again, he sat deep in thought, going over every detail of the case, imagining in his mind's eye the rooms of Chelwood Manor on that fatal evening. One thing that had worried him at the time, but which he had subsequently put to the back of his mind, was that no one had heard anything, and yet five shots had been fired. If Chelwood Manor had been surrounded by extensive grounds, it wouldn't have been surprising, but on the left-hand side of the house, screened by a brick wall and trees, were several cottages, the pub and a newsagent's. At six-thirty in the evening there would have been people about, and yet no one had reported hearing anything.

Grindley went out into the corridor to help himself to water from the large blue plastic dispenser that stood on a table. Then it struck him with an awful suddenness that, if no one had heard the shots, the answer had to be that the .22 rifle had a silencer. *Yet when the gun had been found in Christopher's hands, it hadn't been fitted with one.*

The garden had a disconsolate air about it, the flowerbeds choked with weeds, the grass overgrown and starry with crops of daisies. Carol was the first to get out of the car when Neil stopped in front of the three-pillared entrance. She looked about her with a scandalised expression.

'The place is going to rack and ruin,' she exclaimed. 'Surely someone should be looking after it? Look at the state of that lawn! If David plans to sell the place, he'll never get a good price at this rate.'

Neil clambered out of the driving seat more slowly, his joints stiff. He looked up at the shuttered windows and the strange portico.

'Well, it's not our responsibility, love,' he replied, 'and thank God for that! I've always hated this place. My worst nightmare would be to be lumbered with a bloody edifice like this.'

'It's nice in the summer,' Carol said defensively. She'd always been rather proud that her sister had married money and lived in such a grand house.

'What summer? This is England,' he retorted almost crossly. Coming back to the scene of the tragedy was unnerving him, and he suddenly wished they hadn't decided to do a bit of private detective work. It was ridiculous; what could they hope to find that the police had overlooked? At this moment he didn't even know where to start. Cursing himself for having let Linda persuade him that they must do all they could to clear Christopher's name, he took the keys out of his pocket and unlocked the forbiddingly heavy front door. As they crossed the threshold, a damp smell of unheated and unused rooms hit them with force. Carol wrinkled her nose.

'Ugh! Isn't it horrid!'

'Let's open a few windows,' Neil suggested. He thought the place had the taint of a butcher's shop, too.

Everything was covered by a layer of dust, and dead flowers standing in vases of foul water added to the piquancy of the odour. No one it seemed, had been into Chelwood Manor since the police had finally locked it up, after they'd removed the bloodstained carpets and bedding.

'My God, this is worse than I thought it would be,' said Carol. 'Where shall we start, Neil? What are we supposed to be looking for?'

Neil was standing in the middle of the panelled hall,

recalling how it had looked at Christmas with its magnificently decorated tree, piles of gift-wrapped presents and crackling log fire. Now it was a bleak place, devoid of physical warmth or charm.

'I'm not sure,' he admitted.

Carol made a grimace and strode off in the direction of the kitchen. Neil followed her, hands dug unhappily into his pockets.

The scrubbed table in the centre of the room reminded Carol that they'd always had tea in here. She could see Virginia now, with her quick, nervous movements, always darting about, bejewelled hands fluttering as she poured out the tea. Tears stung the back of her eyes, and she brushed them away impatiently. Weeping was not her style. Crying would not bring Virginia back.

Neil wandered aimlessly around, opening and shutting cupboard doors.

'Chris died in here,' Carol remarked.

'I know.'

'How are we going to prove Chris is innocent, if all the evidence has been destroyed? I think we should search the bedroom he was sleeping in. And maybe Holly's room, too.'

Neil frowned, thoughtfully. 'I think we should start looking for clues in the precise place this murder started.'

'In the hall? Where Edmund was found?'

'No, in the gun room. Remember, it was Edmund's own gun that was used. Let's have a look and see what we can find.'

'But there might be some evidence upstairs,' Carol protested. 'After all, we think he hid Holly in the spare room to protect her.'

353

'The question is from whom?'

Carol nodded. 'OK, let's take a look in the gun room first.'

Across the corridor from the kitchen, what was always referred to as the gun room was also used as a cloakroom. Coats and macintoshes hung on rows of brass hooks, and on a low shelf several pairs of gumboots were neatly arranged. Fishing rods stood in one corner, and along the wall facing the small window, there was an old-fashioned built-in cupboard. Beside it, four foot high and a foot deep, stood the grey metal gun safe.

'Damn! It's locked,' Carol exclaimed.

'Edmund always kept it locked, but I know where he hid the key.' Neil strode over to the window and reached up to the ledge along the top. He felt layers of dust which left his fingers black, but there was no sign of a key.

'Hell! I wonder where it's gone?'

'Perhaps it's on top of the cupboard,' Carol suggested.

He found it almost immediately. 'I suppose the police must have put it there. There's no doubt whoever took Edmund's gun must have known where the key was kept.'

'Who did know? Apart from the family?'

Neil shrugged. 'I don't think Edmund made a secret of the hiding place, so I suppose it could have been anyone.'

He unlocked the door and saw a gun, old and rarely used, propped up in the corner. He recognised it as the spare gun that was kept for the use of guests who came to stay during the shooting season.

Carol started poking about in the built-in cupboard. A row of shelves on the left-hand side held ammunition, cleaning rods, cans of oil and rags, tossed in amongst a collection of household oddments including shoe polish and carpentry tools.

'What a mess,' Neil observed, picking out a fishing fly that had got entangled in a ball of string. Suddenly he stopped and looked at something more closely.

'What is it?' Carol asked.

'What's this doing here? I thought it was—'

'What?' She peered over his shoulder.

Without touching anything, he pointed to a black metal object half hidden by a cleaning rag.

'What is it?'

'A silencer.'

She snorted derisively. 'I know *that*! I do know my way around a gun, you know! I mean, what are you getting at?'

'This silencer belonged to Edmund. He used it because the sound of a gunshot aggravated his tinnitus. Don't you remember he was complaining about it at Christmas? And he said he was getting deaf? He put it down to shooting.'

'So . . . ?'

'On the day of the murder, I wondered why no one had heard gunshots, especially as some of the village people live nearby. I presumed Chris must have fitted the silencer on to Edmund's gun before he shot his parents. Or maybe it was already in place? So what's it doing here now? I suppose the police still have the rifle?'

Carol shrugged.

'If this *is* Edmund's silencer, and I'm sure of it, it proves without a shadow of doubt that Chris couldn't possibly have committed suicide.'

'Yes, he could. I don't see the significance about a rifle with or without a silencer.'

Neil looked at her, suddenly every inch the schoolmaster addressing a dim pupil.

'*Think* about it,' he said sternly. 'Let's suppose Chris loaded the gun, fitted the silencer so the shots couldn't be heard by the neighbours, then proceeded to kill his parents before going to the kitchen where he bumped himself off?'

Carol winced. 'Yes?' she asked doubtfully.

'Well?' He paused to look at her. 'How the hell did he manage to shoot himself twice, and then when he was dead, nip back into the gun room to hide the silencer? Remember it was not on the rifle when they found him holding it?'

Carol looked stunned.

'Yes, I see,' she said slowly. 'Whoever killed Chris took the silencer off the gun . . . and . . . but *why?*'

Neil stared at his wife, horror etched on his face. 'Someone put the silencer back in this cupboard,' he said, 'because there was no way Chris could have shot himself with the silencer in place. *It would have made the gun too long!* He'd have had to have arms the length of a gorilla's to have reached . . .'

Carol closed her eyes for a moment.

'Oh, my God!' she said softly. 'So it means the murderer shot Chris after he'd killed the others, then he removed the silencer and put it in this cupboard . . . and the gun itself in Chris's hands, so it looked as if he was the killer?'

'Exactly. And the silencer had been fixed on in the first place so that people wouldn't come running before the murderer could get away.'

Carol leaned against the cupboard, her knees suddenly weak. 'What do we do now, Neil?'

'You go to the kitchen and see if you can find one of

those transparent plastic freezer bag things, just in case there are fingerprints on it. Then we'll take this to the police station.'

He stopped and carefully lifted away a corner of the cleaning rag.

'Look! Look at this, Carol.' His voice was tense. 'Blood! There's blood on this rag and I think it's come from the silencer.'

'Don't touch anything,' she warned.

'You're right. Let's phone the police and get them to come here right away. How the hell did they manage to overlook this?'

As they hurried back to the kitchen, Neil privately hoped he wasn't about to make a fool of himself. Perhaps it was rust and not blood he'd seen on the rag. Maybe the police knew all about the silencer after all, but didn't do anything about it because it belonged to another gun? Round and round his thoughts jangled confusedly. He'd never played amateur detective before. Suddenly he felt out of his depth.

Carol, sitting down while Neil made the call, wondered if she should make a cup of tea.

Then they both heard it. Shocked, they looked at each other, eyes wide with alarm. A click like a key turning in a lock had broken the sombre silence of Chelwood. Then there was a footfall scraping against stone, and a thud as a door shut again. In that moment they realised they were not alone in the house.

Chapter Nineteen

Holly nodded slowly as she always did when she wanted her mother to agree to something. She continued to nod as she said, 'Yes. I'll talk to Betty.'

'You'll tell Betty everything that happened, sweetheart?' Linda asked softly, trying to control the excitement in her voice. After weeks of refusing to talk about what had happened at Chelwood, Holly had at last been persuaded to talk to the police child psychologist and counsellor. Betty Owen, a kindly woman in her forties who had a way with children, had been visiting them regularly for some weeks, but without success. Holly would play with her dolls and chat about things in general, but when the subject of staying at Chelwood came up, she clamped her small lips together and looked away. No amount of subtle coaxing would induce her to speak.

It had been Randal, Denzil's brother, who had finally suggested a little bribery might do the trick.

'I may not know much about children myself,' he'd admitted with an engaging smile, 'but I know a lot about human nature. Both adults and children respond to a little healthy corruption.'

Linda smiled at him. She and Rand, as he was always called, had got along famously from the start and, to Rand's amusement, she was always introducing him to her single girlfriends in the hope he'd fall in love with one of them. In her opinion, no good-looking young man should remain single, especially if he had all the makings of a perfect husband.

'What are you suggesting?' she asked.

'Is there anything Holly specially wants?'

'A toy, you mean?'

'Yes.'

Linda thought for a moment. 'She'd love a doll's house. She's often asked for one, but really nice houses are very expensive.'

Rand's smile broadened, making him look much younger than his thirty-one years.

'Let it be my birthday present to her,' he suggested.

'Oh, Rand! I couldn't let you do that. They cost several hundred pounds, unless you get something really tacky. You can't possibly give her something like that.'

'Look,' he reasoned. 'You're being kind enough to let me stay here until I find a flat; the least I can do is to give my thank-you present to Holly. I honestly believe if you phrase it the right way she might tell you what happened at Chelwood, in exchange for a doll's house of her choice.'

Linda burst out laughing. 'Now I know why you're such a successful lawyer,' she said. 'In fact, why don't *you* suggest it to her, using your persuasive tactics?'

Rand looked serious. 'I will if you like, but I don't want to push my ideas on to you. Think about it first and discuss it with Denzil.'

'No.' She spoke positively. 'Let's do it. When she gets back from nursery school, you suggest it to her. It might just do the trick, and I believe the sooner she tells us what happened, the quicker she'll get over the trauma.'

'Good.' Rand looked pleased. 'I've seen an amazing shop near where I used to live in Parson's Green. It's called the Singing Tree and they sell spectacular doll's houses and all the furniture, too.'

'Oh, you're so sweet, but don't spoil Holly.'

'Why not?' He sounded delighted with his plan. 'As you are so frequently reminding me, I'm not married with babies, but there's nothing to stop me spoiling other people's children.'

To Linda's relief, Holly had agreed to tell Betty Owen everything.

'And then I get my doll's house?' she said for the third time.

'Then you get your doll's house,' Linda assured her. 'You and I will go with Rand to a shop called the Singing Tree.'

'You can choose whichever house you want,' Rand added.

Holly looked up at him in adoration. 'Any one?'

'Any one you like.'

Her face was radiant as she spread her arms expansively. 'A *big* house?'

'As big as you like.'

Linda shot Rand a quizzical look. 'Steady on, Rand. Don't go mad! You're into serious money, especially if you're going to get any furniture. I think Denzil and I should do that bit.'

Rand swung Holly off her feet and held her at arm's length above his head so that she was looking down at him, giggling uproariously.

'This is going to be my present to Holly and I want her to have anything she wants.'

Linda looked at him fondly. 'You *must* get married and have children, Rand. You'd make a terrific father.'

He laughed. 'I fully intend to, but give me a chance to meet the right girl first, for goodness' sake!'

Carol and Neil stood rock still in the kitchen, listening to the approaching footsteps. They were coming along the stone-flagged corridor, getting nearer and louder all the time. A moment later there was the crash of the back door being slammed shut, and then a second set of footfalls joined the first.

Carol blinked nervously, her face paling, her eyes darting around the kitchen as if searching for something – anything – with which she could defend herself. Neil's hands, she noticed, were clenched into tight fists, and his jawline was taut. Second by second the footfalls were coming closer.

Suddenly Neil sprang into action, as if he'd discarded the invisible bonds of fear.

'Who's there?' He shouted so loudly that Carol jumped.

The footsteps halted, one set stopping abruptly, the second with a shuffle.

'Who the hell is it?' Neil shouted again, staring at the open doorway.

At that moment a figure stepped forward from the darkness of the corridor and stood there looking at them. It was Detective Inspector Grindley.

Neil's jaw dropped open, relief making him feel suddenly weak. 'What the hell . . . ?' he began, a look of bewilderment crossing his face. 'How did you get in?'

As if he guessed what Neil was about to say, Grindley extended his hand. In the palm lay a bunch of keys.

'I borrowed this set from Gladys Scovell. May I ask you, sir, where you obtained yours?'

'From David, my nephew you know . . . David Farrell. He said he didn't mind if we came here to collect . . . er . . . you know . . . some things that belonged . . . er . . .' Neil, stumbling over his words, thrown by the shock of seeing Grindley, turned to Carol.

She seemed composed and decisive.

'Inspector, the real reason we are here is because we are not happy with the findings of the autopsy. I'm certain, having talked at length to Linda Blake, that a terrible mistake has been made. I do not believe Christopher killed his parents before committing suicide, and so we've come here today to try and find some evidence that will prove him innocent.'

'That's right,' Neil chimed in, making a great effort to pull himself together. 'And I think we've stumbled on something of supreme importance; perhaps vital evidence that would prove Christopher is innocent.'

Grindley looked from one to the other as Chief Constable Ron Franklin joined him in the kitchen doorway.

'You have, have you?' Grindley inquired dryly. 'What would this "evidence" be?' he asked Neil.

'We were just about to phone you, actually, to ask you to come and examine something we found in the gun room.'

Grindley frowned. 'I hope you haven't been touching anything that might conceivably be evidence?'

'Certainly not,' Neil replied, offended. As he led the way out of the kitchen, he retorted, 'One thing is sure: Chris didn't commit suicide. He was murdered like Virginia and Edmund.'

'What makes you think that, sir?'

'Wait until you see what we've found.'

In the gun room he opened the cupboard door, and pointed to the shelf.

'That's the silencer to Edmund's gun. I think you'll find bloodstains on that, and on the rag that's partly hiding it,' Neil explained.

Grindley froze as he looked into the cupboard, then he swung on Franklin with an accusatory look.

'I thought I gave orders for every inch of the place to be searched,' he barked.

Franklin blushed a deep crimson, but he kept his ground. 'That was when we were searching for the little girl, sir,' he replied. 'We had a good look around, of course, but we were only looking for the child. We saw there were boxes and stuff in here, but the girl obviously wasn't, so we moved on to other possible hiding places.'

Neil, proud of his discovery, wanted to enlarge on his theory.

'It struck me,' he said, 'that as no one heard the shooting, a silencer must have been used. So why wasn't it fixed to the gun you found in Christopher's hands? More to the point, he must have been murdered like the others, because the silencer would have made the gun too long for him to handle. The murderer must have realised that, and that is the reason it was hidden in the gun room, covered by a rag.'

Grindley looked at Neil coldly, wondering how, in front of Franklin, he could make it look to headquarters that this was his idea; that it was his initiative that led them to vital evidence?

'Got it all worked out, haven't you, sir?' he said

patronisingly. 'You'll be after my job next!' His tone was so dry it crackled.

'We're anxious to clear my nephew's name,' Neil said.

'Which nephew would that be?' inquired Grindley.

'Christopher, of course. None of us believes, now that the dust has settled, that he committed these terrible acts.'

'And what about his brother, David Farrell?'

Neil was taken aback, unsure of his ground for a moment. Carol stepped in, as she'd done before, in complete control of the situation.

'We're not talking about David,' she said sternly. 'We just want it proved that an innocent man isn't being blamed for something he didn't do. It's up to you to find out who really did it.'

Grindley turned to Franklin again. 'Get forensic to come back here at once. I want this house to be thoroughly searched, every inch gone over with a toothcomb. Especially the contents of this cupboard. In fact, I want this room sealed off right now.' He addressed himself to Neil and Carol. 'Would you mind? I'd actually like to have this house cleared of everyone so that we can work from the top to the bottom.'

They all withdrew to the corridor again, suddenly conscious of not being allowed to touch anything.

'If you wouldn't mind leaving right away,' Grindley suggested.

As Neil and Carol walked along the corridor back to the main hall, they could hear Grindley explode with exasperation at the unfortunate Franklin.

'You bloody *fool* . . . !' The words echoed from the gun room. 'We'll be the laughing stock of the county for not having discovered that silencer until now! How the hell could you have overlooked . . . ?'

His voice faded as they stepped out through the front door and went to their car.

'I'm glad they've reopened the case; and how lucky you spotted that silencer,' Carol observed.

Neil nodded slowly. 'Though it's not going to make them appear in a very good light, that's for sure,' he observed thoughtfully.

'Did you hear that, darling?' Charlotte inquired excitedly as she put down the phone. 'That was Linda.'

David glanced away from the television screen on which he was watching the nine o'clock BBC news.

'What did she want?' he asked distractedly.

'Holly has promised she'll tell everything she saw to the child psychologist.'

David's blue eyes sharpened suddenly. 'Really?'

'Yes. Linda's thrilled. It will be so good for Holly to let it all come out at last. Apparently Denzil's brother, Rand, had a hand in persuading Holly. Linda says he is a brilliant lawyer.'

'Don't you think it's very dangerous to put pressure on a small child? It could do more harm than good, and affect her in later life,' David said, looking shocked.

'I suppose so.'

'My God, I wouldn't put a child of mine through all that. We don't even know if she saw anything in the first place. And supposing they want her to give evidence in court, what will that do to her?'

Charlotte frowned. 'God knows, but Linda's convinced

that Chris had nothing to do with it; that he was as much a victim as your parents. She thinks he only hid Holly in the chest to prevent her being killed, too, and she's determined to prove that's what happened.'

'What rubbish!'

'It isn't rubbish. Linda told me . . .'

'Haven't you got a mind of your own? What's all this "Linda said" and "Linda told me . . ." stuff?' He sounded deeply irritated.

Charlotte shrugged. 'I suppose she's anxious to clear his name for Holly's sake.'

The silence in the room almost crackled with tension. David rose to fetch the newspaper from her desk where he'd thrown it down earlier, while Charlotte poured herself another cup of coffee.

'There's nothing on the box tonight,' he grumbled. 'We should have gone to the cinema.'

'I've got an early start,' she observed for the sake of something to say. 'I think I'll go and have a bath.'

Standing in the middle of the bedroom she started to undress, all the while pondering on the sequence of events that had brought her to this moment. Linda had a lot to answer for, she concluded, with her obsessive attitude in proving Chris's innocence. It was upsetting David and that, in turn, upset her.

On impulse she decided she must talk to her family. She'd always been able to go to them for advice, and that was what she most needed now. Someone who would understand and listen to her.

Slipping into her white terry-towelling robe, she sat on the edge of the bed and reached for the phone. To her surprise, as she lifted the receiver, she could hear a woman's voice.

'Don't you dare threaten me like this!' the woman said angrily. 'And stop phoning me like this! No matter what you say, I'm prepared to give evidence because I cannot bear to live with the knowledge . . .'

Charlotte, listening intently, thought she'd got a crossed line, until she heard a man's voice reply.

'Drop dead, you bitch! I'll see you in hell before you do any more damage!'

Charlotte gripped the phone to her ear as an icy frisson swept through her like a great tidal wave, leaving her sick and faint. The man's voice belonged to David.

Charlotte stood in the doorway looking at David as if she was seeing him for the first time.

'What was that all about?' she asked, stunned.

He hurriedly replaced the receiver, but he was smiling up at her confidently.

'I was talking to Connie,' he said, almost breezily. 'Telling her to stop running around making mischief just because I won't give her any money.'

'That's not what it sounded like.'

'How did it sound, then? Don't be silly, La. She rang me a couple of minutes ago, pestering me again . . .'

She rang me a few minutes ago . . . The words caught a hook in Charlotte's memory, taking her back to the night of the shootings. She could see the scene clearly in her mind's eye. She had just come out of the shower and David was standing in the middle of the room holding the receiver and saying, 'My mother rang me a few minutes ago.'

'You rang *her*,' she said quickly before she could stop herself. 'If she'd phoned you I'd have heard the bell ringing.'

David's blue eyes glittered. 'I don't know what you're talking about. Why should I ring Connie, for God's sake?'

Charlotte looked at him, sickened with misery. 'I know you did.'

He shrugged. 'Believe what you like, it's no skin off my nose.' He flopped back into the armchair and picked up the newspaper again. 'You're getting to be a bore, La.'

Tears stung her eyes and her throat constricted painfully. She wanted to believe David more than anything in the world, but she also had to believe the evidence of her ears.

Charlotte dropped on to her knees in front of him, resting her hands on his legs. Unwaveringly she looked into his eyes.

'Please, David. I want to know what's going on. I'll stand by you but I can't help you while you keep me in the dark. Why did the police keep you overnight for questioning? And why should Connie be involved?'

David stared blankly at her for a moment and then he threw back his head with laughter.

'You actually think I'm involved in the murder of my family, don't you?' he said with amazement. 'Go on! You do, don't you?'

It was a direct challenge, and she met his gaze unflinchingly.

'I *know* you didn't shoot them, because you were in Derby all day, and then you were here with me in the evening . . .'

'Yes?'

'So you couldn't have committed the murders . . .'

'Yes?' His expression was still challenging, and amused.

369

'So . . . Oh, I don't know, David,' she said, tears running down her cheeks. 'Your mother couldn't have phoned you that night,' she couldn't stop the words pouring out. 'So why did you say she did? Who are you protecting? And why are you protecting them?' Angry now, she stood up and walked towards the window. Her back towards him she muttered, sulkily, 'I didn't think there were any secrets between us. Now I'm not even sure if you love me.'

'Oh, little angel.' He followed her, wrapping his arms around her from behind and pulling her close, rubbing his cheek against hers. 'There's nothing to worry about. I can assure you I'm not involved in any way. I don't understand about my mother phoning that night – supposedly four hours after she'd died – any more than you do. I can only imagine it was someone impersonating her. Someone who knew her well, because the voice certainly fooled me.'

Charlotte turned towards him and linked her arms around David's neck. She looked up into his face. His expression was earnest and his blue eyes intense.

'It hurts me to think that you could believe nasty rumours about me, La. It's Linda who has been poisoning your mind against me, isn't it? She's so desperate to prove it wasn't Chris that she'd trample over anyone. You don't know Linda like I do; she's always hated me. She'd say anything to get me into trouble. She and Connie.' He shook his head sadly, then nuzzled her temple and kissed her neck. 'Thank God for you, little angel. I'd be lost without you. You know that, don't you? I love you more than anything in the world. You *are* my world, sweetheart.' Then he kissed her tenderly, his mouth lingering over hers.

'I love you too,' she whispered back. She meant it. She

did love him, and when she was in his arms like this all she wanted was to spend the rest of her life with him. It was only at odd moments that the fears and doubts, fuelled by her imagination, started undermining her confidence in their relationship.

'We're so good together,' he murmured, opening her robe and sliding his hands around her waist. They felt warm to her naked skin and, as he stroked her back, goose pimples broke out all over her body, so that she was tingling with anticipation.

'Baby, baby,' he crooned, sliding his muscular thigh between her legs. She pressed herself closer, burying her face in the warmth of his neck, feeling his rising hardness against her groin and, as desire swept through her like a forest fire, making her want him with a passionate fervour, all she could do was say his name, repeating it over and over, like a mantra.

'David ... David ... David!'

'My sweet angel,' he breathed, cupping and stroking her breasts with gentle hands, kissing her throat with tender butterfly kisses, driving her crazy as he thrust himself against her.

Her hands explored him too, knowing his body as well as she knew her own, loving the glistening blond hairs on his forearms and legs, and the triangular bush of golden hair from which rose his manhood. As she stroked him in the way he'd taught her to, he closed his eyes and groaned in ecstasy.

'Oh, bliss ...' he whispered. 'Don't stop ... don't stop ...' His voice became dreamy and he was breathing faster.

'I love you,' she whispered, 'I love you so much.'

For answer, he half carried, half pushed her over to the sofa, so that she sank down among the feather-filled cushions. With his weight on top of her, her desire increased. Almost dizzily, she felt as if they were bound together by something sublime, an eternal bond that nothing could sever. She loved this man and he was hers . . . would always be hers . . . they were locked together by a force she could not deny and did not want to deny. The fact that he loved her meant more to her than she could even admit to herself, and she clung to him fiercely, giving herself to him with abandonment. Everything else was forgotten as his kisses inflamed her and, clinging together, they moved as one, equally matched in desire, pacing their passion with silent understanding, reaching for the same peak together until they collapsed in fulfilment, gasping and crying out in joy.

'I love you . . .' Charlotte cried out, or was it the voice of David she heard, ringing in her ears? She felt so at one with him, she couldn't be sure.

The ringing of the front door bell was loud and persistent. Magda, alone with her charges and just about to give them lunch, swore under her breath as she hurried to answer it. Linda had only gone out to do some shopping a few minutes before. Magda wondered why it was that, as soon as her employer left the house, either the phone of the front door bell started ringing demandingly. Why, for goodness' sake, did the London Electricity Board choose to send a man to read the meter at that precise time? Why did the Gas Board do the same? Then there was the window cleaner, or a nun collecting for charity, or a parcel post delivery? Magda found the interruptions most distracting, especially as her English was limited.

Now, making sure Ben was strapped into his highchair, and leaving Holly to spoonfeed him, she went to open the door.

'What is it?' she demanded crossly as the door swung back. As soon as she saw who was standing there, her face relaxed into a welcoming smile.

'Ah, it you, Mr Farrell!' she exclaimed, pleased. 'Please come in. Mrs Blake, she gone shopping, but you wait?'

David stepped into the hall, eyeing Magda with an appreciative expression. His smile deepened.

'It isn't Mrs Blake I've come to see.'

'Oh?' Magda looked confused. 'Mr Blake, he not here during the day.'

At that moment Holly ran into the hall, her little face glowing with pleasure. She looked at David expectantly.

'Hi there, Holly!' he said, bending down to kiss her.

'Hello.'

'I've got a surprise for you,' said David.

Ecstatic sparkles filled her eyes. 'What is it?' she breathed hopefully.

'I'm going to take you out, but where we're going is the big surprise!' David winked at Magda, as if he was sharing some delightful secret with her.

'Oh!' Holly digested this bit of information before saying, 'Are we going now?'

David nodded, but Magda protested.

'Holly has her lunch now. She must finish.'

'I want to go now,' said Holly determinedly.

'Yes. Come along now,' David agreed. 'We can always

get something to eat where we're going.'

'Is it a restaurant?'

'No, Holly, it's not a restaurant. It's somewhere much more exciting.'

'I get my coat.'

'Good girl.' He turned to Magda, who was hovering anxiously, wondering whether she should let Holly go or not.

'I'll bring her back after tea, Magda.'

'Does Mrs Blake know you're taking Holly out?'

'Of course. We arranged this "surprise" some days ago. Don't tell me she's forgotten.'

'Mrs Blake not mention it to me.'

'Well, never mind,' David said easily.

Holly came hurtling across the hall, dragging her red anorak behind her.

'I got my coat,' she declared sturdily.

'You no finish lunch,' Magda protested.

'Never mind.' David's tone was placating. He smiled at Magda again and gave her another little wink. She blushed slightly, before helping Holly on with her coat.

'OK, if Mrs Blake says she can go, it all right.'

'Great. Let's be off, then. I've got a taxi waiting.' He took Holly's hand and, without a backward glance, she trotted off with him, out into the street and into the waiting cab.

Chapter Twenty

Linda plonked her bags of shopping on the kitchen table and looked around. The kitchen was strangely quiet for that time of day, and it was also unusually tidy. Normally, during the school holidays, Holly would have her box of paints out, and there'd be damp watercolour 'pictures' scattered all over the place, while Ben, crawling now, usually dragged half the contents of the toy cupboard on to the kitchen floor.

'Magda?' she called out.

Linda heard footsteps running down the stairs, and then Magda appeared in the doorway.

'Yes, Mrs Blake?'

'Where are the children?'

Magda beamed. 'Ben, he have his afternoon nap. Holly, she go to get her surprise with Mr Farrell. They back after tea.'

Linda frowned. 'Mr Farrell?' she queried. 'Don't you mean Mr Blake? My brother-in-law? We are going to take Holly to the Singing Tree, but not today. Not for several days in fact.'

'Mr Farrell say today. Say you must have forgotten.'

Linda felt a surge of fear. 'David Farrell? She went with David? What did he say? Why did you let her go?' Linda's voice was sharp with anxiety.

Magda looked back at her defiantly. 'He say you know. You must have forgotten. He say it was all arranged.'

'Oh, my God!' Linda covered her face with her hands for a moment. 'Oh, my God!' she repeated. She tried to pull herself together. 'Where did he say he was taking her?' she demanded.

'He say it a surprise. Holly very happy to go with him. He is her uncle, no?'

'You should *never* have let her go,' Linda said frantically. 'Have you any idea where they've gone?'

Magda shrugged her thin shoulders. 'He no say,' she replied flatly. 'You never tell me not to let her go out with Mr Farrell; how am I supposed to know? Holly's OK with him, no?'

'When did they leave?'

'It was two moments after you go to shop.'

Linda looked at her watch. It was now three-fifteen. She'd left to go shopping at twelve-thirty, so Holly had been out for nearly three hours.

'Did he have a car?' she asked urgently. Fear made her so angry she'd have liked to have shaken Magda and wiped clean the foolish bold smile on her face.

'No, he take a taxi. He tell Holly to hurry. He says he has a lovely surprise for Holly. What's wrong?'

Linda looked at her for a long moment. 'Everything's wrong,' she said trying to sound calm. How could she blame Magda? Normally it would have been perfectly all right to let Holly go out with her uncle. But now she felt deeply frightened for the safety of her child; Holly, the prime witness.

Reaching out she put her hand on Magda's shoulder.

'I'm sorry I was angry with you. I should have warned you . . . but I never damn well thought this would happen.' She shook her head distractedly. 'I must phone Charlotte.' As she hurried out of the room, Magda looked after her with a baffled expression. This was a strange family, for sure, she thought as she went back to her ironing. What possible harm could there be in letting Holly go out with her own uncle?

Charlotte, going through some swatches of curtain fabric, trying to decide whether to advise a client to choose the crushed raspberry damask or the deep crimson silk for her drawing room, was delighted to hear Linda on the line.

'How are you?' she exclaimed. 'And how's Holly?'

'That's why I'm ringing.' Linda said shakily. 'David's taken her out somewhere – I don't know where – without asking me. I don't know what he's up to but I'm scared.'

'What do you mean, "up to"? Look, calm down, Linda.'

Linda ignored her, coming bluntly to the point. 'Did you tell David that Holly had agreed to talk to the child psychologist?'

'Yes, of course,' Charlotte said. 'Why?'

'Oh, my God, I should have told you in confidence. David is the last person who should have been told.'

'What do you mean?' Charlotte repeated, stunned. 'Why shouldn't he know? With Holly's help, we have a chance of finding out the truth.'

'And that, I think, is exactly what David doesn't want.'

'How can you say a thing like that?' Charlotte demanded, irate. 'He wants this whole business cleared up as much as any of us.'

There was a pause and then Linda spoke again. 'I don't know how to say this, La,' she said awkwardly, 'but I believe David was somehow involved in the murder of his family, and if Holly *did* see something, and she talks about it . . . Don't you see, he'd want to shut her up!'

'I'm not listening to this!' Charlotte exclaimed. 'This is because his ex-girlfriend had been spreading rumours about him, isn't it? And you believe her.'

'No, it goes deeper than that. The detective inspector also thinks David is guilty. I know he does. He hasn't said so in so many words, but that's why he spent nearly two days questioning David.'

'David is right! You'd trample on anyone in order to clear Chris's name! But how can you possibly think David had anything to do with it!' She was shaking all over with shock and rage. It defied belief that Linda should think David might have had a hand in the killings! Last night, as she lay in his arms, she felt committed to him in a way she'd never felt before. Weaving his magic, bewitching her with soft words of love and hands that were gently powerful, she'd felt herself surrendering to him all that was hers: her body, her mind, her soul and all her love. The very fact that he loved her was an aphrodisiac, a drug that bonded her to him, and no matter what people said, she was his for the rest of her life.

'I can understand how you feel, love,' she heard Linda saying, more gently this time. 'It was how I felt when everyone thought Chris had shot his parents.'

'You *can't* imagine how I feel!' Charlotte responded, her eyes filling with tears. 'You were divorced from Chris. I *love* David and I hope we'll get married one day . . . You're getting this all out of proportion, Linda. What do you think he's going to do with her, for God's sake?'

'That's what frightens me, La.'

'You're being ridiculous! He loves Holly! He wouldn't hurt a hair of her head. What the hell are you insinuating?'

'He might try and stop Holly from talking. Or from collecting her inheritance.'

'How?' Charlotte demanded. 'You're letting your imagination run away with you, and I'm not going to listen to any more of this crap! For God's sake, Linda, pull yourself together.'

'Did David tell you he was taking Holly out this afternoon?'

'No, why should he? He probably decided on the spur of the moment to give Holly a treat! What on earth's wrong with that?'

'So you've no idea where they could be?'

'No, of course I haven't, but does it matter? Perhaps they've gone to the zoo. Or the Natural History Museum. Or to a cinema to see a cartoon. They'll be back in due course, and I hope you'll have the grace to apologise to David for imagining he had an ulterior motive in taking Holly out.'

'I bloody well hope you're right,' Linda replied fervently. 'Will you let me know if they turn up at your flat? Please? I can't help being seriously worried, La.'

Charlotte knew the anxiety in Linda's voice was genuine, but also knew it was absurd for her to be so concerned.

'Linda, David wouldn't harm a fly. You are overreacting! Of course Holly will be all right. Stop worrying.'

There was silence on the line, and she could hear Linda

sighing. After a long moment she spoke. 'There's nothing I can say that will make you believe me, is there, La?'

'As far as David is concerned, no,' Charlotte replied flatly. 'He knows *nothing* about the murders; if you'd been with him, like I was, when the police came round to tell him all his family were dead, you wouldn't be doubting him now. He was absolutely devastated, Linda. He couldn't even bring himself to tell me what had happened. All he could say was "my family . . . my family". He's lost everyone; except me. I'm the only person in his life he's got to hang on to and it really makes me furious that you should even *suggest* he is somehow involved.'

'I didn't mean to upset you, La, but you must realise I'm worried about Holly being with him. The child's been through enough. If he does anything to hurt her, I'll kill him,' Linda retorted with passion.

'Holly will be fine, you'll see. Just calm down. I'll leave a message on my answering machine at home, telling him to call me when he gets in, but I expect he'll take Holly home to you first. You've really no cause to worry, Linda.'

'Are we going to the Singing Tree?' Holly asked for the third time, as the taxi swung and rattled along the Gray's Inn Road, towards the City of London and the Thames.

David glanced at her, eyes sharp. 'I expect so,' he said without conviction.

'The Singing Tree is where I get my doll's house,' she persisted, anxiously. 'Are *you* going to buy my house instead of Rand?'

'You'll see where we're going when we get there.'

'Will there be lots of dolls' houses?'

'I don't know. Maybe.' Engrossed in thought, he turned to gaze absently out of the taxi window.

Holly wriggled back on the seat beside him, her legs straight out in front of her. Then, in an old-fashioned gesture, she folded her hands on her lap. For a moment she was silent, her face serious.

'Are we meeting Rand?' she asked at last.

David shook his head. 'No.'

'Or Mummy?'

He stifled an impatient sigh. 'No.'

'Are we meeting anyone?'

'Oh, for goodness' sake, shut up!' he said in exasperation.

Holly's mouth drooped at the corners, and she looked down at her hands.

'And before you ask again,' he continued, 'we are not buying you a doll's house, either.'

A tear trembled on her eyelash before sliding down her cheek. If David noticed it he gave no sign, but continued to gaze out of the window. They were approaching the Monument at the bottom of Bishopsgate, and he pointed to it.

'The great fire of London started there, in a bakery,' he told her.

Holly appeared not to hear, but steadfastly looked at her folded hands.

As they crossed London Bridge, he tried to interest her in the boats that moved slowly on the turgid waters.

'I might take you on one of those big boats one day. That is if you're a good girl.'

'I am a good girl,' she pointed out in a small voice. 'Are we going to the Singing Tree tomorrow?'

'That depends on how good a girl you are today.'

The taxi, once over the bridge, turned into Tooley Street, and drew to a shuddering halt at what looked like the entrance to a cellar under a railway bridge. There was a grim greyness about the place and, scrawled on the grey brick wall in red paint to resemble dripping blood, were the words: The London Dungeon.

As the cabbie handed David his change, he looked askance at Holly, and spoke in a broad cockney accent.

'You ain't never going to take that little 'un in there, are yer?'

David's polite smile froze. 'I really don't see that it's any business of yours.'

'Well, I wouldn't go lettin' no child of mine see the likes of it,' he continued stubbornly. 'It's enough to give 'er nightmares, it is.' He nodded in Holly's direction. 'Surprised they allows anyone under ten or twelve years old in there.'

'It so happens that I checked and children of any age are allowed in, so I don't think you've cause to worry,' David replied with heavy sarcasm.

The driver pulled away from the kerb, muttering angrily to himself.

David grabbed Holly's hand, hurrying her towards the entrance. Once inside, the high-vaulted darkened cellars seemed to close over their heads, plunging them into semi-darkness. The air was dank and musty. A howl of pain broke the stillness and was followed by a burst of manic laughter. High above them, where cobwebs shivered on suspended skeletons, and bats' wings flapped fitfully, there was a distant ghostly chanting. Terrified, Holly clung with tight hands to David's jacket, her face suddenly pale in the dim light of guttering candles.

David fished in his pocket for money to buy their tickets, under a sign which read: ABANDON HOPE ALL YE WHO ENTER HERE. Holly's legs began to tremble, and when she spoke her voice was very small.

'I don't think we need go in here,' she said, voice quavering, eyes widened in fear. At that moment, a figure with metal clawed hands and a face inflamed with painful-looking nodules and sores, stepped out of the black shadows and spoke.

'Tickets, please,' the voice was gruff behind the hideous mask.

Holly screamed and David jumped in shock.

'I . . . I d-don't want to go . . .' she wailed, but David dragged her forward, deeper and deeper into the stone-flagged dungeons, where wax figures portrayed the most savage of tortures carried out on prisoners in the sixteenth century. Realistic-looking bodies lay disembowelled on beds of straw, the blood gushing from their stomachs; while others, screaming with pain, lay stretched on the rack, or were branded with red-hot irons, or beaten until their backs were raw. Spiked heads impaled on wooden stakes stared with agonised eyes from the dark alcoves of the cellars, while ahead of Holly's stricken gaze, a guillotine smashed down on to the neck of a victim, beheading him in a flood of gore.

'I want to go home! L-let's go . . .' shrieked Holly, trying to drag David away, but inadvertently leading him deeper and deeper into this dark museum of horror. David was laughing, enjoying himself, examining the tableaux with interest, but a group of German tourists looked at him angrily, appalled at him letting Holly suffer so much distress.

'I want to go . . .' Holly yelled again. She was shaking all over and her face was ashen as she caught sight of waxwork corpses lying strewn in a filthy hovel, depicting victims of the bubonic plague.

Chilling organ music and Gregorian chanting filled the air now with sinister overtones, as the high damp walls rose into the darkness, and then a cry of terrifying despair broke out just behind them, and bony hands rattled the iron bars of a mock window, behind which a figure lurked.

Hysterical with fear, Holly howled and clutched at her suddenly wet panties.

' . . . I want Mummy!' she screamed. 'I want Mummy.'

David regarded her for a moment, and then, taking her hand, led her up a murky alley lit only by a guttering gas-lamp, to where visitors were invited to take part in "The Jack the Ripper Experience".

Detective Chief Superintendent Alex Osborne looked sternly across the clear expanse of his polished desktop, and glared at Grindley with a mixture of amazement and disbelief.

'I hear you've ordered a house-to-house; a bit late in the day, isn't it?' he asked tersely.

'We are looking for witnesses in order to make this case stick,' Grindley replied, trying to muster all his dignity. He'd been summoned to a meeting with the head of the local CID in order to report on the progress of the newly reopened case, and he was doing his best to give the impression that he had everything under control.

'Just what made you assume, in the first place, that Christopher Farrell had shot his parents before committing suicide?'

'To start with, all the windows and doors of Chelwood Manor were locked. There was no sign of breaking and entering, nothing had been stolen, and no damage had been done to the interior of the house,' Grindley replied. 'It was Mrs Scovell, the domestic help, who, on letting herself in the next morning, entered by the back door and discovered the bodies.'

'Yes, yes, yes,' Osborne said impatiently. 'I know all that: *everyone* knows all that; and about the rifle being found in Christopher's hands, without the silencer which was subsequently found, not by you but by Mrs Farrell's sister and brother-in-law, incidentally . . . But why in God's name, man, did you accept the obvious? For one thing, first police reports indicate that Christopher Farrell was "too clean". He was only stained with his own blood, not that of his mother or father. The soles of his shoes were clean, too. No one committing those murders would have emerged without looking as if they'd been through a bloodbath.'

Grindley looked sullenly down at the papers in his hands, wanting to make some remark about no one being perfect, and that overworked police officers had human failings like everyone else, but he desisted. And it was obvious that Alex Osborne was looking for a scapegoat.

'Coupled to that,' Osborne was saying, struggling to contain his fury, 'you and the other scene-of-crime officers were far too ready to believe David Farrell. What proof did you have that his mother phoned him at ten o'clock at night? Why was the rifle removed from Christopher Farrell's hands without the use of rubber gloves to avoid smudging any fingerprints? Why wasn't a thorough search of the premises carried out after you'd found the child? We're dealing here with a multiple murder of a very serious nature, yet you seemed content to wrap it up as fast as you could! You even authorised cleaners to go into Chelwood in order to burn the evidence! It's the most appalling cock-up I've ever come across in all my years in the force. Not only have you brought disgrace on yourself and your officers, but you've involved me by giving me misleading information, resulting in my going off to play golf when I should have been at the scene of the crime!' Osborne's face had become flushed as he talked. Grindley could see he was seething with barely controlled rage.

'Did you know,' Osborne continued, 'that it was the first shot that killed Christopher? Not the second? So how did you suppose he shot himself again after he was dead?' Disgust spun every word out of his mouth with biting venom. Grindley continued to look at the papers in front of him, not venturing to speak for fear of incurring more wrath.

'How do you account for these cock-ups?' Osborne suddenly barked.

Grindley looked up then, and his expression was pained. 'With the benefit of hindsight, I realise we are looking at a very different picture to the one David Farrell painted; nevertheless, we do not have any evidence against him, and we have been unable to break him. He's sticking to his version of events and won't budge.'

'Then *find* some evidence, man!' Osborne roared, bringing their meeting to an end.

Outside in the corridor again, Grindley felt as humiliated as if he'd been an ordinary police constable who'd been hauled over the coals for neglecting his duty. He strode hurriedly out of headquarters and into his car. The sooner he got back to Barrow, the sooner he'd get this nightmare buttoned up. That is, providing he could find a shred of evidence that would put David Farrell in the dock.

Charlotte sat at her desk, feeling sick to her stomach, wondering how anyone could believe that David would do anything to hurt Holly. She glanced at her watch. It was only four-thirty, and yet it felt as if she'd been waiting for hours to hear some news. At last she could stand it no longer. Grabbing the phone, she dialled Linda's number.

Rand answered, his voice warm and relaxed as usual. 'How are you, Charlotte?'

'I wondered if David had brought Holly back yet?'

'Not yet, but I expect they'll turn up soon. I wouldn't worry about it.'

'I'm not in the least worried about him taking Holly out, Rand, but I am upset by Linda's attitude,' she confessed. 'I don't know why she's so against David.'

Rand's chuckle was gentle. 'I think it's the lioness protecting her cubs syndrome. She'll be OK when Holly gets back.'

'What on earth does she think he's going to do with Holly? He's one of the kindest, most gentle people I've ever met . . .' Her voice caught and she paused for a moment. 'He wouldn't hurt a fly!' she added vehemently.

'Then we needn't worry, need we?' Rand said soothingly. 'Look, would you like us to give you a ring when they return?'

'Yes, thanks. Could you ask David to ring me?'

'Of course. Will you be at home?'

'No, I'm at the office.'

'Right. We'll call you as soon as David gets back.'

'Thanks, Rand,' she said gratefully. She'd never met him but he sounded kind and sincere, like Denzil.

It was now nearly five o'clock. On the off-chance, she phoned her own flat, but as she'd expected, there was no reply. For the first time a flicker of anxiety crossed her mind. She wondered why David hadn't mentioned he was taking Holly out this afternoon.

David looked up, fascinated by the body swaying gently as it hung by the neck from a rope suspended to a beam high in the darkened roof of the dungeon. The feet, in coarse wool socks and worn shoes, dangled above their heads with realistic inertia, while the hands hung white and lifeless.

All around them the piercing screams of damned souls rang out, hollow and terrifying. Loud rumbling seemed to make the damp walls shake from time to time, as if a tumbrel was passing over their heads on its way to a place of execution.

Holly, clinging to David, could no longer bear to look at the terrible sights. She buried her tearstained face against his thigh.

'Holly?' David eased her grip and bent down so that his face was level with hers.

'Holly, listen to me,' he said firmly. 'I want you to promise me something.'

A dry sob broke from her throat and she buried her face in his shoulder.

'Now come on, Holly. Be sensible. You're a big girl now and we'll go home as soon as you promise me something.'

There was a long pause, broken only by another heartfelt sob.

'Holly! Are you paying attention?'

She nodded very slightly, but remained silent.

'This is what I want you do to.' His tone was more kindly now. 'I want you to forget all about Granny and Grandpa and your daddy. D'you hear me? When anyone asks you any questions about them, or what happened the last time you were staying with Granny, when you were locked in that chest, I want you to say you don't remember anything. Will you do that, Holly? Will you promise me that you'll say you don't remember anything?' As he spoke his voice had become more urgent, more penetrating, repeating over and over the same phrases, as if he hoped to brainwash her.

After a few minutes she withdrew herself from his shoulder and looked at him with stricken eyes.

David gave her a little shake. 'D'you understand, Holly? You're not to say anything. You didn't see anyone. You were locked in the chest and you didn't know what was happening. Have you got that, Holly?'

There was a wildness in his hot blue eyes now, and a compelling note in his voice.

Tears rolled down Holly's cheeks as she stood twisting her hands.

'Promise me, Holly,' he commanded. 'Promise me you'll say nothing.'

Suddenly wilting under his domineering scrutiny, she began crying again, a woebegone little figure in her short kilt and red T-shirt, standing before him like a picture of pitiful innocence in the macabre setting.

'Say you promise!'

'I . . . I w-want to go home,' she wept as if her heart would break. 'I . . . want M-mummy.'

He gripped her by the shoulders, holding her firmly before him.

'Listen to me, Holly. If you don't promise I'll leave you here all night! In the darkness! You'll have to stay here, by yourself, until you promise.'

'No . . . I want Mummy!' Hysterical now, she screamed in panic. 'I don't want to stay here! Don't leave me here . . . !'

'You'll have to promise. You'll have to tell me you won't say anything about Granny and Grandpa and Daddy, or staying at Chelwood . . . or anything else you might have seen.'

Holly nodded and looked at him with eyes shot with fear.

'Say it, Holly. Say it or I'll leave you here.'

With great effort she tried to control her tears, but sobs still shuddered through her body.

'I . . . I . . .' she began.

'Yes?'

'I promise and can we go home now?' she asked all in one breath.

David straightened up. 'Yes. Let's go. I'll buy you an ice-cream.' He took her hand and started walking slowly towards an exit sign. 'I don't think we'll tell Mummy we came here, do you? That will be our little secret, too. Mummy will say you're silly to be frightened and make such a fuss.'

They walked on in silence, Holly looking at the ground all the time and still giving the occasional hiccuping little sob.

'OK?' David asked breezily now. He looked quite cheerful and pleased with himself.

She didn't reply, and a minute later they were out in the street once more.

'Are you all right now?' he asked, not unkindly.

Holly held on tightly to his hand as they walked towards a nearby café, where he told her she could choose any flavour of ice-cream she liked; but her lips were pressed together and she refused to say anything.

While David had a cappuccino, she spooned a strawberry ice-cream into her mouth, never once raising her eyes to look at him. He might not have been there, so thoroughly had she seemed to decide to ignore him. He found it unnerving. Tears and howls he could understand; a traumatic switching-off of communication he could not. He felt a need to press home one more time that it was vital she remain silent when she was questioned about the murders.

'You understand what I was saying just now, Holly?' he persisted. 'You won't tell anyone what you saw at Chelwood?'

For the first time she looked up, meeting his gaze with red-rimmed eyes and a mouth that drooped at the corners. Then she spoke, 'And I mustn't tell that I saw you, either?' she asked.

'Holly!' Linda rushed forward, relief making her suddenly feel weak. 'Where on earth have you been?' She dropped on her knees in front of the child as she tugged off her anorak in the hallway, while David watched from the open front door, smiling languidly.

Holly allowed herself to be hugged and kissed, but she

seemed to Linda to be as withdrawn as she'd been after they'd lifted her out of the chest.

'Are you all right, darling?' Linda asked with concern. She looked into Holly's flushed face, trying to penetrate the emotional shutter that had descended over her eyes once more, but Holly didn't respond.

Linda bit her bottom lip, trying to stay calm. In the past few weeks Holly had really started to blossom again, even to the point of agreeing to tell them what she'd seen, but now she was back to square one, almost entirely mute and regressed. She'd obviously been crying and she had retreated once again into a world of her own. What on earth had that monster been doing to her?

Linda picked her up, and at that moment Denzil and Rand came out of the living room into the hall.

'I'm going to give Holly a bath,' Linda told Denzil. Her voice betrayed her barely suppressed anger, 'and I want to know *exactly* what's been happening.'

Denzil looked with sympathetic concern at Holly. He reached out to stroke her golden hair. 'Poor baby,' he murmured sadly.

When he turned to David, his manner had changed completely. Gripping him by the elbow, he propelled him into the living room.

'What the hell's been going on?' Denzil asked angrily. 'You had no right to come here and take Holly out without our permission! Linda's been frantic with worry.'

David's expression was mildly incredulous. 'I can't believe this!' he said with a chuckle. 'I do my good deed for the day by taking my niece out and giving her a good time, which, I may add, Magda did not object to, and then you jump on me like a ton of bricks!'

Denzil's eyes flashed dangerously. 'Let's cut the crap, David! Where the hell did you take her? She's scared witless again!'

'Well, I don't know why. We only went to Madame Tussaud's and saw the usual waxworks! The Sleeping Beauty, and Winston Churchill, and oh! of course, the entire royal family,' David replied blandly. 'I think she's a silent sort of child.'

'That's a load of shit and you know it,' Denzil said in fury. 'You've done something to her to make her shut up, haven't you? You're afraid she'll say something that will incriminate you in the murder of your parents and Chris. You took her out today to frighten her into silence once more, just when she was beginning to open up! God, I'd like to see you punished for this.' His right fist was clenched and he was breathing heavily.

'The only thing you're likely to see is yourself charged with slander,' David replied coolly.

Rand spoke out, quietly and clearly. 'Don't underestimate Denzil and Linda's intelligence, David. Being both Denzil's brother and a lawyer, I have a double interest in this case, and I have to say there are a lot of loose ends.'

David glared at him with sudden anger. 'I don't think this has anything to do with you. You're not even related to Holly, except by marriage. She happens to be my brother's child . . .'

' . . . Your brother by adoption,' Denzil cut in.

' . . . My brother's child,' David said again, 'and I have every right to take her out and give her a treat if I want to.'

'Not without the parents' permission,' Rand pointed out.

'Christ Almighty!' David sprang to his feet. 'What the fuck did you think I was going to do with Holly? Beat her up? Sexually abuse her?' He was shaking with rage and his face was flushed. For a moment Denzil thought he was going to burst into tears because his eyes seemed to brim, but then he realised it was a paroxysm of wrath.

'No, but I think you've frightened her into silence,' Rand said quietly. He used the soft, unexcitable tones that had so often proved invaluable when he was prosecuting someone in the law courts.

'Rubbish!' David said scornfully. 'How could anyone be frightened into silence by a visit to Madame Tussaud's!' He threw back his head and laughed. 'You'll have to do better than that.'

'Don't worry, we will.' Denzil spoke grimly. 'Meanwhile, Linda and I don't want you coming anywhere near Holly. You acted behind our backs by taking her out when there was only Magda here, not to mention lying to Magda by saying Linda knew all about your plans for this afternoon, and we cannot allow it to happen again.'

'If you think I'm going to listen to this fucking nonsense, you're mistaken,' David shouted. 'Who the fuck do you think you are, talking to me like that? As it is, I've suffered about as much as I can take, losing my parents and brother like that. I don't need *you* on my back as well.' He strode out into the hall and a minute later they heard the front door slam.

Denzil looked questioningly at his brother. 'What d'you think? Have we made a terrible mistake by thinking he's guilty?'

Rand downed the last of his gin and tonic. 'He's as guilty

as hell. I know all about that hard-done-by reaction! Almost every criminal I've ever met has overreacted in the way David did just now.'

Chapter Twenty-one

Linda phoned Charlotte as soon as she'd settled Holly for the night. Sick with worry, she was anxious to find out if Charlotte knew anything more about Holly's outing.

'Denzil says David took her to Madame Tussaud's, but I don't believe it,' Linda explained. 'Has he told you where they went?'

'Why don't you believe him?' Charlotte demanded. 'Anyway David isn't back yet, but I don't know why you're fussing.'

'But he left here over an hour ago,' Linda protested.

'Then I suppose he'll turn up any moment now. Holly's all right, isn't she?' she added defensively.

'If you call being practically catatonic "all right"!'

'How do you mean?'

'David has managed to scare the living daylights out of her. God knows what he did or what happened, but she's as bad, if not worse, than she was on the day she was found in that chest! She's refusing to say anything.'

Stunned, Charlotte's heart pounded uncomfortably.

'Do you think you can find out what happened?' Linda continued. 'I'm frantic with worry, La. This has set her back so badly, I'm not going to even try to get her to talk for the time being. I'm going to phone the child psychologist first thing in the morning to ask her advice. Meanwhile, I've given her a warm bath and put her to bed.'

'But you surely don't think he's done something to frighten her, do you?'

'Yes, I'm afraid I do.' Linda sounded positive. 'He knew she'd agreed to talk about what happened at Chelwood, and he's done something to frighten her into silence.'

'Oh, he wouldn't, Linda. He'd never do that. You're making him out to be a monster!' Charlotte protested angrily.

'Then ask him what happened. I tell you, La, the child has been traumatised, and after all the care we've taken to help her get over that last ordeal, it's heartbreaking to see it happening again. She's terrified. She looks at me like a little dumb animal, too scared to say a word.'

'Oh, God! I'm *sure* David hasn't done anything to scare her; I don't know how you think he could. He loves Holly. He'd never hurt her.'

'Well, I think Denzil's right to forbid David to see her again. If he's done anything to hurt Holly, he must be kept away from her at all costs. All this trouble could give her lifelong psychological problems.'

'Linda, don't be too ready to blame David. I honestly don't think he's involved,' Charlotte protested, feeling hurt now. David was the man she loved, and she hated the way Linda was acting.

'Who are you trying to convince, love? Me? Or yourself?' Linda questioned.

At that moment Charlotte heard his key in the lock. 'I've got to go, Linda. I'll call you tomorrow,' she said hurriedly. For some reason she knew it would be a bad start to her evening with David if he found her talking to Linda on the phone.

David came into the room as she put down the receiver.

'Hello, darling!' Charlotte said, trying to smile normally. 'Had a good day?' she added, realising it made her sound like the clichéd wife, but anxious not to upset him if he'd already had a hard time with Linda and Denzil.

'Who was that on the phone?' he asked, taking off his jacket and throwing it down on the sofa.

'Myra,' she said lightly, shocked at how easy it was to deceive.

David switched on the television. 'What's for dinner tonight?'

'Steaks and salad.'

He grimaced. 'Let's go out. I could do with something exotic to eat.'

'Would you like some wine before we go out?' she asked.

David looked at her, giving her a little smile.

'Now you're talking!' he replied, cheerfully.

Sitting side by side on the sofa, they watched television as they drank their wine, in companionable silence, while Charlotte racked her brains to think up a plausible remark which would lead them to talking about Holly.

The programme came to an end, and David drained his glass.

'Let's go then,' he said, rising and stretching his hands above his head as he yawned widely.

'Tired, sweetheart?' she asked ingenuously.

'Exhausted. I took Holly out this afternoon, to give Linda a break. I must say, children are very tiring.'

'That was nice of you,' Charlotte replied, amazed at her own composure, although her heart was hammering now. 'Where did you take her?'

'Madame Tussaud's. It's years since I've been there myself. She's rather spoilt, though. Wants everything her own way. I think Linda should be stricter with her.'

'In what way?'

'Oh, you know . . .' His tone was casual, half amused. 'She didn't want to go home; made an awful fuss when I said we couldn't stay any longer. Then she didn't know what flavour ice-cream she wanted . . . ! Children! Who'd have 'em?' he chuckled.

'That doesn't sound like Holly,' she said carefully.

'Oh, doesn't it! I know that child better than you do. She's as stubborn as a mule; she wasn't even speaking to me by the time I got her back to her mother. Spoilt brat!' But he was smiling indulgently as he said it.

Charlotte gave a secret sigh of relief. Nothing had happened except a clash of wills, followed by Holly sulking. She'd phone Linda in the morning and explain it to her. Then she had an afterthought.

'You didn't take her to the Chamber of Horrors, I presume?' she inquired lightly.

'Are you kidding?' David laughed. 'I'm too scared to go to a place like that myself.'

He put on his jacket and ran his hands through his hair in an attempt to smooth it down. 'Are you ready? I'm just going to have a pee.'

'Yes, I'm ready.' She felt light-hearted again. Everything was going to be all right. They'd have dinner and some wine, and then afterwards they'd return home and go to bed . . .

Suddenly she noticed two small pieces of pink paper on the floor. Thinking them to be bus tickets, she idly picked

them up and was just about to throw them into the waste-
paper basket, when something caught her eye. They were
tickets, all right, and they had been torn in half, but on the
parts she held was printed NDON DUNGEON and, in
smaller lettering, RIL 26th. Shattered, she stood in the middle
of the room feeling as if she were being sucked down into a
black hole. Today was April 26th.

Grindley had had a long day. He was exhausted. A minute
search of Chelwood Manor had produced nothing
untoward, apart from the silencer, which had almost
everyone's fingerprints on it apart from David's.

'He'll have worn gloves,' remarked the head of the
forensic team, who had been at the house since early
morning.

Grindley grunted. 'We'll have to search the grounds.
There's got to be something that can be used in evidence
against David Farrell. I'm as sure as hell he's guilty.'

'He's certainly covered his tracks very well.'

They were back in Grindley's office at the Longley Police
Station, having been over at Barrow all day.

At that moment, Franklin knocked on the door before
entering Grindley's office. There was a triumphant gleam
in his eyes.

'What is it, Franklin?'

'That alibi of David Farrell's has collapsed,' he
announced.

'Collapsed? What do you mean?'

'He told us he was in Derby that day, visiting a prospective
client for P.N.G. Links.'

'Yes?'

'And the company he visited, Preston International, initially confirmed he'd been there that day and had talked to the managing director.'

'Yes.'

'It wasn't him. Someone else went in his place, posing as him.'

Grindley's jaw dropped as the implications sank in. He'd been assured Farrell's alibi was watertight.

'Why had this only just been discovered?' he asked hollowly.

'When we checked again we showed them a photograph of Farrell. They'd never seen him before. On the other hand, our first description matched that of the rep. who did visit him. P.N.G. Links also confirmed David Farrell had gone to Derby that day. We had no reason to suppose it was anyone other than David Farrell.'

Grindley looked stunned. 'Then who the hell was it?' he demanded.

'Someone who looks very like Farrell; his cousin, in fact. Andrew Newton.'

'But in God's name, *why*?' Grindley roared, filled with chagrin that it was Franklin and not himself who had turned up this vital piece of information. 'How did you find this out?'

Franklin did his best to look modest, but he couldn't keep the satisfaction out of his voice.

'He came forward earlier today, sir. While you were at Chelwood Manor.'

'This cousin, Andrew Newton, came forward? Of his own volition?'

Franklin nodded. 'He said he didn't for a minute think

402

David Farrell had anything to do with the murders, but it was nevertheless on his conscience that he'd been standing in for his cousin in Derby that day.'

'Why did he do it? Did Farrell pay him?'

'No, sir. He wasn't paid. Apparently he's done it on several occasions when Farrell didn't want – or couldn't be bothered – to make distant calls for his company.'

Grindley looked confounded. 'So what the hell does Newton get out of it?'

'Andrew Newton is a junkie. He and Christopher Farrell used to do it together, but it was Newton who started it. He supplied Chris with all he wanted until Chris wanted out. David Farrell is now blackmailing Newton, and threatening to tell his family and the police, unless he does him the odd favour. Like standing in for him as a rep., and lending him money.'

'I wonder if Newton is the "hit-man" Connie Westcott was talking about?'

'He might have been, originally, but maybe David Farrell thought he was untrustworthy, and so decided to commit the murders himself, while Newton provided an alibi for him by taking his place at the meeting in Derby.'

'Well, Farrell was right about one thing, wasn't he?' Grindley remarked thoughtfully.

'What? That Newton was untrustworthy?'

Grindley nodded. 'He loses his nerve . . . or has an attack of bad conscience and comes blabbing to us. Do we know what Farrell was actually doing while his cousin stood in for him on the day of the murders?'

Franklin cleared his throat. 'From what I understand, Farrell spent the day with Natalie Newton. In London.'

'Doing what?'

'In Newton's words, screwing,' Franklin replied, blushing.

Grindley's eyebrows shot up into his furrowed brow. 'Was he, indeed? Connie Westcott, Charlotte Taylor and now Natalie Newton. Humph! He's quite a one with the ladies, isn't he?'

'Yes. This doesn't provide the evidence we need to arrest him though, does it? He'll probably admit he spent the day in bed with his cousin, before going back to Charlotte Taylor in the evening! And no doubt this woman, Natalie Newton, will corroborate his statement,' Franklin observed.

'It's possible he did both; spent the day in London with Natalie Newton, and then drove down to Devizes, committed the murders, and then returned to London, telling Charlotte Taylor he'd spent the day in Derby.'

'That is conceivable, sir.'

'I'd like to have a talk with this young woman. She lives in London, I gather?'

'She lives in London during the week. She has a job on a glossy magazine, according to her brother. At weekends she goes to the family home in Newbury.'

'Newbury's nearer than London. I'll go over and interview her first thing tomorrow morning. What's the address?'

'Tomorrow is Thursday, sir.'

'Hell, so it is,' Grindley grumbled. Then he thought about spending a day in London. All expenses paid.

'I'll go to London,' he said, 'I shall be interested to hear what she has to say.'

* * *

404

Charlotte's first instinct was to hide the torn-off part of the tickets as if she herself was guilty. For a moment she clutched them in the palm of her hand, which she then thrust deeply into the pocket of the coat she was wearing. She heard David flush the loo in the bathroom, and then there was a pause and she knew he would be checking his appearance in the mirror, and then the bathroom door opened and . . . She turned away swiftly so he would not see her expression, wanting a few moments to herself, to think this thing through . . . to face so much more than the mere findings of the tickets; to face the reality that he might not be the person she thought he was at all. David, her lover, her soul-mate, all she had ever wanted in life, and he might be guilty of . . . No! her mind reeled as the shock waves hit her. It was impossible. It was too terrible to contemplate. It simply couldn't be so.

'What's the matter, La?' she heard him ask from the doorway.

She stood rock-still, trying to gather her thoughts.

'La?'

'It's all right, David,' she heard herself say, and it sounded as if she were reassuring a child or someone very old.

'What is it?' He strode into the room and stood behind her, and looked over her shoulder to get a glimpse of her face. 'Are you ill?'

She was dying, inch by inch, disintegrating into nothingness but she didn't say so. Instead she took her hand slowly out of her pocket. The remains of the entry tickets lay crushed in her palm like crumpled rose petals.

For a moment David looked perplexed, as if he didn't know what she meant, and then he laughed.

Charlotte turned to him then, her eyes filled with pain. 'Why did you lie to me?'

'I didn't, La!' he said blithely. 'I bought those tickets but when I realised what a bloodthirsty place it was, I took Holly to Madame Tussaud's instead. I should have those tickets on me, too.' He started rummaging through his pockets, pulling out a handkerchief, a bus ticket, a sweet wrapping.

Charlotte started to cry. For Holly, for herself, and strangely for David, too. Everything had gone so hideously wrong just when she thought her future was going to be perfect. The terrible realisation that she could no longer trust him was a savage blow; almost a betrayal of life itself.

'It's no use, David,' she sobbed bitterly.

'What's no use? La, what's the matter with you? You find a couple of torn-off tickets for the London Dungeon and you go berserk!'

'I'm not going . . . berserk,' she sobbed.

He tried to put his arms around her, but for some reason she could not bear his touch at this moment.

'No, David. Leave me alone,' she begged.

'Little angel, what's come over you?'

She looked at him then, long and hard, through her tears. 'As if you didn't know.'

Natalie Newton opened her front door, still in her dressing-gown. It was, Grindley was to recall later, a pure white silk creation that had probably cost a great deal of money. She stood, posed in the doorway, with her long blonde hair draped over one shoulder, like the pictures he'd seen in fashion magazines his wife read.

'I'm sorry to trouble you, Miss Newton,' he began,

holding out his identification badge. 'Can I have a few words with you, please? It won't take long.'

Natalie flashed smouldering eyes at him, before opening her door wider. 'Come in,' she said huskily.

Grindley entered a room unlike anything he had ever seen before. More of a stage-set than a living room, he found himself surrounded by antique lace drapes tumbling from brass curtain rods that were fixed along the tops of the walls. More lace, dingy and old, was festooned over an equally battered-looking gilt-edged screen, which stood in front of the window blocking out much of the light. Cream-coloured ostrich feathers, amber beads, ivory ornaments and grubby pink satin cushions were placed around the room in an artfully casual style, making Grindley wonder where he was supposed to sit.

'Coffee?' Natalie drawled, waving him to a chaise-longue over which a silk shawl had been thrown.

'Thank you,' he replied uncertainly. He'd been thrown by both the young woman and the room, and needed a few moments to gather his wits about him again.

She glided out on satin-slippered feet, giving him a chance to look around. When she returned a few minutes later carrying two tiny cups of pungent near-black liquid on a Chinese lacquered tray, she sank gracefully on to one of the cushions on the floor.

'Do you always call on people this early?' she asked languidly.

'I wanted to catch you before you went out to work,' Grindley replied, discomforted.

'Oh, I never get into the office until ten; none of us do,' she explained.

'How very nice for you,' he replied with a touch of irony, which was not lost on her.

'You see, we work until late in the evening; on the days we go to press it's often eight o'clock before I get away.'

Grindley sipped the coffee, almost shuddering as his tastebuds were hit by the bitterness of it.

'I'd like you to tell me about your relationship with David Farrell,' he said bluntly.

She looked at him unwaveringly. 'What do you want to know? Are you shocked at my having a relationship with my cousin? David and I have been fucking each other since we were both fourteen, but we don't intend to get married or anything like that.'

'And you're not really cousins, anyway, are you?'

'Aren't we?' She raised fine blonde eyebrows and looked at him quizzically.

'I'm aware that David Farrell was adopted,' said Grindley.

'That doesn't mean we aren't cousins.' She leaned back, resting against the lace-festooned wall.

This was a game Grindley wasn't familiar with. He liked straight answers to straight questions, and this young woman was talking in riddles.

'*Is* David Farrell a cousin of yours?' he asked with a touch of frostiness.

Natalie cocked her head on one side so her hair fell like a thick strand of silk down to her breast. 'Sort of,' she replied mysteriously.

'What exactly does that mean?'

'It means my father had an affair with his secretary, after he married my mother. They had a son. When Edmund

Farrell heard about it, he asked if he and Virginia could adopt the baby. That's how they came to have David.'

'That actually makes David Farrell your half-brother!' said Grindley, startled.

Her smile was mocking. 'So? Brother . . . cousin . . . ? What's the difference? They say incest is best, and it's true! We feel the same, we think alike. Anyway David's not the only man I sleep with, you know. And I'm not the only woman in his life. So it's great. We get together when we feel like it.'

Grindley regarded her with eyes that bulged slightly, and he looked flushed.

'Am I shocking you?' Natalie asked sweetly. 'I suppose it is a fairly sophisticated arrangement, but who the hell cares? But I don't suppose you've come up all the way from Wiltshire to ask about my sex life.'

'I actually wanted to ask you about your movements on the day the Farrell family were murdered. Where were you?'

'Here, of course. I was in bed with a bad cold, I remember.'

'Were you alone that day?'

Natalie chuckled warmly. 'No. In fact I'd arranged to have the day off so I could be with David. He came over shortly after breakfast.' Suddenly she laughed. 'He told that plump girl he's living with – what's her name? Charlotte something – that he was going to Derby on business, and she believed him.'

'And your brother Andrew went instead, didn't he?'

Startled, she looked at him cagily. 'I don't know about that.' Her tone was vague. 'All I know is that David was here with me.'

'And when did he leave?'

She shrugged. 'I can't remember, really. In time to get back to his girlfriend for dinner, I suppose. She supports him financially, so . . . he who pays the piper calls the tune, as they say.'

'You must remember if he left in the middle of the afternoon? Or late afternoon? Maybe early evening?' Grindley coaxed.

With a languid hand, she pushed back her hair, tucking it behind her ear. Then she gazed up at the ceiling, as if she'd find the answer to his question written large upon the white plaster.

'I really can't remember . . . It was true I had a cold . . . I think I fell asleep and when I woke up he'd gone, but I've no idea what time it was. Can I get you some more coffee?' She rose in one swift movement, uncoiling her long legs like a dancer, standing before him with her white robe slightly open so that he was aware of her nakedness beneath.

'No thanks.' Grindley struggled up from the low chaise-longue, aware of his clumsiness beside her gracefulness.

'I think I've got all I need,' he continued, flustered, afraid that if he stayed any longer she would weave some dangerous spell under which he would find himself helpless, unable to resist.

'Call me if you think of anything else,' she said softly. Her hips swayed as she went ahead to open the door, and a delicate drift of jasmine followed in her wake, making him realise just how long it had been since he'd had an exciting sex life.

Chapter Twenty-two

Charlotte was trembling as the taxi swung into Mulberry Avenue and came to a halt outside the Blakes' house. Through the uncurtained windows of the brightly lit living room, she could see Linda and Denzil talking to a man she'd never seen before. For a moment, as she hurried up the stone-flagged path to the front door, it reminded her of watching a play on television with the sound turned down. Linda was gesturing with her hands, while the men seemed to be listening intently to what she had to say.

Magda opened the door, looking subdued and rather sullen.

'Please to come this way,' she said to Charlotte, walking ahead of her into the living room.

Linda was the first to come forward, arms outstretched to hug her.

'Bless you for coming over like this,' she said, her voice solicitous. 'How are you bearing up, love? Are you all right?'

Charlotte had managed to hold herself in check until this moment, but Linda's compassion, as well as the sympathetic looks of the men, made sudden tears spring to her eyes. Unable to speak because of the lump in her throat, she nodded unconvincingly.

'Poor lamb,' said Linda, putting her arm round her shoulder.

411

'Come and sit down and I'll get you a drink,' Denzil suggested. Then he turned to Randal. 'This is my brother, Rand. He's living with us for the time being.'

Charlotte looked up and through her tears saw a younger, better-looking edition of Denzil, with warm brown eyes and thick dark hair. He came forward and clasped her hand in a firm grip.

'Hello. I've heard so much about you,' he said. He had a soft, soothing voice.

'Let's get you that brandy and soda,' Denzil said briskly. 'In fact, I think we could all do with a drink.'

Seated on the sofa, Charlotte allowed herself to be pampered. After a few minutes she stopped shaking, while the brandy made her glow warmly inside.

'You've had such a shock,' Linda said. 'Are you really all right?'

'I'm fine,' Charlotte said.

'How did you discover David had taken Holly to the London Dungeon? I nearly died when you phoned to tell us.'

'The tickets must have fallen out of his coat pocket, because I saw them lying on the floor. I didn't know what they were at first.'

'Then what happened?' Denzil asked, leaning on the mantelshelf facing her, while he sipped his drink.

'He *lied* . . . ! He lied and lied,' Charlotte said, distressed. 'I can't stand being lied to. I'd rather he'd admitted what he'd done. Poor Holly! I can't bear to think what she must have gone through.'

Linda sighed deeply, and looked troubled. 'I know. I'll never forgive him for this.'

'How could I have been so blind?' Charlotte murmured. 'I didn't believe a word when Connie Westcott said David had hired a hit-man, but now I realise it must be true! And Holly must have seen who it was, and that was why he was trying to frighten her into silence.'

Linda and Denzil exchanged looks, but said nothing.

'Tonight I saw a different side to David . . .' She shook her head and closed her eyes for a minute. 'I can hardly believe it.'

'Love is blind,' Linda told her. 'Don't blame yourself. No one likes to think bad things about someone they love.'

'Even so. All these months . . . He's lied to me about almost everything. This is the man I've been living with, the man I love . . . loved,' she added brokenly.

'I think something went very wrong that night at Chelwood,' Denzil observed. 'I think the plan was to kill Edmund and Virginia. I don't believe David realised Chris and Holly were going to be there too.'

Rand, who had been sitting quietly listening to the conversation, turned to Denzil. 'You could be right. Didn't you say David was shocked when it was realised Holly was somewhere in the house?'

Charlotte intervened. 'David was very surprised,' she agreed. 'I don't think he had any idea Holly was staying. Oh, God . . . it was a terrible day . . .'

She covered her face with her hands, remembering the awfulness of it all and how heartbroken David had seemed. Looking back, of course, she realised how he had put the blame squarely on Chris, and how not only she, but the police, had believed him. But supposing Edmund and Virginia had been alone? How would that have changed things?'

413

'The hit-man, whoever he was, must have been told to make it look like a burglary that went wrong,' she mused. 'But then when Chris appeared . . . Maybe he shot him in panic?' She paused for a moment. 'With Chris dead, David stood to inherit everything; or so he thought. I don't understand why David didn't arrange for the murders to take place when Chris *was* at Chelwood.'

Again, Linda and Denzil exchanged looks, and this time Charlotte noticed.

'What is it?' she asked fearfully. 'What are you keeping from me?'

Linda reached out to grasp Charlotte's hand before she spoke. 'The police are of the opinion that there was no hit-man, no hired killer instructed to carry out the shootings.'

Charlotte looked puzzled. 'Then it *was* an intruder after all?' she said.

'No, love.' Linda shook her head sadly. 'Detective Inspector Grindley,' she said carefully, 'is of the opinion that it was David who killed his family.'

'*No!* Oh, God, no!' Charlotte cried out, jumping on to her feet, her glass of brandy and soda spilling everywhere. 'Oh, Linda, you're wrong! There's no way . . . no way in the world that David would be able to kill his own family!' she said vehemently.

They all looked at her, and there was deep compassion in their faces.

'It probably wasn't planned or premeditated,' Denzil observed.

'I think it *was*,' argued Linda. 'The only thing that went wrong, as far as I can see, is that he forgot Holly would be there.'

Charlotte turned on her. 'You've been determined it was David from the start, haven't you? Anything so long as Chris wasn't blamed!'

'That's not entirely fair!' Linda flashed back. 'I know how awful you're feeling, La,' she continued, 'but you have to face the facts.'

'You keep saying you understand, but you don't!' Charlotte wept. 'David has been my whole life for the past six months. I can't believe this is happening. How could he have shot his parents and Chris? And then turned up for dinner that night as if nothing had happened?'

Linda spoke apologetically. 'La, I didn't mean to upset you, but you're going to find out sooner or later that Grindley is searching for concrete evidence so he can have David charged, and I thought it better you heard about it from us, rather than him.'

'I can't take it in,' Charlotte confessed. 'I can't believe he'd do such a thing. David is so gentle, so . . . so vulnerable himself.'

'Do you know where he is now?' Linda asked.

'No. He stormed out of the flat because I accused him of lying, saying he never wanted to set eyes on me again.'

Linda looked questioningly at Denzil. 'He could be at Natalie's, I suppose?'

Charlotte looked surprised. 'Natalie? His cousin? I met her and her brothers at the funeral. Why would he go to her?'

'He might have done.' Denzil sounded noncommittal.

The way he spoke made Charlotte suspicious. 'Was she a girlfriend of his, too?'

'I don't know about that,' Linda said with equal

nonchalance. 'As cousins go, they were good friends, though.'

'She came back with us in the car to London, after the funeral,' Charlotte said thoughtfully. 'I remember they did seem very friendly. I didn't like her,' she added.

'Not many women do,' Linda observed. 'She's only really interested in other women's husbands or boyfriends. She was making eyes at Denzil at the funeral; can you imagine anything so gross? She was even after Neil at one point.'

Charlotte didn't need to hear any more. If David had been seeing Connie during the past six months, he had no doubt been seeing Natalie, too. Miserably, she sipped her drink, thankful she wasn't on her own at this moment.

'What happens next?' Rand asked.

'We'll have to tell the police about today. Holly can't be questioned now. She's been through enough,' Linda said. 'You did keep the tickets you found, didn't you, La?'

'Yes.'

'It means, I'm afraid, you'll be forced to give evidence, if he is charged with murder.'

Charlotte looked aghast. 'Oh, no! Not really?'

Denzil turned to Rand. 'Ask the lawyer,' he said.

'I'm very much afraid you will. You'll be one of the key witnesses for the prosecution.'

Her hand flew to her mouth. 'Oh, my God! How can I stand there and give evidence that might implicate David? I'll feel like Judas!'

'I'm afraid you'll have no option; you'll be subpoenaed,' Rand explained quietly, 'and put on oath.'

Charlotte covered her face with her hands, trying to block out the vision of herself in the witness box while David, the man she'd loved more than anyone in her life, stood in the dock.

'I don't think I'll be able to do it,' she said at length. 'It's asking too much of anyone to expect them to give what might be damning information about the person they love.'

'Well, it hasn't come to that yet,' Linda said practically. 'What we've got to concentrate on is helping Holly to get over her shock.'

Denzil topped up their drinks and they sat talking for a while. Gradually Charlotte began to feel a little comforted. She was deeply touched by the way the Blake family were showing how much they cared about her. Between them, and her own family, she'd survive, somehow.

'I'm going to make us all scrambled eggs on toast,' Linda announced. 'You must be starving.'

Charlotte glanced at her watch. She'd lost track of time; it seemed only minutes since she'd found the tickets. Now it was eleven-thirty.

'I'd no idea it was so late!' Denzil exclaimed. 'We must phone the police right away.'

'You're going to spend the night here,' Linda said to Charlotte in a brisk, motherly tone. 'On no account are you to go back to your flat on your own.'

'Linda's right,' Denzil agreed. 'You must stay with us.'

'Thank you,' she replied gratefully.

Charlotte awoke with a start, wondering where she was. Then the memory of what had happened the previous evening came winging back, overwhelming her with a strange mixture of fear and heartbreak. There were things she hadn't told Linda and Denzil, things she'd never tell anyone about that last hour she'd spent with David before he packed and left.

When she'd challenged him about lying, he'd looked at her with glaring eyes and an expression she'd never seen before. Even his smile was chilling. For a moment she'd felt as if she were in the presence of evil, as he'd scoffed at her accusations and subjected her to a barrage of abuse but it was the immense cruelty in his manner that had struck her most.

As she lay in the Blakes' spare room, tortured by memories, the tears slid down her face into the pillow. Suddenly she was aware of the bedroom door being pushed open very quietly. Thinking that it might be Linda she sat up, quickly wiping her tears away with the palms of her hands.

'Why are you crying?' inquired a small voice. It was Holly, in a rose-patterned nightdress, her blonde hair tousled and Flissy clutched under her arm.

'I'm crying because I'm not happy,' Charlotte replied, giving her a watery smile.

'When I cry,' Holly informed her solemnly, 'I cry loudly.'

'Do you, sweetheart?' She reached out to stroke Holly's head.

'I cried a lot yesterday,' she announced.

Charlotte looked into the exquisite little face. 'Were you very frightened?' she asked quietly.

Holly nodded. 'I wanted my Mummy. Do you want your Mummy?'

Charlotte nodded, smiling. 'I expect I'll see her later on today.'

Holly climbed up on to the bed, tucking her little pink

feet under her, and settling Flissy by her side. Charlotte looked with fondness at the dimpled arms and hands, as the child arranged her nightdress neatly around her legs.

On impulse, and as Holly seemed to be in a confiding mood, she decided to question her very carefully. Surely it would do no harm, as long as Holly wasn't pressured?

'What happened yesterday, Holly?' she asked almost casually.

'Uncle David took me out. I wanted to go to the Singing Tree to get my doll's house.'

'Is that where you went?'

'No.' Holly shook her head sadly. 'We went to a bad place. I didn't want to go but he said . . .' She stopped abruptly and for a moment she looked scared as if she'd remembered something. Charlotte immediately put her arms around the little girl and hugged her.

'What did Uncle David say?' she whispered coaxingly.

There was a pause before Holly answered. 'He said I mustn't . . . I mustn't tell . . . or he'd leave me there. All night! In the dark. I didn't want to stay there so I cried.'

'Poor Holly.' Charlotte kissed the crown of her head and it smelled sweetly of baby shampoo. 'You needn't be frightened any more, sweetheart, because none of us will be seeing David again.' At that moment the pain of knowing he was no longer a part of her life, swept through her as if someone had driven a knife into her side, and she wondered if anyone realised how agonising the past few hours had been.

Holly's eyes widened. 'Never?'

'Never, Holly. Your Mummy and Denzil have said they never want to see him again . . . and I've . . . I've said the

419

same,' she added, trying not to break down.

Holly digested this piece of information silently, as she adjusted the dress on her doll.

'I didn't want to stay in that place by myself,' she said at last. 'It was horrid.'

'And you're not going to have to,' Charlotte told her robustly. 'Have you told Flissy all about it?'

'No.'

'Are you going to? Flissy would like to hear where you went, wouldn't she?'

'She might be frightened,' Holly said earnestly.

'What was it Uncle David didn't want you to tell?' she asked, hoping she wasn't pushing Holly too hard.

'Nothing.' The small mouth was tightly shut.

'OK,' she said easily. 'You don't have to tell me, but perhaps Flissy would like to know.'

Holly looked at her in surprise. 'But Flissy might tell.'

'Oh, no, Flissy would never tell,' Charlotte assured her. 'Look, her lips don't move; she knows how to keep a secret.'

Holly looked doubtful.

'Why don't I put my hands over my ears,' Charlotte suggested, 'and then you can tell Flissy what Uncle David said?'

'And Flissy won't tell anyone?'

'Of course Flissy won't tell anyone,' Charlotte assured her.

Holly giggled. Then she watched as Charlotte placed the palms of her hands over her ears. She giggled again and then held the doll's head near her own face. With blue eyes that watched Charlotte carefully, she started whispering in Flissy's ear.

* * *

Grindley was also up at dawn, anxious to get to the police station. As soon as he arrived he was informed by the night duty officer that they'd been told by Denzil Blake that David Farrell had threatened Holly in a bid to silence her. The heat was on. Grindley issued the order for David to be found and brought in for further questioning. Maybe, this time, they would be able to make the charges stick.

He'd only been at work a few minutes when Franklin burst into his room, breathless and windblown.

'We've got something on him, sir!' he said triumphantly. 'We've actually got the little bugger!'

Grindley's eyes narrowed. He didn't have to ask Franklin to whom he was referring. 'What have you found?'

'A jacket. It was buried in the garden under some bushes.'

Grindley's heart leaped. 'How do you know it belongs to David Farrell?'

'One of his business cards, from when he was working for Flight Records, had slipped into the lining through a hole in the pocket.'

'Is there any reason for it to be buried?' Grindley asked.

'I'd say so, sir. It's covered in bloodstains.'

Linda was grilling bacon and tomatoes for breakfast when Charlotte came rushing in. She looked up inquiringly and, as soon as she saw Charlotte's white face and tear-filled eyes, she hurried over to her.

'What's the matter, La?'

Charlotte didn't mince her words, so stunned and shocked she felt in a daze.

'Holly's just told me what happened at Chelwood,' she

said in a low voice. 'At least she didn't tell *me*, but I suggested she tell her doll, while I pretended not to listen.'

'Oh, La!' Linda said gently, seeing how upset she was. Then, 'What did she say?' more urgently.

Rand, taking the milk out of the fridge, turned and pulled out a chair from the table and gestured her towards it.

Thankfully, Charlotte sat down and tried to control the dry sobs that were rocking her body.

'It's not as we thought,' she said almost breathlessly. 'There were two murderers at Chelwood that night.'

Chapter Twenty-three

Killer . . . killer . . . killer . . . The word swirled around Charlotte's brain as she heard Linda talking on the phone to Grindley. Killer . . . the man she loved, the man she'd hoped to marry . . . the man who had shared her life night and day for the past three months. Killer . . . the enormity of the situation was overwhelming and she felt dazed as she surveyed the wreckage of her shattered dreams. Killer . . . but not the only killer on that night. That was perhaps the most surprising thing of all.

When Linda replaced the receiver she turned to Charlotte, eyeing her apprehensively.

'They want to interview you, La,' she said. 'Grindley also wants to know where David is; they have a warrant out for his arrest.'

'Already?' Charlotte gasped, feeling as if the breath was being sucked out of her body.

'They've found evidence against him.'

Stunned, she shook her head, letting this new knowledge sink in. Although she had not doubted Holly, this confirmed everything. 'What did they find?'

'A jacket of his, buried in the garden. Covered in blood. The forensic department are examining it now.'

Charlotte looked back at her, dry eyed, numbed by the

horror that was closing in on her.

'I don't think I can stand much more of this.' Her mind was spinning, out of kilter, trying to cope with this never-ending nightmare.

'And the police want to see me, too?' she asked in a small voice.

Linda came over and gave her a hug. 'I'm afraid so, love. For one thing they want you to make a statement telling them what Holly said. I'd rather they didn't question her directly if we can avoid it; she's been through enough. They also want to question you about David, I expect.'

'Oh, my God.' Charlotte pulled away, covering her face with her hands, wanting to nurse her unhappiness to herself, unable to be comforted. 'I never thought it would come to this.'

'I'm afraid they want you to go to Longley police station right away. Detective Inspector Grindley asked me to pass on the message to you when he heard you were here.'

Rand, who had been listening quietly, spoke. 'I'll run you down. If we leave right after breakfast we can be there in less than two hours.'

Charlotte looked at him, surprised and touched by his kindness. She felt tempted to accept. Her parents were in America on a business trip, and Susie was up to her eyes promoting the new Antonia Design Collection. The thought of making the journey on her own was depressing. Nevertheless, she felt it would be taking advantage of his generosity.

'No, really . . . !' she protested.

'I insist,' he said firmly.

'But what about your work? This might take all day.'

'That's OK.' He was a partner in Reynolds, Gough & Blake, an old-established firm of solicitors in Lincoln's Inn; it was up to him if he spent a day away from the office.

'Yes,' said Linda encouragingly. 'Let Rand drive you down and give you moral support.'

'Thank you,' Charlotte said, looking at Rand. 'It really would be very nice to have someone with me.'

Upstairs they could hear Holly chattering to Ben as Magda dressed him for breakfast. Then she started singing 'Itsie-bitsie-spider' in her small, piping voice and Linda stood stock-still, listening, with a rapt expression.

'It's a miracle,' she said softly. 'Especially after what happened yesterday.' She looked at Charlotte with amazement. 'What did you do to make her talk?'

'I honestly don't know. I don't think it was anything special. I just think the timing was right. She was suddenly ready to talk, and I happened to be there. It's really the doll who should be thanked,' she added with a rueful smile. 'It was Flissy she talked to, while I eaves-dropped!'

As soon as they'd had breakfast, Charlotte and Rand set off in his car and headed for Longley. She had no idea what the day ahead held for her, or whether she'd see David. All she wanted was for this nightmare to end and the pain to lessen, because what Holly had told her made what had happened even more tragic than anyone had supposed.

'Why didn't you tell us this before, Mrs Scovell?' Grindley demanded, barely able to contain his anger.

Gladys blinked, feeling confused. 'I didn't think it was

important,' she confessed. 'I'm not one to gossip, you know, and I've worked for Mr and Mrs Farrell for many years. It didn't seem like nobody's business but theirs,' she added self-righteously.

Grindley managed to suppress the groan that rose to his throat.

'And I suppose you're going to tell me that it was none of your business that you thought you'd seen David Farrell driving through the village when you were on your way home from Chelwood Manor, on the evening in question?'

'I wasn't *sure*, sir. It wasn't the car he was driving when he came down at Christmas with his young lady.'

'People do sometimes change cars,' he observed sarcastically.

Gladys Scovell's face reddened and she twisted her hands uncomfortably.

'Now are you sure you're ready to make a fresh statement?' he continued. 'Are there any more vital details you've forgotten to mention?'

'I don't think so, sir. I didn't say anything before because I didn't want people thinking Mrs Farrell . . .'

'It's of no concern to either you or me what other people think,' he said firmly. He rose from his chair in the interview room. 'I'm going to leave you with Constable Maxwell. He will take down your statement, and then you will be required to sign it. All right, Mrs Scovell?'

'Yes, sir.'

Back in his own office, Grindley summoned Franklin.

'Has he been picked up?' he barked.

Franklin allowed himself a moment's self-satisfaction. 'Yes, sir. We arrested David Farrell an hour ago at Natalie

Newton's flat. They're both being brought here now, for questioning.'

Grindley tried to stifle the memory of white silk and the scent of jasmine. There was a knock at the door. It was the police sergeant on desk duty.

'Just to let you know, sir, that forensic have been on the line. The blood group on the jacket matches that of Mrs Virginia Farrell.'

'Very well,' Grindley replied. 'Oh, and when David Farrell arrives, put him in one of the cells for questioning later on. Bring Natalie Newton to me. I want to get a statement from her,' he added.

'Very well, sir.'

Franklin and the police sergeant left the room while Grindley mentally reviewed Gladys Scovell's latest statement, coupled to what Holly was reported to have told Charlotte Taylor. It most certainly put a whole new perspective on the case, and he had to admit he felt deeply shaken.

'I can't think why the police should want to see us again,' Carol complained as they followed the roadsign to Longley. It was mid-morning, and Grindley had summoned them as they were having breakfast. 'We made statements at the time. I really think it's too much to expect us to go through all that horror once more. Thanks to us, they've found the silencer which proves Chris was innocent. Surely that's enough?'

'No doubt there's a reason,' Neil said patiently. Carol had been grumbling ever since Grindley had called them, and he found it more trying than usual.

'But there's nothing more we can tell them,' she continued querulously. 'Why don't they leave us alone?'

They drove on in silence for a while, as the cloudy sky cleared, giving way to a fresh early summer's day.

'A picnic would have been nice today,' Neil reflected amiably, as they crossed the border from Hampshire into Wiltshire. 'It's a long time since we had a picnic. D'you remember how we used to drive into the New Forest when we were young, and I was starting out as a teacher?'

'We had picnics then because we couldn't afford to go to a restaurant . . . or even a pub,' Carol retorted tartly.

Neil suppressed a sigh, and wondered at her bad mood. She'd been as keen as him to find out what had really happened and to clear Chris's name, but ever since Grindley's call this morning, when he'd talked of 'startling new evidence' which would 'turn the case on its head', she'd been in a terrible mood.

As Rand's dark blue BMW drove into the car park of Longley police station, a police car swished past, stopping immediately outside the entrance. For a moment Charlotte glanced at it idly, wondering why there were so many people inside. Then she gave a little cry and her hand flew to her mouth.

Rand, braking to see what she was looking at, saw a tall, well-dressed blonde girl emerge from the back seat, followed by a police officer handcuffed to a young man of equal blondness and good looks.

'So he went to her place last night,' Charlotte burst out, pain giving her voice a hard edge.

The police hustled the couple into the building, while

Charlotte sat in Rand's car, feeling sick.

'Who is she?' Rand asked.

'That's Natalie Newton, David's cousin,' she said bitterly. 'Let's stay here for a moment,' she begged. 'I don't want to run into them.'

'Sure.' Rand parked the car expertly, and switched off the engine.

'You've nothing to fear, you know,' he said gently. 'You'll only be asked to repeat what Holly told you. David is not going to know where the information came from. Anyway, I expect they'll concentrate on questioning him about the jacket they found.'

'We had such a terrible fight last night,' she said, her voice shaking. 'I'm sure he'll blame me for everything.'

Rand's expression was stunned. 'What are you talking about?'

'He'll know that I reported finding the ticket stubs. He'll think I shopped him.'

'It's Holly's version of events that will do that.'

'Even so . . . I know I couldn't protect him, but I still feel like a terrible traitor. If we'd been married, I wouldn't have needed to give evidence against him, would I?'

'That's true,' Rand agreed. 'But you shouldn't feel guilty, La. When you feel badly about it, think of Chris, who was only twenty-six when he died. Think of Edmund and Virginia, who had at least ten or fifteen years of useful life ahead of them. They are the ones to feel badly about. And Holly, losing her father and grandparents.'

'Of course you're right,' Charlotte admitted. 'It's just so hard . . . so hard . . . when it's the person you love,' her voice broke, and her eyes were full of tears.

'I understand that,' he said comfortingly. 'You're in a hell of a position and I think you're being very brave about it. There are some women who go to great lengths to shelter their husbands or boyfriends rather than expose them, but that's the coward's way out.'

'And at the end of the day I have to live with myself,' she added. Then, in a sudden burst of emotion, she exclaimed, 'I wish I didn't love him so much! I wish I could feel that there's life after David Farrell. But I'm a hostage to a family tragedy. Is it *ever* going to end?'

Rand placed his hand on top of hers for a brief moment. 'I promise you, it will,' he told her gently. 'Let's go, shall we?' He opened the car door. 'The sooner you do this, the sooner it will be over.'

Charlotte nodded, feeling her legs heavy with dread as she got out of the car and walked the short distance to the entrance of the police station.

They stepped straight into a square lobby, with black linoleum on the floor, and a wooden bench down one side. Notices and announcements were pinned to a large cork board on one wall, and on the far side two uniformed policemen sat behind a counter equipped with phones and a computer.

'Can I help you, miss?' one of them asked as Charlotte, accompanied by Rand, walked over to them.

As soon as she told them who she was, she was aware of a flicker of interest in their expressions.

'Take a seat, Miss Taylor,' the elder of the two suggested. 'Detective Inspector Grindley will see you in a minute.'

Charlotte and Rand sat down to wait. Then a door by the side of the counter opened and Connie Westcott appeared, accompanied by Franklin. As soon as she saw Charlotte she smiled sardonically.

'Hi there!' Her manner was familiar.

Charlotte didn't reply. Everything about Connie jarred on her nerves. She looked up at her stonily, remembering it was she who had first cast doubts on David, tearing away all Charlotte's illusions. The messenger always gets the blame, she thought with irony, and Connie was no exception.

'In time you'll realise I did you a good turn,' Connie remarked cheerfully. 'I'm surprised it took you so long to find out what he's really like.' Then she turned and followed Franklin into another room which led off the lobby.

Rand raised inquiring eyebrows. 'A friend of David's?'

'They were engaged last year,' she replied briefly.

Rand nodded in understanding once again. In spite of everything he could see that Charlotte was still having difficulty coping with the truth about David.

Charlotte sat facing Detective Inspector Grindley, repeating once again everything Holly had said to her doll. He watched her closely, looking for a sign that would indicate she might be making it all up in order to seek revenge on David, but there was none. Soberly and sadly she repeated everything Holly had said, even at times quoting the childlike phraseology, such as when Holly had whispered, 'Granny's face was all gone.'

'And you think the child was telling the truth?' he asked as length.

Charlotte looked at him steadily. 'Yes. I do.'

'It certainly puts a different complexion on the whole case, doesn't it?' he remarked, almost as if he were talking to himself. 'It also bears out Gladys Scovell's statement . . . about what had been going on at Chelwood Manor earlier that afternoon.'

Charlotte looked puzzled. 'I don't know about that; what happened?'

Grindley looked guarded. 'Let's just say her newest statement was of interest. At this stage, I would like, of course, to get a confession from David Farrell, but I think it's unlikely.'

'So do I,' she replied with feeling. 'I know David . . . very well. He'll never admit to anything. He'll lie . . .' Her voice drifted off painfully.

'Quite,' Grindley agreed. 'That will be all for the moment, Miss Taylor,' he said briskly. 'But I'd like you to remain here for a while yet. Just in case I need to ask you any further questions.' He ushered her to the door. 'I'm sure the duty sergeant will get you some tea or coffee.'

In a daze, she found herself back in the lobby. Carol and Neil had arrived and were talking to Franklin. She introduced them to Rand, and then Carol grabbed her arm as soon as Franklin left, saying he would be returning in a few minutes to interview them.

'What's going on, Charlotte?' Carol asked. 'We've been told they've arrested David, charging him with the murder of Virginia and Chris. But what about Edmund? Why hasn't he been arrested for Edmund's murder too?'

Charlotte knew she was going to hurt Carol deeply, but there was no way of avoiding the truth now.

'Because David didn't kill Edmund,' she said, looking into Carol's puzzled eyes. 'It was Virginia who shot him.'

* * *

Fresh statements had been made and signed, and one by one they were all allowed to leave the police station and go home. Gladys Scovell was the first to go, accompanied by Ruby and her sister Mabel, all declaring that she had been right at the time not to mention the fight between Virginia and Edmund on the day in question.

'I didn't think as it was anyone's business,' Gladys said for the umpteenth time. 'Mrs Farrell wouldn't have wanted everyone to know their business. It was just unfortunate that she picked up the phone that day as Mr Farrell was talking to his lady friend on the extension! Proper wild it made her!'

'And Olivia Middleton never mentioned it to the police, neither, did she?' Mabel added. 'She was a lady who knew how to keep herself to herself.' Mabel cleaned for the new owners of Magnolia Cottage these days, and in her opinion they were a dull lot compared to the exotic mistress of both Edmund and Christopher Farrell.

'Was you there when Mrs Farrell loaded up the gun?' Mabel asked. 'Surprised me she knew how!'

'I heard her in the gun room, but I didn't know what she was doing,' Gladys replied.

'But how could she do a thing like that with little Holly in the house?' Ruby asked, scandalised.

'I think she'd forgotten about Holly, in the heat of the moment, or else she thought Holly had gone out with her dad. I heard Holly upstairs playing with her doll. At one point she was talking to her grandad. I left early because I wanted to get to the shops. I'd no idea that Mrs Farrell was going to kill her husband as soon as my back was turned!'

* * *

Carol and Neil set off wearily for the journey home. Her face was red and puffy from crying, and she felt ill with shock.

'Virginia must have been terribly unhappy,' she said after a while. 'He drove her to it, of course. Edmund was a bastard. He always treated her badly.'

Neil remained silent, lost in his own thoughts. 'The one I'm really sorry for is little Holly,' he said at last. 'Imagine hiding on the landing, watching while her grandmother went berserk and shot her grandfather!'

'Not to mention what happened after that,' Carol added, darkly.

Connie Westcott left the police station shortly after Carol and Neil Whittaker, thankful it was all over. The best thing she'd done was to dump David Farrell. He was a loser, a waster, and a lying bastard. But he was an opportunist; she had to admit that. If things hadn't got out of hand at Chelwood Manor that night, he might have got away with it. He'd confided in her a long time ago that he planned to pay a hit-man to stage what looked like a robbery in which both his parents would be shot. He spoke grandly of his inheritance and how rich he'd be. She knew it was largely talk; he liked to brag and show off, and make out he was successful, and so she hadn't taken him seriously . . . until after the murders. She really thought he'd pulled it off then, but of course he hadn't.

David always managed to screw up, Connie reflected. It was the story of his life.

Natalie Newton had been the only one who had known all

along what had happened on that fateful night. David hadn't been able to resist telling her the sequence of coincidental events that had overtaken even his most carefully laid plans. Not that he'd blurted it out all at once. Bit by bit, in the confidential aftermath that followed love making, he'd eventually told her everything, and it had been an amazing story. Now that it was all over, and she'd made a full statement, she felt, as did her brother Andrew, a sense of relief. David was fun in bed, but not sufficiently exciting to go to prison for.

David's original plan, he told her, once he'd given up the idea of involving a hit-man because he couldn't afford it, was to stage a break-in and robbery, which resulted in Virginia and Edmund being killed. It should have been straightforward, carried out after Gladys and Ruby had gone home. He bought a sawn-off shotgun from an East End dealer who asked no questions, and armed with this, he entered Chelwood by the back door, which was never locked until the family retired for the night, so that Mackie could be easily let in and out of the garden.

The first shock he got, as he crept into the hall, hoping to catch them unawares, was finding the body of Edmund shot through the chest. Then he heard a noise on the stairs, and looking up saw Virginia standing there, brandishing Edmund's rifle which was permanently fitted with a silencer because of his tinnitus.

In a flash, David rushed towards Virginia but she fled to her bedroom, where he managed to grapple the gun away from her. As she flopped on to the side of the bed, seizing the phone and saying she was going to phone the police to confess what she'd done, he shot her at point blank range.

Then, taking Edmund's rifle back downstairs, to wash the blood both off it and also to try and clean himself up, he returned to the kitchen.

Unbeknownst to him at that moment, someone else was about to enter the kitchen by the back door, but on seeing what was happening through the kitchen window, slipped away through the twilit garden to enter Chelwood by the front door with his key. Someone David had not expected to be staying at Chelwood that Friday evening.

Ten minutes later, David was just about to go to the pantry to grab the family silver and stow it away with both Edmund's rifle and his own shotgun in the boot of his car, which he'd left in a clearing in the woods some distance from the house, when Chris walked into the kitchen.

David never told Natalie the details of the confrontation he'd had with Chris, but he said that as they stood there, looking at each other, Chris had accused him of killing both Edmund and Virginia. David was still holding Edmund's gun. In seconds a whole new plan formed in his mind; a perfect plan that would not only make it unnecessary for him to stage a robbery, but put the onus of blame for the murders on his 'unbalanced brother'.

There was only one thing David had overlooked. He'd forgotten that Holly would probably have been staying for the weekend too.

'Chris must have found her upstairs when he discovered Mum's body,' David had told Natalie bitterly. 'Maybe Holly'd seen too much and Chris hid her because he knew it would be the end of her if I'd realised she was around. I had to kill him, of course, and make it look like suicide.'

But it hadn't been quite the perfect crime, Natalie

reflected as she picked up her pen to sign her statement. Why on earth had David buried his blood-stained jacket in the garden of Chelwood when surely he could have disposed of it some other way?

Even the most devious mind, she mused, can be fatally flawed.

Charlotte was silent on the drive back to London. Rand, glancing at her from time to time, didn't try to force the conversation. It was enough that she seemed composed, as if she'd come to terms with what had happened. As they came to the Cromwell Road extension, Rand asked her where she'd like to go.

'Go?' she echoed, as if she'd been in a dream. 'What do you mean?' She looked at his profile, almost as if she were seeing him for the first time. He turned and smiled.

'Where would you like me to take you, La? Back to your own flat? Or your parents'? Or we could go to Linda's? I know she'd like to see you. Or we could go to a quiet restaurant . . . but maybe that would be better on another night,' he added softly.

Charlotte remembered her parents were away, and Susie was bound to be out. The thought of being on her own tonight didn't appeal.

'I think perhaps . . . Linda's,' she said.

'Good.' He nodded in agreement.

When they arrived in Mulberry Avenue, Holly was still up, running around the house in her nightie, with her bare pink toes showing beneath the frilled hem, and her blonde curls tied back with a white ribbon. As soon as she saw Charlotte she ran towards her with her small arms outstretched and a rapturous smile on her face. For once Flissy was not to be seen.

'Hello, sweetheart,' Charlotte exclaimed, lifting her up into her arms.

'Have you come to stay?' Holly asked. 'Are you going to sleep here tonight?'

Charlotte and Linda looked at each other, smiling.

'I hope she is,' Linda replied. 'We'd like her to stay, wouldn't we?'

'*Yeah!*' shouted Holly, clapping her hands. 'Can you sleep here every night? In the room next to me?'

Charlotte gazed into the eager little face, and marvelled at the resilience of children.

Linda caught Rand's eye, and then she stared at him with delighted astonishment. He was smiling hopefully at Charlotte, and there was no mistaking what he was thinking.

'La can stay here as long as she likes,' she said warmly. Then she turned playfully to Holly.

'But meanwhile, it's time you went to bed, young lady.'

Eight months later, David Farrell was tried for the murder of Virginia Farrell and Christopher Farrell. It was, said the judge in his summing up, 'an evil act carried out by a ruthless young man who thought only of his own financial advancement.' The jury took six hours and twenty-five minutes to reach a ten-to-two majority verdict on both counts. As he was driven away to begin two concurrent life sentences, he smiled arrogantly at the public gallery where his previous girlfriend Charlotte Taylor, now married to lawyer Randall Blake, sat watching the proceedings.

MARTINA COLE
GOODNIGHT LADY

SHE KNOWS EVERYONE'S SECRETS...

The infamous Briony Cavanagh: quite a beauty in her day,
and powerful, too. In the sixties, she ran a string of the
most notorious brothels in the East End. Patronised by
peers and politicians – even royalty, some said. Only Briony
knew what went on behind those thick velvet curtains, those
discreet closed doors, and Briony never opened her mouth
– unless she stood to benefit.

Only Briony knew the hard and painful road she'd travelled
to get there. From an impoverished childhood that ended
abruptly with shocking betrayal, she had schemed and
manipulated, determined to be mistress of her own fate.

But her flourishing business brought her into contact with
the darker side of life at the violent heart of London's
gangland. Along with her material success came risk and
danger. And the Goodnight Lady had her own secret place,
a place in her heart that was always shadowed with loss...

Don't miss Martina Cole's bestsellers, *The Ladykiller*
and *Dangerous Lady*, also from Headline:
'Move over Jackie [Collins]!' *Daily Mirror*
'Sheer escapism...gripping...will definitely keep you guessing
to the end' *Company*
'Graphic realism combined with dramatic flair make this a winner'
Netta Martin, *Annabel*

FICTION/GENERAL   0 7472 4429 4

More Compelling Fiction from Headline:

CATHERINE
ALLIOTT
THE OLD-GIRL
NETWORK

A SPARKLING FRESH TALENT
FOR ALL JILLY COOPER FANS

Why didn't anyone warn her that the path to true love
would be filled with potholes?

Dreamy, scatty and impossibly romantic, Polly McLaren is a secretary in an advertising agency, but the day a stranger on a train catches her eye, her life changes for ever. This American Romeo, who's recognised her old school scarf, begs Polly to help him find his missing Juliet. Over an intoxicating dinner at the Savoy, Polly agrees to play Cupid – St Gertrude's girls must, after all, stick together – and her investigations begin. The last thing she needs now is trouble from the men in her life...

...like Harry Lloyd Roberts – Polly's madly attractive but infuriatingly elusive boyfriend. It's he who goads her into turning detective – on the grounds that it might give her something to do for a change. Not to mention distract her from his own lustful pursuits...

...and Nick Penhalligan – Polly's rude, arrogant and ridiculously demanding boss, who's not best pleased that her mind is everywhere but on her job. But even he gets entangled when the old-girl network turns into a spider's web of complications, deceit and finally, love.

FICTION/GENERAL   0 7472 4390 5

A selection of bestsellers
from Headline

THE CHANGING ROOM	Margaret Bard	£5.99 ☐
BACKSTREET CHILD	Harry Bowling	£5.99 ☐
A HIDDEN BEAUTY	Tessa Barclay	£5.99 ☐
A HANDFUL OF HAPPINESS	Evelyn Hood	£5.99 ☐
THE SCENT OF MAY	Sue Sully	£5.99 ☐
HEARTSEASE	T R Wilson	£5.99 ☐
NOBODY'S DARLING	Josephine Cox	£5.99 ☐
A CHILD OF SECRETS	Mary Mackie	£5.99 ☐
WHITECHAPEL GIRL	Gilda O'Neill	£5.99 ☐
BID TIME RETURN	Donna Baker	£5.99 ☐
THE LADIES OF BEVERLEY HILLS	Sharleen Cooper Cohen	£5.99 ☐
THE OLD GIRL NETWORK	Catherine Alliott	£4.99 ☐

All Headline books are available at your local bookshop or newsagent, or can be ordered direct from the publisher. Just tick the titles you want and fill in the form below. Prices and availability subject to change without notice.

Headline Book Publishing, Cash Sales Department, Bookpoint, 39 Milton Park, Abingdon, OXON, OX14 4TD, UK. If you have a credit card you may order by telephone – 0235 400400.

Please enclose a cheque or postal order made payable to Bookpoint Ltd to the value of the cover price and allow the following for postage and packing:
UK & BFPO: £1.00 for the first book, 50p for the second book and 30p for each additional book ordered up to a maximum charge of £3.00.
OVERSEAS & EIRE: £2.00 for the first book, £1.00 for the second book and 50p for each additional book.

Name ....

Address ....

....

....

If you would prefer to pay by credit card, please complete:
Please debit my Visa/Access/Diner's Card/American Express (delete as applicable) card no:

Signature .... Expiry Date ....